SEEKING THE STORYTELLER

Happy Hunting!

Jessi [signature]

read this, ok?

Briana Zauner [signature]

SEEKING THE STORYTELLER

Jessica Walsh & Briana Lawrence

Dedication and
Acknowledgements

Our thanks go out to the numerous people who - through intention or complete accident - made this book possible. To the members of our families who assisted in their own ways, thank you for letting us be our geeky selves. Thank you for being in our corner when we needed you. To our mothers – Helen Berry and Valerie Walsh – and our fathers – Gerald Lawrence and Gerald Walsh – thank you for everything. To our siblings, one in spirit – Glenn Berry – and one who shows up in time for food – Don Walsh – thank you.

We'd also like to thank the anime clubs, yahoo mailing lists, conventions, and nerdy friends who cheered us on while we worked to make this dream a reality. Thanks for the late night chat sessions, the fanfiction, fanart, and discussions on different anime and video game series. We're indebted to our geek community who encouraged our creativity and spurred us down the path to make this happen.

Also, thanks to our good friend Peter Liethen for helping us reformat, typeset and re-release our book.

Prologue

The basement door opened with a long, dramatic groan; the hinges completely against the idea of moving. Alix's arms were hit with a sudden gust of cold air as he took the first couple of steps. Creak. Creak. Each step sounded older than the last, each piece of wood more wrinkled than its predecessor. The florescent lights whined overhead like an unfed toddler and Alix made a mental note to have his much taller partner, Fagan, change them out. He let out an annoyed sigh when he realized that he had made the same observation to the stubbled gentleman a week ago. Between the lights and the stairs it was an orchestra of noise that made Alix swear under his breath. As functional as Fagan's basement was, it certainly wasn't in the best repair.

As another wave of cold ran down Alix's arms he added the basement's cold temperature to his permanent list of complaints. There was a furnace, but it only worked when it damn well pleased, which translated to, "not when Alix was downstairs." His partner never complained, instead claiming that Alix just wasn't used to the Minnesota weather. *"The basement is fine,"* he always said, *"Maybe you should invest in a sweater."*

Alix frowned at the thought; he wasn't so pathetic that he couldn't last a few minutes in a crummy basement. Besides, the cold in the basement had nothing to do with the state itself. "It's always cold in Minnesota" was always Fagan's excuse for, "Didn't get the heat fixed yet," or, "I'll call *the guy* right away." Alix had definitely heard of the cold weather, it had been the main topic of discussion when he moved here as a child – besides Vikings and fairs with strange concoctions on a stick. He had visited much colder places in his life thanks to his parents having to travel for their careers. Minnesota winters weren't all that hard to survive in comparison, unless if you had a partner that seemed allergic to heaters.

As he stepped off the stairs and moved to the back of the basement the fluorescent lights grew dimmer, one failing after the other like an obedient soldier. One light remained defiant, struggling to stay on to give Alix enough light to see up ahead. He ventured forward into the area that had been turned into a makeshift cell, thick iron bars protruding from the ceiling and meeting the cold, basement floor. Brushing a stray lock of blond hair out of his eyes, Alix crossed his arms and looked into the darkness behind the bars, waiting.

"The lights hurt. I left one on." The voice was quiet and smooth, caressing Alix's arms like the freshly dried linen in laundry detergent commercials.

Alix frowned as he looked inside the cell, his eyes focused on the shadows in the very back. "Step out to where I can see you," he said, speaking directly to the shadows as if they were a living thing.

The shadows in the corner remained still for a moment before Alix heard a deep sigh. "If you insist."

Alix watched as the shadows pulled back in a receding wave of dark black. A figure stepped out of the darkness as the waves parted for him like a curtain. Its feet were silent against the uneven concrete, gently touching the floor with the elegance of a trained dancer. It was tall and skinny, the type of thinness that reminded Alix of news reports of war torn countries where the people looked like they never ate. Despite its malnourished appearance no bones showed through his skin, but the texture of its flesh looked like a frozen liquid with small ripples flowing down its arms and chest. Its skin was a color similar to runny ink pens, the black bleeding into the concrete. The creature's eyes were hollow and missing pupils, the emptiness deep like endless black holes. It made Alix wonder how the creature could see anything at all.

In contrast to its creepy, elongated features, two large ears flopped down around its head. It gave the creature a strange resemblance of a playful puppy, something that could be a loyal and trusted friend.

But Alix knew better.

To think that creatures like this shadow dog – the closest thing that Alix could associate the demon with – sparked nightmarish stories of demons and other religious fodder was laughable. What stood in front of him now certainly didn't look like the demons the rest of the human world whispered about during campfires and claimed were underneath children's beds. In fact, there was a good portion of them that probably would have thought that this inhuman thing was, dare he say, *cute*, something to keep as a pet and make do tricks for spoiled little children.

Alix was disgusted by the thought.

The figure nodded politely to Alix and sat down on the chair it'd been given in an effort to look more approachable. Alix noted there was a metal piece hanging from its ear. An insignia of some kind? It had to mean something, Alix thought, since it was the only thing the demon seemed to be wearing as far as clothing or accessories were concerned. But he could worry about the creature's fashion sense later; there were more important matters to discuss.

"You're a different kind of demon than the ones we've seen. Why wouldn't you try to escape? You obviously could. I've seen you move through shadows before."

The demon shrugged. "What would be the point of escaping simply to be hunted down again?"

"We kill demons here."

"So why haven't you killed me?"

Alix couldn't resist the urge to smirk. This demon was different from the mindless mass that he hunted down with Fagan. Unthinking creatures who rushed after their unsuspecting targets, demons were to be killed swiftly because they never listened to reason, nor did they feel things like remorse or regret. But this one was actually civil and Alix could feel a spark of intelligence behind those empty voids that served as the creature's eyes. This demon was patient and didn't seem like the type to give into bouts of uncontrollable rage that he'd seen in so many others.

It made him a threat, but it was a risk Alix was willing to take. Perhaps this was the demon who could assist him.

Alix pulled up a chair and straddled it backward. "There is a story I've heard before, during my hunts." Alix paused for a moment, deep blue eyes searching for the proper words. "It was a rather interesting tale and I want to know if there is any truth to it. I want to know if there are demons who have the power to... change things."

The creature in front of him thought about that for a moment, silently rubbing its chin in an almost human behavior. "I am assuming you mean larger things, possibly past things. There are indeed stories of a specific type of creature who can do that, but you won't find him in your world."

Alix nodded. "I figured as much. Tell me about him."

"In my world they call him the Storyteller. According to our world, every living thing has a book where its life and stories are recorded and written down. These books are stored in a room."

"A room full of books? You mean like a library?"

"Library?" The creature tilted its head in what Alix assumed was a curious gesture. "Yes, I suppose that is a good word for it if these 'libraries' of yours are endless."

"Endless? No, nothing like that."

"I see. Well, I suppose calling it a library will do for now," the demon chuckled before speaking again. "The Storyteller is the one who collects these books and watches over them. But he also has the power to write new books and rewrite events." It stopped and tilted its head again. Unlike the previous demons that Alix had become accustomed to killing, this one seemed curious about a lot of things, particularly in Alix's reactions during their conversation. The empty holes in its head focused on Alix, studying him, its body shifting in its chair each time Alix frowned or let out a soft breath. Soon it spoke again and crossed its arms at its chest in the same way Alix had his arms crossed around the back of his chair. "Why? Is there something you wanted the Storyteller to change about your story?"

"That is nothing for you to worry about," Alix said quickly. "Where can I find him?"

The creature shook its head, the movement liquid against the rippling shadows behind him. "You can't. The Storyteller doesn't leave his library and no one else can enter there."

Alix looked at the demon in disgust and stood up, pushing his chair aside. "So he doesn't actually exist and you're wasting my time." Turning, he moved toward the steps to leave. He was forced to stop as the light directly above him snapped out with a small pop. Alix glanced back at his prisoner.

"In exchange for my life. If you swear that I will not be harmed by you or your associates, I will tell you what I know about him."

"You've already told me everything I need to know. You also just said that no one could go there or see him."

"No. I told you what my world *believed*. *I* have met him."

This was a trick. It was obviously a trap that the demon was using to extend its life. Alix already knew that light hurt it, the creature clinging to the shadows and darkness. He and Fagan could easily wound it, if not kill it, by flooding this entire space with lights bright enough to replace the new stadium that had been built for the "Twinkies" – the terrible nickname given to the city's baseball team. The creature was at their mercy and now it was negotiating for its life.

Perhaps Alix could use this beyond his own personal desires.

Alix turned back to the creature and crossed his arms. "In exchange for your life, you will give us any information we ask for of **any** demon, including this Storyteller."

The creature hesitated, mulling over the choice and the consequences. The shadows shifted, as if they too were trying to figure out if this was a good idea or not. Seconds felt like an eternity to Alix, each one ticking down as he waited for the creature to make a decision. Finally, Alix was given a small nod of acceptance as the demon stood up and extended a dark hand past the bars.

Alix did not step forward; he simply acknowledged it with a nod of his own. "Then you have my word that neither I nor my associates will harm or kill you."

The creature lowered its hand. "A word is worth nothing without a name."

"Alix. Alix Andre DeBenit."

"Dox. Son of the Lurkhamara," the demon nodded. "I accept your word."

Alix turned and headed back up the stairs. He needed to talk to Fagan and decide how to proceed. As he walked up the stairs he did his best to ignore the shadows around him. They were all rippling now, like water drizzling down a clear pane of glass. There was something about that name - or was it a title? It felt like mentioning the *Lurkhamara* had made the very shadows respond. Was it a sign of respect, perhaps? Halfway up the stairs Alix gave into curiosity and glanced back. Dox had returned to simply sitting in its – *his*, he had said *son* – chair, waiting. He couldn't tell if the creature's eyes were open or closed but there was an itch down the back of his spine that made Alix feel like he was being watched.

Pushing those thoughts from his mind he left the basement, closed the door behind him, and made sure to lock the door securely. He didn't let himself think of the fact that the lock would probably do nothing. The shadows on the wall, even if they didn't move at all, confirmed that the thing residing in Fagan's basement was far too powerful for steel and a deadbolt to stop him.

Perhaps they would need to invest in something stronger, though Alix had a feeling that Fagan would "call the guy" just as quickly as he had called to get the heat fixed.

Chapter 1

Something wasn't right. He could smell it in the air.

The moon lit the sky and the rocky ground where plants struggled to gain footing and survive in places they were never meant to grow. His bare, taloned feet were used to the ground as he silently darted forward. Before him, the plants disappeared and the ground dropped off into a valley. He stopped on the edge of the drop-off and knelt down, sniffing the air again. The scent was faint, a tingling on the air around him, but he could tell it was there and he could smell it growing just a little stronger. He leaned forward, clutched the edge of the rocks with his jewel encrusted metal glove, and narrowed his eyes as he looked over the forest canopy below.

He knew the other creatures that lived below in the trees. They were many in number, but scavengers by nature and not the sort to raise trouble if they could help it. The Scough presented little threat, so he knew the smell couldn't be from them. No, it had the scent of something older, deeper, like spoiled food or the stench of a rotting carcass left in the sun for days.

Around him the darkness wavered as if taunting him for his suspicions. Yvonne slowly rose to his feet and kept his eyes on the forest below. Jumping wasn't an option; he couldn't fly and he didn't much like the idea of trying to catch the wall of rock on his way down. Turning, he felt the air around him growing warm as his body waited for the attack he knew was coming.

For a moment the darkness was silent, then the blackness of the night began to knot together in front of him. The shadows grew from the ground and shot forward, attempting to wrap around him. Yvonne didn't stop to wonder how the darkness was moving. Instead, he rolled to the side and sent a wave of heat after the shadows. The blistering wave took on a physical substance of blended oranges and yellows, the few plants on the ground disintegrating from how hot the wave was. The shadows adjusted their direction, shifting away from the fire and moving after him again. Yvonne was already running, reassessing his earlier decision about the edge of the cliff. No matter where he moved, more shadows twisted out of the ground, intent on keeping him from returning to warn the others who had been patrolling with him.

He would have to deal with this on his own.

One of the shadows came close, nearly catching one of the braids on the side of his head. Yvonne twisted out of the way and turned, deciding to attack rather than run away. Running into the thick of the shadows he let the air around him broil, feeling the rocks grow soft under his feet from the heat as they began to melt. The shadows pulled back for a mere second, but then they were on the move again. Yvonne swore he could see a word sliding across them.

Powerless.

Powerless? Was that the word he just-... and immediately the heat from his body disappeared and he was left feeling like a helpless child. Yvonne could taste the fire at the tip of his tongue, his fingers itching to call upon it, but suddenly he had no access to the years of training he had gone through.

Yvonne didn't have time to react as the shadows pounced in, wrapping tightly around him while another layer stalked around the area, pacing like a predator surveying its caught prey. Yvonne growled lowly, watching the night beyond the shadows. "Show yourself," he hissed.

Stepping out from behind a rather large rock - one that Yvonne knew had nothing but a drop off behind it - was a strange and quiet creature. As it walked, the shadows and darkness rippled across its skin, adding shape to its form and turning it more solid with color washing about. When it came to a stop in front of him, Yvonne was surprised to see that it was a Scough, the very creature he was sure would never attack due to their nature of scavenging and not causing trouble.

Though, he'd never heard of a Scough being able to manipulate the shadows.

The Scough walked on two legs just like Yvonne, but that's where the similarities between them stopped. The fox like creature was more animalistic than Yvonne and his brethren. His ears were atop his head with long hair that continued down his back and ended in a large, bushy tail that moved slowly behind him. The Scough had grey and white fur and wore a loose jacket made of scraps of sewn together fabric.

The Scough regarded Yvonne with curious, gold tinted eyes. He wasn't like the other Scough Yvonne had seen in his lifetime; normally their eyes were more earth colored. Scough also weren't raised as warriors nor did they leave their forests. They certainly didn't climb this far up the cliffs to pick a fight.

That explained the stench Yvonne had detected earlier.

"I wasn't aware the Reina sent her son on simple sentry duties."

Not just picking a fight, but picking a fight with *him.*

Yvonne growled. Whatever this creature in front of him looked like, it wasn't really a Scough. As it walked, he noticed that the ears didn't twitch with the sounds in the air and its tail swished with a repeated movement, not at all natural. This thing had the ability to change shape and imitate others, and Yvonne doubted he would have noticed the subtle differences if he weren't being threatened.

"You'll be perfect. Now, stay quiet for me." A smirk crossed the creature's lips as it stepped forward and touched Yvonne's cheek. He could feel something sliding along his cheek and over his lips, brushing against them in an almost soothing manner. Then, he heard a single, whispered word. *Silence.* Suddenly, Yvonne's lips and throat felt numb. He tried his best to growl in anger at the creature but nothing came out, even if he could feel the vibration in his throat. He couldn't make a sound, his ability to speak washed away.

The thing stepped back and motioned to the shadows.

They rose, wrapped around both of them, and disappeared. In the blink of an eye Yvonne found that he was no longer on the cliff. Now he was kneeling in the middle of the forest, beneath the thick canopy cover. Leaves and branches were scattered about and the thing he'd encountered was standing a little ways away, brushing off his outfit. It was in worse condition than it had been when Yvonne encountered him. There were now a couple tears and dirt beaten in, as if the Scough had been through a tough battle. The shadows were gone and Yvonne's arms were twisted behind his back, held there with a thick scrap of fabric. Had he had his powers he could have easily reduced it to ashes, but for the moment it was frustratingly effective.

How insulting that a collection of thin fibers could hold him captive.

"Thierry!"

Another Scough was running toward them on all fours, weaving between the trees and stopping near the false Scough. This one was younger and looked more like the Scough Yvonne was used to. His fur was a light brown, with black freckles scattered across his cheeks and down his back. The young Scough slowly stood up, staring at Yvonne with an open mouth.

"Is that a Red Dragon?"

The first one, Thierry, nodded. "Yes. I suggest you stay behind me, Lyree. He attacked me." His voice was softer now, friendlier than it had been up on the cliff.

Yvonne glared at the two and struggled against the fabric again, trying to growl and call the creature a liar but no words came out. He focused his attention on the younger Scough's face, his narrowed eyes making him stumble back and raise his hands in the air. Yvonne mentally smirked. At least he was still intimidating to someone.

"He looks really angry. Maybe we should let him go."

Thierry shook his head. "We should take him back to Jahren and everyone else before any of the others of his kind notice that he's gone."

"Others?! Here? They don't ever come down into our area!"

"They do now, it appears."

A few minutes later found Thierry and the younger one, Lyree, in a small clearing with three other Scough. This spot showed no signs of habitation, but Yvonne wasn't too surprised about that. It made sense for them to bring him to an area away from their main camp; it was always best to be overly cautious with a "hostile" captive. Aside from the two that had led him here there was now an older Scough with faded grey hair who scowled with every look. Another leaned against a tree near him, looking younger with black and red fur and dark brown eyes. Finally, there was one more with the same coloring as the older one, though much younger and stronger looking. He regarded the group with a serious expression and they all seemed to be waiting on him to say something. Yvonne guessed he was the one in charge, the name Jahren coming to mind from who Thierry had spoken of earlier.

"I don't like this." The elder Scough spoke before their leader did, his voice louder than it needed to be due to his hearing working only on certain occasions – food, sleep, and night time activities. He glared at Yvonne who glared right back, baring his teeth in distrust.

The Scough with the black and red fur beside him shook his head and murmured, "Saraisai," in an attempt to calm him down.

Saraisai was larger than the rest, stomach a hefty size since he was too old to be in charge and could spend his days leisurely eating whatever the others brought in. Lyree now paced near him, skipping from foot to foot and looking uncomfortable until the older fox creature caught his tail and yanked him to sit down and stop moving about.

"Ow!" Lyree swiped at Saraisai's leg out of annoyance but he didn't move.

If the Scough functioned the same way as Yvonne and the dragons there was no way someone so young would be included in this kind of meeting. While dragons were trained young in their lives, meetings such as this were reserved for the Reina and her most trusted warriors. But Yvonne noticed that Lyree stayed close to Saraisai and the Scough with the black and red fur, probably using whatever relationship they had to make sure he always knew what was going on.

"What would ever possess ya to fight one of them, much less bring it near our home?"

Thierry regarded Saraisai with a patient look, as if he was used to the old man's temper. He also seemed used to his inability to follow simple requests – hadn't the Scough with the black and red fur been trying to get him to lower his voice? "I didn't want to fight him, he attacked me. I told you earlier there was something dangerous in the woods and this was it."

"Saraisai's right though – for once. He shouldn't be here."

Saraisai frowned at the Scough with the red and black fur, "Watch yourself, Amari."

"I was giving you a compliment," Amari said, scratching behind one of Saraisai's ears as if trying to emphasize the point. The old fox responded with a grunt, but it was hard to miss the content smile on his face from Amari petting him.

"I brought him here because I didn't want to leave him in the woods," Thierry said, answering the earlier question. "What if he attacked again, or worse, came closer to our camp with the children?"

Yvonne chuckled silently to himself, watching their reactions to Thierry's words. So whatever this creature was – though they seemed to be convinced that he was a Scough – told them that there was something dangerous around their home and they believed him. It was an old trick, drawing attention away from yourself to get others to not suspect you were the one acting strange. That meant Yvonne was a scapegoat for whatever this creature had planned. It sounded so much like one of his Reina's tactics that he wanted to laugh.

Ignoring the worried looks from the others, Jahren finally moved forward. He crouched in front of Yvonne and slowly looking him over. His eyes went from the two braids in Yvonne's hair to the carefully crafted sleeve of metal and jewels that covered his right arm. Yvonne wasn't sure if the Scough knew what the braids or the metal ornaments meant, but he had to assume he knew part of it from how long his eyes lingered. The braids were linked back to the Reina, his mother and the ruler of the Red Dragons. They were reserved for only those closest to her and the amount of jewels on his arm showed his status among his people as the Reina's son. Yvonne willed the Scough to understand any part of that, meeting his eyes and holding the look, unwavering.

After a long moment Jahren stood up and stepped back, turning to face the others. "We should take him back to his people. It's clear from the jewels that he has ties to the Reina."

Yvonne mentally breathed a sigh of relief, happy that Jahren had been able to make the connection.

"Yeah, like that will help anything," Amari muttered, effectively ruining Yvonne's moment. "I don't feel like getting all of my fur burned off. I hear their Reina has quite the temper."

"And that would be a waste," Saraisai said, his fingers combing through Amari's tail, "I rather like this fur."

"Dirty old Scough," Amari chuckled.

"What if we just let him go right now and he leaves?" Lyree asked.

"Considering the fact that he attacked me first, I doubt he will leave peacefully," Thierry said.

Jahren walked over to Thierry and looked over his messy clothes, frowning, "Are you hurt, my friend?"

Thierry shook his head and smiled. "Thankfully no."

"You're lucky ya even managed to handle him," Saraisai said.

Jahren frowned. Saraisai had a point. He had known Thierry for quite some time and had never seen the Scough fight. To be able to take down a Red Dragon was quite the feat, particularly one related to the Reina.

Amari let out a frustrated sigh before sitting himself in Saraisai's lap. "Can't kill him, either. That'd make things worse."

"You can kill Red Dragons?" Lyree looked up at them, his eyes much too wide with curiosity.

"'Course ya can, anything can be killed," the old Scough responded, resting his head on Amari's shoulder.

"I-I know, I just meant that they're dragons, and dragons are dangerous."

Amari smiled and leaned forward, rubbing his nose against Lyree's in a calming gesture. It seemed to work, Lyree closing his eyes with a sweet smile on his face.

"We will not be killing this one," Jahren said in a firm voice.

Thierry spoke again as he took hold of Jahren's hand to get his attention. "We have to consider what this means, Jahren. If the Reina sent him here it means they are leaving the mountains and they will be coming here after him."

Lyree scratched one of his ears, looking confused at Thierry's words. "But the Red Dragons live in the mountains, why would they want to come here?"

"Stupid child, don't ya listen to any of the stories we tell ya?" Saraisai took a moment to unwrap his arms around Amari's waist to swipe at Lyree like a cat lazily playing with a familiar toy. "The Red Dragons were chased out of their lands when *they* attacked them and the Kurai. They fled to the mountains because they had to. No one in their right mind would want to live up there."

"*They?*" Lyree asked. When Saraisai growled at him his eyes widened and he quickly nodded. "R-right. I remember now," though no one could tell if he actually did or if he was just saying that so he wouldn't have to face Saraisai's wrath.

"The mountains are scarce with food and water," Thierry said with a deep frown. "It's hardly a place anyone would want to live. It's surprising that they stayed for so long."

Yvonne glared at that. He didn't like this creature speaking as if he knew him and his people.

"So then he came down here to what? Live down here with us?" Lyree waited for Saraisai to snarl at him but the elder Scough remained silent, actually seeming to agree with his question.

"It's a fair assumption," Amari frowned, "And it would be fine except... Thierry said he attacked. That don't sound like he came down here peacefully."

Thierry began to look more concerned. "So then, perhaps, he came looking for a fight."

The word *fight* seemed to silence all of the Scough, each one looking worried. "We're not equipped to fight them in any way." Jahren dug into the ground with his feet as he continued. "We aren't ready to fight their metal weapons or their fire. We have to talk with them and find out what's going on."

"Talk?" Saraisai let out a low growl, "Clearly, this one ain't feel like talkin' when he attacked Thierry."

"That may be the case with this dragon, but he is our captive now. For some reason he can't talk and we can't learn his intentions, so we must go to the Red Dragons directly. I will not assume the worst until I know for sure." Jahren stopped and looked over at Thierry. "Can you read anything from him?"

Thierry shook his head with a regretful look. "He's too angry. It's all jumbled and nearly impossible to read."

Yvonne would have been angrier at those words, but there was something about the way they'd phrased that. Being able to read him? There was only one creature who could do something like that and Yvonne had only heard stories about him.

The Storyteller.

His mother had mentioned the Storyteller a couple times, a being who could read someone like a book and control them by writing words across their skin. Suddenly what had happened on the cliff made sense. The fake Scough in front of him was the Storyteller, and that was why he couldn't talk or access his heat. But it also meant that he was more helpless than he thought. These Scough had no idea that while this Storyteller might be their friend, the shadows he'd controlled told a very different story. Nowhere, in any of the stories and legends, did the Storyteller use shadows. That talent was reserved for the Kurai, and they were all dead. Only one other creature could do it and that was the last person in the world anyone wanted to be alive.

The Lurkhamara.

"Saraisai and Amari," Jahren nodded to the older fox and the one sitting in his lap, "You can watch over him tonight. Lyree, I want you to go back to the camp and quietly warn the others to be on the lookout, but they don't need to know we have him here. Let's not start more trouble."

"Ok." Lyree was up on his feet as soon as Jahren was done, disappearing into the trees as instructed. Meanwhile, Saraisai started grumbling about how old Scough weren't built to stay up late doing guard duty. Amari chuckled and reassured him that he would keep him company, the playful sway of his tail making Saraisai's grumpiness fade away.

While Yvonne was left to glower at the two Scough now assigned as his personal guards, Jahren turned and motioned for Thierry to follow him away from the group. The two walked silently through the trees until they were out of earshot, then Jahren stopped and faced his friend.

"Thierry. I don't think this is a good idea." Now that they weren't near the group, Jahren could show how worried he was about the whole situation, his tail swishing back and forth as his ears drooped and flattened against his head. "We would have been better off letting him run back to the dragons. I can't believe he just attacked you out of nowhere."

Thierry stepped closer to Jahren and leaned in, nuzzling his face just slightly against the younger Scough's neck. The movement seemed to calm Jahren down as he closed his eyes and leaned into it. "We already discussed why letting him go isn't a good idea," Thierry said. "Him blindly attacking me is reason enough as to why he can't roam free."

"It just doesn't seem like the Red Dragons. We have no quarrel with them," Jahren whispered.

"You're worrying too much." Thierry began running his hands over Jahren's back then up to his shoulders. He slowly began massaging them as he spoke again. "We already spoke about that, too. Perhaps they're tired of being in those mountains."

"But if they are, why not just talk-" Jahren's eyes widened when Thierry tilted his chin up, his thumb slowly brushing over his lips. "Thierry?"

"Shh."

The kiss was soft, a gentle breeze against Jahren's lips that began to put the Scough leader's mind at ease. He was starting to forget what he had even been worried about in the first- *Forget.*

Jahren broke the kiss and stepped away from Thierry, staring at him. "W-what was that just now?"

"My apologies," Thierry said with a smile. "I just wanted you to relax."

"Yes, but you've never used your powers on me."

"I've never had to." Thierry stepped closer and brushed his fingers against the side of Jahren's face. "I can tell how worried you are. I don't like seeing you like this."

Jahren leaned into his fingers, his eyes sliding shut. "I appreciate your concern, but it won't do me any good to forget what's happened."

"Of course."

After a long moment of silence Jahren opened his eyes and looked up at Thierry. "Since you're so willing to use your abilities on me, can those powers of yours tell you if the Reina's going to burn my ears off when I try to talk to her Red Dragons?"

Thierry chuckled. "Now you know I can't do that. I can't show you how future events will turn out."

"Yeah yeah, I know, you've told me that before. But... if things start to go bad, you'll help, right?"

Thierry smiled and reached over to gently scratch behind his ear. "I assure you I will do everything in my power to make sure that this plan works."

Jahren closed his eyes and took a moment to enjoy the motions of Thierry fingers running through his hair. "Thank you my friend."

"Of course," he chuckled. "There's no need to worry, Jahren. This will work. I guarantee it."

Thierry's fingers were soothing and his lips soft against Jahren's ear, but the words seemed misplaced and slowly began to kill the moment. There was something chilling with Thierry's words and Jahren couldn't place it. Among his kind, he knew Thierry the best. He knew him as a quiet and smart creature who usually kept his distance, but cared about those he was close to.

What had happened tonight didn't feel right. The Red Dragon picking a fight was one thing, but Thierry fighting back and capturing him? Then there was his attempt to make Jahren forget. Thierry didn't use his abilities often and to use them on his own friend was not something he would do.

Right now, however, Jahren needed to focus on the task at hand. They now had a Red Dragon on their hands whose Reina wouldn't be pleased. It was Jahren's job as leader to set things right and that would be accomplished by speaking with the Reina and trying to explain everything.

Jahren flashed Thierry a small smile. "I'm going to go for a walk. I need to figure out what I'm going to say to her. I'll see you back at the nests."

He didn't wait for Thierry's response as he turned and walked off, his large ears listening to the sound of his friend moving to follow, then thinking better of it and disappearing among the trees back toward their nests. Only when he was far off did Jahren slow his steps and pause near a tree at the edge of the clearing. Beyond it was a small lake and a break in the canopy of the sky, letting the faint moonlight come in. Jahren leaned against the tree, closing his eyes and enjoying the cool breeze.

"You can come out, I know you're here."

"…but I was quiet," came a soft voice in a comfortably familiar pout.

Jahren couldn't help but laugh. "You were, but even if I couldn't hear you, I knew you'd follow us." He looked over at the tree next to him and smiled as a young girl stepped out.

Mira was the daughter of Thierry and she'd picked up Lyree's habits of always wanting to know what the others were talking about. Even though she was always told to stay put when they had meetings, she never failed to sneak over and listen in. She was dressed much like the others of their kind, wearing a top and dress of tanned leather held together with a couple wires twisted around the edges. Her ears and hair were a rich amber, her skin a light, cinnamon shade that perfectly matched her father's complexion. Draped around her shoulder was a brightly colored bag, decorated in different scraps of fabric that were similar to Thierry's robes.

Behind her a small, black fox scampered over, walking around Jahren and yipping for attention before he smiled and gave in. Jahren knelt down to pet the animal behind one of her gray-tipped ears. "At least Zee is quieter than you," Jahren said.

"Hey!"

"I'm kidding. Mostly."

It was an old conversation the two engaged in, back when Mira had been much younger and barely reaching past Jahren's knee in height. Thierry hadn't been nearly as trusting back then, but Mira had run right over to Jahren and actually hugged him, proclaiming that he could be trusted and saying something quite strange.

"The book told me so."

Oddly enough, as soon as she had said that, Thierry was all smiles and put at ease. Jahren had made a mental note at the time that Mira's book was powerful and he'd had a suspicion of what kind of creature Thierry was. In the years that followed, the three had lived as a family among the Scough and Thierry had grown more comfortable with them. If the Scough noticed how different he was, they didn't talk too much about it. His living with Jahren was approval enough and things were relatively quiet.

Until now.

"I'll do better next time," Mira murmured with conviction, breaking Jahren out of his thoughts. The little fox he had been petting yipped in agreement, walking over to Mira and rubbing against the side of her leg.

"Of course you will."

The two were avoiding the inevitable topic at hand, Mira kneeling down on the ground to run her fingers along Zee's back. Jahren let himself become distracted with the motion of

Mira's fingers, his throat suddenly feeling tight when she looked up at him with a concerned look on her face. "That meeting just now…"

"Yeah," Jahren whispered as he sat down on the ground, letting his back rest against the tree. "The Reina will not be happy. It's her son."

"That's what the jewels on his arm mean, right?" Mira frowned as she moved closer to Jahren, letting her rhetorical question hang in the air. Zee decided to nestle herself in Mira's lap, settling against her legs. "Something about all of this doesn't feel right. My father fighting him, capturing him…"

"He says that he was attacked first."

"Yes, but he would try and avoid the conflict. He would use his powers to get away, not fight."

Jahren frowned. "He… did try to make me forget, to help me relax, he said."

"Forget?" Mira's eyes widened and she quickly shook her head. "Oh no no no. He would never do something like that. That would change the story."

"The story?"

"You know, the story? The book. *Your* book," Mira whispered. "Making you forget something would greatly affect it."

Jahren frowned. Even if he knew what Thierry and his daughter were capable of, it was strange hearing things like "story" in terms of a person's life. "Is there a way to find out for certain if there's something wrong with him?"

Mira shook her head, reaching into the bag around her shoulder. Inside was an old, worn book, the cover a faded brown with scratches along the edges. It was one of those old books you could find in the back of a musty library, one of those ancient structures that gave the sense of old worlds you could discover with just the turn of a page. Unlike the books stored in regular libraries, the one in Mira's hands contained no words. Each page was blank like a sketchpad waiting to be drawn on. Mira moved her finger along a blank page, writing out Thierry's name in the middle of it. The name was visible for only a moment before the letters began to come apart, fading away into the paper until it was left blank once again. "I can't read my father," she whispered. "The book doesn't let me."

"Is there a reason why?" Jahren asked. From what he understood – which was very little – Mira's book could see anything. He had never seen it not be able to show them something.

"I'm not sure. I-I'm still learning."

"I don't like any of this," Jahren whispered as he looked out into the lake. "If he's wrong, or if we do this wrong, people could get hurt."

"He wouldn't want anyone to get hurt. My father hates hurting people."

The worried frown on Jahren's face deepened, his voice getting softer. "So maybe… there's something wrong with him."

Jahren normally wasn't a worrisome person, but this whole situation warranted it and he didn't like it at all. Right now, all he wanted to do was curl up in his nest and talk with Thierry like old times. He wanted to listen to his stories of the different parts of their world he had traveled to, the places that no Scough had ever been. Their world sounded so vast when Thierry talked about it, giving Jahren curious images of lands beyond the forests where they lived. There were the creatures who stayed near the deep waters, swimming around for hours and only coming up if they had a taste for foods that didn't consist of fish or other water creatures. There were the creatures who sang the most beautiful songs, but Thierry always warned him that going near them meant a brutal death. Even with that warning it was all so magnificent to Jahren, his eyes always wide as Thierry smiled and placed a gentle kiss on his lips that would make his heart flutter.

"Jahren, look," Mira whispered, breaking Jahren out of his thoughts.

Jahren opened one eye and glanced over at the girl. He watched as light pencil marks began to spread across the open book page, sketching out what appeared to be a tall, old tree. There was a viney plant twisted among the branches, small flowers scattered along it. Jahren tilted his head, one of his ears twitching. "I know that tree. I've seen it in the forest."

Mira nodded as she ran her fingers over the picture. The tree changed, shifting into what looked like an open door. The picture started to move forward, making Jahren feel like he was stepping through the door and entering into a new area. On the page now stood two people facing one another. One was a taller man who looked to have several years on him, a large scar curving down his face and throat. The other was shorter, thinner, and dark skinned with messy braids tied back in a ponytail to keep them out of his face. There was a sketchy figure kneeling behind the bushes, watching the two figures as the smaller one rushed toward the other, a smoky mist forming around his hand.

Mira squinted her eyes, trying to make out the person in the bushes. Her eyes widened and she shouted, "I think that's me!"

"How do you know that?"

"It has to be me! Why else would the book be showing me these people?"

Jahren frowned. He wasn't sure he liked where this was heading. "So what if it's you? That might not mean anything."

"Of course it means something. And look at this one," she said as she pointed to the young boy, watching as mist began to build around his fingers.

"That mist… I've never seen mist like that before."

"Me either, but this man…" she pointed at the taller man as he watched the younger one, smirking as he waited to see what the boy would do. "From what I've heard others say, he almost seems…"

"Human." Jahren scowled down at the book before he slammed it shut, not letting it show them anything else. "No Mira. Absolutely not."

"But the book…"

"No."

Their world was separate from the humans' world and he'd heard of doorways marked with small, pink flowers. Every now and then there were stories of those who wandered through the doorways and disappeared, but oftentimes it was rare for them to return. The few that did tended to look scared, or like they had just come from a battle, telling stories of awful humans with swords and loud weapons that released something called "bullets." On occasion, around the tree with the flowers, there would be scraps of things from the world of the humans. There was the bag that Mira used, the patches in their clothes, and other such things that humans discarded on their side.

Travelling to the human world was dangerous for any creature, but for a Scough? Jahren shook his head, showing his disapproval again, but Mira stood her ground. "If this is what the book is showing me, it means I need to go. My father is in trouble, Jahren, I know he is. I-I need to do something."

"Going to the human world is out of the question, Mira." Jahren stood up, crossed his arms, and narrowed his eyes at the girl. "It's too dangerous."

"I have to!" She stood up, face set in determination as she looked up at him. Zee stood between them, whining and uncertain about whose side she should take in the argument. Mira opened her book, another image drawing itself on the page. It was a group of people standing behind the two men who had been facing each other before. She couldn't make out their faces, but she knew there had to be a reason why the book was showing her the silhouette. "I think I can trust these people. I think that's what the book is trying to show me."

"You think, but you're not sure."

"Jahren…"

Jahren sighed and stepped closer to her, relenting in his disagreement. When it came to Mira he knew that he could tell her no all day and she would still do what she wanted. It was why she ended up listening in on all the meetings despite being told to stay behind. Mira never listened to direction, not when it was something she felt she needed to do. What's worse, her gut feelings were usually right. He sighed and rested a hand on top of her head, muttering, "You're set on this, aren't you?"

"He's my father and something is wrong with him. I have to do this, even if you don't like it."

"Your father isn't going to like this, either."

"True, but… I have a feeling that my father isn't really here," she whispered, ears drooping down as she looked at her book again.

The air between them was silent for far too long. Even Zee had stopped whining, eyes focused on Jahren, quietly hoping that he would continue to argue until Mira changed her mind. Finally, Jahren took a deep breath and glanced away from her.

"I'll take care of Zee while you're gone."

Mira's eyes widened and the little fox growled, barking at Jahren in an attempt to get him to change his mind. Mira knelt down and pet Zee, giving her a reassuring smile. "It'll be o.k., girl," she said. "I'll be o.k."

"Just promise you'll be careful," Jahren said.

Mira nodded and jumped to her feet, clutching the book close. "I will be, I promise." Leaning forward, she wrapped her arms around Jahren and curled up against him. Jahren closed his eyes and held the young Scough close, his fingers slowly running through her tail. He didn't want to let her go. He didn't want her to have to do this at all. He was scared, a feeling he wasn't used to since his people always kept their heads down. No one had reason to quarrel with them, now all of the sudden they were on the brink of war and he was letting his most trusted friend's daughter go into a dangerous world.

"Jahren? Let go..."

"Not yet," he whispered. "Just a moment longer."

Mira smiled and nodded her head. "All right. Just a moment longer."

The call came through about a week later during that magical time of night when, if you weren't sleeping, you were studying, partying, or taking part in unmentionable activities that Fagan would've preferred over leaving their warehouse home. Still, the call was important, and as much as he wanted to stay curled up in bed watching some late night talk show with a rather enticing special guest, the job beckoned.

After he rolled out of his bed he and Alix were in their SUV in no time, driving down the empty street. It was the dead of night so there were hardly any cars in the warehouse district. It didn't take long for the neighborhood around them to change from the city to the university.

"It's amazing how many people think they're invincible, waltzing across the street whenever they feel like it," Alix commented from the passenger seat as two college students almost wandered into the street in front of them.

Fagan expertly pulled to a stop, "It's a Midwest thing, I think," he said as he waited for them to cross.

"No, it's a stupid people thing."

"Can't be as bad as overseas. You people don't even drive on the right side of the road."

Alix rolled his eyes as Fagan finally started to drive again. The streets were clear, for now. "For the last time, Fagan, that's in London, not France."

"Isn't it the same?" He was joking, of course, but he still enjoyed saying it because it always ruffled Alix's feathers.

The rest of the ride was spent listening to Alix discuss the difference between the two countries, complete with a few French expletives that Fagan only knew the meaning of because he enjoyed giving his partner a hard time.

The conversation was familiar, something that Fagan enjoyed poking fun at with Alix to pass the time while in the SUV. The strange addition to the night, this time, was Dox sitting in the back of their vehicle, listening to them curiously. Since making the deal with Alix, Dox had started playing the part of a civilly captive demon, waiting patiently to answer whatever questions they had. Clearly, he couldn't be left at the warehouse – said Fagan – but it would be dangerous to bring him along – said Alix. Fagan's logic had won in the end, but Alix insisted that they do *something* to keep the demon at bay. As a result, Dox was now sitting with a metal collar around his neck with two battery shaped pieces on each side, putting him in an odd state of probation.

"You do anything I don't like and I will light that collar up like a Christmas tree," Alix had said, slipping a small remote in his pocket.

Dox wasn't sure what a Christmas tree was. When he'd asked, Alix had demonstrated by pressing the button and making the collar light up bright enough to leave a small, painful red ring around his neck. Dox still didn't know what a Christmas tree was, but he assumed they were painful and distasteful things he had no desire to encounter.

Fagan pulled away from the campus area to the highway for an easier and faster drive. They were soon turning off into a different neighborhood full of newer homes that were left untended and empty from a string of recent foreclosures. The yards were kept in decent shape, "For Sale" signs long forgotten and left to fade over time. Few cars dotted the driveways of the one or two occupied homes while windows and doors were covered in dirt and grime from lack of being opened. Even the street lamps had long since burnt out and given up, but one remained illuminated on the corner where the buses would drop off the few people who bothered to live on this block.

Their nondescript SUV drove silently around the block once, getting the lay of the land. Several years ago the vehicle had been a brilliant gray, the kind of car that people tried to win on game shows where you had to guess how much money grocery items cost. Now it was dull and out of date, though kept in good running condition because the hunts that Fagan thrived on were always the most unpredictable. The last thing either of them needed was for their car to not be able to start.

What few residents the neighborhood had were already fast asleep, the streets quiet except for the occasional stray cat yodeling into the night. The SUV finally pulled into a driveway surrounded by trees, the engine going silent. Alix stepped out of the passenger side, dressed in a mixture of black and brown to blend in with the night air. He kept his hand on the gun on his belt as he surveyed the adjoining yards, a second gun ready in his shoulder holster under his jacket. After a moment of complete silence Alix nodded his head, signaling to his partner that it was time to move.

Fagan – "Randall" to his parents, but only because they believed in calling him by his dreadful first name – stepped out of the driver's side and silently closed his door. He was a tall man, well built with lines of muscles pressing through his dark shirt. Stubble covered Fagan's chin and his black hair reached past his shoulders, held back with a simple hair tie to keep it out of his face. Unlike Alix, he wore no jacket, claiming that the cool night air kept him alert and refreshed. Alix had retorted with a comment about Fagan being stubborn and not being able to understand why Minnesotans always seemed to be in denial over how cold it was. Fagan, in response, kindly reminded Alix that, technically, he too was a Minnesotan since he'd lived in the state for a number of years.

Rather than a gun on his belt like his partner, Fagan wore a long, ornate sword across his back made of a black stone that resembled obsidian. He preferred close combat and liked having the ability to see his opponent's face rather than keeping a distance, a method that Alix had perfected. Scars on his body would have proven his love for close combat, but Fagan was good enough to not have any worth mentioning. The few he did have had mostly faded with time or remained as pale blemishes against his skin. He used to pass them off as common injuries. *"I just slipped on a patch of ice, mom,"* but that was back when he still cared enough to make up excuses.

The minute he was out of the SUV Fagan was all business, his usual cocky grin traded in for the serious look of a Hunter, his eyes ready to catch anything. Behind them the back door of the SUV opened and Dox slid out in silence. "This has been an interesting trip," he said with an amused chuckle. "Please tell me more about this London and France you speak of. The stories about the lack of 'flair' British cuisine has compared to the 'elegance' of French food was rather intriguing."

Fagan's serious look cracked immediately and he covered his mouth with his hand, trying not to laugh too hard when he saw the look on Alix's face. To his credit, the shorter man had managed not to go into a monologue about how dull fish and chips were. "That is not important right now," Alix said with a frown.

"It seemed rather important to you on the trip here. In fact, I believe you spoke a different language."

"Alix does that when he gets emotional." Fagan couldn't keep the smile off his face.

"Is that a human characteristic?"

Fagan shook his head and smirked. "Only if your name is Alix."

"Let's get going," Alix hissed to both of them. "I would rather not stand outside in the cold for longer than I have to." It was bad enough that his lips were already becoming chapped, but now he could actually see his breath in the air.

"You're just not use to the-"

"I know. I know. Minnesota cold."

"Minnesota? Is that what this world is called?" Dox asked.

"Just the state." Fagan watched as Dox tilted his head, clearly confused. Fagan chuckled and spoke again. "A state is a part of this country. The country makes up a large part of this continent. There's seven continents that make up our world."

"Wonderful. You passed junior high geography," Alix muttered. Before Dox could ask more questions Alix frowned. "I'll explain later," but he didn't mean it. The last thing he ever wanted was to have a discussion about school systems with a demon.

The group made their way across the decaying yards, mindful of stepping on the few leaves and branches that remained from the trees suffering through the remains of autumn. The neighborhood around them remained silent, even the stray cats calling it a night as their yodeling died off into the darkness. But now it was too quiet, a queasy feeling of uneasiness making their stomachs churn. Fagan stopped at the house next to their target and leaned against the wall to survey the area and get his bearings.

They had received a call from Xaver Knoxton, a former member of their group who had stopped being Fagan's partner three years ago. He was one of those Hunters who preferred to work alone, not answer to anyone, and not be responsible for anyone else but himself. When Alix had begun training under Fagan, Xaver was already mostly out the door and, a month later, he'd moved out. The two had split on good terms and while Fagan and Alix shared the same warehouse home, Xaver had returned to a more nomadic style of living that included abandoned buildings and the basement of foreclosed houses like this one. They would hear from him on occasion, get some leads to particular jobs and demon hunts that Xaver wasn't interested in. Other times, Fagan and Xaver would hang out at a bar, drinking tall mugs of beer that

Alix would find *distasteful* since he preferred a classy, well-aged wine.

Receiving a call from him in the middle of the night with just a place and a time was not Xaver's style. He was all about the details, always telling them the specifics before they would meet up.

This stunk of a trap.

Now that they were here, the sickening feeling of paranoia had only intensified in Alix's stomach. The silence was becoming unnerving and left a dry taste in all of their mouths. Dox watched the edge of the building, one hand pressed against the dirt covered stucco. He knelt down and pressed his hand to the ground, the shadows slithering to embrace his fingers. Dox frowned as he lifted his hand and rubbed his fingers together.

"There's blood, a lot of it." He paused and pointed past the house. "Over there."

"Damnit. That idiot," Fagan swore under his breath. He touched the handle of the sword on his back and pulled it out of the sheath. Now he was certain that Xaver hadn't called them to give them a job.

He had called them for help.

"What the hell did you get yourself tangled in?" Fagan whispered.

Alix held his gun at the ready as he stepped past Fagan and nodded to Dox to follow him. Silently, the three crossed the last backyard to the house.

As they approached they could make out a limp body in their path. It was tossed carelessly between the trunk of a large tree and an old fence that had been worth something once upon a time. Bullet holes were lodged deeply into thick flesh, the crushed grass soaked with blood that led around the yard and back to the house. Bullets could be found in the fence and the side of the house along with long sword slashes and broken twigs from hurried feet running through the yard.

There had obviously been a battle here, and recently. What was surprising was the fact that Xaver had lost, his preferred Japanese style sword lying flat on the ground next to his body.

Xaver had been a large man of Asian descent, made of muscle from head to toe. The thick scar across the side of his cheek was etched down to his throat, a reminder of a young Xaver's first hunt that had gone horribly wrong. The scar had given him a raspy voice, something a casting agent would have seen as gold for portraying a hit man or an intimidating bodyguard. Xaver had been well known for hunting down demons with precision and expertise, but whatever happened in this backyard tonight did not reflect that. This was something desperate, rushed, an attempt to stay alive and…

Alix looked up from the body and frowned at the house, his eyes scanning the windows. They were all closed, the glass still intact and not a victim of the violence that had taken place. Whoever had attacked Xaver hadn't ventured inside. Xaver had met them outside, drawing them away from the house.

Something was inside, something worth Xaver's life.

"Inside."

Fagan took a deep breath to readjust his thoughts and look away from his fallen comrade. "Thinking the same thing," he said as he led the way to the back door.

Dox followed them in complete silence, all three standing at the thick, concrete slab that led to a door that had once been white. The house was a simple two story, the outside made of stucco with edging on the windows and door that had fallen off a long time ago. A piece of plywood was nailed over the door's window while a completely new door knob and deadbolt stood out against the rest of the house.

Fagan lowered his sword long enough to quietly test the door knob. Click. Click. Completely immobile, locked tight. No doubt the deadbolt above it would be the same.

"We should back away." Dox murmured as he looked up the side of the house. "There's someone inside."

"How can you tell?"

"I can't." Then Dox smirked, a gesture that he had seen Fagan do that seemed to irritate Alix. "The shadows are telling me."

Alix nodded, turning his attention back to the house. If someone – or some*thing* – was inside, the best course of action was to go in and attempt to take it off guard. The lock presented a problem since the door was the most silent way to get into the house. Knowing Xaver's style, the man had probably found a loose window frame in the basement and worked on it until the window popped out enough to open. Repeating that effort would have been pointless as neither Alix nor Fagan were the best at breaking and entering. Their attempts would surely be heard by whoever was inside.

The problem solved itself a few seconds later when the door actually blew out, broken pieces of wood flying back with Fagan and Alix. The two found themselves on the ground just beyond the steps, Dox somehow managing to land safely next to the fence though he looked stunned. There wasn't time to react as something heavy and hard settled on Alix's chest. Cold shot through his body like electricity, confusing his senses and making the gun completely useless in his hand. He couldn't move his fingers, much less his body, to respond to the threat. All he could do was lay there in shock as his vision focused on the person crouched over him, literally freezing him to death.

The young man on top of Alix was fast and built as thin as a willow tree, his skin a deep, dark brown. Long, black hair fell down his back in messy braids that were held out of his face by a single band that struggled to keep hold of all of it. His eyes burned with a pale blue, a look of seething hatred choking Alix as he glared at him. Then, a second later, he was away from Alix and jumping back across the yard. The ice cold disappeared with him, letting Alix roll over on the ground and gasp for breath.

"Are you all right?" Fagan knelt beside him, his sword at the ready and his eyes on the inhuman boy. Alix noticed that there was blood on the end of his sword, showing that Fagan had cut the boy and shoved him away. Alix pushed him back and sat up, immediately aiming his gun. Two shots rang through the night and he heard one snap into the tree trunk next to the boy, the other hitting the middle of a strange white tattoo covering his arm.

He didn't know what that tattoo was or what it meant, but from the boy's earlier attack it was obviously the source of some sort of power, the cold having disappeared the moment he'd let go with that hand.

The boy cried out, the sound from his mouth sounding more reptilian than human. The bullet seemed to have the opposite effect of pain and now the boy was on the move again, seconds after his arm was hit.

"Don't hit that arm again, you'll only anger it. You need to knock him out." Dox's voice carried across the yard to whisper directly into Alix and Fagan's ears, giving them advice through the darkness. The two moved without so much as a look at each other and split, moving to surround the boy and divide his attention. Neither anticipated the sharp icicles the boy threw in their directions with precision that rivaled Xaver's own accuracy. Alix ducked and rolled, the icicles narrowly missing while Fagan blocked them with his sword and kept charging. The larger man reached the boy first and took a hard, quick swing that was strong enough to break right through the ice shield the boy was creating between them. It shattered like glass, scattering across the ground in small pieces as the boy caught the edge of Fagan's sword. He shoved him backward, not even wincing from the cuts the sword had put into his hand, small lines of blood sliding down his fingers.

"You need to knock him out," Dox spoke softly.

"I heard you the first time." Alix growled, his eyes combing across the yard. A full on run and attack wouldn't work. They were out matched and they had no idea what type of demon this boy was, but maybe there was another option.

Alix smirked to himself and pushed away from the ground, running straight for the boy. At the last moment he dropped into a slide across the cold, wet ground next to him, and aimed his gun right up at the branches above them. Shots fired in quick succession, hitting the wood perfectly. Alix rolled away as he heard the wood cracking above them. The boy looked up at the branch too late as it came crashing down painfully across his shoulder. He stumbled back, clutching his right shoulder and throwing himself into the fence to dodge Fagan's next sword swing, the old wood whining and cracking in protest. The boy ended up crouching on the ground, panting as he watched them.

"He's getting ready to attack again. Careful-"

Dox's voice stopped as the boy turned his head, those ice blue eyes now focused on him and making him his new target.

Fine then. Let him be distracted while we take him out, Alix thought to himself as he quickly reloaded his gun. Dox's information was valuable, but this rogue demon was a more pressing matter. Might as well use the demon as bait, and if their captured demon ended up killed in the process that was fine. The collar hadn't been working the way it should've and Alix was sure that it would only be a matter of time before Dox let his demonic nature take over and attack them both. He would just have to find another way to get more information on the Storyteller, getting rid of two dangerous demons was first priority.

Their target darted across the yard, the shadows around him rippling but not responding fast enough to catch him. As he moved, ice gathered around the bleeding arm with the tattoo, swirling like its own little blizzard before he threw it straight at Dox, leaving him with nowhere to escape. Alix leveled his gun to fire a shot, eyes trained on the back of the ice creature's head, but he never got the chance to fire.

Instead, the ground around the boy reared up, plant roots breaking through the dead grass and slithering up. They tangled around him and, without warning, yanked him down to the ground in a hard crash. The ice attack crumbled away before it could hit Dox, the cracked, gray roots wrapping around the boy's tattooed arm until the mark was no longer visible. The young man cried out in protest and pain, the rough branches squeezing around the wound on his arm and the small cut on his side from Fagan's earlier attack. He struggled against the branches but they only grew thicker, keeping him locked in place.

"What the hell are you doing, you fucking idiot! Are you trying to get killed?!"

The sudden voice was female, coming from the front yard through the broken entryway in the fence. She stepped around it, wearing a pair of loose black pants with a black tank top. Fishnet covered her arms and the small exposed area of her waist. Her hair was a dark color, possibly red, but it was too hard to tell in the middle of the night. As she walked up to Dox she looked ready to slap him across the face.

"Cyn? What are you doing here?"

Alix was surprised to be able to read an expression on Dox's face despite his lack of normal eyes. It was a mix of concern, surprise, and a touch of intimidation as the new girl, Cyn, continued to berate him, her fist balled up at her sides.

Alix swore softly under his breath. He didn't even consider Dox having some sort of partner.

"Saving you, you moron!"

Forget slapping, this was the type of girl who threw punches and she looked very close to the point of bashing Dox's face in.

"This isn't a good place for you to-"

"Shut up. I'm not going to take advice from someone who was just going to stand there while an Ice Dragon froze his head off!"

Ice Dragon. So that's what the boy was. Now that Alix had that tidbit of information he could attempt to make some sense of the situation. However, with a very irritated demon girl – he assumed she was demon, no human could make roots erupt from the ground like that – he only had one sure fire way to calm things down. Alix stepped toward them, careful to step away from the roots as he aimed his gun straight at the new girl. "Don't move."

Behind them Fagan crossed over to the boy trapped by the roots and turned his sword, delivering a quick blow to the back of his head and knocking him out. The boy's body slumped against the roots as the air around him stopped feeling like the inside of a butcher's freezer. Despite this, Fagan stood with his sword ready in case he woke up or if the roots decided to choose a new target.

Cyn turned and glared right at Alix. "You're a Hunter."

"I am. And you're a demon."

"Cyn, back down." Dox's voice was low, showing an authority over the girl despite the level of rage she had been directing toward him earlier. He seemed older than her, more experienced, but then these were demons with unpredictable powers and their looks didn't always match up with their ages. This much closer Alix could tell that she had dark red hair, almost blood colored strands that were long enough to brush against the back of her neck. One of her ears was sprinkled with piercings, small silver loops that dangled around her earlobe. Her other ear only had one earring but Alix recognized it as the same symbol that Dox wore in his own ear.

Terrific. An emo, gothic demon. Alix didn't know that such a thing existed but it certainly was the last thing he needed to deal with right now.

There was also something else through the fishnet, just on the edge of the right side of her waist. It looked like a mark, maybe a tattoo, but Alix's gut insisted that it was something more. The mark almost looked like a rash, but it wasn't red and inflamed. Instead it had scabbed over with strange, crusted over pieces that almost looked like scales. The mark reminded him of snake skin, or maybe a frog. Alix wondered about it, but that was a distraction that he couldn't be bothered with right now.

"Who are you and what is your connection with them?" Alix asked.

Cyn crossed her arms and gave a small snort. "Dox is my idiotic friend who decided to get himself captured." Then she turned her attention to the unconscious boy trapped in the roots. "That kid? I've never seen him before in my life."

"And why should I trust that?"

"Hey, you asked." Cyn frowned, the annoyance clear on her face. "Are we going to stand out here all night? It's cold."

Fagan stepped closer to them and nodded to Alix to relax a little. "Our friend was killed here. We need to look around in that house and you need to come back with us."

"That's bulls-"

"Cyn." Dox snapped at her, effectively cutting off her protest before turning to look at Alix and Fagan. "I won't let you harm her."

"Fine. Alix, stay out here with them. If she or that boy move, shoot them." Fagan moved past them and gave them no chance to argue as he disappeared into the house through the broken doorway. Alix made a grand show of reloading his gun while Cyn just rolled her eyes.

Away from the bickering group Fagan was free to look around the house. It wasn't in bad condition, but he could tell no one had lived here for a couple of years. The floorboards were exposed, covered in dust, leaves, and sticks that had managed to collect inside the house. Every once in a while there were signs of someone moving the shavings and leaf carcasses aside, attempting to make the place at least a little bit livable. The point was to make the old house look uninhabited, especially if anything happened to Xaver. It was what the man was good at: details, even down to the small rat droppings that were across the edges of the kitchen.

Details. With the exception of the quick call made that night.

Fagan closed his eyes for a moment and took a deep breath. There were memories floating through his mind of hunts and tall mugs of beer shared with a friend. Memories of a former partner, someone who had helped him become a better Hunter, someone who Fagan had, once upon a time, looked up to. When Xaver left to work on his own it had been on good terms, but in the beginning Fagan had felt a touch bit sore about it.

"You don't need me around," Xaver had said. *"You and Alix will be fine. 'Sides, ain't like I'm not gonna still be around. You still owe me drinks for that bet last week."*

The man had been right. He had still been around, still came by the warehouse, and still sat in the same spot at the bar they would go to. At that point Fagan realized that they were equals and Xaver had been absolutely right: he didn't need him as a partner anymore. Instead, Xaver had been upgraded to a trusted friend.

"Ain't like I'm not gonna still be around," Fagan frowned bitterly. "Liar," he whispered, forcing himself to take another deep breath. Now was not the time for grief, he knew he couldn't stand in the house for too long. Alix was still outside with three demons – one unconscious, but the point still stood. Fagan knew that if the mouthy one didn't annoy him enough to make him shoot, the shadowy one would. "Get it together, Fagan," he said softly before opening his eyes, continuing his investigation of the house.

Fagan turned his attention to the stairs, stepping around an old, rotting door that was quietly hanging from its hinges. The wallpaper curled and hung in waves off the walls and revealed worn hints of dull, white paint, the previous color of the walls. Once he was at the bottom of the stairs he listened to the silence for a long moment before he reached back and gently touched the hilt of his sword.

"Eegil."

The word was a soft whisper across his lips and, for a moment, nothing happened. Then a light hum emanated from the sword followed by a soft glow from the blade. Around him the basement slowly came into focus as if he'd been carrying a flashlight the entire time. The light had a blue hue to it, bathing the room in faint color as Fagan looked around. Pulling the sword out of the holder strapped across his back, he held it at ready, using it to shine light on the nooks and crannies of the deserted basement.

Eegil was actually shorter than most swords, reaching nearly the same length as Fagan's arm. In its true form the hilt and blade were made of a deep, black metal that almost looked red in the right light. The hilt was smooth but it wasn't slippery at all, and Fagan had never felt a sword that fit better in his hands.

The edge of the hilt, just before the blade, actually resembled a hand. Long, spiny fingers came out and twisted around the blade that protruded from the palm. Red veins spread over the blade itself and more than once Fagan had seen them pulsating with life when he hadn't expected it. Now, as the blade glowed with light, the veins were pulsating again, but he'd had the sword for so many years he was used to it. "Don't worry," Fagan said as he looked around the room, "Alix isn't here to complain about you."

He felt the hilt of the sword warm his hand as if responding to his statement. Fagan chuckled softly to himself. His partner absolutely hated his sword, always commenting about how there was no way a demonic weapon could be trusted. Fagan may have felt the same way once, but ever since he quote, unquote, "won" the sword in a fight against a demon shortly after Xaver had left he somehow knew that the sword would never turn against him.

As Fagan looked around the area he could see that, unlike the top of the house, the basement showed clear signs of habitation. A box in the corner contained various cans of food and army rations in need of hydration. Two jugs of water, one partially empty, hugged the corner. Fagan recognized a duffel bag beside the water as one that Xavier had owned. Usually, all of the food and water Xavier needed fit neatly inside his duffel bag.

This was too much for Xaver, had his habits changed?

Fagan crossed the room, looking under the stairs and behind the furnace before he found what he was looking for. There was a space where the shavings and pellets had been brushed away to make room for two full bedrolls. Had the ice demon been staying with Xaver? Or was there someone else? The door had been locked before it was broken, so maybe the demon had been inside while Xaver was killed.

Had Xaver been protecting the demon? That thought seemed completely absurd, but Fagan had to admit that there might be some substance to it.

Xaver's call had been so quick that the man had to know that he was in trouble. He probably kept it short so he could have enough time to hide anything that could have been important. But where would he hide it?

"Come on old friend," Fagan whispered as his eyes scanned the area. "At least give me something." He stopped when his eyes spotted the old furnace pipes that were spreading across the underside of the house. Acting on a hunch, Fagan walked over and felt above the pipes. His fingers met with cobwebs and dust for a moment, but a few inches over he felt a collection of newspaper pieces. Once he pulled the papers down he could see drawings on top of the finance section – stocks were dropping, what a shame. There were symbols and a diagram, the type of things he and Xaver used to draw all the time before a hunt.

"What are you doing?"

Fagan glanced over at his new partner, the blond haired young man sitting across from him at the table, a bored look on his face. Fagan chuckled before he responded with, "Drawing a map."

"On newspapers? And what's with the triangles and circles?"

"You never write down something as simple as words. Words can be read. So, instead, we use symbols."

"Is this from the great philosophy of Xavier Knoxton?"

"Watch it, kid," Xaver said as he walked into the warehouse, still acting like he owned the building even if he had left a month ago. *"And Fagan's right. This way, only the two of you will understand this map."*

"It makes for great secrecy," Fagan frowned as he looked over the newspaper, "But not so much if you're dead."

It would have to be enough because a thorough search of the basement revealed nothing else. Fagan folded up the papers and shoved them in his pocket before whispering the word, "Eegil," once more. The light from his sword faded out, the blade looking like a normal weapon as the pulsing veins shrank back into the metal.

"You can't kill him. He didn't do anything wrong. Even I could tell he was defending himself. *You* shot his dragon."

Fagan stepped out of the house and right into an argument between Cyn and Alix.

"Dragon? You mean the mark on his arm?" Now demons had actual creatures that slept on their arms? "That does not concern me. He attacked us first," said Alix, pulling away the roots from the young demon's body. He still had one hand holding onto his gun, tugging and breaking the roots with his other hand as he freed the boy, waiting for him to open his eyes just so he'd have an excuse to shoot him again.

Dox had taken a place sitting on the concrete steps as if he were spending the night looking up at the stars and not dealing with a hostile man out to exterminate anything remotely inhuman. And then there was Cyn, standing next to him, a glare of disapproval set across her face over the entire situation. Maybe she didn't know any other expression but pissed off. She was pissed at Alix, pissed at Dox, and probably pissed at the steps for daring to let Dox sit on them in such a calm fashion.

"You're both coming back with us. We will sort this out there. No one dies, yet." Fagan knew that Alix would not approve of that last part and a hard glare sent in his direction confirmed that, but he was taking charge on this current series of events and Alix would have to listen to him. Fagan wanted to know what had happened to Xaver and, at the moment, the dark skinned demon with the dragon was their only clue.

Cyn toyed with the idea of using that moment to slap the gun out of Alix's hand just to knock him off of his self-righteous *demons are scum* pedestal, but for some reason Dox was set on playing the part of captured demon. So she would play along, for now, and at least the larger man – Fagan – didn't seem to want to kill them.

"Fine, let's head back then," Alix muttered.

Fagan lifted the unconscious demon up and put him across his shoulder as the group began to filter out of the backyard. As they walked, Alix nearly tripped over a large tree root that he swore hadn't been protruding out of the ground before. He turned and glared at Cyn who simply blinked at him. "What?"

"Nice to know that demons lack any sort of maturity."

"I have no idea what you're talking about," Cyn said, watching as Alix turned and headed toward the parked SUV.

"So is it time for another discussion on British versus French things?" Dox asked as he slipped into the back of the vehicle with Cyn.

"There's no discussion required," Cyn smirked. "British people are much, much better. Better accents. Cooler shows on T.V. And London is an amazing city."

Fagan didn't need to look at Alix to know that he was gritting his teeth as he spoke. "Excuse me?"

"French people suck. They're rude little pricks that think they're better than everyone else."

If Alix were in a right state of mind he'd wonder how a demon seemed to know so much about their world, right down to television programs. It was dangerous for one of them to know so much and unnerving to think that some demons were so deeply involved with their culture. But, at that moment, all Alix could think of saying was, "I'm French!"

"Well then, my point is completely valid."

Fagan took a moment to breathe in the cold night air before slipping into the driver's seat, bracing himself for a long, long drive.

Xaver had picked a terrible night to get killed.

Chapter 2

Later that night, away from the now abandoned house and back toward civilization, stares and murmurs followed a beautiful woman as she crossed the floor in a local bar. To be fair, *beautiful* wasn't enough to describe her, but it was a word that the drunk men and scattered college students in the bar could comprehend.

The bar was on the other side of the suspension bridge that led into the downtown area, not suffering from explosions of loud music and too many people grinding against one another. This bar wasn't themed, didn't get attacked by the city's radio stations, or offer cheaper prices for single ladies on certain nights of the week. Instead, it was quiet and relatively low key, perfect for her to get away from work for a night. Here she could sit by herself at the bar and relax, not thinking about whatever mission her boss and his partner were on or what danger they might encounter.

As she made her way over to her normal seat all eyes were locked on her. She had long, slender legs of ebony skin that ended in a pair of stylish heels the color of fresh grown lilacs. She wore a dark business jacket that matched her short skirt and a button down shirt that complimented her heels. What really made the outfit stand out was the black men's necktie that was tied around her neck and gently falling against her chest. It couldn't be helped; the men's eyes immediately started to undress her, imagining the stunning woman lying across a bed with her short, stylish haircut becoming wrinkled and disorganized after a night of breathless sex.

A hard glare in their direction made the message clear, interrupting the pleasant scenarios they had worked so hard to create. She wasn't interested in any of it, so their eyes had no other choice but to turn back to their games of darts, pool, and touchscreens, drinking their fantasies away with bottles of beer.

The bartender, a young woman with more tattoos than hair, flashed her a welcoming smile as she wiped a glass clean. "What can I get you?"

The woman blinked. She didn't recognize this woman as one of the regulars who worked at the bar, she definitely would've noticed the glorious amount of ink over her skin had she seen her before. Perhaps the stubborn, heavyset owner had finally hired some extra help.

"She'll have sparkling water. She doesn't drink." A second woman sat down at the bar, a complete contrast to the first. Her thin, blonde hair was starting to show hints of premature gray, further accenting the severe angles of her face. She wore a comfortable pair of jeans and a shirt that was stylish, or had been more than a couple of years ago when the logo was still fresh and new. A bag at her shoulder held a notepad that never left her side and a hidden tape recorder at the ready. "Good evening, Katalynne."

"Liza." The name left the dark beauty's lips with more than a little disdain as she placed her work tablet on the bar. Instead of unlocking it to see the screen, she left the cover closed, turning on the bar stool and lacing her fingers together. "I thought I made it very clear that I wasn't interested in assisting your career."

"Oh, you did. But then this interesting little tidbit came up and I just knew you could help me out with it." She pulled the notepad out so quickly that Katalynne swore that she could summon it with just a mere thought. "Seems they found a body a couple hours from here dumped in a quarry. Victim of a particularly nasty blade. Or sword." Liza's eyes glanced up at Katalynne as she said that part, making sure she caught it. "Victim is a young man in his early twenties, sliced apart by a large blade with an unidentifiable white mold covering plants nearby." The notepad was closed and Liza smirked. "Is your boss out sharpening that strange sword of his on college students' bodies again?"

Her drink arrived and Katalynne set out a few bills for the bartender, not willing to accept anything from the woman sitting beside her. "He was cleared of those charges," Katalynne said, remembering the pointless mess she had to deal with a couple of months ago. Three dead bodies, two of which were students on campus, with the same evidence of a brutal sword attack but no proof that the sword belonged to her boss. "In fact, I believe you were in the courtroom at the time."

"Doesn't mean Randall Fagan isn't a psychotic killer. The public has seen the pictures. There are bodies and sightings of him during the night in different neighborhoods. Just because the police can't link the bodies doesn't mean he's not responsible."

Katalynne rolled her eyes, disinterest in anything the woman had to say. "And I suppose you believe in his partner, Bigfoot, as well?"

Liza ignored the jest and kept pushing. "How about you, Ms. Cove? What exactly do you do for him that pays your bills? You left a highly lucrative job as a personal assistant for one of the leading law firms in the state to work for this man? What does he pay you for?"

"I pick up his dry cleaning."

Liza set down the notepad, obviously not happy with that response. Katalynne could practically see the gears turning in the poor woman's head as she tried to come up with another angle to strike from. Katalynne turned her attention to her drink. There was a hint of cherry that she wasn't used to but it wasn't necessarily a bad thing.

"Where is your boss tonight?"

Katalynne tapped her tablet screen, pulling up his schedule like a good little personal assistant. "I'm not sure, I clocked out over an hour ago. What he does after work isn't my business. And I believe you've run dry for the night."

"What's your rush? All the dry cleaning shops are closed by now." Liza bit the words off sharply. The notepad was closed now and she was flying solo, that well trained mind looking for another place to pounce. "You're sleeping with him, aren't you?"

That brought the raising of a perfect eyebrow but Katalynne remained calm. "Now you are reaching. Good night, Liza. I would like to enjoy my drink in peace."

"I'm right, aren't I? He's significantly less attractive unless you like the rugged type. That is entirely possible... – you're frowning. You don't like this idea. How about you tell me what's going on and I won't plaster the front of the paper next week with lewd details of your secret sex life."

Katalynne turned her attention back to the woman sitting next to her and decided to do away with the pleasantries. "I wasn't aware that your own sex life was so stagnant that you have to fantasize about mine."

"Don't believe me? I'll post it, and believe me I have quite a few pictures of you just waiting to be fancied up in Photoshop–"

"Hmm, that sounds like harassment." This came from the bartender who still had her lovely tattooed back toward them, the lyrics of some song curving over her shoulder blades in small, delicate lines. Her hands still worked in precision, wiping clean another glass. As she leaned forward to place it away she turned her head just slightly, her gaze settling on Liza to make the threat clear.

Liza stood up and grabbed her notepad, shoving it hard enough into her purse that both women could hear the keys jingle in protest. "We'll talk later." With that, she turned and stomped out of the bar.

"I don't think she likes me." The bartender smirked as she wiped the spot where Liza had been sitting.

Katalynne chuckled and finished off her drink before sliding it forward for a refill. "Thank you."

"No problem. I don't like her much anyway. This one's on me." The refill appeared with little effort and this time there was a cherry floating on top of the liquid. Katalynne relaxed in her seat as her cell phone vibrated in her pocket. Leaning back a little she fished it out and brought it to her ear. She turned so that her back was to the bartender who had already gone back to serving another patron.

"Katt. Got some overtime for you."

She could almost hear the smirk on his lips as Randall Fagan spoke. No matter how serious the situation he was always a hairline away from pressing her up against a wall in a less than professional way. It would have been sexual harassment if Katalynne didn't find his attempts at seduction so amusing. She had made it clear on several occasions that she wasn't interested, but he kept stalking her like a clever little puppy. Fagan knew how to perfectly walk the line between creepy and cute so that she was never really tempted to quit.

"I work hourly. You know I don't do overtime." A touch unlocked her tablet and she slid her finger across the screen to begin taking notes.

"Xaver's dead. Killed by bullets mostly, so it doesn't look like a demon attack. We found him at the house he wanted to meet at. I found some papers which Alix is sending you scans of now. I've also got two demons for you to try and find information about."

Katalynne listened quietly, a soft pain in her heart from the news of Xaver's death. She had been the one to take his call but she had no idea it would lead to this. In their line of work being hurt – or killed – was always a possibility that lingered at the edge of each mission. A successful track record over the years, however, had Katalynne convinced that her boss and the people he associated with were damn near invincible.

Until now.

The table the men used to enjoy drinks at wasn't too far from where she was sitting, currently occupied by a couple who were drinking until the other looked attractive enough to sleep with. Katalynne had been hired after Xaver left so she didn't know him as well as Alix and especially not as well as Fagan. Still, she did speak with him often enough, always being the one to answer the phone when he called or the first to greet him when he came by to have drinks "like the good ol' days."

Xavier "Xaver" Knoxton and Randall Fagan were more like brothers than colleagues, Katalynne could tell from the moment she first met the large man. Despite his intimidating voice and scars Xaver was friendly, immediately welcoming Katalynne as if she had been part of this crazy group of Hunters since day one. She had memories of enjoying a drink with them on occasion, Xaver calling out the nickname "Legs" when referring to her. At times he'd even play the role of possessive boyfriend when someone got a little too friendly with her and ignored that she clearly wasn't interested.

"The first demon is young, looks about late teens, early twenties," Fagan said, breaking her out of her thoughts. "He's tall and thin for his age, skin color a bit darker than yours. He has a large mark on his arm, white, looks like it's made of some sort of scales and it's in the shape of a dragon. The other one called him an Ice Dragon more than once."

She was tempted to say something to Fagan but decided to save it for later, her fingers flying over the tablet with focused ease. "Got it."

"The second looks a couple years younger, but not by much. Very human looking, the kind you see hanging out at that dark and moody store in the mall. She's got a mark on the side of her waist, some burn or something, but there's a definite shape and it looks different, like frog skin. She made the roots come out of the ground and attack. She's also acquainted with Dox."

"I'll see what I can find on them but you know that's not much to go on."

"It'll have to do for now. They'll be here when you show up tomorrow. We invited them over as guests for the next few days until we find out what happened with Xaver."

Katalynne opened the attachments on her email and found a photo of Xaver's body. Her eyes widened and she was sure that Fagan could hear her gasp quietly through the phone.

The first photo showed him lying between the tree and the fence while the second was obviously taken in the back of Fagan's SUV under much better lighting. She silently counted the bullet holes. Seven. Whoever had killed him had wanted to make sure he was dead and fast before he could catch up with them. Each hole was aimed perfectly at a vital part of the body. This killer was an expert shot. "Fagan, I'm so sorry," she whispered.

There was no response for a moment and Katalynne almost spoke up again but Fagan beat her to it. "We'll discuss it later. I'll see you in the morning." With that the phone snapped off. If the pictures didn't point to the seriousness of the situation his lack of flirting certainly did. It wasn't like Fagan to be so businesslike if he wasn't in the middle of a hunt.

Pocketing her phone she glanced over the notes she'd taken, clearing her mind of concerns over her employer's less than flirtatious mood. Tapping a perfectly manicured nail on the bar she considered where to start. The details of Xaver's death were pressing, but the more important matter was probably the two demons Fagan had told her about. They were the more immediate issue due to them being in such close proximity now. If Fagan and Alix hadn't killed them already that meant two things: they were trying to find out information from them, and that they'd be held in the "cells" Fagan had constructed in the basement of the warehouse. It was a gamble that that place would hold anyone, but it had worked so far with Dox and a couple other demons over the years. It was better than nothing.

To be honest Katalynne had a feeling that those cells only worked with Dox because he was fine with staying put. If that shadow demon really wanted to leave he'd be gone by now. To add a demon that used ice and another that moved roots to the mix was so dangerous that it was bordering on stupid. Dox was much too intelligent for Katalynne's comfort, nothing at all like the few other demons that Fagan and Alix had brought to that warehouse over the years. Those demons, at least, couldn't be reasoned with and would normally end up with a bullet in their head. Creatures like Dox didn't mind sitting, waiting, being patient, and negotiating with them. Who knew what these two new demons were capable of, especially if one of them associated with Dox.

But then, that was Katalynne's job to find out.

In the years since these demons had started to show up more around the world, certain fringe groups calling themselves

"Hunters" had popped up and eventually began coordinating their efforts. It was almost a crime to call the variety of creatures *demons*, but the old term stuck and seemed to be universally understood, making things simpler. What came out of the effort, at least recently, was a spanning global collection of records, all arranged online behind the strongest of firewalls and every other electronic defense conceivable. The owner of the records decided who had access to the records and seemed to choose Hunters and groups only after a trial period. Most Hunters who didn't have access were either too inexperienced or had betrayed the others in one way or another. Having or not having access to this database was a surefire way to determine who had the skills needed and who could be trusted.

Fagan, who had never been one to make friendly with computers, had given his information over to Katalynne. Now, sipping on the last of her drink, she put in the multiple passwords required and entered her search terms. She could do a few quick searches for the time being and get the information back to him before the night was over. Then she could spend time later being more thorough; that was the best course of action.

She found no mention of Ice Dragons in the entire database, which was odd since there was a significant amount of information on other dragons. They certainly weren't the giant, fire breathing creatures that humans wrote about in fairy tales, video games, and roleplaying get-togethers. These dragons were more like parasites, creatures made of a certain element that attached to a host and lived off their energy. The most common were Red Dragons, creatures who controlled fire. The Ice Dragon was probably the same type of creature, meaning that it would most likely be vulnerable to heat.

Demons that controlled plants were common, but Fagan had said roots specifically so that was important. In her quick search she did find one or two demons with such powers, but they were rare on account of how inhuman they looked. Most had been spotted in the marsh areas of the southern states and had been killed on sight due to being mistaken for mutated alligators. They would make it onto the front page of joke newspapers sometimes, ranking up there with aliens and UFO sightings, something that a majority of the population decided to not believe in. Aside from the frog skin like scar, that sounded nothing like what Fagan had described. He had specifically said that the girl looked human. In fact, she looked so human that she had a style: gothic, like the kids who hung out at the "dark and moody store in the mall."

"Hey. How's the reading?"

Katalynne blinked and looked up from her research to find the bartender leaning over with another drink. She was politely keeping her distance, not reading over Katalynne's screen, and smiled as she slid the drink over. "I wanted to give you a refill but you were so caught up in your work. Didn't mean to disturb you."

"No, it's fine. Thank you." Katalynne saved the information and pushed the data aside on the screen, locking the system. "I need a break to process it anyway."

"Seems important." Her hands moved with studied perfection, fetching a glass from under the bar and mixing another alcoholic drink as they talked, stepping away just for a moment to pass it to a patron and then back to talk and mix another. "It's late and a week night. Shouldn't you be planning a date out to a local club? Or maybe slipping on a hot dress for some fancy restaurant and play?"

Katalynne chuckled. "The shows would be over by now and all the best restaurants are closed, but that almost sounded like an offer."

"It almost is." The woman winked as she moved to deliver another drink, weaving around one of the other bartenders with practiced ease to do so.

"Almost?"

A pause in the service and she leaned back against the ice chest. Katalynne could see the tattoos on her back from before matched the ones encircling her arms. The designs were made of sweeping lines and curves, a physical representation of a warm autumn breeze that flowed over her arms. "Almost depending on what?" Katalynne pressed.

"Depending on if you're interested in that sort of thing." There was nothing subtle about that smirk and Katalynne liked it. This type of flirting was completely different from the men with their invading eyes and Fagan with his not so serious remarks. This was an honest woman actually asking her out.

"I might be."

"Then I might have to take you up on that." The bartender smiled. "Harper Blake. And you?"

"Katalynne Cove."

"Dude, you two are so hot together."

The moment shattered, crashing to the floor as Katalynne turned her head and looked at the table just behind her. She wasn't surprised, but very annoyed, to find a young man sitting there with short hair and dark, brown eyes. There was no mistaking the familiarity behind that grin, it was the same one she saw on Fagan's lips every morning when she came in for work.

"Zach. How long have you been sitting there?" Katalynne tried not to sigh in exasperation.

Zach was Fagan's younger brother who attended the local community college thanks to his parents who had insisted that he didn't turn out like, *"That screw-up of a brother of yours."* She'd crossed paths with him a couple of times while working for his brother, but seeing him outside of the workplace was not what she needed right now. At least at work Fagan was there to act as a buffer, insisting that Zach leave and not be a part of his Hunter lifestyle.

"Long enough to see you two undressing each other with your eyes." The grin widened, spreading across the young man's face like a striped cat whose head could turn in a full circle. "It's hot and I'd hate to break it up, but I figured I should ask for a ride before you two disappeared back to the stock room to make out."

Harper chuckled, seeming much more amused than Katalynne – who hated being turned into a spectacle when it wasn't on her own terms. Just as politely as before, Harper stepped away to service another patron coming up to the bar. The moment was completely gone, but it wasn't like Katalynne didn't know where she worked.

She turned and frowned deeply at Zach. "You have your own bike. Where is it?"

"Broken at home in the garage. I had to catch the bus for class today." An apologetic look crossed his boyish features. "Please give me a ride back? I can repay you for the gas."

"Class huh? It's pretty late, Zach, I'm fairly certain they don't have classes this late at night..." Katalynne checked her phone to see what time it was then rose an eyebrow at Zach, "...or this early in the morning."

"Um... I'm an astrology major? Classes run late for star gazing?"

Katalynne sighed. There was no way she was going to drive all the way out to the lush suburbs where Fagan and Zach's parents lived, but this way she could at least go back to the warehouse and get the information she'd found to Fagan as quickly as possible. "Fine. But I am dropping you off at the warehouse, you can catch the bus in the morning from there."

"Sweet!"

Katalynne suddenly felt like someone's mother, "And you are not interfering with your brother's work."

"Of course not."

"And I don't want to hear another word about tonight and the bartender leave your mouth, especially not around your brother. If you say anything I will make sure you regret it."

"Word of honor, I won't tell a soul."

Katalynne believed that about as far as she could throw him and his bike, but there wasn't too much she could do about it. She dug in her purse to grab her car keys and a couple of bills to leave on the bar for the drinks then she stopped, remembering that the bartender had said that they were on the house. She looked over to see the woman passing out more drinks as the bar began to fill with more people. Terrific. It would take too long to catch her attention now, especially with Zach standing and watching her every move. She would have to come back tomorrow night to see exactly how serious the bartender had been with her flirting.

━━━━◆◆◆━━━━

The building had once been a warehouse for a paper company. When Fagan bought it he'd split the building up for living and business but was still working on the remaining back area. A portion of the building was sectioned off into what could almost be called apartments that housed Fagan and Alix in their own areas. These areas had full bedrooms, bathrooms, and normal living spaces. More apartments, with smaller space, were also sectioned off in a more or less finished state with various pieces of cheap furniture Fagan had picked up. The hallway to these apartments was closed off by a large, thick metal door, just in case some rather unpleasant guests decided to visit unexpectedly.

Those guests tended to be treated to the basement, where Haven had finally woken up after a few short hours of being knocked unconscious.

Shadows crossed the floor, slithering slowly around the spots of light. Haven's eyes were just barely open, face pressed against the cold and hard comfort of the concrete floor. He could see the shadows rippling, moving toward him like cautious little snakes. His body wanted to jump up and move despite still aching from being shot and attacked in the backyard earlier, so he compromised by sitting up and glancing at the darkness around him.

There was a soft, purring voice in the back of his head that advised him to stay put. *We don't know this place well enough, we need to wait.* As it spoke to him Haven felt his arm grow a touch bit colder, over the scale like markings that rained over his skin.

Haven listened without question, giving a small nod in response. "Are you all right? They shot you."

A chuckle, then, *it's more annoying than painful. Humans have irritating weapons.*

"And what do you make of this?" Haven looked over at the shadows as they moved, the dark wisps of black coming from somewhere just outside of his line of vision. Haven watched the darkness and silently held his breath as it stopped short of his face and moved in a circle around his body.

They're sizing you up for their master.

"So what is your dragon saying about me?"

This new voice was quiet and whispered in Haven's ear from the darkness. He immediately recognized it as the one who had been giving the other people tips on how to fight him. His mind started to piece everything together, gathering everything he needed to complete the jumbled puzzle. Twisted roots. A blow to the head. Now he was in a dark room, underground or under some large building with thick walls keeping out the light and noise from the outside.

He had been captured.

Some mix of plastic and cloth was wrapped around his hand and when he breathed he could feel the same thing over the cut across his waist. He flexed the muscle in his arm just slightly and felt the same there. Someone had gone to the trouble of dressing his wounds which meant that they, at least, wanted to keep him in decent shape.

"We can talk," the voice said from the shadows. "I won't hurt you."

Haven considered the words, unsure. This person had been with the other two who had attacked him and there was a high probability that he was working with the person who'd killed Xaver. Sitting up and talking could be a trick.

It could be a trick, yes, but if this creature wanted to hurt you he could've used his shadows to do it by now.

Haven's dragon was old, much older than Haven, which meant he had plenty of experience and he always seemed to know what was best. As a child he had his moments of testing his dragon, challenging what he suggested and often times ignoring his advice. It didn't take long for him to realize that when you had a much older creature as part of your body it was best to listen and take advantage of their knowledge.

Haven opened his eyes and sat up in the cell. He frowned when he found that his wrists were bound tightly with a cold piece of metal. He could hear the sound of metal on metal echoing through the room, the cuffs far too noisy for his taste. It would make getting out that much more difficult.

Now that he was sitting up, the small shadow snakes retreated and disappeared into the darkness at the edge of his cell. With his widened frame of vision he could see the bars were made of a thick metal that was securely bolted at the ceiling and the floor. There was a door to one side locked just as tightly as the metal around his wrists. Beyond his door there was another room, this one without bars. Instead this room had a thick metal door, most likely for their more dangerous captures. He couldn't tell if there was someone inside but he could see that there was a light on through the crack at the bottom of the door.

"Where am I?"

"In the basement of a warehouse, a distance from the house we met you at. The people here were friends of the man who died." The shadows responded, the sound coming from beside his head. Haven looked directly across from his cell into another cell where he could make out the faint outline of someone in the darkness.

"I don't believe you." Haven looked down at his restraints, turning them slowly in the faint light. The mechanism was made of several pieces of metal, interlocked. He'd seen them a couple times before he'd met Xaver, worn on the belts of some humans in uniform. Looking closer at it now he could see quite a few thin places, places where he could easily snap the metal if it were cooled to the right temperature. But if he attempted it now without a clear plan they might wise up and put him in something much more complicated.

It was better to wait.

Instead of addressing his doubtfulness the shadows whispered a different question to him. "Do you have a name?"

"Haven," he responded, still letting the edge of mistrust stay in his voice.

"Dox."

Lurk, his dragon hissed lowly.

Haven had heard of Lurks before, in passing and from his dragon. A Lurk was something made completely of shadows, a type of slithery creature that could blend in with the darkness. They were used by the Lurkhamara as a way to watch over other beings and attack silently, dangerously, leaving no evidence behind. Haven had never heard of one who could talk, much less take on such a solid form as he had seen during the fight. The only creatures that had a solid form and could command shadows to such an extent were the Kurai, but his dragon had told him that they had been wiped out before he was born.

Now he couldn't help but be curious despite the warning hiss from his dragon. "My dragon says you're a Lurk."

"I am."

"How is that possible? From what I know about them, they aren't-"

"Intelligent?" This was said with a chuckle. "That's funny that you're asking me questions."

"What do you mean?"

"You're asking about my heritage when I can certainly ask about yours. You possess an Ice Dragon. I was under the impression that they no longer existed."

It had been a while since Haven had heard his dragon hiss so loudly, the sound making him wince. He was sure that there was a bigger story, something between his dragon and this dark creature, but his dragon's anger was the last thing he wanted to deal with at the moment. "That is not something we need to discuss," Haven said, frowning at the darkness around him.

"In that case you don't need to question me about particular subjects."

"Fair enough. How about this, then. You were helping them fight, so why are you locked up down here?"

The shadows rippled, almost as if they were laughing along with their master. "They do not exactly trust me."

"Yet you still helped them kill Xaver."

"I already told you they weren't the ones behind it. Your friend called them for backup."

"Liar!" Haven stood up and glared at the shadows, growling dangerously at them.

Calm down, Haven.

"You're lying! They killed him!"

"Look, I only helped them because they're holding me here. They're Hunters. They hunt demons, but I made myself useful so they wouldn't kill me."

"Hunters?" Haven slowly began to calm down when he heard that word. "Do… you know their names?"

"The taller one calls himself Fagan. I believe there is a Randall somewhere in there but he doesn't like using it. The other one is Alix Andre DeBenit."

Haven slumped against the wall. These people were the friends Xaver had mentioned more than a few times, the ones he would go and meet on occasion. He had never taken Haven with, always saying it was too dangerous for him to be seen by too many people.

"My dragon says the same thing. He doesn't even want me staying with you."

Xaver laughed. "Is that right? So why do you stay?"

"Why do you let me? You're a Hunter, right? Just like those friends you go to see. Aren't you supposed to kill me?"

"Aren't you supposed to be running?"

"Hey. Are you still listening?"

"What? Oh… yeah, I hear you," Haven whispered, shaking off the memory.

The Lurk had been telling the truth before about them not being the ones who killed Xaver. In fact, these people had to be the ones Xaver had called before telling him to stay inside the house. Now here he was, alone in a cell with nothing but shadows to talk to. He had just made enemies with the wrong people because of one simple mistake. Xaver had told him to stay put, to not look out the window, but he couldn't help himself when he heard the gunshots echo around the backyard. He still remembered hearing his dragon protest when he went to the door, the old creature trying to remind him of Xaver's words about staying inside. But there was no way he could do that, not after seeing Xaver's lifeless body spread out across the lawn when he had finally looked out the window.

How was he supposed to know that the people who had showed up were friends?

Somehow he'd have to convince them that he'd been travelling with Xaver if he had any chance of getting out of this. Unfortunately, since he'd attacked them, they now knew about his dragon and how dangerous he could be. Haven had no doubt the only reason he wasn't dead right now was because these Hunters thought he knew something about Xaver's death. As soon as they found out he had no idea what had killed the larger man, his life would probably be worthless to them.

Stupid.

Wait…

Haven's eyes widened in realization and he stood up, moving to the bars. If Dox was in the barred cell across from his, "Who is in the other room?"

"My friend, Cyn. She was the girl who protected me."

"… oh."

"Were you expecting someone else? You sound disappointed."

Haven…

"I thought maybe they'd caught the one who killed him," Haven whispered.

"They're working on that. I'm sure they'll come down here with more information soon. Fagan seems more understanding, but Alix has a short temper around us."

"If that's true why keep us around?"

"Well, clearly, they can ask you about what happened to that man. As for me, I have something that Alix wants."

"Which is?"

"The Storyteller."

Haven stared into the darkness. "Y-you have the Storyteller?"

"I don't have him, I simply told Alix that I have seen him before."

"Him? You mean-"

Haven. Now is not the time to discuss these things.

"I mean what? What were you going to say?"

"… nothing. It's not important."

The shadows rippled along the edges of the wall as Dox spoke again, a little more threatening this time. "I'll be the judge of that."

"We're locked in the basement of a warehouse. That's more important than you using other demons to your advantage."

"Says the one with a dragon on his arm."

A couple hours passed in silence, Haven sitting and watching the door while the shadows remained quiet. Every once in a while they would ripple, but there was no other movement in the cellar, giving Haven plenty of time to think and ask his dragon for advice.

Wait for now. It hissed, the chilly consciousness curling in the back of Haven's mind. Waiting was best when one was unsure. It gave them more time to be cautious and come up with plans. Haste and anger only created more problems, ***much like the situation you're already in.***

Sometimes Haven hated having a dragon party to all of his thoughts. *I get the point.*

"STOP!"

The shout shot through the cellar like a physical bullet and Haven jumped to his feet, his body shivering from the sound. He watched the shadows across the room surge forward like a wave, recoiling and reacting, but the wave tapered off and fell short, melting across the floor and walls as a sound of pain came from the other cell.

The Lurk couldn't control the shadows as much as he wanted to.

"STOP IT!"

The screaming continued, high pitched and desperate, coming from the room where Cyn was being kept. Haven could feel the dragon mark on his arm grow ice cold, ready for any threat that might materialize in the room. The door at the top of the stairs flew open and the two Hunters came rushing down, sword and gun at the ready. The blond one aimed his gun at the metal door.

"What is she screaming about?" He demanded of the Lurk, not taking his eyes off the door.

"She's having a nightmare, you have to let me in there to help her!"

Now that there were other people in the basement, the shadows were thinner and Haven could see the familiar dark shape from the night before. It was a far cry from the snarky, confident attitude the creature had spoken to him with. The Lurk was now standing right at the bars where he was being kept, actually pleading with the two Hunters. A collar of dim blue light encircled his neck, obviously something to curb his abilities. Haven remembered seeing him wear something similar when he'd attacked.

It certainly explained why the shadows had seemed to die off earlier at Cyn's first desperate cry.

"Is that all? I didn't realize that something so trivial could bother demons, too." Alix lowered his gun. "It's just a nightmare."

The screaming continued and everyone, except for Alix, winced at the sound of it.

"You can't be serious!" Dox snapped, the panic clear in his voice. "I need to get in there to calm her down. She has a demon inside her, if she gets too worked up she'll lose control of it!" Dox gripped the bars, pulling at them as he tried to reason with the blond. "You have to let me in there!"

Alix glanced over at Dox, clearly confused by that statement. "Demon inside of her? What exactly does that mean?"

"It means exactly what it sounds like! There's a demon inside of her!"

"You mean someone put one inside of her? Is that even possible?" Fagan asked. That certainly explained how she looked so human. That also explained how she knew so much about their world.

"The details don't matter!" Dox yelled back at them. The shadows were edging past the bars and Dox winced, the collar flaring up. Alix had insisted on adjusting the collar after the incident at the house and it seemed to be doing the trick.

"He's right, Fagan, they don't, because we're not letting him in there."

"What?!"

"You expect me to let you be in the same room as your friend? Why? So you can wake her up and attack us? Why don't I let you in the same room as the Ice Dragon over there?" Alix shook his head. "No chance. It's just a dream, it can't hurt her. She'll wake up on her own."

"That doesn't even make any sense! I helped you two bring the dragon here!"

"And now we have three of you to worry about and a deceased Hunter."

Haven covered his ears as he heard the scream again, this time sounding even more desperate. He didn't know what the humans were hearing, but to him it sounded like the girl was in physical pain, as if actually being attacked. Did they really hate demons so much that they'd let something like that continue? "Can't you just let him calm her down so she stops screaming?"

Idiot. Don't draw attention to yourself.

The blond Hunter turned a look of disgust in his direction. "You don't need to be concerned about them. But you can tell us what happened to Xaver."

"She's screaming over there and you're going to waste time interrogating him?!" Dox's own voice was nearing the point of hysteria. Haven could see the shadows on the edge of his cell straining, struggling to do something for him, but whatever he was trying they weren't able to help.

Haven. Don't.

"This is stupid. I'm not going to sit here and answer questions while she's screaming." Haven muttered, closing his hands into loose fists. He could feel the cold sliding down through his arms, swirling in the small space between his fingers as it spun and gained speed.

Haven! Don't be so rash!

"Shut up."

Alix frowned. "Who are you talking to?"

Haven!

The metal around his wrists was the first to go, cracking from the cold and sliding off his skin like thin sheets of shattered paper. In seconds Haven was moving forward and shoving his hands against the two bars in front of him. At the same moment, the gathering balls of ice broke apart, the cold surging up the metal and freezing it in a matter of seconds. The now weakened metal shattered like glass that danced across the floor in sparks and shards. The two Hunters were stunned, and Haven used that split second to run across the floor and duck around the one with the gun. Guns took slightly longer than swords to aim and that difference was a blessing to Haven as Alix tried to recover and aim. Haven made it across the room and used a second ball of ice against the lock on the metal door, shattering it in the same way as the bars of his cell. Haven kicked it open and ducked inside as the bullets whizzed past his head, just narrowly missing.

He found the girl in the cell, curled up in the corner and shaking as if she were having a seizure. Her hands were clenched around her head and she had pulled her body into the tightest ball she could make, still screaming and shaking her head back and forth, pleading with whatever she was seeing and hearing to

"STOP STOP STOP PLEASE STOP."

Haven stepped toward her and knelt down, forcing his hand to not be as cold as he lightly touched her shoulder, trying to wake her up.

You stupid boy, look out!

She moved at the touch, lashing out in his direction. Her eyes never opened but her body reacted, incorporating his touch into her dream as something she didn't want. A hand and a kick flew in his direction and Haven jumped back out of reach, watching her with wide eyes. He knew the Hunters were probably at the door watching him, aiming their weapons, ready to fire. He knew he was being stupid and would probably get himself killed, but he couldn't believe that someone would just let her scream like this.

To think that humans claimed that his kind were the vicious ones.

Stepping forward again he grabbed Cyn and wrapped his arms around her. There was something wrong with her skin. It felt too dry, almost scaly, and Haven suddenly remembered what Dox had said earlier. The girl had a demon inside of her, one that she could lose control of if she got too worked up. As if responding to his thoughts Cyn began thrashing in his arms, her screams turning louder, the fear shifting into anger. Her voice had a rougher edge to it, an animalistic growl that sounded deadlier with each yell. Haven could feel the ground shifting through the concrete, a soft hint of a rumble brushing against the walls.

In her dreams she was calling to the roots, begging for them to rescue her from this perceived threat. Haven did the only thing he could think of. He let the cold slide through his body and into hers as he restrained her arms.

The screaming stopped and the ground stopped shaking. For a moment Haven had the horrible thought that he'd killed her, freezing her to death with a single careless thought in an effort to stop whatever she was seeing. However, a quick look at her chest as he loosened his grip revealed her shallow breathing. She was alive, at least, but Haven had given her enough cold for her teeth to start chattering and her lips to turn a tint of blue.

Calm down. Keep holding her and concentrate on slowly pulling it back. Ignore everything else in the room because I'm watching them. Just slowly draw the cold from her body.

Haven nodded and took a few deep breaths. He was good at calling on his dragon's cold during panicked situations because adrenaline made it easier. Now that he was trying to call it back, the cold didn't want to listen. It was easy pushing it out, but pulling it back was a completely different story, especially with the two Hunters watching behind him. He could hear the impatient sigh from Alix and knew the man was waiting for an excuse to shoot him.

"I-I can't..."

Haven. You need to concentrate on it more. I've taught you how to do this.

Haven closed his eyes and forced himself to focus. He could feel the cold coming from her skin as she started to tremble against him, trying to grow warm again. He mentally latched onto that, trying to convince the cold to flow back into his body. Time dragged around him and he knew that Alix's patience was wearing thin. He wasn't sure what Fagan was doing, but he could only imagine that he was equally frustrated – with whom was anybody's guess.

Eventually Haven could feel the cold slowly starting to surge back. He drew in a breath and knew that when he exhaled the others could see it in the air from his own change in temperature. Slowly, Cyn's body grew warmer and the shaking stopped, her skin not as rough as it had been before. Sighing softly in relief he watched as the girl's eyes slowly fluttered open to look up at him.

Without warning he was shoved back, hard, the girl retreating to the corner to glare at him. "Don't fucking touch me!"

"Hey!" Haven stood up and glared back at her. "You know a thank you would be nice!"

"Thank you? For what?! You tried to kill my friend, remember?!"

"I just helped you out of whatever nightmare you were just having!"

"Why? So you could kill me when I woke up? And- shit, it's fucking cold!" The girl wrapped her arms around her thin body, the adrenaline wearing off to remind her of the sudden drop in temperature her body was experiencing.

Haven almost felt sorry for her, *almost*, but the girl did just snap at him after he had been nice enough to help her out. "Wake you up and then kill you? That is the stupidest thing I have ever heard!"

"Um... hello?"

Both Cyn and Haven turned to see Alix frowning at them, gun still aimed at the both of them. Cyn rolled her eyes.

"Great, he's still here."

"It's my basement," Alix said, training his gun on Haven. "You will not be pulling anymore stunts like that, correct?"

"She can't even say thank you, so no." Haven ignored the sound of his dragon chuckling in amusement.

"Excuse me, but the last time I saw you, you were about to attack my friend. Where is he, by the way?"

"In his cell," Fagan said as he stepped over to the girl. Shrugging off his coat he wrapped it around her shoulders. "This might help a little. The cold is bad enough as it is, having him use the ice like that has probably made it worse."

Alix frowned at Fagan, not at all pleased with his sudden sympathetic tendencies toward the demons. He also wasn't pleased that it had taken a demon for him to admit that it was actually cold in the basement. Meanwhile, Cyn turned a hard frown in Haven's direction and yelled, "So you were trying to kill me!"

"I was not! The Lurk said-"

"Dox. His name is Dox."

"Hey!" Alix snapped at both of them. "Remember me? With the gun?"

"Enough, all of you," Fagan frowned, the serious, deep tone of his voice immediately cutting their argument. "Clearly, there are a lot of things we need to discuss. Starting with you," then he turned his attention to Haven, "can we trust you to be calm enough for that?"

Haven nodded. He had already learned his lesson when it came to doing rash things around these people.

"As for you. Stay put," Alix said to Cyn.

"Fuck you. You think I'm staying in this room? The door is broken."

"We still have your friend locked up. And he still seems fine with staying here."

Cyn's eyes narrowed. She would have to have a long talk with Dox about that. "Fine. But I want to speak to him."

"Absolutely not." It was no surprise that this came from Alix.

"Well then, I'm not staying here."

"Our top priority is Xaver, Alix," Fagan said.

Alix glared angrily at Fagan. "Our top priority is the Storyteller!"

"That changed when Xaver was killed," Fagan hissed, glaring back at Alix. "Whatever you had going on with Dox changed when that happened," then he turned his attention to Cyn, "You can speak with him, but we'll still be down here. The second you try something we'll know it."

Cyn nodded, watching as Fagan and Alix led Haven to the corner next to the room she had been kept in. Stepping out, Cyn walked over to the cell where Dox had to be – it was much too dark, the shadows still lingering around the edge of the bars. "This is quite the mess you got us in."

"You're shaking," Dox said, deciding to sidestep her statement by pointing out the obvious.

"Yeah, no shit. That dragon decided to wake me up by freezing me to death."

"Can't be *to death*, you're still here."

"Ha ha," Cyn muttered, pulling the coat tighter around her body. "So tell me, how does the angry blond know about something like the Storyteller?"

Dox watched as Cyn moved her fingers across the bars of the cell. The shadows gently slid over her fingers, Cyn smiling a little as she quietly played with the darkness, a motion that always seemed to calm her down.

"It's a long story, Cyn."

Cyn just nodded, quietly enjoying the shadows brushing between her fingers as she leaned against the bars and closed her eyes. She was used to Dox being secretive about his motives, and she was mostly fine with it. For now, she could relax and maybe later, when she was up for dealing with his annoying personality, she'd pester him for more answers.

———◆◆◆———

The area where Haven was taken had a couple of chairs and a table, serving as a makeshift interrogation area. Haven took a seat in one of the chairs, relaxing against the cold metal and letting the feeling sink into his skin. There were so many things in this basement he could draw cold from. They would probably realize it eventually, but for now he would use it for as long as he could. His arm had stopped throbbing from where he had been shot before, now it was down to an annoying sting. He was lucky that the bullet had missed anything major, though bullets weren't something that a dragon as old as his was ever concerned about. *Even if they do hurt. A lot*, his dragon hissed, still a bit irritated at Haven's rash behavior.

"Why were you at Xaver's house?" Fagan was the one asking as he took a seat directly across from Haven, looking much more relaxed than his partner. His sword was back in its holder, crossing his back from shoulder to waist. Alix took a seat next to him, still much more tense and uneasy. He wouldn't stop glaring at Haven and made it clear that he thought this whole line of questioning was a waste of time.

"I was living with him."

"Xaver wouldn't live with a demon." Alix's words were sharp and so sure.

"Maybe you didn't know him as well as you think." Haven couldn't help the comeback; he was really starting to get annoyed with this human.

Alix opened his mouth to respond but Fagan frowned at him "Alix." The tone was warning enough to make Alix close his mouth. Fagan continued his questions. "Why didn't Xaver tell us about you, if you were living with him?"

"He always said it was dangerous for other Hunters to know, that they would kill me. Or worse. And from the way he's glaring at me I can tell that Xaver had good reason to worry."

"Our job is to kill demons. Why would he bother to keep you alive?"

"I don't know," Haven frowned, "but you don't seem to be killing the demons who are here."

Before Alix could respond Fagan spoke up first. "Our job is to kill demons who harm others, not just any demon we run into." He decided to ignore Alix as the smaller man rolled his eyes. Instead, Fagan continued. "Clearly, Xaver saw some good in you."

Haven thought it was pretty funny that Fagan said that. His first meeting with Xaver hadn't been pretty. The man had been ready to kill him and the flash of that sharp sword so close in the moonlight still gave him chills. Xaver had never said why he stopped, but he had always called him "kid" so maybe it had something to do with how young Xaver thought he was. Dealing with Xaver that night had been one thing, but from his short time around Alix he knew that Xaver had been right to keep him away from other Hunters. If it weren't for Fagan, Alix would be more than happy to kill him, no matter how young he looked.

"You seem to know him pretty well," Haven spoke carefully, watching their reactions.

"We were partners before." Fagan could feel the edges of a memory trying to play through his mind, of the first time Xaver Knoxton had entered his life and introduced him to a world of demons, hunts, and unwinding at the local bar. He shoved it aside. There would be time for that later.

Haven looked up at Fagan. "Partners? So you would travel together in the same way we did?"

"I suppose you could look at it like that, sort of. This warehouse was going to be a spot for us to stay, but Xaver decided to work on his own... until he met you, I suppose."

"I don't mean to sound rude, but-"

"But you do sound rude," Fagan said to Alix. "Though I suppose you raise a good point, we can discuss our relationship with Xaver later. There's something else I want to ask you. Do you know what these were for?" Fagan set a pile of papers on the table between them. Haven immediately recognized them as the ones he'd seen Xaver sketching out the night he'd made the phone call. Haven reached over and took one of them, looking at the words and symbols he had seen once before. Something about the papers made Xaver's death hit home and he didn't want to talk anymore. Haven quietly set the paper down and clasped his hands in his lap so the Hunters wouldn't see that they were shaking.

Xaver was dead and he was alone again.

The earliest memory Haven had was his dragon whispering in the back of his mind for him to get up and move, find someplace different, find someplace safe. Every night it was time to move again, time to find somewhere else. He'd never stay in a place for more than a few nights and then it was always time to go somewhere else. It even continued when he'd met up with Xaver, but something about travelling with another physical person made it more tolerable.

He had a feeling that Xaver had felt the same way. When Haven came along he'd spent more than a few nights telling the boy he'd have to leave in the morning, then promptly forgot he'd said it when the sun rose. His dragon had told him he should leave more than once, but instead Haven did his best to work around Xaver and stayed out of his way. He was rewarded with a companion who didn't seem to mind him sticking around. Xaver had even spent time training him, the two finding empty park areas in the middle of the night to face one another. Like his dragon, Haven had gotten used to listening to Xaver's advice. The two had gotten along and he'd seen the scarred Hunter smile more than once while Haven got used to living on canned goods for dinner and sleeping in abandoned houses.

Now that Xaver was gone, Haven knew he was going to be back to moving and hiding again – assuming, of course, he made it out of this situation alive. There'd be no more nights where the two would spar until Haven collapsed. There'd be no more times where Haven could actually sleep longer than two hours. With Xaver, they never moved until Xaver said they should, and the man always seemed to wait until Haven was awake and ate some sort of meal before telling him they needed to go. Xaver always had his back, and Haven liked to think that he had his.

But he'd failed at that, hadn't he? Because now Xaver was dead.

The thought of going back to a life alone, a life without Xaver, curled in the pit of Haven's stomach and he felt sick. He brought his knees up on the chair, looking down at the papers sadly.

"He's not going to answer anything else," Alix said, rolling his eyes. "This is pointless."

"Maybe we should give him a little time. It's obvious that Xaver being dead is affecting him."

"Don't talk to me like they have feelings, Fagan." Alix's voice was sharp enough to cut across the room.

It sounded like an old fight, even to Haven's ears, but it was also one that didn't need to be fought at the moment. Luckily, Fagan and Alix seemed to feel the same way, because Fagan walked with Haven back over to the cell he'd broken out of and advised he spend the night there even with the broken bars. Haven didn't protest and went back to sitting in the corner, barely noticing when Fagan dropped a blanket and pillow inside the cell. He would allow himself a night to feel depressed about the whole situation, then tomorrow he would decide where to go next.

"We'll talk more in the morning," Alix said, then he looked over at Cyn. She was still standing by Dox's cell, watching them. "And as for you…"

"Yeah yeah, stay put. Got it."

Alix nodded and headed for the stairs, Fagan nodding to Cyn and Dox before following after. He stopped and looked back at where Haven was, frowning for a moment before he decided to walk back over. "Hey."

Haven looked up in surprise, watching as the hard frown on Fagan's face turned a bit softer, almost sad.

"Xaver was a good man," he said. "I..." Fagan wasn't very good with words, stumbling over what should've been an easy thing to say.

Fortunately, Haven seemed to get the message and he nodded. "Yeah. I... me too. I-I only attacked because I thought you were the ones who..."

"Right. I'm fairly certain we thought the same about you."

"So that fight happened for no reason?" Cyn asked. She was now standing next to Fagan, frowning. "This is why people need to talk about stuff first."

"Says the one who bit my head off when I tried to help her," Haven pointed out with a small smile.

"Goddamnit, kid, that was in the past. Let it go."

"Kid?" Haven raised an eyebrow, chuckling. "There's no way you're older than me."

"Children," Fagan said, giving both a stern frown. "Play nice. We still have a lot of things to discuss later."

"Yes sir," Cyn muttered sarcastically, crossing her arms at her chest.

"Sir?" Haven asked, giving Cyn and Fagan a curious look.

Fagan tried not to laugh as he turned and walk off, but he could practically feel Cyn's brain trying to process how Haven thought she was being serious about the "sir" comment. Alix was waiting by the stairs, glaring as he spoke up, "Do you really have to entertain them?"

"Come on, Alix, you know that kid is hurting."

"*That* is not a kid, it is a demon."

"Yeah well, Xaver saw something in him."

"And look where Xaver ended up," Alix whispered, getting to the top of the stairs and stepping through the door.

Fagan sighed, rubbing his forehead to try and make the impending headache go away. There was a mean-spirited thought that rang through his head, a time when Xaver had told him that he and Alix worked well together, that he didn't need to stick around because the two were fine as partners. *"Don't like bein' a third wheel,"* he had said with a chuckle.

Fagan could feel the bitter irony of that statement. Still, deep down, Fagan knew that this was Alix's way of dealing with Xaver's death. Alix wasn't good with the death of those close to him, and the way he dealt with it was by shutting others out.

It was a mechanism he used to deal with other people. If you shoved them away, they left you alone and didn't ask awkward questions. Fagan had learned when to give Alix space and when to focus on other things. Now was one of those times, time to focus on something else until the dust settled.

But what to focus on?

Fagan smirked as he heard the familiar clicking of heels against the floor, watching as his secretary walked over to greet him. "Mmmm now that is an attractive sight to see after all this shit."

"Hello to you too, boss." Katalynne greeted his large, stubble dotted grin with a small, teasing smirk of her own.

"Can't you keep it in your pants for once, Fagan?" Alix asked.

"My brother? No way in hell."

Everyone turned to see Zach leaning back against the warehouse door, smirking. The smirk immediately wilted when Fagan gave him his most serious of frowns. "What is he doing here?" Fagan asked. It was almost frightening how authoritative he sounded when Zach was around.

"Found him at the bar looking for a ride."

"Then why didn't you take him home?"

Katalynne frowned. "I shouldn't have to go through the finer points of my job summary, but I am not your brother's babysitter, nor am I his chauffeur. Besides, I thought this issue was more important, boss."

"Issue? What issue? There's an issue?" Zach walked over, practically bouncing from one foot to the other, eyes lit up with the promise of adventure.

"No. There is no issue."

"Awwwwww, come on! Is there some giant demon to kill? Something like that? Tell me!"

Alix sighed and looked up at Fagan. "We certainly can't discuss anything with him here."

"Sure you can!"

Fagan was practically growling at Zach now. "You will go up to the living quarters and stay there until morning. In the morning Katalynne will bring you to campus."

Both Katalynne and Zach frowned at Fagan but Katalynne was the first to speak. "Again, I am not-"

"Katt. I know, just... please?"

Katalynne sighed when she saw the look on Fagan's face – exhaustion, with a hint of sadness. It was at that point that she remembered that the man did just lose his best friend. Taking a deep breath she nodded. "Will do, sir."

"There's enough space for Zach and Katalynne to stay here tonight," Alix said. Katalynne didn't look too thrilled with the idea, preferring her own apartment to the warehouse, but she knew now wasn't the time to argue.

Zach smiled brightly. "You hear that? We get to spend the night together, *Katt*."

"No," Alix said, grabbing onto Zach's wrist. "Come on, I'll take you to one of the spare rooms," then he turned his attention to Fagan and Katalynne, "I'll be back down so we can discuss the situation."

"Hey! I know my way around the warehouse!"

"Yes, and this is my way of making sure you make it to the living quarters."

Once the two walked off – Zach grumbling the entire time – Katalynne looked over at Fagan. "How are you holding up?"

"The kid with the Ice Dragon was traveling around with Xaver. He kept him hidden from us."

Katalynne's eyes widened. "He travelled with a demon?"

"More than that. They were close. The kid is really upset about all of this."

"And it's bothering you."

"When we were down there Alix said to stop acting like they have feelings. I guess as a Hunter, we're under the impression that they don't. But obviously they do and Xaver saw that." Fagan chuckled sadly, "I guess I still have a lot to learn from him. *Had* a lot to learn," he whispered.

"Fagan, anything that's living and breathing is capable of feelings. Even Alix."

"The jury is still out on that," Fagan muttered. It was meant to sound like a joke but there was no laughter in his voice.

"I suppose so," Katalynne returned a hesitant smile she didn't completely mean.

The air between the two was quiet for a moment before Katalynne stepped forward, speaking again, "This is only because I feel bad, so don't read too much into it."

The kiss on the cheek was a nice touch, Fagan thought, but it was the arms that were around him that finally made him slump down, giving into the various emotions that he had originally kept bottled up when he first saw Xaver's body. They all clumped together to form that one memory he had pushed away, but while in Katalynne's arms, he decided that it was o.k. to think back and remember his friend.

Back then, Fagan had been "Randall," the perfectly groomed and intelligent, wealthy son poised to take over his father's company when the time was right. Randall spent every day behind a desk, repeating his father's words of this being the life for him while secretly dreading putting on pants for the sheer purpose of calculating facts and figures. That all changed when he met Xavier "Xaver" Knoxton. Xaver had been everything that Randall wasn't, the Hunter equivalent to that roommate in college who your parents thought was a "bad seed." They had met by chance, Xaver stumbling down the street with a nasty bruise on his shoulder while Randall was making his way to his car late at night after working overtime.

Xaver had simply asked for a light for the cigarette he said he so desperately needed. Randall, unfortunately, didn't smoke, and it should've been left at that, except Randall made the mistake of asking one simple question.

"What happened to your shoulder?"

Xaver chuckled and said, "A fight taken too far."

Randall thought of leaving it at that, but it was hard to ignore the fragments of blood on the man's shirt and hands. When Randall started to look worried about where the conversation was headed Xaver smiled and shook his head. "It ain't what ya think, trust me," and, again, it should've been left at that.

But Randall pressed on. "What is it, then?"

"Do ya really wanna know?"

All it had taken was that whisper of something more than cubicles, computers, and numbers. There were sayings for moments like this, analogies of picking doors or taking a certain color of pill. Randall had decided to take whatever choice that led to *more* and hadn't looked back since, abandoning all traces of *Randall* to stand as *Fagan*, a Hunter, a demon killer.

It was ironic, Fagan thought to himself as he rested against Katalynne, that he was always chasing his little brother away from doing the very same thing he had done. But, just like him, Zach didn't know the risks involved with this lifestyle. It had all been so fresh, so new, that Fagan hadn't even bothered to worry about the dangers of being a Hunter. Sure, he had been told about the hunts, the prospects of being hurt – or worse, killed. At the time those risks had sounded more like perks than anything else. Adventure, excitement, the stuff in movies, and he knew that was exactly how his brother saw it.

He wasn't a novice this many years later, but that didn't stop it from hurting. The thrill and excitement was worth it, but that didn't stop him from missing those safe cubicles every now and then. Those cubicles knew nothing of hunts gone wrong, of ex-partners and old friends found dead in an empty backyard. So, just for a moment, he let himself relax and imagine he was back in that drab office. In a minute he'd think of business, but Katalynne was right.

He needed a moment for himself, just this once.

The vast majority of the finished space in the front of the warehouse was devoted to "business." Along with the cells on the basement floor, the first floor contained an entry and receiving area where Katalynne normally worked. Once Alix came back downstairs, free of Fagan's annoying little brother, the group moved to the small sitting area right by the front desk. It was safer to speak somewhere where they had a view of the door to the cells since Haven had already disabled his own cell and the door to Cyn's cell. Fagan stole Katalynne's chair, reclining back in ergonomic bliss that looked ridiculous with his larger frame. Katalynne took a seat on the couch while Alix perched on the armrest on the opposite side, too uneasy to sit normally, as usual.

Katalynne unlocked her tablet, her eyes moving over the search terms she had looked up earlier as Fagan and Alix brought her up to speed. She already knew that the Ice Dragon had been travelling with Xaver, what she didn't know was that the girl with the plant roots apparently had the demon put inside of her. On top of that, she had suffered from some sort of nightmare that threatened to make her lose control. "So essentially... there's a shadow creature, an Ice Dragon, and a plant rooted time bomb in our basement."

"Sounds like the opening to a bad joke," Fagan said.

"Well here's the punch line. We might need to discuss a pay increase if I have to work with that much of a threat below my feet."

Fagan chuckled. "Add another zero to your next paycheck or something."

"I think the last time you said that to me was when you brought back that demonic sword of yours."

"Didn't you know? Alix and I have an ongoing bet as to who can bring back the most dangerous thing. This time I think Alix is winning." Fagan's tone was playful and both recognized it as a habit of laughing off serious problems so they were easier to deal with.

"You're the one who wanted to bring back the dragon and angry girl," Alix pointed out.

"Right, because she would've stayed put while we left with Dox."

"Gentlemen. While I'd love to listen to you bicker like the old, gay married couple that you are, I have a report to give you." Katalynne didn't look up from her tablet, simply waiting for the words to set in.

"W-what?!" Alix's eyes widened as he stared at Katalynne. "W-we're not-"

"You always get like this, sweetie," Fagan said, his voice doing a poor imitation of sounding higher pitched. "Why do you have to be so mean?"

"Ta gueule!"

"Well that didn't take long," Katalynne said. "Only a couple of minutes into our meeting and Alix is already speaking French."

"I'm trying to remember what that phrase means…" Fagan stared up at the ceiling, attempting to remember some long forgotten French teacher who claimed to drive a Porsche and never stopped talking about her pet kittens.

"Shut the fuck up," Katalynne supplied.

"Mmmm. I love it when you say *fuck*."

Katalynne rolled her eyes. She swore that the scene that had transpired before this meeting was an exhausted Fagan who actually needed a little bit of comfort. His recovery time for depression was record breaking. "May I move on to my report?"

"Yes, please do," said Alix.

"There isn't much in the database about Ice Dragons, but if they're anything like their fire controlling counterparts, heat will at least slow him down. I would be careful about where you aim it though. Apparently the marks they have on their bodies are actual living dragon parasites and you can either hurt them, or just make them angry. Think of the boy as the dragon's host."

Alix frowned. "Dox did mention to not aim for the dragon during the fight. The bullet to the arm certainly didn't seem to slow him down. What about the other girl?"

"She looks nothing like the demon who is normally associated with those abilities. However, you mentioned that she had the demon put inside of her?"

Alix nodded. "That's what Dox said. I've never heard of such a thing before. Who would want to do something like that? Is something like that even possible?"

Fagan swung back and forth in the chair, thinking. "We can figure that out later. I think the more pressing matter at this point are the papers Xaver left behind. We can safely say that none of the people below killed Xaver, so we should focus on the clues he left behind for us."

Katalynne pulled up the scans and glanced over them. "He has horrible handwriting, but it almost looks like he was drawing a map of some sort. Of course, without any idea of what these symbols mean, there's no way to match it with physical locations."

Fagan moved his chair closer and spread the papers out across the glass coffee table between them. Drawn over the newsprint they could see sharp lines that traced a shape resembling a map. The articles the lines were drawn on were pages from the financial section, providing words with almost no pictures. The downside was that the endless paragraphs of numbers, company names, and financial predictions weren't at all relevant.

It felt like they were staring at some sort of optical illusion, trying to find the hidden picture within the picture of a picture. Every time one of them thought they figured something out it turned out to mean nothing. Certain aspects of the paper were underlined, others left blank, and as the minutes ticked away their eyes were beginning to grow tired.

"Should I make us some coffee?" Katalynne asked, stretching and forcing herself to take a break.

"It's too late for that," Alix said.

"Or too early depending on your definition," Katalynne muttered. She remembered making the same observation about the time with Zach in the bar, which meant that she should definitely be in bed by now.

"Maybe a small break would be nice. Is there any of that canned crap that Zach drinks?"

"He may have left the case from the last time he 'just so happened to be in the area'."

As Katalynne stood up to work on getting drinks Alix took another look at the papers. He tilted his head, a curious look on his face. "He underlined this one."

"Hm?" Katalynne sat back down and asked, "Which one?"

Alix pointed to a section in the paper where a single word in all capital letters was underlined.

TMDD.

There seemed to be nothing significant about the article. Stocks were going up and down, though this particular one had gone up recently. "I'm not familiar with this," Alix frowned, scanning the rest of the article.

"It's a company tag used for identifying a company in the stock market."

Both Alix and Katalynne gave Fagan a blank stare, the man sighing at them. "Do you two always have to look surprised when I know something?"

"Yes," they both said at the same time.

"What part of 'I grew up with wealthy parents' do you not understand?"

"The wealthy part," Alix answered.

"The 'grew up' part, sir. Saying such a thing implies that you no longer act like a child."

"Insert perverted joke in your general direction here," Fagan said. "Now, are there any other articles about TMDD that were in the paper from this same date?"

Katalynne looked through her tablet, everyone waiting silently for a moment before she nodded. "TMDD is the identifier for Tobias Maddson LTD. It's some company that's taken an interest in the local zoo and their botanical gardens. It says they sponsored a rebuild of part of the botanical gardens site and are funding some research the zoo is engaged in."

"Research on what?" Fagan asked, still frowning.

"The Middlemist Red." Katalynne pulled up a picture on her screen, setting it down for the others to see. The picture, in color on her screen, matched the one in the paper. It was a dark, pink flower that almost resembled a rose, but it didn't open quite as far. "According to the information on it, it's the rarest flower in the world. It originally came from China, but now it can only be found in a greenhouse in the UK, a garden in New Zealand… and the Tobias Maddson sponsored remodeled building here in Minnesota."

"So it's something with that garden. Can you bring up a map of it?" Fagan rearranged the papers again so they could see the map. No one was surprised when they found it matched almost perfectly with the map of the garden on their official website.

Xaver had done it again.

Now, with that frame of reference, Xaver's map looked more like a war general's plan of attack. They could now see the true purpose of the various symbols that had been drawn out. The symbols represented security guards and park attendants with corresponding times scribbled along the edge of the paper. All of the paths on the map led to the newly remodeled area and its several gardens. According to the website, there were flower displays in this area that changed every season.

"Why would Xaver be interested in this flower?" Katalynne whispered.

"More importantly, why would he be so interested that he would take the time to make a map like this? Was he going to go to the gardens?" Alix asked.

"Or…" Fagan frowned, crossing his arms at his chest. "Did he make this and purposely leave it for us?"

"Maybe if we can figure out what the flower is-"

"It's a door. A gateway."

All three turned to the door leading down to the basement where Cyn now stood, still clutching Fagan's jacket around her body to scare away the lingering cold. The coat fit her thin frame like a blanket, completely covering the fishnet shirt she was wearing, her baggy pants worn around her shoes. A well placed glare hid how weak and tired she actually was. While she'd shown quite a bit of attitude and power at the house it was now obviously an act to hide a young woman who was barely over fifteen and hadn't had the easiest life.

"We told you to stay down there," Alix said.

"It's fucking cold. Unlike ice boy and Dox I don't do well in the cold. Him freezing me certainly didn't help."

"Let her stay up here, at least for a moment," Fagan said. "Besides, she seems to know something about that flower."

Alix motioned to the other side of the couch, watching her with a distrustful look as she took the seat at the end, huddled under the jacket.

"I can make you some coffee," Katalynne offered. "Or hot chocolate."

"Hot chocolate would be great."

Katalynne stood up to make the drink while Cyn looked over the papers laid across the table and the tablet with the photo of the flower pulled up. "The Middlemist Red is nearly extinct and can only be found in a couple spots in the human world. Each time, that spot corresponds with a doorway, leading to their world. Their world is like ours, with oceans, continents, tribes and kingdoms."

"And how do you know all of this?" Alix asked, moving to lean against the front of Katalynne's desk, his hand resting on his belt, just above his gun.

Cyn didn't seem to be intimidated by the gun and looked up at him with an unreadable expression. "Simple. This thing inside of me came through that gate. Oh, and Tobias Maddson is my father."

Chapter 3

Tobias Maddson was a well-known businessman across much of Europe with holdings in many other countries, including New Zealand and China. He didn't own an actual company, instead, Tobias Maddson LTD operated more like a foundation, sprinkling its money across different medical companies that specialized in things the name holder was interested in. He would purchase stocks and shares in the companies that showed the most promise, usually those that worked with equipment and ground breaking research.

Thanks to the hefty donations of Tobias Maddson, major breakthroughs and vaccinations had been the talk of several medical journals across the globe, including a couple of Minnesota news prints that whispered about the man's interest in renovations to the Marjorie McNeely Conservatory attached to the Como Park Zoo and how promising that would be for the future. Cyn had no doubt that he was already bidding to take some sort of ownership of the conservatory, especially since he already owned the other two gardens that housed the flower. A few taps of her tablet and Katalynne confirmed that the man had already placed a hefty bid and was currently in negotiations.

The gothic girl also explained – after downing most of the hot chocolate – that her father wasn't a stranger to the higher up corporations. When she was younger he'd made no attempt to hide the different companies he owned a majority of shares in. She remembered there were always businessmen coming in and out of their houses at all hours of the day and she'd spent most of her meals eating either by herself or with her father and one man or another discussing business that she didn't care about.

"And at times we would travel around, a lot. Hence my knowledge of French people being assholes, like you," Cyn said to Alix with a sweet smile.

Alix graced her with his deepest of frowns. "Can we try and stay on topic?"

"It's my life story, I'll tell it how I want to."

"You said he put the demon inside of you," Katalynne said, attempting to keep the peace. "Does… that mean you're human?"

Cyn set down her mug and pushed off Fagan's coat. Tugging at her fishnet shirt she pulled it up, rolling up the side of her tank top so they could see the full mark at her waist. The patch on her skin was about the size of the young woman's hand. Greenish, red scales mixed with scabs covered the area, almost melting into her skin at the edges. It was as if someone had actually removed the skin in that area and grafted on skin from something else in its place before her body could attempt to repair itself. Cyn extended one of her arms that the dark fishnet had been covering. Just above her wrist to her elbow, her skin was freckled with little angry scars, testifying to what was probably years of injections.

"Your own father experimented on you." Katalynne whispered sadly. "But how could he have put a demon inside you?"

"I don't know. I wasn't awake during most of it, I just remember this huge chunk of time feeling incredibly sick and I couldn't keep my eyes open for more than an hour. I now know that he kept me heavily sedated through the whole thing. I woke up with a massive headache and a burning pain where the scar is. The pain doesn't go away."

Katalynne grabbed her tablet and flipped through her notes, pulling up the information on the demons she had looked up earlier. "Is it this type of demon?" She asked, showing Cyn the notes on the database that centered on the demons that preferred the marsh areas in the south. The picture on the screen was faded and grainy, like some poor quality phone picture that was supposed to prove the existence of extraterrestrials. Next to it was a sketch of something crouched on four legs with large eyes and hair across its head and down its neck like a raggedy beard.

"I…" Cyn took the tablet and read over the information. "It sounds the same. I… guess I don't really know since I was so out of it. I've never seen anything like that before."

"So his charitable donations for research go into things like this?" Alix asked. He tried to keep his voice steady but this new information was a bit disturbing. In the world of humans versus demons, demons were always the bad guy, not some rich human who decided to experiment on his own child.

"Pretty clever, huh? Side effects include a shitty adolescence, running away from home, the occasional series of fucked up dreams, and – if you get me pissed off – I can make roots come up and crush your ass." She crossed her arms, her annoyed expression completely returning now that she was starting to regain her body heat. "Other things have happened, too. Dox saw me with slitted yellow eyes and claws for hands more than a few times. I can only control it a little now because Dox taught me how after I left home."

"If I can take you off topic for a moment, I'm curious how you met Dox. Was he something else your father experimented on?" Katalynne asked as she refilled Cyn's mug with more steaming hot chocolate.

Cyn took a drink before answering, her expression lightening more than she probably realized. "You know how kids talk about the monster that hides in your closet? Well, Dox was mine. It's stupid, but when your only family is your father and he treats you like this, well... I clung to that 'monster' that hid in my room."

"Weren't you scared?" This question surprisingly came from Alix. "I mean, you were a kid and he's a demon."

"Considering the things my father is interested in demons weren't new to me, especially after having one put inside of me." Cyn took another drink, avoiding their eyes. "Compared to my father, Dox was a godsend."

"If he wasn't an experiment do you know how he got into your room?" Katalynne asked as she took a seat on the couch next to her.

"I don't know all of the details. I just know that he wanted to get away from his father and, somehow, ended up in our world. I can only assume that it was with that same flower my father is interested in."

"The Lurkhamara," Alix whispered. "He mentioned him when we first spoke."

"After he helped me get away from my father we've been hiding ever since. You won't believe me, but he's actually more curious than mean. Kinda like a kid brother."

Fagan chuckled at that, remembering the conversation in the van. "You two are safe here for now, we have no reason to hurt you. We're actually more interested in finding what killed our friend."

Cyn was surprised that Alix had nothing to say to that. She had at least expected a glare of some sort. Katalynne pulled her out of her thoughts as she spoke up, "These doorways, what do you know about them?"

"I know they aren't always open. My father had people watching them, waiting for things to cross through. Last time I was there he still hadn't figured out the pattern for when they are open, or how to get through to the other side."

Alix stood up and paced a bit around the room, picking up part of the map to look at it. "We should go check out this door. This is obviously what Xaver was searching for and what he wanted to tell us about before he was killed. He probably knew where the door was because of the Ice Dragon. Maybe he was holding him to get more information about when this door would open and where it would lead."

"Yeah, because the kid totally wasn't fighting out of anger and grief because his friend was killed," Cyn muttered as she finished off her hot chocolate. Katalynne leaned over and poured her yet another cup with a soft smile, catching more than a little gratitude hidden carefully in the girl's bitter eyes.

"I agree, we should go check out the door, but we can't leave those two alone downstairs and packing up the SUV wouldn't be ideal."

Alix nodded. It was good to see that Fagan hadn't started to completely trust these creatures despite their backstories. "You can stay here, Fagan. Cyn and I will go in the morning."

Fagan frowned, considering that plan for a moment. He didn't have any good reason to go against Alix's plan but something felt off. It wasn't like Alix to be all gung-ho about a plan like this. Alix was the type to kill his prey, not work with them. An in-depth plan about investigating a doorway to the demon world didn't fit him or his intense hatred of their kind. Whatever it was, Fagan decided it wasn't wise to bring it up in front of the others. He'd just have to find a better time to bring it up and confront him. "Sounds like a plan," he said.

"Then it's decided. We'll leave tomorrow morning. In the meantime, Cyn, I'll show you to a place where you can sleep."

"Seriously?" Cyn gave Alix a wary look as she took another sip of her hot chocolate. "What's the catch? Are you going to shoot me in my sleep?"

Alix laughed, "No, nothing like that. You said it was too cold down there, right?"

Alix's sudden fit of generosity worried Fagan even more. Alix certainly wasn't the type to invite a girl – demon possessed or not – to spend the night anywhere near him.

Damnit. Alix definitely had something else on his mind, and Fagan had a feeling he knew what it was.

Alix woke up early that morning and moved right into his morning routine. He pulled on a loose t-shirt and white pants, buckling the gun holster belt around his shoulders and across his chest. Boots tied tight and blond hair brushed out of his face, he headed down to the large practice area on the main floor near Katalynne's work area.

The practice area was full of a few "rescued" gym floor mats and various pieces of equipment gathered over the years. A set of mismatched weights, weapons for practicing, and benches were spread across the area for a range of exercises. The back area contained wooden and metal replicas of different weapons for practice, but a few actual weapons – primarily guns – were kept in a locked case for more serious training.

Alix used an area where the rafters were lower for pull-ups and a couple simple pads on the floor for stretching, pushups, and a host of other strengthening exercises. Once that was done, he moved to picking up one of the scraps of wood leaning against the wall and proceeded to move around the room, practicing his skills with a sword.

The routine was old, familiar, and comfortable. He could feel the strain on his muscles from the quick movements and the air brushing past his face with each thrust, cooled by beads of sweat. No matter how many demons crossed his path, returning to this every morning brought back his sense of balance and control. In the field, he preferred the sureness of a gun. It allowed him to take out the demons before they got close enough to do any major damage. Thanks to this he didn't have nearly as many scars as Fagan and Xaver, but practicing with a sword was still important for when he ran out of bullets or lost his gun in a fight. There was security in knowing firearms and melee. He wasn't so much as practicing to use a sword as he was practicing to use that random tree branch, abandoned golf club, or even a strong crowbar.

As an added bonus of the morning routine Alix was able to forget the demons sleeping below his feet and the strange girl resting on the couch back in his living area. He still wasn't quite sure how the situation had gotten to this point. All he wanted was information on the Storyteller, but now he was left with a dead hunter, an Ice Dragon, and some girl whose father apparently experimented on his own child with a demon.

At least this single hour in the morning was completely in his control; and he dominated it.

* * *

"When you can't control the world around you, you can at least control yourself."

At the time, Alix looked up from where he was attempting to practice as Xaver set down his can of beer and walked over to him. This was one of the few times that Xaver had approached him without a joke or a sarcastic comment, actually offering advice. "You're holding it wrong. Your grip should be here, and like this."

Alix let the taller man move his hands, adjusting them on the roughly carved piece of wood. He'd seen the two men practicing nearly every morning and he'd started imitating them. This morning he'd thought they were done and he hadn't expected Xaver to actually be watching him, much less giving him pointers.

The new grip felt strange, straining muscles he wasn't used to using. He decided to push past the pain by making a snide comment at Xaver. "Beer this early in the morning? Your breath stinks."

"Hey, we all have our coping mechanisms. You want this lesson or not?"

Alix simply nodded as the man picked up another piece of wood and began slowly moving across the padded floor so Alix could copy his movements. Shamefully, Alix only lasted a few minutes before he was forced to drop the piece of wood, the unused muscles in his hand smarting in pain. Out of frustration he kicked the piece of wood across the floor and watched it clatter against the concrete block wall.

"Not bad. You lasted longer than I thought."

"Doesn't sound like much of a compliment," Alix muttered, rubbing his hands together and flexing his fingers to try and relieve the stiffness.

"Hey, kid."

Alix looked up, ready to scream at him about how he wasn't a kid, but stopped as he saw a water bottle flying for his face. Somehow he managed to catch it, even though his hand cried out in protest. Xaver favored him with a smirk as he finished off his own can of beer. "Take a drink and relax. And if you're really serious about this, you're going to need this." Xaver stepped over and dropped a thin piece of leather string next to him. Alix looked at it in confusion, unsure of what it meant.

"I don't-"

"The ring. It's a distraction."

Looking down at his hand, Alix now knew exactly what he was talking about. He hadn't thought it was a distraction during the sparring, but overall it was, wasn't it? He didn't want to take it off, but he did want to show the man he was serious. Hesitating for a moment he slid the ring off his finger and onto the piece of leather.

"Good. Now, relax. You've got two minutes before we go again."

Alix opened the water bottle and took a long drink before tying the string around his neck and tucking it beneath his shirt. The metal felt cool against his chest and he found it to be an oddly comforting feeling as he closed his eyes and caught his breath. Two minutes later and they were at it again as Xaver said they would be. By the time noon had come along Alix had learned how to properly hold a sword and at least defend himself without feeling like his fingers were going to fall off, Fagan watching from the doorway with a small smile on his face.

* * *

It had become a morning routine that adjusted and changed over time. After he got the movements down with Xaver, Fagan had stepped in, helping Alix learn how to hold his own with a sword and a gun. Occasionally, Fagan would join them, mixing the random exercising and practices with sparring and facing off until one of them won, or one ended up collapsing to the ground to catch their breath. In the beginning, Alix was always the one who ended up finding a home against the cool floor mats, but over time he was finally able to catch them off guard. The routine changed as Xaver left the warehouse and Fagan gained his demon sword, but Alix like the familiarity of what Xaver had originally taught him. The morning practice was something stable he could hold onto in a world that was largely unpredictable and overwhelming. No matter what they faced, this was a place he returned to every morning and he used it to clear his thoughts, rebuild his resolve and remind himself why he was here and what he needed to do.

Stopping and putting back the piece of wood, Alix took a moment to lean against the cool concrete wall and catch his breath. As he took a couple of breaths he began to think about the task at hand. Today, he and Cyn were going to the gardens to check out the strange flower that was supposedly a doorway into the demon world. In the solitude of the practice room, Alix allowed himself to think about the objective he originally had before Xaver's untimely demise.

The Storyteller.

He remembered that Dox had said that the Storyteller was from the same world as the demons. This meant that finding the doorway would have many advantages. The Hunter part of his mind took a moment to whisper to him, speaking about how it could be the ultimate chance to close off the doorway and stop the demons from crossing over into their world. Granted, Cyn did mention that the flower existed in two other places, but closing one door would at least take out a third of the problem. Hunters existed in other parts of the world, Alix was sure that Katalynne was using that network Fagan had given her access to for spreading the word about the Middlemist Red.

However...

There was the potential of being able to cross over and find the Storyteller himself. A plan like that would involve him stepping into complete enemy territory, but he didn't plan on going alone. Once this morning trip was over and they confirmed that's what this place was, he planned to come back and hold Dox to his word. Dox would take him through the doorway and lead him to the Storyteller. Xaver's killer would have to wait, no matter how he or Fagan felt about the situation.

It wasn't a decision that sat well with Alix. He valued his relationship with his partner and knew what the man had done for him. He had taken the time to train some angry guy he barely knew, teaching him to hone that anger into something useful. Now would be a great time for the roles to be reversed, for Alix to be there for Fagan instead of the other way around. But this was an opportunity he couldn't pass up.

Alix looked down, reached under his shirt, and pulled out a small chain that never left its place around his neck. Hanging from the chain was a simple gold band. The small diamond had fallen out a long time ago, during some fight or another, and the gold was tarnished from the numerous showers and sweat which had crossed over it. Alix had never wanted to take the necklace off long enough to clean it, he always needed to feel that small weight resting against his chest.

It represented his family, his life. It represented the very thing he would make the Storyteller give back to him.

"You don't seem like the type for jewelry."

Alix immediately dropped the chain behind his shirt and nodded a quick good morning to Cyn, the girl now standing across from him. She had changed into the small, black, button down shirt Alix had left out for her, choosing to button it only to the center over her fishnet so it covered her chest and flowed open over her stomach. Her hair was matted from sleep, clinging to one side of her head for dear life. On second thought, Alix was pretty sure the girl had left it that way on purpose.

"Did you find food in the kitchen?"

"It's too early to eat, or do anything for that matter, but thanks." Cyn walked over and lifted one of the scraps of wood shaped like a blade, turning it over in her hand. "Effective, I guess. They're heavier than I thought. Maybe I could talk you into teaching me after this, provided you're not still bothered by the thing inside me."

"I haven't decided yet." Alix grabbed a towel to wipe off the sweat, still relaxing against the wall. "If you're telling the truth and it wasn't your fault, then it just comes down to how much that thing is affecting you."

Cyn gave a snort, looking more amused than annoyed. "You really hate demons, huh?"

Alix didn't bother nodding. It wasn't worth it, especially since he was sure it was a rhetorical question. He'd made his view of demons quite clear the day before.

Instead he looked over Cyn's small figure, trying to evaluate how useful she'd be if they had to defend themselves. He didn't want to have to rely on her power over roots, if it came down to it. Walking over to a combo locked case, he twisted the dial and pulled it open.

"Do you know how to use a gun?"

"You mean aside from pointing and firing? No."

Alix pulled out a smaller gun from the case, loaded it with a cartridge, and handed it to her. "Try and shoot the red board over there," then he gestured to one on the far wall.

"Paranoid much? Aren't we just checking out the doorway? Are you planning on getting into a fight?" Cyn clenched her fists around the gun handle and held it up, attempting to aim. She frowned and pursed her lips before pulling the trigger. In spite of it being a small gun the sound was loud and the kickback was a surprise. It forced Cyn to step back, her hands shaking as she lowered the gun. The bullet didn't make the mark, not even close, becoming lodged in the concrete wall next to the red board. It didn't need to be said, but, "I suck."

Alix couldn't resist a small chuckle at that. "Hold the gun again, but don't fire." He waited for her to raise the gun then walked over to stand behind her, putting his hands on the handle. "Line up with the small bump at the top of the gun. Since your first bullet skewed off to the left, you want to aim a little more to the right of the target. Account for that difference. Now try."

A loud shot echoed through the room as Cyn tried again. This time they both watched as the bullet hit much closer to the target, still missing, but in the general area. Cyn made a face.

"It'll do for now. But you're better off pulling a fire alarm if you can. If I yell, toss me the gun. I've switched the safety on, so it won't accidently go off. You can practice more later."

"You never answered my question. Are you planning on a battle when we get there?" Cyn put the gun in the belt of her pants, hiding it under the loose shirt. Apparently, Alix didn't like that, as he shook his head and handed her a shoulder holster, helping her adjust the size so it was barely visible under the shirt. "You're ignoring my question," Cyn muttered as she moved her shoulders, getting used to the feeling of the holster.

Alix shrugged as he grabbed his towel and relocked the gun cabinet. "No, not planning for a fight. But I would rather be prepared for one than not. I'll be back down in ten minutes." Then he turned and headed back to the apartment for a quick shower.

"Not to sound needy, but you do have a coat or something for me, right?" Cyn called back to him, "It's still cold."

"Yeah. Just don't mention the cold around Fagan."

"Huh?"

"Trust me, just don't."

———◆◆◆———

Known for its free admission, the Como Park Zoo was the home of the Marjorie McNeely Conservatory in St Paul, Minnesota. Sitting right next to the zoo and part of the overall campus, the Conservatory was a large, white building that was sectioned off into several different gardens whose attractions changed with the seasons. The Sunken Gardens were in the back of the building, beginning with a pair of glass doors that opened to a long, rectangular section. Two paths moved down from the door, parallel to each other, and met at the end in a large sitting area where one could admire the flowers. Between the two paths was a small man-made river, ending in a bronze classical style statue of a stunning woman pouring water from a jar.

The Conservatory building was old, but kept in modest repair, just enough to make the high domed and glass covered building look antique with a bit of age and taste mixed in. The outside was surrounded by the zoo, acres of plant life, bird houses, a golf course, and even a Japanese style garden off to one side. Normally the campus would have been full of families taking pictures and having picnics, but since November in Minnesota tended to mean early winter, the amount of people had significantly decreased.

From the article and the signs in the building boasting about the new renovations, Alix and Cyn easily found their way into the Sunken Gardens. In contrast to outside, the room was warm, the air thick with heat and the smells of the exotic flowers arranged in an array of orange, white, red and pink. Following the path and weaving around the few patrons, it didn't take much work to locate what they were searching for.

The Middlemist Red.

At the very back, where the cobblestone path bowled out into a sitting area, a large white trellis had been added to frame the back door and almost hide the glowing emergency exit sign. The small, pink flower grew on two large bushes, placed on either side of a white wooden doorway – the ideal picture taking spot for the private parties and weddings the garden was popular for. There were a couple of flowers on the bushes themselves, but the majority grew out of the vines that curled up around the doorway, as if it were part of the bushes rather than a foreign piece of decoration.

Alix found this interesting since Katalynne's research hadn't said the flower had a vine, just that it was a rare bush.

In front of the plant there was a young woman who wore a deep, red coat and a brown belt made of fur that was wrapped around her waist. She was looking over the plant, brushing her fingers against the small flowers that were sprinkled along the vines.

"Great, this is exactly what we need right now," Cyn whispered to Alix.

"Just follow my lead," then Alix walked over to the girl, smiling a little. "Beautiful, isn't it?"

The girl jumped back in surprise, the bag slung over her shoulder falling to the ground. "I-I… yes, it is really pretty," then she knelt down to grab her bag, two thick ponytails bouncing with the movement. Alix knelt down with her, helping her pick up her bag and the book that had fallen out of it.

"I didn't mean to scare you. I apologize."

"It's all right," then she stood up, smiling. "I shouldn't be touching the flowers anyway."

Cyn watched from where she was standing, surprised to see Alix being so nice. She was under the impression that the man didn't know the meaning of the word. More amusing, she thought, was that you could almost call the conversation flirtatious.

"Is this a rose bush?" Alix carefully stepped up to the bush on one side and moved his hand along the wooden doorway as he looked up at the vines that crisscrossed over his head.

The girl shook her head. "No, it's not. It's a vine, actually. The plant that's growing around the door is the Middlemist Red."

"I don't know much about plants, but this is a bit strange. I read an article that said this was recently put in. Either the plants grew like this over the last week or someone hand threaded this."

"They grow rather quickly," the girl said. "A week is plenty of time."

"You seem to know a lot about them." Cyn walked over to the two of them, giving the girl a questioning look. "Have you seen this plant before?"

The girl smiled and nodded her head, the pigtails bouncing with her. "I've seen one back at home."

"Back home?"

Alix tilted his head. "And where might that be, miss..."

"Um... n-nowhere special." Now her smile was faltering, her body fidgeting as she spoke to them.

"There's only two more places in the world that have this plant," Cyn said.

"There's two more? Really? It never said anything about that…"

"What didn't?" Alix asked.

"My… f-friend didn't. I-it's not important, I should get going. Bye!"

Cyn watched as the girl ran off and frowned. "That was strange."

"Not really," Alix said, looking at the plant. "She said 'back home', and was surprised when you mentioned the other two places."

Cyn's eyes widened. "Wait, you think she came through the door?"

"It's possible."

"So she was a demon? But she was wearing human clothes."

"So was Haven," Alix said. "The fact that she didn't take off running immediately means she's new to this. I would guess she hasn't been around humans for very long."

"Should we go after her?"

"There's no reason to cause a scene. What matters is how interested she was in this plant. Now I'm positive this is what Xaver was looking for." Alix stepped closer to the plant. Was there something that needed to be done to get it to work?

Could he just walk through and-

"Excuse me? Can I help you?" The voice was quiet, speaking softly behind them. Both Cyn and Alix turned to see a young, portly woman wearing a simple summer dress covered in a pattern of flower petals and leaves. Her tightly curled, red hair was held back by a headband that barely fit behind her ears. She wore a little white name tag with the name 'Hailey', a small plastic clear case filled with about five beautiful silver and gold butterflies clutched tightly in her hands. She smiled at them nervously. "Please don't step off the path. It's there to protect the flowers."

"Of course." Alix hadn't even noticed he stepped off the stone path onto the dirt, but he stepped back and offered a rare smile of apology to the young woman. "My mistake, do you work here?"

Hailey nodded. "Just as a volunteer, really. Did you have any questions about the plants or display?"

While Alix was deciding how to phrase his question, Cyn decided to just go for it. "This display looks brand new. We were interested in speaking with someone who's been working in this area for the last week since it was set up."

Hailey didn't do a good job at hiding her discomfort with that question. She set down the case of butterflies on a bench behind her and twisted her hands together. "T-that would be me. But I'm just a regular volunteer. I can get you the general manager of this area, she just got back from her vacation…"

Alix flashed a comforting smile. "Unfortunately if she was on vacation she wouldn't have been here during the times we're interested in." Alix pulled out his wallet and opened it, showing what appeared to be a badge, "Alix Andre DeBenit."

The girl's face lit up, her mood immediately changing to a more relaxed one, "Hailey Grace. You must be here about the break in."

"Break in?" Cyn asked.

"Yes, we are," Alix said smoothly.

"I could've sworn the police already came by though…"

"We're simply following up. It's nice to meet you, Ms. Grace. This is my partner," then he nodded over to Cyn, who was trying hard not to stare at the Hunter. Where did he even get a badge from? "Cyn, don't be rude, introduce yourself."

"You just did," she said.

Alix chuckled and looked back at Hailey. "Please excuse my partner. We're sorry for showing up unannounced, but we assumed you didn't want to disrupt business any further, especially with the new display and changing season."

"O-oh, that's fine officer, I'm glad you're both here."

"What can you tell us about what happened?"

Hailey glanced back at the room, making sure no one was wandering too close to overhear before she spoke. "About a week ago someone broke in through one of the windows, but nothing else was damaged. We've already had it replaced and the flowers have mostly recovered from the temperature change." She stopped and pointed to a window behind them in the greenhouse that shone a little brighter in the sunlight then the others. "I wasn't here and don't really know anything else. If you need more information I can take you to the main office. I know they want to keep it quiet since this is a new attraction..."

Alix flashed another smile and shook his head. "We're on our way over there, we just want to finish taking a look around this area. Thank you, though."

"Of course. Is there anything else I can do to help?"

"Does this place have any surveillance cameras?" Alix continued speaking with the young woman while Cyn turned away from them and knelt next to the edge of the display of flowers. Quietly, she reached her hand past the edge of the path and touched the dirt next to the sign detailing where the flower was native to. Cyn took a deep breath and closed her eyes, exhaling slowly as she mentally reached beyond her hand.

She could feel, below the dirt, the roots spreading out across the span of the greenhouse. Every size, shape, and angle wove its way beneath her feet and she could feel all of them pause, as if waiting for her to give an order. The sense was unnerving. Even though Cyn had had about three years to get used to it, it still weirded her out in more ways than one. She didn't like how the plants around her seemed to be holding their breath, waiting to see what she would do.

Pushing past the feeling, Cyn focused on the flower bushes in front of her. She had no idea what she was actually doing – interrogating nature itself, perhaps? Mentally, she tried asking the roots if there was anything strange about them, but of course they couldn't answer. Roots didn't talk, mentally or otherwise. Even if they could, would they consider themselves to be strange? Cyn almost pulled back from frustration but tried one more thing she'd learned from Dox. Feeling for the roots again, she tried to remember their earlier days together, back when she had no sense of focus and back when he had to muster up all the patience in the world. He had taught her to focus on one target instead of many, one source instead of several, so she paid attention to the flower bush in particular, noticing the difference in that single plant compared to the others. Buried somewhere, deep inside those roots, there was something.

Something different. Something familiar that whispered softly in her ear.

Cyn stood up and shook the feeling off, brushing her hands against her pants. She hated doing things like that because she always felt dirty afterwards, the strange demon power sticking to her skin like honey. She stopped moving her hands when she noticed Hailey was staring. "Ants," she said quickly. "I hate those things."

"Actually, a lot of people don't realize it, but ants are very useful in gardens."

"Ah. Um… yeah, of course. I suppose they do more than just ruin picnics, huh?" Cyn let out a shaky laugh. If Alix could pull this bullshit off so could she, right?

It seemed to work because now Hailey was smiling, even giggling at Cyn as she picked up her box of butterflies. "I'm really sorry I couldn't be more help, but you can always stop by. I'm usually here somewhere."

"Thank you, we'll remember that." Alix nodded to her. "We should be going."

"Just remember to walk on the path on your way out," the young woman called with another giggle as they left, going back to whatever she had been doing before speaking with them. She actually started humming as she was stopped by a taller man with a long, gray pony tail, the man smiling and asking for directions to another part of the garden.

"I can't stand people like her," Cyn said darkly, brushing her hands over her pants again as if trying to wipe the girl's infectious smile away. "Always smiling and happy, for no reason at all." She decided to change the subject before she ended up ranting about smiles and rainbows. "Did she say anything important? I was distracted."

"Nothing too useful. The cameras were part of the remodel, but the ones they received were broken, so the replacements are still on the way and useless to us. What were you doing?"

"Touching the… roots- it's not important. The plant feels strange, not like the other ones. Three years later and I'm still not too sure how this whole thing works. I can't explain it, but it doesn't feel like it belongs in this world."

"How convenient," Alix frowned, "There's a break in and then we see a demon girl at the doorway."

"You think she did it?"

"Nothing was stolen. If she entered our world she may have broken the window for a way outside." The two exited the greenhouse and Alix leaned against a tree far away from the other guests. "We still don't know how the doorway works. Maybe we should've gone after that girl after all."

"Maybe the door isn't permanently open. Maybe it only opens at certain times."

"You've seen the plant before too, right? With your father?"

"I remember seeing the one in London. Chiswick, actually. That girl was right about the plant growing quickly. The one I saw grew around a janitor's closet of all places before they realized what it was. It only took a couple of days."

Alix nodded. "I think we need to keep an eye on that plant. Maybe a camera of our own or something, I'm sure there's some gadget Fagan can suggest."

"Works for me. Now let's get out of here, I've spent far too much time in the sun for my taste."

Alix chuckled as they left the building. "Is there anything you like?"

"I'd like to know where you got a badge from, 'officer'."

"Katalynne is extremely useful. So is that database she uses."

"So you and Fagan go around pretending to be cops?"

"What, you want a badge too?"

"Hell yeah I do!"

Alix decided to ignore the small voice in the back of his head telling him that this demon girl wasn't that bad after all, but no matter how hard he tried he couldn't stop himself from laughing at her comments on their way back to the warehouse.

———————◆◆◆———————

Stupid.

Stupid stupid stupid!

Mira wasn't sure how long she had been walking. She also wasn't sure where she was currently walking to.

"Mira. You should go."

"But what are you going to do? He said to stay inside…"

"He's dead."

"What?"

"Xaver is dead."

"But… n-no, he can't be, t-t-the book said–"

"The book was wrong!"

"This isn't how it was supposed to work," Mira whispered, arms wrapped tightly around herself as she walked down the sidewalk. "I found them, but then…"

How did everything go so horribly wrong?

Finally tired of walking Mira sat down on a bench. This world had too many twists and turns, too many different directions to go in. She missed the trees and forests of her home. Back home, she knew how to get around, could tell the difference in the trees and the leaves on the ground. Here there were sidewalks, streets, and traffic lights, all unnecessary methods that humans used to maneuver through the city.

It was all too confusing.

She had finally found her way back to the doorway, only to be stopped by those two people. Now she would have to stay here longer when all she really wanted to do was take the advice that had been given to her.

"Mira. You should go."

Mira pulled her book from her bag, frowning down at it. "You never said that you would be wrong," she said sadly.

In all the times she used the book it had never led her astray. Then again, she didn't use her abilities as much as her father did. She sighed, brushing her fingers against the cover. She missed her home and her father, she missed Jahren and Zee, she missed everyone back at home – even the always grumpy Saraisai. She hated that she needed to cover her ears with her hair, hated wrapping her tail around her waist all the time, hated all of the commotion of this world. It had been interesting at first, but with everything that had happened…

It would be o.k. to go back home, right?

Maybe she had read it wrong, misunderstood the image. Maybe she wasn't supposed to come here at all. Would Xaver still be alive had she not shown up? Things had been fine between Haven and Xaver before she showed up. They travelled together, stayed in old houses, and ate meals from cans and plastic trays. They had made room for her, and Haven even let her sleep next to him, making her believe for a moment that she was on the right track.

Then Xaver was killed.

"The book was wrong!"

"A pretty girl like you shouldn't look so sad."

Mira looked up to see a young man standing in front of her. His short hair was a mess, tossed all over his head in a way that reminded Mira of rolling around in the nests back at home. His brown eyes were just as bright as the smile on his face, making it very difficult for her to keep frowning. "I shouldn't look sad because of my appearance?"

"Yeah!" He said, sitting down next to her. "You know, because cute girls look better when they smile."

"... I don't feel like smiling," she said, looking down at her book again. "Everything is a mess."

"Why, what happened?"

"Just..." she knew there were parts she wouldn't be able to share, not with some random boy she just met, but she felt the need to say something. "I was only trying to help, but I ended up upsetting a friend."

"Did you apologize?"

"I didn't get the chance to! He told me to leave!"

"Well then, you need to go apologize. You can't just leave it like that," the boy said, putting a hand on her shoulder. "You still want to be friends with him, right?"

"It would be nice," she whispered. "A-and then maybe I can still help."

"No." He shook his head, "One mess at a time, o.k.?"

"But-"

"No," he said again, cutting her off. "Fix things with your friend first, then worry about the other stuff. Otherwise, all you'll do is sit here and worry about mess after mess after mess."

"... o.k.," Mira said as she stood up. "That... is good advice, thank you."

The young man chuckled. "You wanna say that again while I call my brother? He always thinks I screw things up."

Mira blinked. "Screw things up?"

"You know, I make a mess of things, I can't be trusted, blah blah blah."

"But that's silly! You helped me just now, you aren't screwing things up!"

"Um... thanks." He looked surprised at her outburst for a moment, but then he was smiling again. "You're the first person to say that."

"Really? Well... I'm glad I got to say it."

"Hey, um... I-I usually don't do this well with girls. What's your name?"

"It's Mira."

"Zach."

Mira smiled, "It was nice meeting you, Zach, but I should get going."

"Wait, just like that? But we just-"

"You told me to go fix things with my friend, so I'm going to do that. Maybe we'll meet again later! I hope we do," then she took off down the sidewalk, clutching her book to her chest.

Zach watched her take off and sighed, slapping his forehead. "Stupid," he muttered to himself. "You should've asked for her phone number."

Once Mira was far away enough from Zach she stopped running, leaning back against the wall to a building that smelled like it had delicious food inside. Taking a couple moments to catch her breath she opened her book and looked down at the pages. "I know I'm supposed to help my father, but Haven…"

The pages became filled with pencil lines and quick sketches, the lines coming together to create a picture. She couldn't recognize the building but it looked old and worn out, nothing like the house she had stayed in with Xaver and Haven. Inside the building, in the sketch, she could see Haven sitting in a room that was closed off with bars that came from the ceiling.

Her eyes widened. Was he being held captive?

On the blank page next to the picture Mira could see the book drawing the group she had been shown before coming to this world. Before, it had been a large silhouette, but now she could see Haven and Xaver – though Xaver was in back of the group, his image faded. She watched as more people became visible in the picture, three faces she immediately recognized. The blond haired man from the gardens along with his red haired companion, but it was the third person in the picture that made Mira smile.

"Zach," she whispered, brushing her fingers against his picture. "I guess I really will be seeing you again."

This had to mean that she was going in the right direction. It had to mean that she was still doing the right thing. Xaver dying was an unfortunate circumstance, but she now had a chance to make things right with Haven. Not only that, she could learn more about this group her book kept showing her.

"I still have a chance," she said, smiling brightly at the picture. "This can still work." Now all that was left to do was figure out how to get to the building in the picture, but once she did that, everything would come together.

Right?

Chapter 4

Night fell across the warehouse district. The houses across the street had their doors shut, their curtains drawn as their porch lights struggled to stay lit. In the receding sunlight the warehouses resembled towering giants of disrepair, some still in use while others suffered from broken bits of concrete wall that were decorated with artful graffiti.

A lone bus pulled up to pick up the last of the tired, straggling workers. Mira stepped off the bus and gave the driver an enthusiastic wave, the older man nodding to her before he closed the door and drove off.

"So this is it, huh?"

The warehouse was nestled between two different buildings. One warehouse boasted the name of some local hardware chain while the other was a newly remodeled building rented out to various artists and community groups. Taking a deep breath Mira walked forward, glancing inside her book at the sketched picture of the locked door in front of her. She tapped her finger on the picture and smiled, the knob turning with no trouble, as if it hadn't been locked at all.

Mira stepped through the door and looked around. A lobby sprawled out before her that only had a few pieces of furniture filling the space. The quietness of the area seemed to echo around her, against the cold, tiled walls and large, circular glass light fixtures. She loosened her grip on her book and opened it, turning it to a blank page. She began tracing her name with her finger in the top corner on the right, then Haven's name on the left. Pulling her hand back, she watched as the curves of their names began to unfurl and move. The lines stretched and rearranged themselves as they sketched out the interior of the warehouse with uncanny detail. As the drawing finished, the lines drew a door before redrawing Haven's name over it, showing her his location.

Mira closed the book and slipped it back into her bag before she headed straight for that door. As she reached it, she heard a mechanical click as the lock snapped shut. Mira stopped and quickly looked around the room. Hadn't it been empty before?

"You know, it's not polite for guests to wander through other people's houses."

To Mira's surprise Katalynne was now standing near her desk. When did she get there? Mira swore there had been no one there a second ago.

Mira mustered up her cutest smile, clasping her hands behind her back. "I was just curious."

"Really?" Katalynne raised an eyebrow. "What exactly is interesting to you about a paper warehouse?"

Mira's smile grew sweeter like fresh made candies. "I like books."

Katalynne stepped away from the desk and walked toward the girl. "I'll walk you to the door, we're about to close anyway."

Mira nodded and turned, walking with the taller woman back toward the front entrance. As she did, her hand slid into her bag, tracing on one of the pages. A moment later Katalynne stopped mid-step, her eyes looking a little hazy as she shook her head and tried to regain her mental footing. Mira took that moment to quickly turn around and head for the door she had been trying to get to before.

"You really must think I'm stupid." The words were low, dangerous, and before Mira could turn and react she found herself shoved against the wall harshly. Katalynne pinned her by her shoulder and quickly snatched away her bag as Mira reached for it, not able to get to it in time. A couple pieces of paper hit the floor with the book, which opened to a random page. Katalynne's eyes narrowed when she saw a picture of the warehouse on that page. Across the street, in the picture, was a girl standing at the bus bench who looked just like the intruder she had pressed against the wall. Katalynne's harsh look melted into one of confusion. "What the hell?"

Mira kicked at Katalynne and scratched her arm with a sharpness that wasn't possible with human nails. Mira landed on the floor and crouched away from Katalynne as her stylish, fur belt actually uncurled, assisting her with her balance.

A tail?

Katalynne winced from the small lines of blood caused by the creature's earlier attack. She was a demon, one of the more animalistic kind.

Katalynne ignored her bleeding arm and kicked the book as far away from them as she could. She had no idea if the book was important but she wasn't going to risk it. She quickly backed up to the desk, reaching under it to press a button hidden from sight. Clicks sounded throughout the building as the silent alarm was triggered, sending the warehouse into lock down.

Katalynne pulled a gun from the desk and took aim. "You really should back up and wait quietly until the others get here."

Mira shook her head. "I don't want to hurt anyone, I'm just here to help a friend."

"You can discuss that with Fagan when he arrives."

"I can't wait that long." Mira darted across the floor, trying to reach the book, but stopped short as Katalynne fired a couple of well-aimed shots at the floor just in front of it. Mira immediately backed up, reassessing the situation.

"Tough luck, kid, you're going to have to."

"You don't understand anything."

Katalynne fired a warning shot right in front of Mira but the girl didn't seem to care as she slid her hand inside the pocket of her dress. Katalynne gritted her teeth and fired again, this time aiming right for Mira; she'd given her enough warning.

The bullet stopped just in front of Mira, making a strange, hollow sound as it came into contact with a piece of paper appearing in the air. That piece of paper grew, other pages furling out from it and spreading out to create a wall between them. Katalynne's eyes widened as she watched the papers as they blocked Mira from sight, giving her access to the book lying on the floor.

She had never seen such an attack before, certainly not from the animalistic demons. Usually they were limited to physical attacks that were exaggerated abilities related to feral animals. She knew that they shouldn't have been able to create walls, certainly not of paper.

Only one creature was even rumored to have such a power.

"That's impossible," Katalynne whispered. She lowered her gun and watched in stunned silence as Mira picked up her book and hugged it close to her chest. She turned her back to Katalynne and headed to the door that led to the basement. Katalynne's suspicions were confirmed when the girl moved her finger over a blank page in her book, the lock clicking and letting her push the door open.

Well, that certainly explained how she got in.

Katalynne stepped back to her desk, picked up the phone, and pressed the button to connect her to Fagan.

"Fagan here-"

Katalynne cut him off. "We have an intruder."

"Yeah, I got the alarm. I'm already on my way, what is it?"

Katalynne winced. The scratches lining her arm hurt more than she thought. She could worry about that later, there were more pressing matters to deal with.

"It's the Storyteller."

She could hear a startled sound coming from her boss' lips, a noise the man rarely made, before he whispered, "Shit."

<hr />

Mira closed the door behind her and slowly walked down the stairs. In hindsight, she wished she'd just been patient and asked the book to show her who else was in the building, but she swore that woman hadn't been there when she walked in.

Only a couple lights were on, illuminating a cell on the far side of the room and another cell that was shrouded in almost complete darkness. Mira didn't like that darkness. It felt familiar and physical, and she swore she could feel it creeping across her skin. Her tail swayed nervously behind her as she walked past that cell. She wanted to get out of the basement as quickly as possible, so she darted forward to the cell she could see. She breathed a sigh of relief when she looked past the bars. "Haven?"

The young man sat up in the cell, his eyes widening when he saw her. "Wha...- Mira, what are you doing?!"

"I came to say I'm sorry about everything. And I came to help you."

"Sorry?" Haven blinked, looking confused. "What are you sorry for?"

"For Xaver. F-for everything. I just-"

"You don't have to apologize, and... damnit Mira, you shouldn't be here!"

"I came to help you."

"You idiot," he hissed. "This isn't a place to play around, the people upstairs are Hunters!"

"I know who they are and I know what I'm doing!" She snapped back. "I'm not leaving you again! Friends don't do that!"

Haven sighed. "I... look Mira, that's really nice of you, but the people upstairs-"

"Don't worry about it," then she smiled, "I'm supposed to talk to them."

A frustrated look crossed Haven's face. "Not that book again," he groaned.

"I know, I know! But I think I understand it better now."

"I'm not sure what you two are going on about, but attacking them wasn't the best idea." Dox stepped out of the shadows and up to his own bars, speaking quietly. "That woman upstairs is already calling them. They'll be here soon, ready to fight you. The blond, Alix, won't want to talk."

So she had been right about the shadows being a physical being. It had to be a Lurk, but she didn't remember hearing anything about them being able to talk. "How are you doing that?"

"What?"

"Talking. The only Lurk I can think of who can do that is-"

"There's no time for that," Dox snapped. "You shouldn't be here. Those Hunters are going to cause trouble for you. Alix-"

"The blond, right?" Mira pulled out her book and smiled. "Oh him! He'll talk to me, I'm sure."

Haven shook his head. "Alix hates us, he won't help at all."

"But he has to! They all have to! The book said they would!"

Dox's eyes widened and the shadows around him pulled back, as if in shock. The book? That meant she was... but that couldn't be, right? "Where did you get that book?"

"It's mine, I've always had it."

"That type of power is something the Storyteller would have. Why do *you* have it?"

Mira giggled. "He's my father. Do you know him?"

Father? The Storyteller had a child? "T-that doesn't matter," Dox said quickly. "Did you use your powers upstairs?" He demanded, sounding more than a little worried.

"So what if I did?"

Dox clutched the bars in front of him. "You stupid little girl," he growled. "Alix is searching for the Storyteller. You need to take that Ice Dragon and get out of here."

Haven's eyes narrowed. "They wouldn't even know about the Storyteller if it wasn't for you."

"Alix was looking for the Storyteller before we met, but even if he hadn't, what I do to survive is none of your business," Dox hissed back, glaring at Haven.

"It is when you turn against your own kind." A low growl followed Haven's words, his voice sounding more reptilian.

Dox chuckled, a smirk replacing his panicked look. The shadows around him rippled with his laughter. "My own kind? I'm not one of you, dragon, I'm a Lurk. Most of you don't consider me as being from your world. Why shouldn't I use you to stay alive?"

Haven raised his hand, an ice crystal growing, reflecting the light from right above his head at Dox with pinpoint accuracy. Dox jerked back, holding his cheek where the line of light touched him and crouched just a little in the darkness. A low hiss came from his throat, seeming to echo through the shadows around him.

Haven kept the ice crystal ready. "Mira, let's go. I'll keep an eye on him."

Mira opened her book to a blank page and watched as Haven's cell was sketched out in front of her. Smiling, she began to rub her finger against the bars in the picture, whispering the word, "Erase." Haven watched as the bars in front of him actually crumbled away, hitting the ground in a cloud of ash. She closed her book and stepped forward, hugging Haven tightly. "I'm sorry it took me so long to come and get you."

"Stupid," but he couldn't stop himself from smiling, wrapping an arm around her waist. "I told you to leave."

Mira shook her head. "I came here for a reason. I need to talk to them, but first… I needed to help my friend."

Haven smiled a bit more. "Come on. Let's get this over with."

Stupid. This came from his dragon in a cold whisper. ***I told you before that this girl was trouble.***

"Yeah well, we're already in trouble, might as well make it worse."

"Is your dragon upset with me?" Mira asked as they headed for the stairs.

"He's upset at everything," Haven said. He followed the girl up the stairs, keeping his eyes on Dox and ready to aim the ice crystal as needed.

When they got upstairs neither Haven nor Mira were surprised to see two guns and a sword pointed in their direction. Fagan had his sword out, while Katalynne and Alix had their guns aimed, ready to fire. Katalynne had one of her arms wrapped in a bandage, her eyes narrowed at Mira and hoping for an excuse to fire at her.

Mira smiled and looked ready to step forward and actually talk to the Hunters as if they were her new best friends. Haven was a bit more skeptical and moved in front of Mira, watching their weapons. He knew he wasn't fast enough to freeze all of them, but he couldn't risk them hurting her.

Sitting on top of Katalynne's desk was Cyn, swinging her legs and watching everyone with a small frown. After exploring the Conservatory with Alix she had somehow ended up staying around the Hunter. For a split second she had almost thought he was a reasonable person.

Almost.

Mira raised her hands in surrender. "My name is Mira. I would just like to talk, I'm not here to hurt anyone."

No one lowered their weapons, though Alix did step forward, signaling that he would be the one to speak with Mira. "Let's go upstairs and talk."

Haven frowned and his dragon reacted, cooling the air around him protectively. He didn't like this situation. The Hunter who hated demons the most wanted to talk to Mira and he wasn't about to let her out of his sight. "I'm going with her."

Alix frowned. "No, go back to your cell."

"Right, because he's going to listen to you with a gun aimed at his head," Cyn said as she rolled her eyes.

Alix looked back at her and frowned. So much for the demons – or part demons, whatever – being agreeable. "I didn't ask for your commentary."

Cyn shrugged. "Just saying. The girl obviously doesn't want a fight, otherwise, she'd be fighting right now. And he obviously doesn't want a fight or he'd be freezing shit."

"She's right," Haven said, smirking. "Besides, I can't go back to my cell, the bars are gone. Again."

Now it was Fagan's turn to frown. He wasn't a fan of his basement being rearranged by these demons. He knew it was a piece of crap, but it was *his* piece of crap and he didn't like the damage it was taking. "You freeze the bars again?"

"No... I removed the bars." Mira gave Fagan a sheepish look. "I don't like my friends being locked up."

"You never mentioned that you were friends with the Storyteller," Alix said, glaring at Haven.

"We were discussing Xaver. In fact, didn't your partner say that Xaver came first?"

"He does. But I suppose we have no choice but to talk to her," then Fagan frowned at Mira, "No more destroying my warehouse."

Mira smiled, "I can draw the bars back on the cell if you want."

"... maybe later," Fagan muttered, not quite sure how he was supposed to respond to that. "Let's head upstairs."

"All right." Mira stepped forward to follow Alix up the stairs. Haven just sighed, quickly walking after her.

"She wasn't supposed to come here, was she?" Cyn asked, following after Haven.

"No."

Cyn chuckled, "Same with Dox."

Haven smiled a little at that. He suddenly wondered if this was how Xaver felt when he had sighed at Haven those first couple of weeks they were together.

———◆◆◆———

"Katalynne here."

"Hey there, hot stuff. Got a free moment?"

The familiar voice on the other end of the phone brought images of flirtatious smirks, free cherry hinted drinks, and a very attractive set of shoulders covered in artistic tattoos.

"Harper, right? How did you get my number?" She hadn't had the chance to get back to the bar. She wanted to tonight, actually, but with the Storyteller's unannounced visit plans had changed.

"That kid you gave a ride to came in and gave it to me about an hour ago. He told me to tell you that he's sorry for last night... and that you owe him."

"How do I owe him after he apologized?" Katalynne took a deep breath. How was Zach giving her a headache when he wasn't even here? "You know what, never mind. I'll deal with it later."

Harper chuckled. "My question is why did you send him to give me your number? I would've preferred seeing you."

Katalynne smiled into the phone as she stepped away from the group heading up to the meeting room. "I didn't send him, believe me. I wanted to go myself-"

"Wonderful. So I'll see you in a few minutes? I can make you that drink you like, on the house."

Katalynne sighed. It was rare for her to feel disappointed about missing a date. In fact, she couldn't remember the last time she even *had* a date. Being Fagan's personal assistant was full of unpredictable hours that didn't work well with a social life. She was fortunate enough to have her own apartment – she had insisted on it, refusing to live in the same place she worked no matter how convenient it was. "Actually, I'm about to go into a business meeting."

"Isn't it too late for that? You're supposed to be here, sitting at my bar," then Harper chuckled, "I'm not as good at flirting over the phone."

"You seem to be doing fine to me."

"Mmmm, but I'm much better at it in person. Come by so I can demonstrate?"

Katalynne glanced into the meeting room, quietly contemplating if the group could survive without her. She knew from the look on everyone's faces that the answer was no. The only one smiling was the so called Storyteller, still holding her book in her arms. "I wish I could Harper, honest, but my boss had some guests show up from out of town and last minute arrangements have to be made. Rain check?" Hopefully Fagan and the others wouldn't require her help for longer than a night. From experience, though, she knew better.

If she were smart she would end things with this woman here and now, she would thank her for the one drink she had given her and move on.

But this one was too attractive to let slip by. The bartender's attempts were much better than Fagan's programmed flirting and Zach's college-aged hormones. It had been so long since Katalynne showed interest in anyone, let alone someone who wasn't involved with unworldly creatures.

"I suppose I can let you get away with a rain check, but I am going to pester you until you let me redeem it."

Katalynne could hear the smirk in her voice and the promise poised on her lips. "I look forward to it. I will talk to you then," then Katalynne closed her phone and headed into the meeting room before she could think about the fact that she had basically locked herself into something that resembled a social life.

Fagan's main meeting room was modestly decorated much like everything else in the warehouse. A large, wooden table filled the middle of the room with various mismatched chairs surrounding it. Fagan took the largest and most comfortable one – a worn out office chair that might have once been a deep green or blue. Alix's chair had once been part of a kitchen set, something that belonged with a glass table and matching china pieces. The seat was padded while the back was made of metal arches that curved together. Katalynne took a seat in the back of the room by the door, watching their guests move to the other available chairs.

The new girl picked out a padded chair covered in some faded flower pattern, sitting down gingerly before she decided it was safe to get comfortable, her tail twisting and adjusting to the seat. Haven didn't sit down, instead, he stood behind her. Katalynne could almost see the gears in his mind turning, surveying the room and determining the easiest way out, just in case. Finally, Cyn sat in one of the plain and worn wooden chairs with her normal pissed off expression, as if she couldn't be bothered to pay more attention to the situation at hand.

Fagan regarded the new demon with a guarded curiosity. He remembered from the abandoned house that there had been two bed rolls, so one had belonged to Xaver and one might have belonged to the Ice Dragon. But now there was a second demon in the mix and something didn't fit. Where had she slept? She looked much too young for Xaver to be interested in – not that he would sleep with a demon, right? Then again, he had been travelling with one. There was also the fact that she wasn't there that night. Had she been hiding in the house or had she left?

Or was she the one who killed Xaver?

That last thought made no sense and Fagan shook his head, frowning. There was no way Haven would be so close to the girl had she killed Xaver. Considering how he had lashed out against them that night he certainly would've turned that ferocity against her. Fagan sighed. This new girl added too many questions to an already messy situation and he didn't know where to start.

"You said you wanted to talk to us." Alix, on the other hand, was more than ready, jumping right into the conversation as Katalynne silently turned on her tablet to record everything.

"I came here to ask for help. It said you would help me."

"What did?" Alix asked.

Mira set her book on the table. "This did. I'm supposed to come here for help."

Fagan leaned back in his chair, considering her words. "Perhaps if you tell us what exactly we're supposed to help you with. And knowing who you are couldn't hurt either."

The girl nodded and reached up to pull out her pigtails. The others in the room sat quietly as she felt the hair fall around her head. The release was relaxing and she could feel her ears twitch as the hair uncovered them.

Everyone in the room – aside from Haven – stared at the fox ears that jutted out from the sides of her head. Cyn was the first one to react. "Great, so you have cat ears. How is that supposed to tell us anything?"

"I am not a cat!"

"You have cat ears-"

"I'm a Scough!" Mira hit the table lightly with her hand to make her point more clear but this only resulted in Cyn smirking in amusement. For a moment it looked like she was going to yell again, but the girl took a deep breath and relaxed in her seat.

"She looks more like a fox," Katalynne said. "I take it cat demons are different?" She moved her fingers across the tablet to pull up information. Once upon a time the question would've been sarcastic, but after dealing with fox creatures, Ice Dragons, shadows, and plant monsters, she wouldn't be surprised if a demonic cat trotted through the front door.

"Demons? Oh right, Xaver said that was what we were called here."

So that confirmed it. This girl, this *Mira*, had been with Xaver. Did that mean that he knew about this book? Did he know that she was the Storyteller and what that meant? Before Fagan could ask Katalynne was speaking again. "What do you call yourselves in your world?"

"We call ourselves the type of… um… *demon* that we are. I'm a Scough. The cat like ones are-"

"Wait, so cat girls are real?" Cyn asked.

"Of course they are," Mira giggled, sounding much too happy about it. "Do you already know about them? Have they been in this world?"

"It depends on what convention you go to."

Both Mira and Haven looked confused, Haven quietly waiting for his dragon to supply an answer for what a convention was. *I'm afraid I don't know what she's talking about.* Haven chuckled to himself. Finally, something his dragon didn't know.

"I swear we came together with a topic in mind. Why is it so difficult to stay on task?" Alix asked.

"Because not all of us have a stick up our asses."

Alix glared angrily at Cyn but before he could respond Mira spoke up. "Is that true? Why would you put a stick up there?"

"Seriously, do demons not have expressions?" Cyn asked, but she couldn't help but laugh at the confused look on Haven's face.

"Look, do you want our help or not?" Alix snapped, Mira shrinking a bit in her chair.

"I-I do, I just... I am not sure how to explain this." Her ears drooped and she looked down at the table and her book, as if searching for answers.

Haven squeezed Mira's shoulder to try and give her a bit of reassurance. "Like she said, Mira is a Scough and similar to a fox. She was staying with myself and Xaver until... recently."

Fagan glanced back at Katalynne who nodded to him, signaling silently that she had information on the Scough which she could share if needed. He turned his attention back to Mira. "What do you know about Xaver's murder?" It wasn't the question Alix wanted to ask, Fagan was sure of that, but he just needed to be sure.

"Nothing," she whispered sadly. "Haven... told me to leave."

"I thought whoever was outside might've been after Mira. Because of her being the Storyteller." At least that's what Haven believed she was. Her abilities matched the stories he'd heard from his dragon about the mythical creature. But, down in the basement with Dox, she had said something completely different, addressing herself as the Storyteller's daughter.

"And are you the Storyteller?" Fagan asked. Haven noticed right away how much Alix seemed to stiffen at that.

"No. No, I'm not." Mira quickly shook her head. "My father, Thierry, is. He's the one who needs help."

With a little friendly prodding from Fagan, Mira finally relaxed and explained the situation concerning her father and the issue with the Red Dragons. She explained that she and her father had lived with Jahren and the Scough for as long as she could remember and her father had become one of Jahren's 'advisors' when he'd taken over as leader of his kind. With Thierry's help, Jahren had been able to unite the different clans of Scough in their forest so that they lived in relative peacefulness without the constant tension that seemed to fill most of her world. The tension came from the fall of the Kurai and their ruler, Hanzo. Since his death, everything had changed for the worse, especially for the leader of the Red Dragons – who had almost been wiped out in the battle that killed the Kurai.

"They say that the Red Dragons lived in the same area as Hanzo, so when everything was destroyed, their home was destroyed, too."

"So these dragons were, what, scouting your forest to take it over?" Cyn asked, frowning. "Sounds like a lame roleplay plot." Before Mira could ask Cyn spoke again, "I'll explain roleplay later. Maybe."

"I am curious about this huge battle you mentioned. What exactly happened?" The question came from Katalynne, who usually didn't take an active part in such meetings, but there was a lot of information to keep track of. Fagan glanced back at her but her eyes were fixed on the tablet in front of her, fact checking against the information in the database.

"Saraisai, the eldest Scough, always talks about how our world has many different types of creatures. Back when he was younger, none of them got along. Hanzo was Era of the Kurai – uh... an Era is what they called their ruler. He made it so everyone stopped fighting and got along. But he and his kind were killed by the Lurkhamara and some other creature named Atticus. It was really bad and no one likes to talk about it. Ever since then, none of us mix. The Red Dragons are in the mountains and the Scough are in the forest, things like that. Even so, the Red Dragons have no reason to attack us. We keep to themselves."

"The Lurkhamara?" Alix frowned. "That name keeps coming up."

Haven spoke quietly, "What you have downstairs is a Lurk, a living shadow. My dragon says that the Lurkhamara is the master of all of the Lurks. Whenever there's a shadow that feels a little too dark in Mira's world you have to assume he's there, listening."

"Mira's world?" Cyn asked, raising an eyebrow. "Isn't that your world, too?"

Haven shrugged. "I have lived in the human world most of my life. I don't remember that world, just what my dragon tells me."

"If you've lived here for most of your life, how do you not know what conventions or roleplaying is?"

"Never said I lived with the humans here, my dragon told me to stay away from them because they weren't safe to be around. Still, this world is safer." Haven's voice sounded a bit sad at that and Cyn was sure he didn't believe what he was saying.

"Your dragon have anything else to say about Dox and the Lurks?" Alix asked, getting back to the main subject.

"Just that he's different. Most Lurks don't speak or do things on their own without the Lurkhamara. Dox seems to think for himself."

"He only does because he's away from his father, otherwise, he has no control. That's what he's told me." Cyn added.

Haven opened his mouth to say something, but stopped as his dragon spoke to him. "He says that Dox reminds him of the Kurai that Hanzo ruled before."

Mira nodded in agreement and explained when the others in the room looked confused. "The Kurai controlled shadows like the Lurkhamara. Saraisai said they were fearsome, but intelligent and peaceful when Hanzo was in charge. Nothing like the Lurkhamara. The Lurkhamara was Kurai once, but he gained more power and it twisted him into something else. Most of the people in my world are scared of him."

"It sounds like we know all we need to know about the shadow things, but what about this Atticus person? Is that something we need to worry about?" Katalynne asked, still clicking through her tablet.

Mira shook her head. "No one has seen him since that day. It's the Lurks that cause concern."

"Was any of that on the network?" Fagan asked.

Katalynne frowned softly. "Just very scattered bits and pieces. Nothing concrete to add."

"So this Lurkhamara helped destroy the stability of your world and we have his son in our basement," Alix muttered.

Cyn glared at him. "Dox is different. He-"

"Not to deviate from the story, but it sounds like this Jahren has everything under control if he's going to talk to the dragons and smooth out the situation," Fagan said, quickly putting an end to a potential argument. "I don't understand where we come in."

"The problem is that I think my father was lying. He says the Red Dragon attacked him, and even if he did, my father isn't the type to fight back, capture him, and bring him back to our camp, especially one related to the Reina – their leader. Also, there's no reason for the Red Dragons to be in our forest. I think he was lying about that, too." Mira opened her book and everyone watched as a picture was sketched in front of them. They could see a forest, then the picture shifted, showing a black smudge that resembled a fox and the Red Dragon, already tied up. "The pictures shouldn't skip like this. Usually, it shows me what happened, even if my father is involved. It would show me the fight that led to this first. Instead, it skips to the meeting with my father, Jahren, Saraisai, Amari and Lyree." She pointed each of the Scough out before she continued, "They are the ones Jahren trusts the most."

"Is it something to be concerned about, that it's skipping?" Alix asked.

"I'm not sure." Mira frowned as she turned the page. This time the sketch was different, showing Jahren at the edge of the forest where the mountains began, speaking with three others. These three were taller, dressed in leather and small pieces of metal armor. Compared to Jahren they looked like warriors, someone you wouldn't generally walk up to for a normal conversation. "He's already speaking with them," Mira whispered in concern.

"So what do you expect us to do?" Fagan asked.

"I'm not sure. I left because my book told me to and it said you would help." Mira didn't take her eyes away from the moving picture as Jahren and the Red Dragons talked. She couldn't hear what they were saying, but their movements were tense. It didn't seem to be going as well as Jahren had hoped it would.

"Mira, you should show them the other picture," Haven said, placing a hand on her shoulder to get her attention.

Mira looked up at him in confusion for a second, then she smiled brightly at him and cried out, "Oh yeah!" Then she flipped to the picture she'd originally shown Jahren before she'd left. Xaver was still a very faint outline on the picture but the rest of the silhouettes were clearly Cyn and Alix. Since she'd last looked at it the rest of the picture had filled in to become Fagan, Dox and Katalynne.

"This... your book showed us to you?" Alix asked, lightly touching the picture in front of him.

Mira nodded. "That's how I knew I could trust you, even if you had those things pointed at me."

"Guns," Katalynne said, frowning, "And we could've killed you with them."

"Could've. But I knew you wouldn't."

"Wait, why is he in the picture?" Fagan pointed to the image of Zach, his brother sporting the trademark smirk that was common to the Fagan brothers.

"I met him earlier today. He was really nice."

"Well, he is not getting involved."

"If the book says-" Mira stopped when she saw the hard frown on Fagan's face. "... well... maybe he's in the picture because he talked to me earlier."

"Back in that other picture..." Alix leaned over and turned back to the meeting with Jahren and the Red Dragons. "There's a black smudge, like in the first one," then he turned the page to the picture of the Scough meeting together.

Mira frowned. The shape of the black spot looked more like a Scough than a smudge. The Scough's skin and clothing were as dark as Dox, but his eyes were all too familiar to Mira. "It's my father," she whispered, "but usually the book can't read him. Usually it doesn't show him at all."

"Could it mean something else?" Katalynne asked. "Could something else be there?"

"Not that I know of. When I spoke to Jahren before I left, we both felt that something was wrong with my father, so maybe the book is trying to show me that."

Fagan leaned back and stretched as he stared up at the ceiling. "If someone were controlling your father, how much damage could they do?"

Mira's ears flattened against her head and she looked uneasy. "I don't know all of my father's powers."

Haven tilted his head a little, listening to his dragon before he spoke. "My dragon says it could be similar to the large battle she mentioned before, with Atticus and the Lurkhamara. He won't go into more detail… which means this is pretty bad."

"So let me get this straight." Fagan sat up in his chair, speaking carefully. "A long time ago there was a huge battle that messed up the demon world. Now something – possibly related to that war – is controlling your father and he's kidnapped the son of this powerful dragon lady who's already pissed about losing her home. And just because your book shows you a picture of us you want us to, what? Run into a completely different world that we know nothing about and help you get him out? Oh, and stop a war?"

Mira recoiled a little in her chair, nodding nervously.

"You realize how ridiculous that sounds? The answer is no. Even if we were on friendly terms with demons, it would still be a no. You're asking us to join a war with you, which is something we aren't equipped or willing to do."

"But I need your help! You know my world better than any other humans because you hunt us down. You would know how to fight!"

"No, we know jack shit about your world," Fagan countered. "We only know about the demons here from experience. We're not prepared to go into a world full of them."

"Hunters hunt demons, they don't help them fight. This war isn't our business." Katalynne added coolly.

"You'll have to find someone else." Fagan stood up from the table and stretched again. "You can stay here for the night and I'll even let you leave with that Ice Dragon you seem close to, but I expect you to leave by tomorrow night."

Mira turned pleading eyes to the others in the room but was met with the same opposition. No one seemed willing to step forward to say anything against Fagan. Defeated, she looked down at the book in front of her, her ears pressing against her head again. "But it said you would help me," she protested softly.

Haven squeezed Mira's shoulder and reached forward, closing her book. "We'll figure something else out."

"But..."

"Come with me, I'll show you a place where you can rest." Katalynne motioned for her and Haven to follow her out of the meeting room. Mira and Haven reluctantly followed while Cyn stood up and made some comment about going to check on Dox, leaving Alix and Fagan alone in the room.

"Fagan." Alix looked up at him as he passed by to leave the room.

Fagan stopped and glanced back at the younger man. "You've been pretty quiet, I take it you disagree."

"Doesn't really matter, you already made the decision for us."

Fagan turned a disapproving look at his partner. "What happened to the Alix I know? Even considering this isn't like you."

"It was a thought…"

"For as long as I've known you, you've hated demons. Why the sudden change of heart?"

"I haven't had a change of heart."

Fagan decided he'd had enough. Now that there was no one else in the room, it wasn't worth holding it in. "Bullshit, Alixandre. You are never this agreeable with demons. This isn't like you, and don't you dare try and tell me it's because you're tired or some crap like that. I want the truth."

Alix's eyes widened at the use of his full name. The shock soon wore off and he glared coldly at Fagan. "I told you to never call me that again."

Fagan glared right back. "I'm still waiting for an answer."

"Fine. I want to talk to her about her father and I want to talk to him. He's the Storyteller."

"God, here we go again with this Storyteller crap. You want to talk to some mythical creature who, even by their standards, is unbelievable?"

"You look at that book and you tell me it's unbelievable."

"Fine, it sketches pictures and-"

"It sketched *us*, Fagan. If she can do that, think of what her father can do."

Fagan took a deep breath. He was trying to stay calm but he was getting more frustrated by the minute, "What makes you think he'll give a crap about anything you ask him for? You're a Hunter. You kill things from his world. Any smart demon would kill us on sight, not ask us for help to stop a war. And, if we help, that's no guarantee he'll turn around and do the same."

"She's here because-"

"Her book told her to come, not her father."

Alix opened his mouth then stopped, pondering his words before he spoke them out loud. "I spoke to Dox when he came here and he bargained for his life by saying that he'd arrange for me to meet the Storyteller. We should learn more, just so this doesn't come back and bite us in the ass."

Fagan frowned at Alix, studying his expression. No, there was something else. He could tell in the calm way that Alix was talking that he was trying to hide something. While his partner was smart, he was usually rash about things. Right now he was carefully considering his words and thinking before he spoke. There was something he didn't want to say.

Fagan knew from experience that there was only one subject that changed Alix's mood like this.

"This is about Roderick, isn't it?"

Alix immediately looked away as if the name physically hurt to hear. His hand moved out of habit to toy with the chain that held the ring hiding under his shirt. "The Lurk said the Storyteller could change things."

"And what made you so sure he was telling the truth? Even if he was telling the truth, we have nothing that says we can trust that thing. I shouldn't have to tell you not to trust them, usually that's your line."

Fagan's body was rigid, his fists clenched tightly. He wasn't comfortable having this conversation, neither of them were. The subject of Roderick was always shaky territory. Alix never wanted to talk about it and Fagan never wanted to bring it up, not after seeing how much his partner would react to it. He'd take a rash, careless Alix any day if it meant not having to deal with the sadness that crossed his eyes when Roderick became the topic of conversation.

Unfortunately, this time, there didn't seem to be anyway to avoid it.

"That book she has… you have to admit, there's something about that book that…" he struggled to find the right words to explain it but he couldn't piece the letters together as his voice took on a more desperate edge, "I have to try. I hate them, but if this can bring him ba-"

"Roderick is dead, Alix." Fagan cut in. He tried to take the edge off his voice. He didn't like saying it, never had, but it was the only way to get through to him. "He's not coming back. You can't just take a book and rewrite the ending to it. Once something is gone it's-"

But Alix shook his head, looking at the table where the book had been. "I have to try," he said once again.

"No. You're taking too many risks on this. You need to accept that he is dead and not coming back. Trusting these demons and getting involved in a war is not worth it."

"It is to me!" Alix actually screamed, the sound piercing the air around them. Fagan took an involuntary step back from the storm as it was released. "You don't understand any of this! You weren't there, I was! I need to do this, and if you're not going to help me then I will do it myself!" He was shaking now, his hands clenched so tightly that they were a ghostly white.

Years of memories flooded his mind, moments with a handsome young man named Roderick, *his* Roderick. Attending university together, their eyes meeting across the classroom like the best of written clichés for romance novels. Moving in together, Alix lining their bookshelves with novels and textbooks, Roderick hooking up wires to a television, video player, and stereo. All that time spent together, working to become a family, shattered in a single moment.

There was no way he was going to lose this chance.

"If Zach had died you'd do anything to have him back, right?!"

Fagan winced. "This isn't about Zach."

"No, this is about family. My family. They're standing right there in front of me, Fagan." Alix finally looked up at Fagan with tear stained red eyes. "I have to do this," he whispered, "With or without you."

"Shit Alix." Fagan sighed, wilting under that look. Stepping forward he pulled the younger man close, attempting to hold him, but Alix pushed him away and shook his head. Fagan wasn't surprised to be pushed aside like that, nodding to Alix as he spoke again, making one last attempt, "Let's sleep on this. Maybe there's something else we can come up with."

"I'm going through with this. Anything is worth bringing them back."

Those words hung in the air, effectively ending the conversation between them. If that wasn't final, the slamming of the door behind him certainly was. Fagan slumped back against the wall as the sound rang through his head. He reached up, rubbed his forehead, and took a deep breath.

"I suppose I really don't have a choice then, you idiot," Fagan sighed loudly in the silence before he left the meeting room to go back to his room. He had a feeling he wasn't going to get any sleep tonight.

Cyn took the opportunity to step away from the group and head down to where Dox was. She visibly relaxed once she was on her own, running a hand through her hair as she walked down the stairs. She frowned, letting the situation fade away in her mind as she gave into a more pressing matter.

Her hair had been dark red for far too long, it was well past time for a new color.

"Dox?"

"I'm here. You're missing quite the show upstairs, they're fighting about something." Dox was sitting on the small bench in his cell, staring off into the shadows as if he could see an entire world deep within the darkness. After a moment he seemed to come out of the weird trance and looked over at her.

"I don't like the idea of staying here." Cyn laid back across the floor, her hands under her head of short hair. She could feel his shadows slithering over, the comforting cold brushing over her fishnet covered arms. "These Hunters are too unpredictable. It was fine when they were just looking for who killed their friend, but now that stupid cat girl has them thinking about a war."

"Cyn, the Scough are not cats."

"You know what I mean. This place is too busy now with other demons. It's a shitty place to hide."

Dox smirked a little and shook his head, his long ears flopping a little like a wet puppy. "No, this place is perfect. We can both blend in among them and the various demons they come across. If anyone shows up we will have advance warning."

"Do I have to remind you that you're sitting in a cell right now? How can you be o.k. with that?"

"Because I can leave when I want. I choose not to."

"Easy for you to say," she grumbled, kicking at a couple of the shadows to blow off steam. "What am I supposed to do up there by myself? Do you really think it's that easy for me to sleep in the same living space as someone who hates us so much? I swear I'm going to wake up and Alix will be standing over me with a gun aimed at my head."

"I thought you were having fun with the dragon, at least," Dox said. Cyn just settled for scowling at him for that. Dox chuckled, "This is certainly better than the empty hotel rooms we used to stay in. You said you were getting tired of that. Something about it being too noisy at night, the beds squeaking next door and the moaning and-"

"I really wish you'd stop remembering everything I say to you," Cyn said, glaring at the shadows now, "And you're missing the point." Cyn rolled on her side, resting her cheek on her arm as she brushed her fingers against the bars between them. "I don't like being trapped here. I don't like seeing you behind these. Even if you're comfortable with it, I'm not. You should have told me about this plan before you disappeared and just did it. You scared me by not showing up when I called."

"I did not mean to worry you," Dox said, suddenly sounding very guilty, "but you would have said no had I brought it up to you. And I had to see if I could trust them, if it would be safe here."

"Being purposely captured by Hunters just for a place to hide? Of course I would've disagreed!"

"Yes, but your father would never think to look for you here."

Cyn's eyes widened at the mention of her father and she frowned at the shadows in front of her. "You don't have to do stupid shit like this to protect me from him."

"Isn't that what friends do?"

"That's not fair," she whispered. "It's not fair for you to say shit like that!"

"But it's the truth, right? At least according to the teddy bears we played with."

Cyn rolled her eyes, trying hard not to smile but the edges of her lips curved upwards anyway. "I told you not to bring that up ever again."

"Dox should be friends with us too," the shadow said, his voice a touch bit lighter. "Friends are always there for each other. Just like his majesty Ted E. Bear and his royal court of Ruff Ruff the Patchy Dog, and Snowflake the Cat."

Cyn giggled, "Royal court?" She made her voice slightly deeper, trying to imitate Dox. "Weren't they superheroes yesterday?"

"That was yesterday, not today!" Dox laughed with her.

The two friends smiled at one another before Cyn took a deep breath, trying to use the moment to calm her nerves about the situation. "I guess hiding out in the demon world is out of the question."

Dox moved to sit on the floor, leaning back against the bars next to her. He reached his hand back, resting it near hers so that Cyn could slide her fingers over his, her pale skin standing out in sharp contrast against his. She closed her eyes and held his hand quietly.

"You'd hate it there," Dox said.

"Would I?"

Dox nodded. "There's no buildings, no soft beds, no cars. All the stuff you like isn't there. The skills it would take to survive are completely different and it would be harder for you to disappear there."

"What about hair dye? Is there hair dye? Red is getting old."

"There is definitely no hair dye."

"Damn. So I'd have to shave it all off if we moved to the demon world? Or at least clean out a beauty supply store."

"Cyn..."

"I dunno, Dox, it might be worth it. My father's not in that world," she whispered, her voice sounding much softer than it usually did.

"Your father might not be there, but mine is. I can't go there, he would find me." There was a slight tremble in his fingers when he spoke of him.

"It's all right. It doesn't sound like they're even going to go to that world. And if they were, there's no way I'd let you go with them."

"Except they would ask, I'm sure. They know I'm his son. If my father is involved the smart thing to do would be to take me with."

"Then tell them no."

"Even for a guaranteed safe place to stay?" Dox shook his head, "It might be worth bargaining for."

"Dox..."

"There's no use debating it until we know for sure."

Cyn wanted to say more but she ended up nodding quietly, letting the subject drop. She only had two options and neither seemed appealing. She could either stay here with Dox and trust him, or run off on her own and try to survive. At least staying with Dox meant she wasn't alone. She felt safe with him, something that most humans wouldn't understand – particularly the ones like Alix who automatically assumed that *demon* was another word for *kill on sight*. Children were supposed to fear the dark shadows that roamed in the corners, but the only monster she ever had to deal with was the very man who was supposed to protect her: her father. The shadows and darkness had always protected her. Dox had never led her astray, but most importantly, he had never hurt her.

She would just have to trust him again.

"Can I sleep with the shadows tonight?"

Dox nodded and the shadows around the cell flowed forward, sliding over her body like a blanket as she lay on the floor. Cyn relaxed under them, not letting go of Dox's hand as she slipped off to sleep, shrouded in the comforting darkness.

Mira sat on the small bed in the room they'd been given after Katalynne left, her ears still folded against her head in disappointment. The book lay in her lap, open to the page she'd looked at before she'd left. The group of Hunters remained on the page in front of her, the picture not changing in the slightest even after Fagan's harsh, "No." She was so sure that the picture had meant they would help her, that she could trust them. Fagan's words could only mean one thing: the book had been wrong again. It had been wrong about Xaver, now it was wrong about the people who stayed inside this warehouse. It wasn't supposed to be wrong. Her father had told her she could always trust it.

"Mira?"

Mira looked up to see Haven leaning against the wall. He'd apparently finished inspecting the room and now he was facing her, looking concerned as he tried to untangle some of the messy braids that covered his head, rethreading them together to keep them out of his eyes. She stood up and crossed over to Haven, leaning against him and closing her eyes. Just being near him was comforting.

"I know you told me to hide and not follow, but these are the people I was supposed to come talk to."

Haven sighed softly and brushed his fingers through her thick hair, ruffling it a bit. "I understand that, but please be more careful next time. Humans are unpredictable, these ones more so than Xaver ever was."

Mira scrunched her nose up and ducked out from under his hand, remembering when she'd run into Xaver. It had been a complete accident, honestly. She'd just been following her book when she'd come across them fighting – or rather, practicing, as Haven had called it after the fact.

Haven remembered that night as well. He remembered crouching in the tall grass, his eyes on the large Hunter's thin, curved blade as it glinted in the moonlight. They'd practiced several nights in the same back area of the park after the sun set and the last police car drove away. Haven could still hear his dragon hissing lowly.

* * *

Mess this up and he'll cut your arm off.

You say that every night, he'd thought back, not taking his eyes from Xaver. Focusing on the cold feeling from his arm he felt it grow. Mist formed around his hand as the cold twisted and created a blade that he could use. He focused on cooling the blade, freezing long pieces of grass between the shards to make the ice stronger.

Xaver was suddenly moving, giving no warning to Haven aside from the movement itself. Haven reacted almost as quickly, shoving himself to roll out of the way as he rolled to his feet and brought the blade up to deflect Xaver's first strike. The metal caught the ice with a sharp sound and Haven staggered at the strength behind the blow, gritting his teeth to push the man back as far as he could. Xaver actually smirked at him, his large scar catching the moonlight and making his face look even more threatening as he pulled his blade back and attacked again.

Right!

Haven listened to his dragon and managed to move just quickly enough to the right to avoid the blade. He could feel a rush of air too close to his skin. If he'd delayed just a second longer... Haven banished the thought and concentrated on putting as much distance between him and Xaver as possible. Making the air colder around him, he watched the small ice crystals form fog between them, slowly making him less and less visible. Xaver moved in to attack a few more times, but he was slower and more cautious, giving Haven time to put more distance between them and think of his next move.

Crouching behind a particularly thick bush at the edge of the park, Haven considered his options. Like the other nights, the point was to get Xaver's sword out of his hand. Haven had never managed it before, but he was determined to do it tonight. He had to figure out some sort of trap that the man wouldn't be able to counter, something that he could create quickly-

Something moved behind Haven.

It's not him, it's something else. Too big to be an animal.

Haven chanced taking his eyes off Xaver for a moment to turn toward the sound. It was quiet, someone slowly stepping through the grass. But if he could hear it, then Xaver–

What happened next was a flurry of movement. One moment Haven remembered seeing Xaver move toward the sound, then suddenly Haven was in front of the Hunter, his dragon screaming in his head for him to move. Another thought filled his mind, stronger and louder than the dragon he was used to.

Protect her.

Haven had never moved so fast in his life. He was able to block Xaver's attacks with scary accuracy and with moves he was sure he hadn't known the moment before. All the while he caught glimpses of a young woman standing behind him, trembling in the trees, watching them fight and clutching a book.

"Least these Hunters didn't try and cut me in half like he did! I'm lucky I was able to control you and make you stop him."

Mira's voice brought Haven out of the memory and he couldn't help but chuckle a bit at her statement. The look on Xaver's face when he'd originally seen the girl had been priceless. Even better was when she demonstrated how she could control anyone by writing in her book, making him smile and hand his sword to Haven.

Xaver had always frowned at her after that.

"If it makes you feel any better he tried to cut me in half when we first met, too." Haven turned to look around the room again. The guest room was sparse, with a couple of beds and a couch that looked like one of the ones Xaver said could be turned into a bed if you pulled it open the right way. There were cabinets in the back for a kitchen, if needed, and a bathroom past a small table in the center of the room. Haven walked over and checked the windows out of habit, not surprised to see them securely attached to the frames. There was no way that glass was going to move unless it was broken.

So even this room felt like a cell.

Haven walked over to one of the beds, lying down and trying to relax. In truth he was very comfortable with the fact that they would be leaving soon and he wouldn't have to worry about the Hunters here. He was better off looking for Xaver's killer alone, assuming that his dragon would actually let him without constant protests of trying to track someone and how it was best to keep on the move. It was obvious that these Hunters weren't concerned with Xaver anymore, not with Mira coming into their lives and mentioning her father to them.

Not that he was going to let her stay here with them in the first place.

Fagan had said they would be allowed to leave and Haven was pretty sure that the hot tempered one would listen, or at least wouldn't try to kill them. So all they had to do was move fast enough to get away.

"Maybe I can talk to them in the morning," Mira said.

Right. He also had to convince Mira that leaving was a good idea.

He had toyed with the idea of pulling her out with him, but knowing what that book was capable of he knew that he would actually have to reason with her somehow. Maybe this wouldn't be so easy after all.

Mira crawled into bed next to him, snuggling under the blanket much like a pet puppy. She nuzzled her face against

Haven's chest until she was comfortable, her ears perked again in contentment as her tail curled against his leg. Haven couldn't resist the comfortable warmth of the Scough lying against him and wrapped an arm around her, closing his eyes and relaxing.

"Someone missed me," she teased quietly, not pulling away.

"I was worried about you." It was nice to have her by his side again. In this place full of hostile humans and a certain shadowy demon he didn't trust, it was nice to see a familiar face again. Having her this close to him reminded him of a more peaceful time, when he was with Xaver, and how Mira had whined about needing someone to sleep against.

"It's what we do!" She insisted as her tail swished behind her. "The Scough always sleep together in packs."

"No offense, I mean you're cute and all, but you're a bit too young for me."

"I'm not that young! And why does that even matter?"

"Because I don't wanna feel like a pedophile."

Both Haven and Mira looked confused over the comment and Xaver sighed, rubbing his forehead in frustration. Finally, he nodded over to Haven. "Sleep next to the kid then."

Chuckling to himself at the memory, Haven couldn't help but feel relieved to see Mira again, even if it had been reckless of her to come.

"Thank you, Haven. It's nice to know that I at least have your help."

"I'm still not quite sure how I feel about this plan of yours, but I'm not going to leave you alone." Haven pulled the blanket around both of them and ignored the disapproving hiss from his dragon. "We already got separated once, I don't want to do that again."

"The people here... I need them to help me, too."

"Get some sleep, Mira. We'll figure it out in the morning." And hopefully, in the morning, she would come to her senses and they could leave together.

Mira reluctantly nodded, closing her eyes and curling a bit tighter against him. Haven responded by forcing himself to relax, mentally telling his dragon to be quiet as he dozed off next to her.

Chapter 5

Early the next morning found Fagan unable to sleep. In fact, most of the night had been spent lying in bed, glaring at the ceiling and silently demanding why it wasn't helping him with the current situation. When this whole mess started he had hoped to find out who had killed Xaver. Now, he was stuck thinking about something completely irrational: going to the demon world. Hunting demons was one thing, but stepping onto the front porch of their home territory was completely insane. If the few humans who knew about demons made their living off killing them, demons certainly had to have a skewed view of them. Going into their world was suicidal, at best, yet somehow Fagan was stuck with a partner set on doing just that.

Was there any way he could convince Alix that this was a terrible idea?

Did he really want to?

Fagan was one of those Hunters who didn't have a tragic back story like most heroes in an adventure story. He had parents who were still around and an annoying little brother. He even had a normal life, once upon a time, and a future in his father's company until meeting Xaver. Meeting Xaver had made him realize that sitting behind a desk for the rest of his life would make him tear out his hair from sheer boredom. He couldn't begin to imagine what Alix was going through, nor did he want to. He had no desire to think of his life without his family – even if he spent his time trying to keep them away from this lifestyle.

Alix had raised a good point. What if this were about his family? Wouldn't he do anything to have that back if he had lost any of them? Especially Zach, though he would never voice that out loud.

A little before sunrise he decided to change tactics. Rather than lie and wait for the answers to come to him he stood up and pulled on a shirt, opting to work out his frustration. Knowing that Alix usually worked off his frustration by practicing, Fagan chose to avoid any chance of contact for the moment and crossed the practice room floor to a large utility door that was generally left closed. Using a key hung next to the frame, he unlocked the door and slid it aside just enough to step through into the back room.

Fagan had bought the warehouse back when he and Xaver had become partners. At the time he'd had the help of Xaver to knock down walls and build new ones that were stable enough to still support the ceiling and take a couple good punches. Once Xaver had gone out on his own, Fagan had been left with a large warehouse that still needed work, but was livable. About a third of the space in the back was left with wide, metal shelves and dusty boxes of unshipped paper and unused equipment. Trying to tell Katalynne or Alix how to do any repairs would have taken too much time to explain. So Fagan treated it like a sort of hobby, using it to work off steam in the way that only a hammer, nails, and a saw could.

Fagan set down his sword by the door and started to clean off one of the large shelves. Lifting the heavy boxes made for mindless grunt work as he carried them to the door at the far end, dropping them into a dumpster outside in an area that use to be a loading dock for semi-trucks. After four boxes he could feel the familiar sensation of his muscles protesting, a few droplets of sweat tanning his arms and forehead. The sun was just barely peeking over the horizon in the distance, taxis starting to crawl out of their resting spots to rush around town and pick up their morning fares. Through the open loading door, he could hear the city buses coming to life, moving down the streets to greet the early risers who armed themselves with heavy coats and cups of gourmet coffee.

He chuckled to himself. That had almost been his life. Even with the current mess he was in he still preferred demons and Alix's temper to dealing with the morning traffic that would lead to the best of cramped cubicles.

Mentally, he knew that hauling boxes and breaking down metal shelves wasn't going to help solve any issues. He knew that, eventually, he would have to talk to Alix or maybe even beat some sense into him. Sympathetic feelings or not, it was still a stupid idea. But, for the moment, the mindless motions felt good and helped him clear his head.

Fagan was used to Alix's personality and very familiar with how the younger man followed things he was passionate about with pinpoint accuracy and determination. They worked so well together because they could set their minds on a goal and Fagan could count on him during a tight situation. It also helped that Fagan had trained Alix and given him most of his skills. In many cases Alix could be hot headed, but when it came to a battle they understood each other's moves and abilities enough to create a force to be reckoned with. The problem came when they attempted to take solo jobs. Alix was too hot headed to work alone, Fagan knew that, but Alix was too stubborn to admit it.

If Alix didn't have someone to cover his back he was going to get killed, which meant that Fagan had to be a part of this foolish plan – even if he hated it – just to keep his partner alive.

Fagan dropped the latest box into the dumpster, watching the bottom of the cardboard give way as random pieces of blank paper slid out to create a new bottom layer over the other boxes he'd already dropped in. Inwardly he sighed, still not liking the choices placed before him.

"Coffee?" Katalynne's voice from the doorway wasn't a surprise to him. His assistant knew his habits enough to know that he always came to this room when things were a bit too hectic and he couldn't leave the building. She didn't wait for his answer. Instead she stepped across the dusty floor, her fashionable heels clicking across the ground as she set the coffee mug on a newly clean area of the shelf. She leaned against the edge of the shelf after making sure it wouldn't leave a line of dust across the back of the white shirt and pinstriped skirt she wore. Fagan would've made a comment about her wearing such nice clothes to an old warehouse full of Hunters had she not looked so good in them.

Fagan walked over to join her and took a sip, making a face as the sharp taste hit his tongue and the back of his brain shot to attention. Despite the drink's bitterness he took another sip, this one much longer, and let the black coffee wake him up like a drag on a morning cigarette. He dropped to sit on one of the spare boxes, the cardboard crumbling a bit under his weight until he hit the solid piles of paper within.

"Why are you up so early?" Fagan asked. Not that he minded seeing her gorgeous face but his assistant never came to the warehouse until the sun was fully up in the sky.

"Your partner decided to call me and request everything I had on the demon world. I've been researching for the last hour, attempting to wake up. He's pretty determined about all of this."

A snort of agreement and Fagan closed his eyes, enjoying the feeling of the bitter caffeine sliding through his body as he took another drink. "That's Alix. He's got a bull's determination for stamping out the color red... and every other color in his way," he sighed.

Katalynne frowned. "It isn't my place to ask, but... what is behind that determination of his?" Usually, Katalynne wasn't the type to worry about the particulars of her boss' motivations. She understood that Fagan and Alix were Hunters and she understood what that entailed. Those details were enough for her and she would go about her business. Asking why Alix or Fagan had gone into this line of work was bordering on the personal and that was something she didn't like bringing up.

Work was work, and personal was personal.

However, Alix's passion for hunting and killing demons was a hard thing to ignore, especially when situations like this came up and it had the potential to put their lives in danger.

"Why is he so determined to stamp out all the demons he comes in contact with?" She raised the question again, this time using the same analogy Fagan had used earlier.

Fagan sighed. It really wasn't his place to tell the story – especially since he didn't like talking about it – but if Alix was set on this plan it would be best if people knew why. Or, at least, if Katalynne knew why, since she was the only person he could turn to who wasn't a demon who posed a potential threat.

"You've seen his ring, right?"

"You mean the thing he nearly snapped my head off for asking about when I first got here? How could I forget it?"

"Alix used to have a fiancé and a daughter. His fiancé's name was Roderick Michaels, some brilliant egghead in genetics or something like that who worked at YH Tech."

Katalynne hesitated. "YH Tech? I know that company name."

Fagan nodded. "The company was doing some sort of genetic testing with demons. A couple of demons decided they didn't like it. They burnt down the building with everyone trapped inside on the day Alix was going to tell him…" he stopped.

"Tell him what?" Katalynne asked.

"On the day Alix found out they were going to be parents. He lost his daughter soon afterwards."

He could hear Katalynne set down her coffee mug, quietly contemplating the story. After a long moment she spoke up again, "I've heard of that company and the fire that burnt it down. I didn't realize Alix knew someone who…" she frowned and glanced over at Fagan. "Wait a minute… what you just said makes little sense."

Fagan cracked an eye open to look up at her.

"You say that Alix lost his daughter but you didn't mention anything about a mother, or adoption." Katalynne tapped her stylus on the tablet. "And in those listed as beneficiaries for the fire at YH Tech there isn't a single person named Alix," then she stopped, her eyes widening, "But… there is an Alixandre…"

Fagan listened to Katalynne's voice cut off as she realized the missing piece to the situation, and once again the long legged beauty proved to be worth every penny he paid her. "Alix is Alixandre. And if you ever tell her I told you, she'll kill us both."

"Alix Andre DeBenit," Katalynne whispered. "Alixandre… A-Alix is a woman." Out of all of the surprises her boss threw at her, from new types of demons, to fallen colleagues, and even perverted little brothers, this one certainly stood on top.

"Yeah. Surprise," though his voice didn't carry an enthusiastic tone, "Alixandre was this mousy little French girl whose parents use to socialize at the rich and snobby parties my parents threw. That all changed when she got to this warehouse. Xaver kept making comments… you know how Xaver is." *Was* he thought to himself, but he didn't feel like saying the word out loud.

"Right," Katalynne muttered, remembering Xaver's personal nickname of *Legs* for her.

"When she found out about what we do, she wanted to help because of what happened to her fiancé. Xaver refused, called her a mousy little girl, and left it at that. I guess it got to her because, one day, she came down the stairs with her hair chopped and a tight sports bra to attempt to hide her chest – she's upgraded to compression shirts since then. Add to that the muscles from sparring and practicing and the fact that she had more confidence... well, people started thinking she was a guy and she never corrected them. Why would she? She's not the mouse Xaver made her out to be anymore, she actually views that as a weakness now." Unless, of course, the Storyteller gave her what she wanted, but Fagan wasn't going to mention that as he took another drink. "She basically imitates Xaver, whether she realizes it or not. Even I get fooled sometimes. It's just easier to think of her as a guy now."

Katalynne stood there in shock, still adjusting to the information. Now that she knew the truth she could see the signs she'd missed before. Alix was shorter than most men and softer in the face. Now that she knew, she felt a little stupid for having missed something that should have been so obvious.

"She miscarried her daughter when she found out Roderick died in that fire. She's been determined to hunt down the demon who was responsible since then. The only clues we have is that it used blue and black flames."

Katalynne tipped up her mug and frowned softly when she found there was no coffee left. For this news she should have brought an entire pot. She couldn't get over how well Alix hid it. Granted, Hunters tended to be male... Katalynne frowned, that thought may have answered her own question. But thinking of the story as a whole made a part of her feel like it was a bit deeper than that. Hiding behind a male persona may have helped the woman mask the pain, at least, until the girl with the book showed up.

"So that's why he-" She stopped, struggling for a moment, "-she hates demons so much. And now? With the Storyteller? Does she have some sort of plan to make him change things back for her?" The ultimate dream for anyone who had suffered a loss. The chance to turn back time, to rewrite events for a chance to have a better outcome. But, "Doesn't she realize everything a move like that would actually cause? Even if the Storyteller could potentially do it, it would change everything. For one, you two would probably never meet, and I'd probably still be working for Florence, Cave, and Cable."

"Hey, I thought you liked your previous job at that law firm." Fagan set down his mug and stood up, he needed to do something to distract himself now that Alix's secret had been revealed. He went about tossing some loose reams of paper into the box he'd been sitting on.

"I did, but you are infinitely more interesting to work for." Katalynne rescued his mug, holding it with her own. "Did you need a refill?"

He was quite happy to be mostly off the subject of Alix's motivations and now felt the need to keep moving. "Nah. I'm gonna move a few more boxes and figure out how to barge head first into the demon world." Mind made up, Fagan gave his assistant a smirk. "I can't let that idiot go in on her own, can I?"

There was a look on Katalynne's face, something that Fagan almost swore was concern. Before he could comment on it the woman spoke, "I guess not." And with that, Katalynne turned and left, letting him work off the rest of his restless energy. If he was planning on going to the demon world for a fight, the least she could do was arm him with as much information as possible.

She would hate to have to look for another job.

Randall Fagan had grown up with an uninteresting little girl named Alixandre DeBenit, who lived down the street. Their families ran in the same circles of the excessively wealthy, people who had so much money that they were beginning to run out of island plots to buy on the ten thousand lakes of Minnesota. The two weren't friends, not really, but he had seen her a few times at the various parties his mother felt the need to throw or attend. She was one of those rich kids whose parents travelled a lot, but had somehow settled down in the suburbs of the Twin Cities, of all places. Cute, blonde, and dressed in plaids of blue and white, Alixandre tended to be quiet and only spoke when spoken to.

According to Fagan's mother, she had gone off to college and met some smart boy who had a promising future at YH Tech. Randall hadn't really cared at the time, he was too busy making a place for himself in his father's shadow. The name YH Tech had translated to stocks and investments, a scientific company that, while interesting, had nothing to do with his father's business. By the time he joined Xaver, any information about Alixandre or YH Tech was buried in the back of his mind, long forgotten.

The day she'd walked into the bar that he and Xaver liked to frequent Fagan hadn't even recognized her.

"Didn't know the preppy girls drank like that," Xaver had nodded his head to a couple tables over. Fagan turned, his drink paused at his lips as he realized who his friend and partner was nodding to.

Two tables down was the quiet and mousy French girl he'd crossed paths with for most of his adolescent life. Years had passed, but she still had the same long, blonde hair, and her style had only been minimally updated to a long skirt and modest sweater over a button down shirt. He couldn't quite believe it was her. She wasn't the type of person he ever expected to see in a bar, much less *drinking* in a bar. Maybe a glass of some fancy wine, but certainly not the liquor they advertised on television.

"Damn, look at how big that glass is. I bet she passes out before she gets halfway through it."

Xaver's words seemed like a cruel jest, but Fagan knew him well enough to know it was a warning, and in Xaver speak that translated to something along the lines of, "Poor stupid girl has no idea what she's doing and is going to get hurt."

"Yeah," Fagan muttered, then stood up.

He had only meant to ask her what she was doing there in the city. Last he'd heard from his mother she had plans to marry the scientist guy she had been dating. Here she was, out of place in more ways than he could count, so the least he could do was offer her a safe ride to her parents' place, or where ever she was staying. Unfortunately, as he got closer, he realized he'd just stepped into the worst type of situation one could come across. Maybe Xaver's words had been a warning for concern about him rather than her.

Her eyes said it all, wide and red from crying as she looked down at the glass. Each step that took him closer made it quite clear this wasn't the type of celebratory drinking that he and Xaver participated in after a hunt. This was the type of drinking someone did to drown their sorrows, to try and forget something terrible that had happened. Placing a hand on her shoulder, he spoke to her quietly, "Alixandre, right?"

Alixandre turned to look at him, squinted her eyes to get a clearer picture, then she broke into a smile. "Ah! Randall, right? Mr. Fagan's son. How are you?"

He let the name slide since he didn't really want to explain how *Randall* was a thing of the past. She was being much louder than he had ever seen her be – not that he had seen much of her to begin with. "I'm fine, but more importantly, how are you?"

"Oh! I'm fine, just fine, living the single life, you know."

"Single? I thought you were with someone, at least that's what my mother said a while ago."

"Nope," then she shook her head and took another gulp of beer. "Single as of nine months ago. Eight, technically, I guess…"

Fagan was not equipped to deal with a heartbroken woman. His immediate response would've been something along the lines of "get over it," "stop wearing his ring on your finger," "fuck him," but he had a feeling that such words would only urge her to drink away her misery more. He glanced over at Xaver, nodding for him to come over. Xaver gave him a disapproving frown, but stood up and walked over anyway like a good friend. "Hey. Uh… who's your friend?" Xaver asked.

"Alixandre DeBenit," the girl's words slurred together as she held her hand out toward Xaver. "Was going to be Alixandre Michaels, but I'm single now."

"That's a shame," Xaver said as he slowly shook her hand. Xaver always did his best to avoid emotional situations and Fagan already knew he was going to catch hell for this one.

"Yeah. YH Tech. Caught on fire. Such a shame, such a biiiig fiiiiiire." The alcohol was clearly taking its effect.

"Shit…" Xaver whispered, looking over at Fagan.

They were both thinking the same thing. There had been a lab fire in the news months ago, but at the time neither had paid much attention to it despite reports of it being "out of the ordinary." There were plenty of other things they had to worry over, a lab fire could wait. Of course if Fagan hadn't been so eager to leave his suburban business life behind, he might have remembered that the girl down the street was with a guy at the lab, and maybe he wouldn't have felt like such an insensitive ass right now.

Fagan took a deep breath. "Look, Alixandre, I'm sorry. I know it must be terrible that that happened but… drinking isn't…" it was an odd feeling, actually trying to talk someone out of drinking. "It's not going to make you feel better."

"Are you sure? Because I'm feeling pretty good right now…"

"He's right, kid. It sucks, but drinking ain't gonna bring him back."

"Blah blah, I know. But I'm sick of people telling me I can't drink, can't still be missing him, and can't still be upset." Alixandre set down her glass and glared at it angrily, then the look immediately wilted and she laid her head on the table. "I wasn't supposed to be single. She was supposed to be here today, you know? Then I could at least have that."

Fagan opened his mouth to ask, but Xaver shook his head sharply. He pulled him aside and whispered to him, his voice low and sadder than Fagan had ever heard it as he explained what Alixandre had to have meant by *her* being here today.

Single as of eight to nine months ago? Alixandre was talking about a child.

Fagan numbly reached back, grabbing a chair from the next table and pulled it over so he could sit down, his legs not feeling so stable. What the hell had he just gotten himself into?

"Was gonna be today," Alixandre murmured, still talking and not noticing their reactions. "Doctor said it was going to be today."

"Fuck," Xaver said softly, shaking his head. "I'm really sorry, kid."

"Alixandre... come on, you shouldn't be here," Fagan said. "Not like this. Let me take you home-"

"No," she snapped at him, frowning. "I'm not going home. I'm not going back there. All they do is coddle me, baby me, and treat me like glass. I'm tired of it," then she started screaming, "It doesn't make it better! It just makes it hurt more!"

"I got it, I got it," Fagan said, wrapping an arm around her waist as he urged her out of the stool she was sitting on. She stumbled right into him and immediately collapsed into tears, shaking and sobbing. Fagan shifted, not quite sure what to do, especially when it felt like the entire bar was staring at them. The man behind the bar – the owner, actually, Fagan knew from frequenting the bar with Xaver – quietly nodded toward the door, trying to get Fagan to take Alixandre outside. Fagan nodded back to the heavy set man, "Just put the drinks on my tab, um, and hers, too," he said, then he took Alixandre's arm and helped her stand enough to walk.

Meanwhile, Xaver walked back to his table and downed his beer. "Gonna need this," he said, and the man behind the bar let out a hearty laugh.

"Tell Fagan the drinks are on me, but you both owe me."

"How many drinks did she actually order before we noticed?"

"Let's just say you two are lucky that you're both handsome."

Xaver smirked and winked at the man. "Thanks, Chuck."

Alixandre ended up at the warehouse with Fagan and Xaver, keeping to herself and walking around like a zombie in a daze. After a week of not even bothering to change her clothes, Xaver had decided that enough was enough. "Pathetic woman," he said. "You said you didn't want them to coddle you but you can't even take care of yourself."

"Xaver!" Fagan glared at his partner. "Don't talk to her like that, you know what she's been through."

"Yeah yeah, fire, baby, I got it. Still pathetic."

Alixandre frowned at him. "No one asked you for your opinion."

"Well you're here wasting space in my warehouse, so you're stuck listenin' to my opinion," then he chuckled, "Though I guess I shouldn't expect such a mouse of a woman to do more than just sit around and do nothing."

Alixandre's frown had transformed into a hard glare. "Shut up! You don't know what it's like to-"

"Oh please, is **that** the excuse you're gonna use? 'You don't know what it's like'," Xaver said, making his voice higher pitched in a clear mockery of Alixandre. "'I lost everything, now I'm gonna sit here and pout'."

"Shut up!"

"'I don't want people to treat me like glass, but I'm going to sit here and do nothing'."

"I said shut up!" She threw a pillow and Xaver easily stepped aside, laughing.

"'I'm such a pathetic woman, all I can do is throw pillows'."

"Fermez la bouche!" Suddenly there was a glass flying at Xaver, the larger man ducking away and the glass shattering against the wall. Alixandre stared at the broken bits of glass, panting softly from how much she had been yelling. Fagan couldn't stop staring at her, completely surprised at her reaction toward his partner.

Xaver, on the other hand, couldn't stop smirking. "Good. That's a start."

It had been the push she needed, both she and Fagan realized. Xaver had actually shoved her into dealing with the issue. As a result of that yelling match, she'd actually stomped upstairs and taken a shower. New clothes were worn and she'd even started cooking, keeping herself busy while they went on their missions, practiced, and repaired the warehouse into a more livable state. The three settled in to a simple living arrangement and Alixandre soon forgot to be sad.

She wasn't quite sure what either man did in the manner of working for a living. She never bothered to ask, though from the weapons she would see them carry she had a feeling that asking would lead to something that she might not be ready for. She liked the balance they all had. It wasn't great but it wasn't bad, something that all three parties could work around. She liked not having to face her parents or their sympathy, their apologies, and the way they were too scared to even whisper Roderick's name around her. Asking too many questions had the potential to disrupt that balance, so she always kept them to herself.

Or, at least, she tried.

"I heard something from my parents one day, before I moved in with Roderick."

"Oh?"

Alix tried to choose her words carefully as she faced Fagan, hands folded in her lap as she spoke again, "You… left your father's company to do something that your parents disapprove of. They didn't go into details."

"Yeah," Fagan said, sitting in a chair across from her. They were both in what could be considered a kitchen area. It at least had tables, chairs, and a half-hearted fridge. "Got tired of the nine to five lifestyle."

"And I'm assuming the thing you do with Xaver is the thing they disapprove of?"

Fagan nodded again but didn't actually say anything. He wasn't going to bring up his occupation until he absolutely had to.

"What is it that you do? I mean… you live in a warehouse, and there's swords, and-"

Fagan sighed, "It's a long story-"

"He's a Hunter."

Xaver stood at the doorway, watching the two of them as they talked. Fagan immediately glared at his partner while Alixandre gave him a confused look. "A Hunter? What's that?"

"You don't want to know," then Fagan turned a glare at Xaver, "Which is why I never mentioned it."

"He's right," Xaver chuckled. "It's not for a mousy little lady like you."

"Excuse me?"

The seed had been planted after that, just like it had been with Fagan. Fagan could tell from the look in Alixandre's eyes that another one of Xaver's small pushes was working its magic. She wanted to know about being a Hunter and Fagan wouldn't be able to dance around the subject anymore. This kind of life didn't suit the girl and he hoped that, eventually, she would see that and return to her parents. But there was another, stronger part of Fagan that Xaver had extracted out of him. That part knew that this was exactly what Alixandre needed. It was the same thing

Fagan had needed the night he met Xaver, only Alixandre needed this more than he could ever begin to comprehend.

She was right with what she had said at the bar: she had been coddled long enough.

So he told her. He told her everything.

And, of course, she didn't believe it. He hadn't either the first time.

"You're telling me that boogeymen and monsters in the closet actually exist?" She laughed, "That's ridiculous!"

"Oh?" Xaver crossed his arms at his chest, a serious look on his face. "I'm sure you heard the news about that fire. How the fire was 'unlike anything anyone has ever seen'."

Alixandre's look of disbelief shifted at the mention of the fire, turning sad in an instant. "I didn't just hear about it," she whispered. "I was there. I was on my way there to tell him I was pregnant."

Fagan winced. She had failed to mention that when they saw her at the bar. "Alixandre-"

But she cut him off, focusing her attention on Xaver. "The flames... they were black, and there were swirls of blue. They didn't just burn the lab, they completely melted it. Does... that sound like a particular type of... demon?" She struggled with the word, still not quite believing it.

"Dunno," Xaver said with a shrug. "Didn't look too much into it at the time, but it's a very real possibility."

"I... want to help you."

Xaver laughed, "Forget it. There's no way."

"Why? Because I'm a woman? Surely there are female Hunters."

"They're rare. And the ones who do exist aren't cute and proper like you."

Alixandre frowned. "Fagan and I come from the same background and he's a Hunter."

"He's also a strong man. You are a mouse not worthy of our time. You can barely look me in the eye."

"I…" she hadn't realized that during this entire conversation her eyes had been focused on the floor. She forced herself to look up at him and hoped that her eyes looked as hard as she wanted them to. "Y-yes I can."

"And you keep stuttering," Xaver sighed. "You're not Hunter material, little girl. If Fagan and I run into that kind of demon we'll let you know," then Xaver walked off.

Fagan already knew that it wasn't going to end there.

In the days that followed Alixandre would make her way to the practice area where Xaver and Fagan would spar together. Xaver never let her stick around long enough to watch, shouting at her, "No mousy women allowed," in a tone of voice that always made Alixandre jump.

"Can't you go a little easy on her?" Fagan would ask as he threw a punch at Xaver. Xaver always knew when to dodge, when to counter, and soon he'd be throwing his own punches at Fagan.

"Demons won't go easy on her."

"We're not demons," Fagan would say, trying to dodge Xaver's attacks, wincing when a hard fist would connect into his shoulder. "Considering what she's been through-"

"That's no excuse. If anything, it's a liability," and Xaver would take a moment to breathe, sweat dripping from his forehead. "No one is going to feel sorry for her, Fagan. They see that long hair and cute skirt and they'll turn it against her in a heartbeat. We're not demons, no. We're worse. We're Hunters, and if she wants this, she needs to learn that."

Fagan, to this day, wasn't sure if Xaver was aware that Alix had been listening from behind the door. He could never figure out if it actually mattered if he knew or not. What he did know was that the next day, Alixandre had walked into the practice room, plaid skirt replaced with a worn out pair of jeans that he didn't even know the girl had. The button down shirt was now an old T-shirt, and her long hair was now jagged layers of blonde that she had obviously cut herself.

Xaver smirked. "You look like a raggedy little boy."

"Better than a mouse," she said, walking over to the wall and taking up one of the swords. As she held onto the weapon Fagan could see that her ring was still on her finger, but that was the only part of Alixandre that he recognized.

"What do you expect to do with that, little boy?" Xaver asked.

"Fight demons. I want you to train me," then she stood and faced him, looking him in the eye, "And my name is Alix."

"We'll see if you can earn that name," Xaver said in response, a smirk growing across his lips.

It was that smirk that Alix remembered as he woke up that morning to the sound of boxes being moved around in the unfinished area of the warehouse. It took him a moment to realize that he had been dreaming and not standing in front of Xaver, trying to convince him that he was capable of fighting. No, that wasn't the situation at hand. *She* hadn't just cut her hair and threw on a pair of old jeans. He had just woken up the morning after being asked to go to the demon world to help the Storyteller.

The Storyteller.

Roderick.

Normally, Alix would have gotten up and began his morning routine. Instead he rolled over in bed and listened to the muffled sounds of Fagan working. Just this once, he told himself, he'd sleep in and imagine those sounds were Fagan and Xaver sparring, just like what *she* used to wake up to.

Just this once he'd let himself be that girl in this strange warehouse again, because if all went well, today would be the last day.

Cyn grumbled to herself as she left the comfort of Dox's shadows to go upstairs to the living area. She'd already passed through the main reception area, nodding to the secretary as the woman typed on her computer, the smell of coffee permeating the room. In Cyn's opinion it was far too early to even consider coffee, but now that she was smelling it, her stomach decided to remind her that she hadn't eaten much the day before. Her first thought was to wander to Alix's room and see if the pissy Hunter had any food to share. Despite his attitude toward demons, he seemed less prickly around her now that he knew about her father's grand experiment. Climbing the stairs to Alix's room, her plans were suddenly thwarted as a sickeningly sweet smile and far too awake green eyes appeared in front of her.

Cyn glared at the fox girl. It was too early for this crap.

"Good morning," Mira said, her tail eagerly wagging behind her.

"Yeah." Cyn silently reminded herself that she was going to have to be more firm with Dox about finding another place to live. This place was completely intolerable with someone so... bright... staying here. Surely he'd understand that, he was a shadow after all.

"Did you sleep well?"

"I sure did. Sleeping in the same building as people who make their living by hunting demons and who have put my friend in a prison cell makes me sleep just fine."

"I'm glad to hear it," then the girl smiled at her. "I slept well, too."

"That was sarcasm," Cyn muttered.

"What?"

"It's-"

"I was actually talking about the creature that keeps you awake sometimes. You know, the one your father put inside of you?"

Cyn blinked at the girl before a deep frown crossed her face. "And how do you know about that?"

Mira giggled as she tapped the pouch that was slung over her shoulder.

"You read about me?! How much did you read?" Cyn sounded more panicked then she would have liked, but she couldn't help it. This was her life and it was upsetting to hear that this happy *thing* suddenly knew all about it.

Mira blinked, her tail slowing. "I wanted to know about you so I-"

"You can't just **do** that! There are things people don't want to share with others, you have to ask! How would you feel if I just read everything about you?"

Mira shrugged. "It's just reading."

Cyn sighed and pushed past the girl, muttering something about stupid cat-... fox-... Scough... whatever. Mira's ears flattened when she heard it and she frowned sadly. "I've upset you, haven't I?"

"You think?"

"Yeah, I do."

"Again, that was sarcasm."

"I still don't know what that is."

"Just forget it."

Mira nodded, her tail swaying nervously behind her as she spoke again. "You said that I shouldn't read about people without asking, right? I won't do it again," then she smiled, "Let's start over. Hi, I'm Mira!"

Cyn's glare faltered against her will. If she was going to be stuck here, it meant being stuck with this creature. It was best to at least attempt to share the same breathing space. "Cyn," she said in response to Mira's introduction.

"Nice to meet you! We should talk more, then I can learn more about you properly!" Then suddenly Mira was urging her to walk into the room where she had slept last night, a determined look on her face as she whispered to herself that she wouldn't use the book this time.

Cyn reluctantly walked into the room and sat in one of the chairs, nodding to Haven since he was perched by the window. He nodded back to her then went back to looking outside. Always tense and alert, it was a good trait to have, Cyn noted. Mira followed her and took a seat on the bed, watching Cyn as if studying her. Cyn glared back and snapped, "What?"

"I'm just trying to think of the proper way to engage in conversation."

Haven raised an eyebrow from the window, trying not to laugh but a couple of quiet chuckles slipped past his lips. Cyn turned her glare toward him and he stopped, deciding it was best to change the conversation. "Was there food upstairs?"

"Dunno, she stopped me in the hall. I can't imagine that they stock food for guests though, especially since they had you in that basement before."

Haven nodded. "I was debating going out for food, but I'm not familiar with this area and there's more people outside then I'm used to."

"I was headed up to Alix's room to see if he had anything, but when I was up there before it was mostly all tea and fancy crap."

"I've heard Xaver talk about tea. He said it was just hot water with dead leaves in it." Haven made a face at that as he stepped away from the window to stand closer.

Cyn smiled a bit. It was nice to have at least one person agree with her about something in this place – she wasn't much for tea, either.

"I'll get us some food. Xaver called it a grocery store, right?" And with that Mira was writing something in her book before she practically bounced over to the door, pushing it open. Much to Cyn's surprise it actually looked like some sort of grocery store on the other side instead of the hallway she had just walked through to get to this room. Either way, Cyn was glad to get some breathing time away from the incessant happiness that seemed to surround the girl.

"Xaver hated her in the morning too," Haven said, finally choosing a chair close to hers where he sat down and stretched out.

"And you?"

Haven shrugged. "She's a person to talk to. And it's safer to be more alert when you're awake."

Cyn nodded, seeing the logic in that. Obviously Haven was one of those people who survived in the moment and only relaxed when he was sure he and those he was protecting were safe. As he sat down in the chair, Cyn couldn't help looking at him, as she hadn't really had the chance to before – that nighttime battle from their first encounter or him nearly freezing her to death hardly counted.

. Every once in a while Cyn could catch a glimpse of a scar on Haven's dark skin. She assumed that they came from whatever he had gone through in his life as a kid with an Ice Dragon. The most striking thing about Haven, aside from the pearly white scales wrapped around his arm, were his eyes. Icy blue, like looking down at a frozen lake just under her feet.

"You're staring."

Cyn shrugged, looking away from him. Were her cheeks actually feeling a bit warm? "Never seen an Ice Dragon before," she said. "Dox has mentioned them, but that's about it."

Haven lifted his marked arm a little. "He told me they were all killed in some war in their world. I believe it's the same war we talked about before with Mira." The young man stopped, tilting his head just a little, obviously listening to his dragon's voice for a moment. "He says you're human, but you can control the ground. How?"

"My father did some freaky shit and put a demon inside me. It's also why I'm messed up and have nightmares," she looked at him again and smiled a little, "Thanks for that, by the way."

Seeing her smile made a smile cross his own lips. It actually made the girl look more approachable, almost cute – but he had a feeling that she'd shove a tree branch down his throat if he said that out loud. "I just wanted you to stop screaming and no one else was doing anything." Haven turned his head and looked at the door, waiting for Mira to come back.

As if on cue the door opened and Mira stepped back in, holding a green grocery basket of what looked like various fruits and some deli-made sandwiches. There was some worker yelling that she wasn't allowed to go in there, "That's employee only!" Mira just closed the door and caught Cyn's confused look, smiling and pointing to her book.

"It's a Storyteller thing my father taught me. Haven likes fruit, so that's what I got."

"You say that like it's normal," Cyn muttered as Mira set the food on the table. She wasn't about to admit that she was glad to have some variety in food because she had a feeling Mira would do something like smile at her again. Haven, meanwhile, picked up an apple and bit into it.

"It is normal. For a Storyteller."

"Right. Nice to know that Storytellers are thieves who steal food."

"It's not stealing. They set it out for everyone."

"That's what Xaver said, too," Haven said around a mouthful of apple, already grabbing a second one to eat.

Cyn sighed, "We're going to have to have a talk about how things work in this world."

Mira smiled as she opened one of the sandwiches to eat, pulling it apart to eat the meat inside before eating the bread and fixings. "I want to check in on Jahren again to see if he's o.k. Oh! I could tell him that I found help... well, sort of."

Haven paused in eating his second apple. "Mira, they said no. We should finish eating and leave. We can talk about how to help your father once we're someplace safe."

"Right," Cyn commented quietly as she took one of the sandwiches. Well, that got rid of the annoying problem of having to deal with furry Ms. Sunshine, but it was annoying how she suddenly didn't like the idea of them leaving as much because it included Haven.

"It'll be quick, I promise. The book showed him on his way to meet with the Reina. I want to see how it turned out."

"Mira..." Haven warned, his voice wary.

"I'll do it right here. It'll be fine, honest." She pulled her book out of her bag and laid it on the table. Haven frowned but didn't protest anymore as he finished his apple and reached for a sandwich, taking advantage of the food while they had it and weren't moving.

Cyn dug through the grocery basket, finding a few packages of string cheese to eat while Mira flipped the pages in her book. Most were blank or had small sketches on them, looking a lot like a child attempting to scribble out the family dog. Mira ignored those pages, not able to make out the images, and finally reached the page she wanted and spelled out Jahren's name with her finger. Both Cyn and Haven watched as a new picture sketched itself, once again showing Jahren talking to the three Red Dragons.

"Hey, that dark spot from before is back," Cyn said, pointing to it as it slithered between the trees behind them.

Mira nodded, then her eyes widened as she watched the dark shadow spread across the page, covering Jahren's image. "Jahren?!"

"Why is it doing that?" Haven asked, immediately setting down his sandwich and standing up to look closer. Cyn swore she felt a sudden cool breeze in the room.

"I'm not sure," Mira said, the worry clear in her voice. "W-what are you trying to tell me?" She asked, actually speaking to the book.

Cyn frowned as she pulled her hand back from the page, rubbing her fingers together. Haven looked up at her as she rubbed her fingers against the back of the chair she was sitting in. "What's wrong?" He asked.

"I'm not sure, it felt like I had something on them."

Mira looked at the book in worry and turned the page to one that had nothing on it. Tracing with her finger, she quickly wrote Jahren's name again. The letters bled out and covered the page in black. "Why won't it show him? What happened?" Mira looked up at Haven, shaking. "You see? This is why I need help, something bad is happening!"

"All right, relax," Haven said. He might not have liked her idea of going into the demon world, but there was no denying that something was going on. "Calm down and close the book. Maybe we can try talking to them again."

"So you're on board with this now?" Cyn asked, finishing the rest of her string cheese before grabbing a muffin. It was the most disorganized breakfast she had ever had, but that didn't stop it from tasting good.

"I'm not sure, but I feel like we need to talk about this again."

Stupid his dragon hissed to him in disapproval. *You need to stop listening to this girl.*

Haven didn't bother answering him and went back to enjoying the sandwich he was eating while Cyn shrugged her shoulders, picking at the top of her muffin and trying to ignore Mira's bright smile.

"Thank you, Haven! Thank you so much! And you too, Cyn!"

"Yeah. Whatever."

None of them noticed the shadows slithering slowly behind them.

———◆◆◆———

She'd met him at a coffee shop, of all places.

Years ago, Katalynne Cove had been working at the prestigious law firm of Florence, Cave, and Cable as one of the many capable assistants in their office. She'd originally been hired as the standard secretary to look good at the front desk and offer coffee to clients while they waited. That was, until, one of the partners had discovered that she had a knack for locating information. That partner had taken her under his wing, making her his personal assistant in spite of her lack of legal knowledge. Laurence Cable had a talent for surrounding himself with brilliant people and it didn't hurt that he had a taste for the finer things in life.

A stylish and intelligent assistant had only added to his image.

Katalynne found the job challenging and to her liking with the odd hours and strange requests. She never knew what he'd need next, though she drew the line at accompanying him to company functions and Laurence had respected that without a second thought, though there had been some playful teasing here and there.

She'd met Randall Fagan in the coffee shop where she spent most of her lunch hours. The Hunter had stood out, his tall frame and muscular arms clashing with the briefcase carrying men on their cell phones and the women armed with laptops and deadlines. He had ordered a plain, bitter coffee in a place that specialized in sugary, expensive drinks that could hardly be called coffee anymore. He always took a seat near the corner where he could look down the street and he'd sit there, scanning the crowd for something – or someone, she was never sure.

A month had passed like that, him foregoing fancy drinks laced with whipped cream, her sipping her chocolate concoction and looking through paperwork. Then, one day, he had broken his routine and sat across from her at her table.

"I'm not interested," Katalynne said, not looking up from the folder of papers she'd brought to read through that day. She was used to this. The problem with the men of the business world – and some men in general – was their disillusioned sense of power, thinking that an attractive lady was an invitation to sit across from her and insist on a phone number. Perhaps this man had spent the entire month trying to work up the nerve to say something. Whatever the case, she already had her answer programmed. She was already weighing her options if this turned out bad. There was a small sandwich shop about a block away that could work as a peaceful replacement, but she would really miss the cream and chocolate coffee mix from this place.

"Wasn't offering." He took a drink from his coffee, the bitter smell wafting across the table to Katalynne's nose. "You work for that law firm across the street."

"Yes." Katalynne kept her answers short, turning the page to scan the next piece of paperwork. She moved in to make a note on the margin when a card slipped across the paper next to her pen. It was a simple business card, with only a first and a last name and a phone number, nothing else. Katalynne inwardly sighed and glanced up at the man sitting across from her at the table. "I already said I wasn't-"

Fagan smirked at her. "I'm in the market for a personal assistant. I'd like to offer you a job."

This was new. She raised an eyebrow at him and shook her head. "I am content where I am, thank you." Katalynne closed her folder and stood up, leaving the card on the table.

Fagan stood up with her and slipped his card in her folder in a fluid, quick movement. "Think about it. I can guarantee that it'll be much more interesting than working for an expensive defense attorney." He ended the statement with a smirk, as if he already knew her answer and left the coffee shop before she could, having successfully planted the seeds of curiosity in her mind. A second later he looked back inside the shop and grinned at her. "Nice legs. There, I flirted with you. Have a nice day."

Those words, ultimately, were what got her – not the statement about her legs, but the promise of something more interesting. Katalynne generally preferred to stay under the radar, or at least as much as her attractive and unique looks would allow. But her jobs always seemed to have the looming promise of boredom creeping up on the horizon. Fagan had timed himself perfectly, offering her the job after she'd grown accustomed to working for Laurence Cable. She knew all of his quirks and she knew how to work with him. Now the job was starting to edge with monotony, making her mind yearn for something more interesting.

In the end she'd accepted Fagan's offer and now it was years later, far past her normal boredom point. Of course, had she known at that coffee shop that the job was to help a man who hunted down demons, she would have never agreed to it – maybe? He had saved that little nugget of information for her "interview" in the warehouse where she now played secretary.

Katalynne was broken out of her memories by harsh boots walking across the floor. She glanced at the laptop screen sitting next to her, rereading the information she'd managed to find on the demon world as Alix stopped in front of her desk.

"What did you find?"

On any other morning Katalynne would have been annoyed with his lack of manners – a greeting would've been nice. But now that she knew *her* back story, she couldn't find any annoyance in her mind. "None of the records show any Hunter having gone to that world and returning here, so there is effectively nothing."

"C'est des conneries," Alix muttered, and only Katalynne's years of working in a law firm and dealing with several nationalities helped her understand the French equivalent to *this is bullshit*. "There has to be something," he spoke in English this time.

"There are… speculations. From notes on how the demons interact with each other in this world, the demon world is likely set up in a system of clans and territories, operating like their own small countries. This fits with what Mira said about the Red Dragon leader coming to take over their area and how the Scough are peaceful compared to other demons. So, likely, each area of the demon world has a handful of related demon types living together that don't cross. Lions in the caves, fish in the water, and deer in the fields. A setup like that."

"And when they do cross fields, they fight. Like a lion hunting a deer." Alix leaned against the wall next to Katalynne's desk, mulling over that information. "A small force would be best and we could use the territories to our advantage, but that might be hard without knowing the edges. Still, it's possible."

"I also looked up what I could find on the Storyteller. He's more of a myth then a person. The idea is that every person – human or demon – has a book that tells their life story. The Storyteller has access to all of those books. If he wants to, he can write in any book and change the things that have happened, or will happen, in a person's life. He can open a door and end up wherever he wants, and he can blend in anywhere. If that's the case, he may not even be a Scough, he could just be blending in with them. The idea is that he's always watching or reading about you. It almost reminds me of Santa Claus." That fact had amused Katalynne when she'd read through the database, but the amusement was lost on Alix who didn't even grant her with a chuckle. Katalynne gave up trying to lighten the mood and went back to business. "You realize there is only supposed to be one Storyteller."

"I am aware."

"Yet this girl is claiming to be related to him, which would almost make her a Storyteller in her own right."

"What's your point?"

"My point is that this girl could be lying about who she is."

"I'm not stupid, I'm aware of that."

Katalynne sighed, "I'm just saying-"

"No one has been to that world nor has anyone actually seen this Storyteller, save for Dox – so he claims – and Mira. The only way to know for sure is to go for ourselves."

Katalynne frowned. She could understand Alix wanting to meet the Storyteller, but wasn't this being a bit too reckless? Mira's abilities were already impressive enough, couldn't she just help Alix? Of course, if the girl were smart, she would force Alix to help her, which would lead them back to square one: going into the demon world. Still, if her father was *the* Storyteller, what was her role in all of this? Was her father training her? And if she was already this skilled and needed help saving him what chance did they have?

"I can't convince you out of this, can I?" Katalynne whispered.

Alix shrugged from where he was standing. "That's not your job."

Katalynne frowned more, not liking the tone his voice had taken. No matter what she had learned from Fagan she still thought of Alix as male. She just couldn't make herself picture him as a woman. She couldn't imagine there being a time where Alix may have been a kinder person, someone with a fiancé and a child on the way. She could understand the pain hidden behind that hard exterior but she just couldn't believe that such sorrow came from Alix, of all people, when he was being so thick headed all the goddamn time. There was no compassion in his eyes, not a care or concern about bringing them into such a dangerous place where they were putting their lives at stake.

She could understand wanting lost loved ones back, could even understand Alix's drive to find the ones responsible for their deaths, but as Katalynne watched him she wondered if he had ever cared about them at all. Did he care about Fagan? Had he cared about Xaver? It certainly didn't feel like it, not when he wasn't willing to listen to anything any of them had to say. It was an effective mask, especially when Katalynne found herself wondering if there really was a mask there at all.

"Alix-" Katalynne stopped in her protest and glanced across the room. There was a minute change in the air, barely even noticeable. One moment it felt fine and then suddenly, before she was able to say more, the air shifted and felt like the mist from a warm shower. She could feel the air catch in her throat, thick and almost wet. Katalynne locked her computer and stood up, frowning. "Can you feel that?"

Alix was already nodding, his body stiff with readiness. Across from them, the shadows on the wall twisted, growing and turning to cover the wall. Alix had his gun out and ready as the shadows ballooned out and Dox stumbled through the wall, the light collar around his neck giving a spark and fizzle as it desperately tried to come back to life. A moment later he stood, his deep and cavernous eyes looking at the two of them.

"Don't move." Alix clicked the safety off his gun, aiming it right at the Lurk's head. The collar may not have worked – again – but he had a feeling that a bullet would.

"You can shoot me later. We have a problem upstairs. Even you should have been able to feel what's in the air."

"Wait, that wasn't you?" Katalynne asked.

Dox shook his head, "I'm not that powerful," he whispered, and they could hear the slight tremble in his voice. "Where are Cyn and the others?"

Katalynne frowned, stepping around her desk and next to Alix. "I'll take you."

"Katalynne, what are you doing? The only place we should be taking him is back downstairs."

"Protest later, the others might be in trouble. Get Fagan. He's in the back."

"Katalynne-"

"You might not care about the wellbeing of the people here, but I do," then she took a moment to glare at him, not even bothering to respond to the shocked look on his face as she led Dox through the thick metal door and up the stairs to where the others were staying.

Chapter 6

The secretary and the Lurk took the stairs at a quick speed. Katalynne ran with expert skill in her heels while Dox's shadowy feet almost seemed to float over the concrete stairs with no sound. Around them the air grew thicker as they moved, a sticky feeling collecting across Katalynne's skin. Dox reached the door first and opened it without hesitation, throwing them both into the thick of what was happening.

What should have been in front of them was a room with a modest sized living and kitchenette area. Katalynne knew from experience that the room should have had at least some furniture for guests. Now, as she stood by the doorway, it didn't come close to resembling the same room as dark shadows of purple and black swirled between the walls, creating a tornado of darkness and glowing white eyes.

The Ice Dragon was crouched in the corner, using his body to block most of the shadows from hitting Cyn as she stared at the darkness in front of them. Meanwhile, in the center of the room and the tornado, Mira was crouched with blank eyes, her book open and the pages rustling in front of her. Her bouncy pigtails had long since come undone and now her hair, along with her tail, were whipping harshly around her, as if it were trying to chase the shadows around the room.

Katalynne frowned even more when she saw Mira's arms. Words were written up them, scrawled out in what looked like hasty marker, the ink dripping from her skin into the pool of shadows under her. Small, clawed hands curved out of the shadows, clutching and pulling at her arms and legs and skirt. Slowly they pulled her down, making her sink into the inky goo as those white eyes moved through the pool, looking far too intelligent for comfort.

Dox ducked through the shadow tornado quickly, not giving it much thought as he swiped his hand at the white eyes, causing the strange little shadow creatures to scamper and scurry away like oily rats, silently letting Mira go. She slumped away from the book and crumbled down to the floor.

"You, dragon, come get her so I can get rid of these shadows."

"It's Haven," Haven grumbled as he reluctantly moved away from Cyn and through a small opening in the swirling shadows Dox had created.

"Wait, Dox! What are you doing?!" Cyn shouted to him.

"Just stay there."

"But-"

"I told you before, remember? If you see their eyes to get to a safe place."

Haven frowned, glancing back at Cyn as she finally moved behind one of the couches. The look in her eyes was too young, too scared, and he was suddenly reminded of Xaver's instructions to stay inside the house and do nothing, forcing him to stay put and listen to him die.

"Come help me, Cyn," Haven said, "I'll grab her and you grab the book."

Dox glared at him, hollow eyes narrowed as he growled at him, "Do not bring her into this!"

"Don't make her feel useless!" Haven snapped back, completely catching the Lurk off guard. "Cyn, come on!"

Cyn moved quickly, doing her best to ignore the howling of the shadows and the angry look on Dox's face. Haven picked up Mira and held her limp body close as Cyn snatched up the book. The shadows continued to bleed off the pages, dripping onto the floor and creating a mess of black around her. There were scattered images peeking through the dark pages. A fox tail, a hint of a fuzzy ear, someone's hand, but the shadows kept moving over everything, burying everything they touched.

"We need to close that book!" Haven yelled to Cyn.

"I can't!" She screamed back, trying to close the book but it didn't budge, the shadows keeping it wide open as they started to move along her fingers.

"Cyn, I told you-"

"Just do what you need to do, Dox!" She looked up at him, keeping a tight hold on the book despite the shadows. "I got it!"

Katalynne stood transfixed at the doorway, watching the Lurk stand in the middle. For a long moment it looked like he wasn't doing anything. The shadows still swirled around him, white eyes visible every few seconds as if battling between watching and hiding among the currents. Dox stood completely still, the edges of the shadows licking at his body as they passed around him. Then, Katalynne noticed him turning his hands outward and the shadows around him slowly began to shift, the swirling moving inward like water rushing toward the shore. Slowly, a handful of the shadows slipped into him, flooding out the details in his body. The form standing before Katalynne shifted, melting into a silhouette with no details. She watched as Dox's nose, ears, and fingers melted into a flat blackness that only resembled a humanistic shape. The oddest thing to see, Katalynne thought, was the beating of a heart underneath Dox's flattened features. It pulsated against his chest, the shadows barely able to keep it covered.

Was this what the shadow creature actually looked like when he wasn't attempting to seem more human?

If it wasn't obvious before, it was clear as day now. Dox had never been trapped in the basement. The light collar clattered to the floor, reaffirming Katalynne's suspicions as his form melted and changed. This Lurk was smarter than that, he'd been using their home to hide from something else, and something that was now, obviously, in this room. The name *Lurkhamara* crossed Katalynne's mind and she stepped away from the doorway, well out of the range of the shadows and watching quietly, ready to rush back downstairs if needed.

The shadows and darkness twisted and struggled, racing forward and straight into him. Dox drew in a slow breath, the shadows flowing into his mouth and his body, completely engulfing him. The shadows around the book were absorbed just as quickly, Cyn quickly closing it as soon as she had the chance.

Suddenly, the shadows were gone, completely disappearing into Dox's body. The movement in the room stopped and Katalynne felt her hair settle against the back of her neck, no longer being tossed around by the wind as the air became much calmer. The room in front of her now looked just as it had before, the same humble living quarters as if the tornado of shadows had never happened.

Haven gently shook Mira to attempt to wake her as Cyn stepped around him and up to Dox. She gently touched his shoulder, some of the shadows clinging to her hand. "Dox?"

"I'm all right." His voice sounded strange, detached, and he shivered for a second. Slowly, his eyes and face reformed on his body and he looked at her, trying to offer a small, comforting smile as his body shifted back to the form they were familiar with. Cyn crossed her arms and concentrated on looking annoyed to hide whatever relief or fear anyone might have seen. "And you? Are you all right?" He asked.

"I'm fine," she said, smiling a little, "I told you I would be."

"Yes, you did. Thank you, Cyn."

Katalynne slowly stepped into the room as she heard Fagan and Alix rushing up the stairs behind her.

"What happened?" Katalynne asked as the two Hunters rushed into the room behind her.

"It doesn't look like anything happened," Fagan said. "What's going on?"

"There was a tornado of shadows a moment ago, but Dox got rid of them," Katalynne explained.

"I see." Fagan frowned a bit as he gently slid his fingers through her hair. "It looks like some got a bit too close to you," he said, pulling his hand back and watching a small bit of shadows move along his skin.

Katalynne frowned, watching as Dox walked over and took hold of Fagan's hand, the shadows disappearing into his skin. "Yeah, I guess so," the woman whispered as she looked over at Dox. "Thank you for your assistance."

Dox regarded her quietly for a moment, then simply nodded.

"So everyone is all right then?" Alix asked.

Cyn nodded as Haven finally managed to wake Mira up, the girl slowly sitting up and rubbing her forehead.

"What happened?" She whispered, looking surprised to see everyone in the room.

"That's what we'd like to know," Katalynne said. "Where did all of those shadows come from?"

"Mira was mentioning checking on things, but we decided against it. I'm not sure how all of this happened after that," Haven frowned.

"The black smudge in the book," Cyn whispered. "It must have come from that."

"That was there before, right? You mean that caused all of this?" Katalynne asked.

"I saw a man made of shadows, like Dox, but it wasn't him at all," Mira murmured, biting her lip. "I think I blacked out after that."

"My dragon says it was the Lurkhamara." Haven glanced over at Dox watching his reaction.

Dox ignored the look, the shadows still rippling and shifting across his skin. "If my father's involved then this is very serious. And dangerous. You shouldn't try that again."

Mira pouted more, jumped out of Haven's arms, and rushed over to Alix and Fagan. "I need your help! Please? I know you don't want to get anyone hurt, but the book said I should come here after Haven and that you would help me. I know you don't like demons, but I don't have anyone else to go to and-"

"Are you nuts?!" Katalynne snapped, her voice more threatening that Fagan or Alix's could ever be. "Those shadows just attacked, through your book, what the hell makes you think that-"

"Katalynne." Alix frowned, crossing his arms at his chest, cutting her off. "If they can come through her book like that, that means they can come through something else. Anything, really."

"Stop being selfish for two seconds and-"

"I'm not being selfish, I'm being realistic." Alix looked over at Dox and Cyn. "You're running from him, right? If that was him she saw, that means he's been here. He knows where you are now," then he glanced over at Katalynne, his voice surprisingly soft as he spoke, "He knows where *we* are now."

Cyn frowned and looked up at Dox. "So does that mean we run again?"

"No." This came from Haven who slowly shook his head. "There's no point in running. It just gives him another chance to find you."

What are you saying? His dragon hissed to him.

"Something like that isn't just a threat to Mira's father, and the Scough, and that world," Alix said, looking at everyone as he spoke, "It's a threat to all of us. Even after all of your running, he still found you."

"So you want to take the fight to him, in his world? You can't possibly think that's a good idea," Katalynne scoffed.

"If we sit and wait for him to make a move he's going to make things worse. With what just happened, we don't have a choice. At the very least we need to go to their world and find out how much of a threat this really is to us. If there's a war in their world, who's to say it won't move to ours next?"

Fagan frowned, but he couldn't deny the fact that Alix was making sense and he didn't have a good counter argument.

"I think my father is controlling the Storyteller. With power like that nowhere would be safe." Dox spoke softly, stepping closer to Cyn as he did.

"Great, so he controls the Storyteller and can potentially cover everything in black ink. What's the point of starting a war with the Red Dragons?" Cyn asked.

To finish what he started, Haven's dragon whispered to him. *He already helped destroy their land once, now he's going to destroy them again. Or, even worse-*

"Control them," Haven spoke up, "Control them in the same way he's controlling Mira's father. This world would have to deal with Lurks and Red Dragons."

Katalynne didn't like the whole situation, but when Alix looked at her, expecting her to protest, she didn't say anything. Instead she glanced away, silently acknowledging they were right.

Mira looked around at everyone, clutching her book to her chest. "So you'll help me?"

"It's not just about you anymore. It's about all of us now," Fagan said.

Alix nodded. "Let's start planning this."

Mira smiled brightly and actually hugged both of the Hunters, her book falling to the floor as Fagan and Alix stared at her in surprise.

"… you… will probably need my help," Dox said slowly. "I should go, too."

"Dox, you can't-"

"No, the dragon is right. There's no point in running anymore, not if he's willing to show himself in this world."

"I swear I told you my name," Haven said with a frown. "It's not that hard to remember."

Dox shrugged, "It's not like I'm not stating a fact. There is a dragon on your arm."

Haven sighed and rolled his eyes, Cyn smiling at him. "Just let it go, there's no point in arguing with his logic."

"You all are insane," Katalynne whispered, interrupting the moment as she turned and headed for the door.

Fagan followed after her, letting her get away from the room before he caught her arm and gently pulled her to a stop.

"Let go." She didn't turn back to face him

"Why are you acting like this? You never act like this with missions."

Katalynne yanked her arm away and turned to face him with a full on glare. "Because this mission is completely ridiculous! Going to their world, with demons?! How stupid is that? You're asking to be killed and don't tell me it's just to gather information about a threat, because we both know you'll end up fighting."

"Katalynne, this is something we have to do."

"No, it's not! You're just agreeing to this because you care too damn much about Alix!"

Fagan frowned more. "You're grasping at straws. You were just in there, this is not just about Alix or the Storyteller or any of that. This is what Hunters do."

"And what happens if the Storyteller gives him what he wants? What happens if he does rewrite it? Do you think Alix would really be here if he hadn't of lost his family? *Her* family? If he rewrites it there's a chance-"

"That none of this would've happened," Fagan whispered, finishing her sentence for her. "We don't have a right to decide what Alix will do."

"Fagan. This may be the last mission you have with him. With… us, as a team. Either you go there and lose to that shadow demon, or you win and Alix rewrites history."

Fagan smiled, seizing the chance to break the serious mood. "Awwww, I didn't know you cared that much."

Katalynne blinked, briefly lost in how she'd given him the upper hand. Damn, he always managed to do this. "Shut up!"

"Don't worry," then he wrapped an arm around her waist, smirking, "I'll still find you if things change."

"Hmph, next time I'll keep working for Laurence. He was less stressful."

Fagan sighed, suddenly looking more serious, "I promise, Katt, I'll be careful. We all will," then he chuckled, "You won't have to find a new job anytime soon."

"Right," she whispered, leaning forward and lightly pressing her lips against Fagan's. The man stared at her, too surprised to give a proper response as the woman pulled away, "Because that's what I'm worried about," she said before she pulled away from him, walking down the hallway to go back downstairs.

Fagan stood in that spot for what felt like a century and a half, but as he pressed his fingers to his lips he knew that it had only been for a couple of seconds. "Well I'll be damned," he whispered, smiling as he turned to head back into the room with the others.

Hours later, the sky shifted from blue to fiery orange as the sun slowly sank in the background. Standing on the roof of the large warehouse, Haven couldn't remember the last time he'd been outside in direct sunlight without desperately trying to dart to another place to hide.

He actually felt relatively safe, all things considered, and in his life that was very rare.

From his vantage point he could see the buildings on the edge of the city spreading out before him. Most were in a mix of disrepair, this area of the city obviously having been abandoned for the newer, taller buildings more than a few miles away. Cars zipped down the streets and people moved about, completely oblivious to the dark skinned dragon watching them. The view was almost calming-

This has to be the stupidest plan that you could have possibly agreed to go along with! I told you not to come here and I told you that Scough was trouble. You should have left them both, her and that Hunter. You should have left them behind when I told you!

Haven sighed as his dragon's voice rang out in his head, shattering the peaceful moment. So much for relaxing and clearing his head. "Wasn't it you who pointed out what the Lurkhamara is probably planning to do to the dragons? That sounded like you wanted me to help." He decided to ignore the other comment, not willing to discuss how he felt about Mira or how he'd felt about Xaver.

Don't misunderstand me, Haven. That wasn't a signal to help. That was a reason to leave. I told you that girl would be a problem, but you decided not to listen to me. And now look where we are. This is why it's not safe to be around other people!

Haven closed his eyes, rubbing his forehead to try and mentally quiet the voice. He knew it wouldn't work, but the action made him feel a little better. This argument about not coming near people had been going on in his head with his dragon for as far back as he could remember. One of his earliest memories was when he had wondered why he couldn't go home with the tall people like the rest of the children at the park. For that matter, he'd wondered why he couldn't just play with the other children. Living with Xaver had been his latest in many attempts at ignoring his dragon's warning words. Yes, that had failed miserably, but that wasn't due to anything he'd done wrong. Hunters were not expected to live long, given their choice of occupation, and he certainly couldn't fault the Scough or Storyteller or whatever Mira was supposed to be.

You're not listening to me.

"I can't help but listen to you, I can't shut you off."

The dragon hissed lowly in his head and Haven winced a little as he felt a sharp, cold pain shoot up his arm. He shook out his arm, flexing his fingers in and out of a fist until it faded.

"I'm not abandoning Mira, I've told you that, so there's no point in you arguing with me. What you could do is actually help me and tell me more about the world I come from so I don't end up going in blind."

There's no reason for you to go there.

Haven wished that he was actually talking to a person in front of him, because with the anger boiling up inside of him right now, punching someone would have been a great release. He would have even settled for glaring dangerously, but doing that at his own arm just felt stupid. So, instead, he glared at the roof of another warehouse a block away and spoke in a low voice to get his point across to his dragon. "I know you are trying to protect me, but this is getting old. You can't keep me locked away from people my entire life. I am helping Mira out, which means we're going to the demon world. So you better tell me about it so I don't go in blind, or shut up, because I'm tired of you scolding me like I'm a child!"

The reaction in his mind was chilly, the dragon curling up tightly in the back of his brain and giving a low, warning hiss. But for once, Haven's dragon actually remained silent. There was no yelling or protesting, there was simply a very tense silence between them. Haven would have preferred that the dragon relent and actually tell him something useful, but he wasn't going to complain about the silence, either. He would make do with what the Hunters could find out and what Mira could tell them.

"I take it he doesn't like listening to you very much."

Haven glanced back to see Cyn standing at the small doorway on the rooftop. He nodded to her and took a seat on the edge of the roof while Cyn walked over and sat next to him. "It's not that he doesn't like listening to me, he just has a habit of telling me to do things and not telling me why."

"Have you always had him?"

"As long as I can remember he's always been a mark on my arm and a voice in the back of my head."

Cyn frowned, her eyes focused on the ground below them. "I can't imagine always hearing something in the back of your head. I can feel the demon inside but it doesn't talk to me, save for the occasional nightmare. It probably hates me, you know, since it was forced inside of my body."

"Do you know what type is inside you?"

Cyn laid back on the rooftop with her hands under her head as she looked up at the sky. "The secretary here showed me some information, but before that I never had an idea. I vaguely remember something at my father's place, kept in this cage when I snuck in as a child. Something with large eyes in the darkness, but I never got close to it."

Haven took a moment to look over at the girl spread out across the roof. He could see hints of the mark on her stomach through the dark fishnet she wore. The thin girl seemed to live in torn clothing and dark colors, a rather attractive-

Earthmover. They're solitary, strong, and live in the Deep Woods. The dragon cut into his thoughts and Haven sighed, "Oh, so now you're sharing your knowledge with me?" Haven rolled his eyes as Cyn glanced up at him, confused. "My dragon says it's called an Earthmover. I guess it lives in the Deep Woods in the demon world. What the heck are the Deep Woods?"

"Sounds like a video game level," Cyn said.

Haven waited for some kind of response but this time his dragon didn't answer. "Figures," he muttered. "Sorry, thanks to this guy my knowledge of that world is limited to what he tells me… which is basically nothing."

Cyn nodded and pushed herself to sit up again. "So the dragon is a part of you. Could he survive without you?"

Haven shrugged. "No idea. All I know is that he has no intention of leaving. He mentioned something a long time ago, that he promised someone he'd take care of me so he's always here." Haven sighed and looked up at the sky.

"Sounds like me and Dox."

She still remembered that day, a younger version of herself who hadn't yet discovered the wonders of fishnet and baggy pants. Her hair had been in blonde pigtails back then – a color she vowed to never be again. At the time she had an unhealthy obsession with pastel, frills, and stuffed animals. The logical reaction for a child meeting their very first monster was to scream, but Cyn had been different. Cyn had seen glimpses of her father's experiments, had heard talks of demons and other creatures, so when she first met Dox she had simply smiled at him and asked if he wanted to play. Of course, it helped that Dox had spent a couple months before that pretending to be a talking, stuffed pink rabbit named Mr. Buns. Despite her comparisons to monsters and closets, when she had first met Dox she'd asked him if he was the Easter Bunny.

Yeah, too embarrassing to tell the truth about.

"That doesn't sound like a Lurk at all. My dragon always told me to stay away from them because they can't be trusted."

"Dox is different." It seemed to be a common prejudice about her friend, one that Cyn was getting used to defending.

"If you say so." Haven ignored the low growl in the back of his mind from his dragon but he got the message. Just because the Lurk took care of Cyn didn't mean his good will or protection would extend to anyone else. That much had been clear down in the cells, back when Dox had admitted to telling the humans about the Storyteller just to spare his own life. Haven silently promised his dragon he'd remember and be careful.

"Oh, before I forget... thanks."

"Hm?" Haven looked over at Cyn, tilting his head, "For what?"

"For having my back before, with the shadows." Cyn frowned a bit, embarrassed. "That's twice you've helped me. We should try and not make it a habit – you know, you needing to save me from situations I can't handle."

"I don't know, I kinda like being your hero," Haven said with a chuckle. "How do human girls repay heroes in this world? A kiss, or something silly like that, right?"

"Thought you didn't know much about this world."

Haven shrugged, "I'm a faster learner."

Are you actually flirting? His dragon sounded somewhere between amused and surprised. Haven chose to ignore him.

"Well, what you're referring to is in comic books and video games. Besides," Cyn smirked at Haven, "You said *human* girls. Clearly, I'm not human anymore."

"You weren't born a demon, so you're still human."

"And what about you? You weren't born with that dragon, were you?"

"Don't know," Haven shrugged, "Don't remember. But we're talking about you right now." Haven smirked at Cyn, "I saved you twice. I should get something, right?"

It was relaxing to have a moment like this, something akin to normal activity that didn't involve dragons, or demons, or Hunters. Cyn, surprisingly, seemed to be enjoying herself, too, as she smiled back at Haven. "If you insist," then she leaned forward, almost kissing him and completely catching the Ice Dragon off guard. He could feel the cold rush over his skin in a tingling sensation.

That feeling was from his dragon, right?

"When you're in trouble, I'll save your ass. Twice," then she pulled back with a laugh.

Haven stared at her for a moment and couldn't help himself, laughing with the girl, the sound echoing around the both of them.

Behind them Haven could hear the faint sound of metal against metal as the roof access door opened just a little. A smirk crossed his lips as he went still and listened for the familiar sound of a bushy tail brushing against the door. "Mira, you make too much noise, still."

The Scough sighed loudly and blew a breath of air to move her bangs. "I was really trying this time! How did you hear me?"

"Your tail again."

"The door, too," Cyn added.

Mira pouted at them. "Fine, but I'll do it next time."

Haven just nodded, struggling not to smile too much. Back when he and Mira had been staying with Xaver he'd started teaching her about stealth and surviving in a world where the majority of the inhabitants would rather kill than help you. It had turned out to be incredibly amusing because she either did an amazing job, or her ears and tail gave her away in a second. The poor Scough couldn't catch a break and even Xaver had been known to laugh at her childish attempts and the expressions she made when she failed.

"What are you two talking about up here? It has to be more interesting than what they're doing inside." Mira jumped up onto the air conditioning unit that was affixed to the top of the building and didn't look like it had worked any time in the last decade. Spreading out her arms she walked along the very edge like a child playing on the curb of a neighborhood street, her bare feet not seeming to mind the cold.

Both Haven and Cyn exchanged a look and the red haired girl chuckled before answering Mira's question. "Comic book heroes and the women they rescue."

"Huh? What kind of books are those?"

"Nothing important, Mira," Haven smiled, but he honestly didn't know the answer to that question. "We were just wasting time until we leave."

"They told me that we're leaving in a few hours, because of what I... err... what happened with the shadows." Mira's ears flattened against her head as she turned around and walked along the edge in the other direction, her tail flicking behind her. "The angry one and the taller one are talking about weapons and maps and stealth. It sounds like how you and Xaver used to talk."

Haven didn't answer that and instead focused on the roofs in front of him. He found himself missing Xaver again, the feeling twisting in the bottom corner of his stomach. Maybe his dragon had been right, maybe he shouldn't have gotten attached to anyone.

"You two were pretty close, huh?"

Haven blinked and turned his attention to Cyn. "Oh… um… y-yeah."

"I didn't mean to bring it up again," Mira said, pouting, "I'm sorry, Haven."

"It's all right, Mira. He was a Hunter. He told me that it would happen eventually." Of course that didn't mean that either had expected Xaver to die protecting them. He would have preferred it to be something random, something that had nothing to do with him, then maybe he could have forgotten that night faster and moved on to hide somewhere else.

"Doesn't mean you wanted him to go out and die." Surprisingly, Cyn reached over and took his hand. "Dangerous life or not, it still sucks."

It goes away eventually, Haven. Just try and think of other things and don't let it distract you too much. Just because you try and move on doesn't mean you forget.

It was a more elegant way to say what Cyn had just said, but the words still meant a lot to Haven. "Thanks," he whispered. His dragon wasn't all bad, he knew that, otherwise it would have let him die a long time ago. As much as he complained about the thing living on his arm and in his head, it was still the one consistent thing he had in this whirlwind life of his and, on occasion, he'd actually say something that really mattered to Haven.

It also helped now to have Mira, all bright and full of sunshine, and Cyn who, he noticed, was still holding his hand.

"Who's that?" Mira asked.

Both Haven and Cyn pulled their hands away, both avoiding eye contact with one another. Mira jumped down from the air conditioner unit to walk up to the edge next to Haven. Her tail thwacked him unconsciously in the back of the head as all three of them looked over the edge of the building.

Standing below them, about three stories down, was a young man wearing a pair of jeans with a ratty and well-loved backpack slung over one shoulder. He had brown hair cut short and they could see him knocking on the front door. When he got no answer he started to pace near the door, waiting.

"That's strange," Cyn commented quietly. "They aren't answering the door. I'm sure whatshername would answer."

"Katalynne," Haven supplied the woman's name for her. "It's good to remember names."

"Don't lecture me-"

"We should say hello!"

Haven pulled Mira's tail back before she could get any ideas and moved away from the edge with her. Hopefully the boy didn't hear them from below but Haven wanted to be careful, especially since they weren't opening the door downstairs. "Mira," he hissed, "Not so loud. They obviously aren't answering the door for a reason."

Mira made a face at Haven, her hands on her hips. "He looks like a perfectly nice human."

"That doesn't mean anything." Cyn countered for Haven. "We should go in and find out what's going on."

Haven nodded and the two headed for the door back into the building, Mira racing after them after a moment. "And don't pull my tail!"

Cyn tugged on her ear for good measure. "Didn't he say not to be so loud?"

"Ow!"

The three reached the main lobby area and found Fagan sitting in Katalynne's chair while she leaned against the side of her desk, concentrating on her tablet. Alix was standing not too far away, an annoyed look on his face as the person outside knocked again, louder. A television screen was up on the side of the wall near the desk, showing the young man's face. Cyn noticed, with amusement, that the young man had a striking resemblance to Fagan. "Someone you know?" She asked with a chuckle.

Fagan frowned. "Yes. My brother, Zach. He tried calling earlier and left me a voice mail. Obviously he thought it was too important to wait until I called him back. He'll go away soon enough. We don't need him here when we leave."

"You should've never told him where this place was to begin with," Alix grumbled from where he was standing.

"He's my brother and he gets along with our parents less than I do, I wasn't going to completely cut the kid off."

"No, seriously, you should have." Katalynne added dryly. She still hadn't forgiven the boy for interrupting her night at the bar even if he had supplied the attractive bartender with her phone number. "In any case, you all should be getting ready for your mission-"

"Hi!"

The entire group turned to find Mira standing at the front door she had just opened, waving to Zach without any regard for hiding her tail or ears. Zach stared at her for a long moment, taking in the ears and tail with a look of childlike wonder. He knew what his brother did for a living but he certainly hadn't seen anything nonhuman before thanks to Fagan always making him leave.

"Zach, right?"

"H-huh?" Zach took his eyes off of the girl's ears – that was certainly a first for him, focusing on ears instead of more voluptuous body parts. His eyes widened. "O-oh! Mira?"

"Yes! And you are Zach!" She said his name again, giggling, "I couldn't tell it was you from the roof."

"The roof?"

Mira nodded. "That's where we were when-" her voice trailed off when Zach reached forward and poked at one of her ears. "Um… w-what are you doing?"

"Whooooooa! They're real, they twitch and everything! Sweet!" Zach said, lightly scratching behind her ear.

"Sweet? Like something sweet you eat?" Mira asked.

"Huh? No, it's a compliment."

"Oh!" Mira smiled, leaning into his fingers with a happy little sigh before she spoke again, "Sweet."

"Yep, you got it now."

"And of course my ears are real, why wouldn't they be? Your ears are real too, right?"

"Well yeah, but they aren't furry, like yours. I know some girls in class who would kill for ears like this."

"They don't have to kill, they just have to be a Scough."

"A what?"

"Zach, get out," Fagan said with a harsh glare.

"Aww come on bro." Zach stepped into the warehouse, looking around and counting on his fingers. Katalynne, Mira, and Cyn, "A party with three hot girls and I wasn't invited? I'm hurt."

Fagan groaned and sank a bit more in Katalynne's chair, looking like he wanted to drop into the floor. Perhaps with Dox's abilities he could have that arranged. "Shut that door behind you."

As Zach turned to close the door Haven looked at Mira, not looking pleased. "What were you doing opening that door?"

"They said the name Zach. I met him before I came here. He's in the picture with the rest of you, remember?" Mira pulled the book from her bag and opened it. "See? Right there." She held the book up and pointed to the picture of all of them. "He can be trusted, I wasn't hurting anyone."

"What the hell? How did you get our pictures in there?" Zach asked.

Mira giggled, something she was doing a lot around Zach. "The book sketched you all in there."

"You depend on that book way too much," Cyn said, stopping Zach before they would be forced to explain magical books and fox girls. "They obviously didn't want him in here, you can't just-" Cyn stopped when she realized that Zach was now standing in front of her, grinning. "What?" She snapped.

"Pissy and hot," he smirked. "I really like the piercings."

Cyn decided to gift him with a full on glare and a middle fingered salute while Haven stood next to her, sharing Katalynne's unimpressed expression. After a moment Haven whispered to Katalynne, "I take it raising that finger is some sort of insult?"

"It is," she whispered back, "It comes in handy against the particularly annoying breeds of humans."

Haven smiled and was surprised when his dragon chuckled softly in the back of his mind.

Fagan finally stood up from the chair and walked over to Zach, putting himself between his brother and Cyn. "So what is it? We have a mission tonight," then he quickly added, "And no, you can't come with."

"But... he's in my book-"

"I said no," Fagan snapped at the girl, Mira's ears pressed against her head.

Zach shrugged. "It's fine. It's not important, it can wait until you get back. I'll hold down the fort."

Fagan didn't believe that for a second. His brother came off to others as rash and annoying due to his constant flirting and vagabond attitude, but Fagan knew better. He knew the difference between the mask his brother showed to other people and the real him that only came out when he felt completely safe. The backpack had to be a clue, as his brother usually kept it tucked under his bed, packed for a quick get away from a mother who was too perfect and a father who expected things that neither of them had managed to attain. The backpack meant he was escaping, and it meant he needed a place to stay for the night until he could go back and pretend like things were normal.

Alix wouldn't approve, but Fagan was willing to deal with him for Zach. It was a silent truce he and his brother had that neither would ever admit to.

"You can stay in my room until we get back. Don't mess with my stuff."

Zach flashed a grin and Fagan recognized a hint of sincere gratitude in his eyes before it slipped behind the well practiced mask. "Thanks bro," then he stepped to the side to turn his smile to Mira, "So are you some sort of cat girl? Or something else? The tail is cool!"

"Scough, remember?" But she was smiling back and not nearly as angry as she'd been with Cyn for making that mistake. Her tail was swishing behind her and a small blush peppered her cheeks. Cyn rolled her eyes and leaned back against the wall, making a soft gagging noise. Haven couldn't help but smile. It was hard not to be amused with Cyn's reactions.

Fagan cleared his throat. "We should get going. Zach, stay here and don't cause Katalynne too much trouble. Please."

Katalynne didn't look too happy with that order as Zach set down his bag, making himself comfortable on the couch against the wall. No one missed his wonderstruck expression as Dox slid out of the shadows next to Cyn, showing that the Lurk had been listening the whole time. To Zach's surprise the girl didn't seem bothered that the shadows next to her had suddenly become a tall, pitch black figure that could walk. Said figure turned its eyes – were those eyes? – on Zach, who sank a bit into the cushions of the couch, as if trying to disappear.

Why couldn't all demons be cute like the foxy one?!

"Asshole," Cyn muttered to the shadow that now stood next to her, but there was no denying the playful smirk on her face.

"Oh! Bye Zach!" Mira turned and waved to the boy, smiling brightly. "I'll see you again, o.k.?"

"Y-yeah." Zach smiled, waving back to her, his uneasiness about the shadow thing disappearing as the girl smiled at him. Katalynne sighed as she walked over to the door. The exchange would've been cute if Mira wasn't leading Fagan and the others into such a terrible situation.

Zach caught the expression on Katalynne's face and frowned. "So how much trouble is my brother in this time?"

"Enough," Katalynne said. She took one last look at the group, watching her boss' back for a moment before she closed the door, whispering a soft "good luck" before locking it tight.

———◆◆———

The Marjorie McNeely Conservatory at Como Park was silent that night, doors locked securely to keep intruders and vagrants from sneaking in for a covered place to sleep. The small group of Hunters and demons took Fagan's SUV and parked it in the nearby parking lot at the far end where most of the employees parked. At this time of night only a handful of cars were present. The SUV blended right in, as if it belonged to an employee working late. Closing and locking the doors, the group headed up the hill to the Conservatory building, quietly watching the large garden for anyone who might notice them. They made it to the building with little trouble, and a quick finger brush in Mira's book let the doors open so they could step inside.

The lone light in the gardens came from an office situated just near a side entrance. Alix approached it with his gun drawn, raising his head only enough to peek inside. Standing inside the office, adjusting her coat, was the young woman he and Cyn had encountered earlier. Alix ducked his head down in time to not be noticed as Hailey stepped out of the office and shut off the light, closing and locking the door. Hailey took a look around the gardens with a quick eye but managed to completely miss the group thanks to Dox's shadows and a particularly deep corner next to the donation box. She walked right past them without incident and, upon reaching the front door, was surprised to see the same man from before with the long, gray pony tail down his back. There was an amused and inviting smile spread across his face, the man decked out in a suit and obviously planning a social night out. "What are you doing here?" Hailey asked.

The man's smile changed to a smirk. "I thought I'd meet you after work. Did you want to get something to eat?"

Alix watched the two, recognizing the man from the day before. Just like before, Hailey blushed just slightly as her hands moved to her skirt to smooth out some of the creases unconsciously. "N-now? But it's late, most places aren't open..."

"There's always a place where a man can take a woman out for the evening. And I have the perfect place in mind." The man slid his arm around her shoulders to lead her out the door and, for a split second, glanced behind his shoulder.

Was he looking at Alix?

Alix swore the man was looking at him in spite of the fact that he was well hidden in the shadows. If the man did see him he wasn't saying anything about it, intent on taking his new lady friend out on the town. In seconds the couple was gone, the security system staying off as the girl had conveniently forgotten to reset it.

The shadows disappeared around the group and Alix stepped forward, nodding back to the others. "Let's go."

The group made it to the Sunken Gardens with no problem. They were greeted with the pink and red flowers of the Middlemist Red, each petal seeming to hold a silver tint in the moonlight that shone through the greenhouse roof. Both Alix and Cyn had already seen the flower before, but Fagan and Haven hadn't.

The larger Hunter spoke up first. "So this is it? This is how you get to the demon world?" It seemed rather anticlimactic.

"It is a bit hard to believe," Haven said. He remembered Xaver drawing on those papers that night, mapping out what apparently led to this very plant. Was all of the fuss over something so simple?

Mira stepped up to the flowers and gently brushed her fingers against one of them. Instead of answering their questions, she figured that it would be best to show them.

The change in the air was instant.

The silver shimmering from the petals spread out, dripping like morning dew over the flowers and leaves to land and float in the doorway. The group watched as it melted together to create a free-standing film of silver that resembled the entrance to a tunnel. Of the entire group, Dox and Mira seemed to be the only ones comfortable with the changes in front of their eyes. Haven tried to not show any sign of hesitation as his dragon hissed a soft protest in his mind. He decided to turn his attention to Cyn, who kept frowning at the doorway to mask the nervous trembles in her fingers. Alix kept his hand clasped tightly on his gun, ready for anything that might jump through the strange doorway while Fagan held his hand on the hilt of his sword, Eegil, stance at the ready.

"Quickly, before it fades." Mira motioned for them to follow her but Haven caught her hand and walked through first, not willing to let her put herself into danger. Mira, Cyn and Dox followed next, with Alix and Fagan holding up the rear of the group.

"You ready for this?" Fagan asked his partner.

"Yes," then he took a moment to clasp the ring he wore around his neck.

Fagan rested his hand on Alix's shoulder and nodded his head. "Let's go then, Alixandre," he whispered.

Alix's eyes widened and for a moment his eyes lost a bit of the harsh edge to them. The smile on his face was soft, genuine, the smile of the woman he had locked away so long ago.

And, for the first time, two Hunters stepped into the demon world.

Chapter 7

Alix didn't know what he expected when he stepped through the doorway, but he certainly didn't expect what he got.

There was barely the sense of a transition. Once he stepped into the silver film, his foot met with solid ground, the slight tingling in his skin the only sign of entering a completely new world. To his surprise, he found himself standing in a forest. The doorway was now gone, leaving a simple tree behind them. The familiar flower was growing in vines up the trunk and over the branches to disappear into the thick forest canopy above.

To Alix, the world looked eerily normal. The forest they were standing in looked no different than the ones in the human world. It was even nighttime, just as it had been back home. Old trees surrounded them that were high enough to touch the sky with smaller, new trees struggling for their own piece of land. Small branches and leaves littered the ground from a recent storm, the forest silent with creatures holding their breath and waiting to see if these new creatures were predators or prey.

"It smells like rain," Fagan commented as he stepped around the group, trying to see the sky through the thick leaves above. "We should find shelter before it starts."

"I know this area. There's a couple caves not too far from here. They would be best for temporary shelter." Dox waited for a nod from Alix and Fagan then led the group through the trees, his long limbs moving smoothly as he walked.

The caves he mentioned seemed to appear out of nowhere. One moment they were in the tree covered area then suddenly the trees stopped against a high stone wall. The side of the wall was a deep gray with white and black speckles, a few stray plants attempting to grow on the uneven surface. Alix ducked into the cave opening with the others as large drops of water began to dance across the leaves above their heads.

"Roomy," Cyn said as she looked around the cave. From the initial opening the ceiling shot up into a cone shape, the insides smooth with a few boulders scattered about and loose rocks swept to the side. A few dead leaves and twigs scattered the front entrance, but otherwise the cave was clean, as if it had been waiting for them.

The cleanliness was unnerving, but Alix took comfort in the fact that there were no smaller caverns inside and, from the entrance, you could see and protect the whole cave. It would be safe for a night, at least. Alix finally let himself relax and took a seat on one of the boulders where he could watch the entrance and the rain as it grew heavier. Outside he could catch glimpses of small animals – demons, they were in the demon world now – darting for cover, the rain chasing them away.

Mira shivered a little, her tail shaking off what water had got on it. Pulling her book from her side pouch, she opened to a blank page and watched as marks started to appear, slowly sketching out a landscape. She sat down, her tail wagging happily as she watched the picture draw itself.

Alix noted that the girl seemed to have a particularly short term memory. She didn't seem fazed by the shadows that had attacked through her book before. She opened its pages and regarded it with complete trust as she watched the pictures forming. Alix decided that the Scough was either very naive or incredibly trusting.

Or both.

Cyn, however, seemed to remember everything with pinpoint accuracy as she walked over and slammed the book shut.

"Hey!" Mira frowned, opening the book again, "It's drawing us a path!"

"Isn't this how you got here? Can't you remember your way home without using that thing?"

"It's not a *thing*, it's my book! And I didn't take this way before, this is new to me. There's more than one path in these forests."

"Did you forget the part where the book tried to eat you with shadows?!"

"She's got a point, Mira," Haven said as he walked over to stand next to Cyn. "Maybe we-"

"That was just one time! Dox took the shadows away, its fine!"

Dox frowned. "I'm watching it, just in case."

"You guys are too paranoid," Mira said as she watched the drawing move along the pages.

"No, you're just too trusting," Cyn countered.

"We can argue about it later." Alix walked over to watch the picture in the book. "We'll just have to be more careful around it."

Fagan surveyed the cave and touched his sword, whispering its name under his breath. A faint glow came from the blade, illuminating the cave for them. Fagan left the blade attached to his back to glow while he leaned over Mira's shoulder. "Lucky for us, this place doesn't seem too different from our world. Forests I can deal with. That cave is us, right?" He pointed to a cave as the lines continued to draw across the page.

Mira nodded. "It should be done soon, then I can show you where my father is." As she said it, the thin lines twisted up and started to draw another area toward the top corner of the page. The new area had more trees and a river running right through the center. A small star appeared on the page, presumably marking her father's location. As the rest of the map drew itself, the star occasionally moved in that specific area, seeming to track his movements in real time.

"That's incredibly useful… but you're still way too trusting." Cyn said the last part quickly, as if trying to remind herself that this book could be a threat.

"But it doesn't tell us what's around him or what we might have to deal with," Haven said.

"I don't want to get that detailed, just in case," then Mira looked up at Cyn. "I'm not *that* trusting."

"Great. She's learning."

Fagan looked at the book before he nodded to Alix. "As we agreed before we left, you'll stay here with Mira and Haven. I'll take Cyn and Dox with me to check out this location."

Haven looked like he wanted to protest but he could hear his dragon hissing in his mind. He knew the older creature wasn't pleased with him being in this world, it was probably best to stay put for the time being.

"Do I get a say about being the sacrificial lamb?" Cyn remarked, halfheartedly.

Fagan shook his head, "If you don't trust us at this point, you should have stayed behind."

"It's not fair if you have a meeting and decide who goes where without telling the rest of us."

"Odd. I could've sworn we told you we were having the meeting and you said, 'Whatever, decide what you have to, I just want to get this trip over with'." Fagan smirked.

"It was a pretty boring meeting," Dox said, "You wouldn't have liked it."

"Wait. I didn't see you in the room with us," Alix said, frowning at the Lurk.

Dox chuckled, "Of course I was in the room with you, I like to know what's going on. I just didn't make my presence known."

Alix's eyes narrowed and he snapped at Dox, "You can't do things like that!"

"My apologies, I'll know that for next time."

Alix looked ready to snap again, but Fagan cut him off. "Why do you even care? I thought you were set on there not being a *next time.*"

Alix's eyes widened and his hard look faltered. If he got what he wanted in the end it really wouldn't matter, but he didn't expect Fagan to throw it in his face like that. He was under the impression that his partner was o.k. with this.

He was o.k. with it, right?

Fagan looked back over at Mira. "Can I take the page from your book without it disappearing?"

Mira ripped out the page and handed it to him. "Why would something that was written down disappear?" Her ears twitched in curiosity, but Fagan ignored the question and simply nodded.

"We should go now. The rain will help hide us and it'll hide our scent if her animal appearance is any indication of the abilities they hold," Fagan said.

"I never agreed to trudging around in the rain," Cyn grumbled.

"Better than the snow, right?" Fagan chuckled, speaking the dreaded word that Minnesota was known for. "It could be a lot worse."

Cyn frowned at him. She certainly wasn't dressed for it, her poor fishnet shirt would never survive in the trees and rain. "This sucks."

Haven smirked at her. "Better be careful, you already owe me twice and I won't be there to save you a third time."

Cyn decided it would be best to use her middle finger in such a situation.

"I know what that means now," Haven spoke confidently, then his voice began to falter, "Well... sort of. I know it's not good."

Dox smirked as he watched the both of them before he held out his hand toward Cyn. She reached over and placed her hand in his, a questioning look on her face. "Please tell me you're not going to try and *save* me, too?"

"This is your game with him. Although I suppose if I save you, Haven can have whatever you'd owe me."

"Oh! Kisses, right?" Mira's ears perked up, her tail eagerly wagging behind her. "Or something like that? That's what you two were talking about on the roof."

"What the hell?! You weren't even out there for that part!"

Mira just smiled and tapped her finger against her book. Cyn's eyes narrowed. She could've sworn she and the annoying creature in front of her had previous discussed not using books in such a way.

"Kisses?" Dox raised an eyebrow. "Is that my payment for saving you?"

"So that's what you were doing instead of sitting in on the meeting?" Fagan asked with a laugh.

"Aren't we supposed to be leaving?!" Cyn glared at them, trying to turn her embarrassment into anger, but the small blush on her cheeks said otherwise. Haven gave Cyn an annoyingly sweet smile but decided not to push the issue. They had more important things to do, but as soon as they didn't, he would definitely be addressing it again.

As Dox held Cyn's hand, small wisps of shadows slid over her skin. He nodded to her to step outside into the rain and Cyn frowned, muttering about the rain one last time before she walked out of the cave. To her surprise she found herself standing in a full on downpour and not getting wet at all.

"How did you…?"

"The shadows are repelling it. It's not something I can do for an entire group, but two people shouldn't be a problem." Dox turned to Fagan. "Assuming, of course, you trust me."

Fagan responded with a shrug. "I never said I didn't."

Dox nodded and repeated the same action with Fagan before the three of them set off. Mira stayed close to Haven, waving to the group as they made their departure. Cyn decided it would be best to ignore the energetic fox girl, but she did give Haven a slight nod, the dark skinned Ice Dragon nodding back to her. Alix watched them from the entrance of the cave, his eyes locked on Fagan as the larger man disappeared through the trees. He was never the type to wish his partner *good luck* or say *be safe* when they went on missions, but watching him leave with two demons – one part human, he supposed – made Alix a touch bit paranoid.

All of this taking place in the demon world only made it worse.

So Alix whispered a soft, "Be careful," as he waited for his partner to return.

———◆———

The further they walked into the forest, the more Fagan couldn't get over how normal everything looked. He would often let his mind wander about the demons he hunted and the world they must have come from. Movies, fairytales, and storybooks from his childhood contributed to the images in his head. Monsters around every tree trunk, cliffs leading to pits of fire, and bat like devil creatures who filled the black skies all claimed equal time in Fagan's imagination. To his inner, adventurous child, the innocent looking forest he walked through now was a letdown.

To his inner Hunter, it was a godsend.

The trees reminded him of the suburban neighborhoods he and his brother had grown up in. He half expected to stumble through a line of trees and come out in one of those perfectly manicured lawns with their fake fountains and outdoor pools. Maybe there'd be a driveway with a basketball hoop, or a woman jogging with a puppy while kids rode their bikes around as if they owned the streets.

As they continued to walk, Fagan found himself thinking of Xaver. He could imagine a drunken night with the man, celebrating a hunt, and haphazardly making their way home rather than driving or dealing with a taxi. Two men lost in stupid, immature conversation wouldn't notice if they tripped through some fancy flower covered garden arch. They certainly wouldn't notice if they wandered into a forest like the one he stood in now, only to realize hours later that they were lost. This place looked so normal that they would never know that they were in a new world until they encountered the danger head on. Meanwhile, back in his world, no one would be the wiser and the two would simply be disregarded as a couple of drunks that stumbled off to die in some alley.

It had to be the same for at least some of these demons. It was just as easy to imagine some demon stumbling through that same doorway, not realizing what world they were in. When confronted with a group of Hunters or scared humans, they would simply be forced to defend themselves out of fear.

It was a sobering thought that put his life and chosen occupation in a completely new light.

Life as a Hunter wasn't nearly as eventful and interesting as it sounded – with the exception of this moment, of course. It worked more like an exterminator service, cleaning the human world of the volatile demons who caused trouble. The number of demons that crossed through these doorways – or any other method – was few and far between. It was enough to keep him busy, he guessed, but there were some days where his time was spent practicing, flirting with Katalynne, and avoiding Zach's phone calls.

Like most Hunters he knew that the demon presence in their world had been happening for years, much further back than his lifetime. Monsters under the bed or campfire stories of monsters that lurked in the woods, there had always been a ring of truth behind these tales. Now he wondered how many of those "monsters" had been lost demons who had accidentally stumbled into their world. More than once he'd run into a demon who had seemed more frightened than dangerous. Seeing that these doorways were completely unprotected in this world the chances of a demon stepping into a whole new world without realizing it were high. Then there was the problem of finding their way back, who would ever think to try a botanical garden in the middle of the night?

It certainly put the whole idea of demon hunting into a new perspective; but it didn't change the core. Like humans, some demons were simply evil and there was a line. Kill other people and you deserved to be hunted down, just like any other animal. Fagan wasn't playing god, he was defending himself and the people who depended on him. This particular mission wasn't about starting a war, it was about protecting a young girl's father. Their job would be over after that, no matter what Alix wanted.

But more than a job would be over this time, wouldn't it? His partnership would be over, too. If the Storyteller really could do what Alix seemed to think he could do, Alix would be Alixandre, engaged to some genius and pregnant with his child.

It wasn't for Fagan to judge what Alix wanted, but would he – *she* – really want something so normal after hunting?

For Fagan it had been an easy choice: hunt or be bored to tears at some office job. For Alix it was clearly more serious than that, but could his partner really be satisfied with such a neat and tidy life now? Though, he supposed, that if all went according to Alix's plan, this life of hunting and demons wouldn't even exist. There'd be no Randall Fagan, no Katalynne, no Xaver, and no warehouse.

Fagan was thankful when the three of them came to a stop, the forest floor changing before them. His thoughts were wandering way too much during this walk and he needed something else to think about.

They could make out various plants that moved up to an edge then gave way to a depression in the ground about five feet across. The plant life was flattened and matted with old and worn leaves with vines and a couple of flowers twisting around one end. Fagan knelt down to get a closer look, frowning to himself.

"A nest." Dox's voice was quiet as he looked around the forest. "We have to be at the edge of the Scough's territory, but there don't seem to be any around at the moment."

"Wait, is this how they sleep?" Cyn was leaning back against a tree trunk, panting softly. Of the group she was the one not used to walking for long periods of time. When she was on the run with Dox, he always let her set the pace, always making sure that he didn't move faster than her. Keeping up with a seasoned Hunter was worlds different. Now that they had stopped she used the small conversation to her advantage, taking the moment to rest without looking like a complete, whiny child. More than anything she wanted to complain that her feet hurt from trying to keep up with Fagan's long stride and that her worn out boots were not made for the bumpy forest floor. That coupled with the stress of trying not to step on every dry, loud branch on the ground had worn her out.

Dox responded to her question with a nod. "Scough live in the forest and sleep curled together in nests like this one. The nests surround a central gathering area. We need to be even more careful from here on out or we'll be noticed. The rain will keep them from smelling us, and I'll try and muffle our sounds as much as I can with the shadows."

Fagan brushed his fingers against the twisted roots and nodded quietly to himself. Now it made sense why the home Xaver stayed in only had two sleeping bags. Mira had probably slept curled up against one of them – most likely Haven, there was no way in hell Xaver would go along with it. "I guess it's a good thing it's still lightly raining," Fagan whispered. "Let's keep going." Fagan stood up and motioned for them to follow, Cyn groaning quietly to herself as she was forced to walk again. Fagan looked back at her and chuckled. "Don't worry about being tired, you should've seen Alix the first time he took on a mission."

Cyn sighed. She should've known that Fagan would be able to tell that she was tired. "Please tell me he cried."

Fagan managed to stifle his laughter. "No, nothing like that. But he certainly wasn't as prepared as he thought he was. This was before we had the SUV too, so there was a lot of walking involved. Compared to that time, you're doing great."

That thought made Cyn smile... just a little bit.

It only took about a minute for them to pass another nest, this one built up much better than the first. Branches interlaced around the curved edge and the inside was a comfortable looking mixture of thick vines and leaves. When Cyn looked closer she was surprised to see that there were indeed Scough sleeping in the nest, curled against each other like cats under the sparse cover the canopy provided from the rain. The creatures were so tightly wound together that Cyn found herself squinting to determine how many were there. She finally settled on two, but she wasn't sure. Turning, she quickened her steps to walk next to Dox rather than behind both him and Fagan.

There were several things scattered around the area made of distinctly human items. A smaller nest, obviously used for a child, had an ornament made of various broken but glinting metal objects hanging above it. Some of the sleeping Scough wore jewelry crafted from braided pieces of brightly colored scrap fabric. Fagan swore some of the cloth pieces had logos he recognized, brands he'd see teenagers wear or the fancy skirts Katalynne would wear until they became *out of style*. Nearly every demon around him had something he recognized and he felt his earlier thoughts about that doorway resurface.

Just how often did these creatures wander into his world?

The nests grew denser around them, each tucked right next to a tree. A beaten path wound between the nests and trees, clear of most leaves and twigs from constant use. In the darkness they could make out an obvious direction to the path, leading them through the nests to a circle of trees. These moss covered trees grew closer together than the others, as if creating a wall or the bars to a cage. As Cyn got closer, she could make out faint symbols and pictures painted across the moss in white. The pictures looked like nothing she'd ever seen before, with thin sharp lines and intricate shapes. She could see that the branches from these trees all grew toward each other. They were twisted together with vines, creating a natural roof just a couple feet taller than Fagan's height. Dox silently motioned for them to follow him and they walked around the edge of the tree cluster where there was the most cover so they could listen.

The tree cluster held a handful of the Scough, each one speaking in a hushed voice. The area was lit by a cluster of moss covered stones that actually glowed with a faint, greenish blue tint. Among the demons they could make out different animalistic features. The majority had fox tails similar to Mira's, some longer than others. Some had pointy ears, others had a thin layer of fur covering most of their skin except for their eyes and mouth. Their fur was more varied than human hair colors, yet it was easy to tell they were all part of the same clan with their similar clothing and mannerisms as they spoke. It reminded Fagan of one of those conventions Zach had spent last summer gushing about, where people wore costumes with cat ears, furry tails, and the women looked especially hot – or so his little brother had claimed.

Fagan wasn't listening to the conversation between them but caught a few words: battle, agreement, and a truce breaking. To him it sounded like a discussion of an army, or a rebel group deciding how to strike against another group. This was obviously some sort of preliminary planning meeting, the last get together before the battle commenced. Shifting his weight carefully he moved to the next tree to get a better view of the front of the tree cluster. Dox and Cyn followed after him once they were sure they wouldn't be seen. To their surprise they could see a small collection of crudely made weapons leaning against the next tree, mostly pointed sticks with scavenged wires and metal pieces attached on the end. The weapons looked small, childish, obviously thrown together by a group of creatures that were used to using their claws. Seeing the weapons further illustrated the grim seriousness of the situation.

At the front of the cluster was another Scough, but this one stood out from the crowd. This one had fur that was too dark to be white but too luxurious to simply be called grey. His eyes were a deep gold and he wore more ornate clothing then the others. The Scough around him wore smaller pieces of clothing that covered their bodies as a necessity, while this one wore a robe a few shades darker than his hair with his tail wrapped around his waist like a sash.

"That's him," Dox whispered, "Thierry, the Storyteller."

"How do you know?" Fagan asked, making sure to keep his voice low.

"I bargained with your partner about him, remember?"

In front of the Storyteller was another figure, kneeling on the forest floor, very different from the group surrounding him. Fagan could only see his back, his thick hair falling in various shades of brown with a couple braids to hold it back from his face. The man was tied up, like he had been in the pictures, but seeing him in color instead of a pencil sketch was a big difference. His skin was bronze, reminding Fagan of the color women strived for when the weather was hot and the air sticky. The strange piece of armor over his arm was covered in many different stones that shone in the moonlight, reminding Fagan of the celebrities who wore accessories that cost more than his parents' wealthy home. A childlike part of him suddenly wondered if the storybooks of dragons guarding treasure was true. At least this one didn't seem to breathe fire.

"The Red Dragon?" Fagan mouthed toward Dox before nodding to the tied up demon, half for confirmation and half a question of what to do with him.

Instead of speaking up this time, Fagan could feel a cool breeze next to his ear as a shadow moved just in his peripheral vision. "Yes," it whispered so soft that only he could hear it. He noticed a second shadow next to Cyn's ear, presumably telling her the same thing. "Those wires shouldn't be able to hold him, he should be able to melt them because of his ability to control heat."

Fagan frowned. So much for not breathing fire. "So why are those wires able to hold him now?"

"Something must be preventing him from using his powers."

Fagan nodded. Just like he'd thought, they wouldn't be able to count on the captive for much help even if they freed him. He was fairly certain that whatever was preventing the dragon from attacking had to be related to the Storyteller.

"This is so strange," Cyn whispered as she watched the Scough. "She showed us this before and now..."

"Now we're seeing it first hand," Fagan finished for her. "I recognize everyone, too, but... there seems to be one missing."

"You're right," Dox murmured quietly.

"Their leader, the one she called Jahren." Fagan frowned more, watching as the small group talked around the Red Dragon, who kept glaring at them as if trying to set them on fire with his eyes alone – Fagan had a feeling he would if he could. He was especially glaring at Mira's father, who was speaking quietly and avoiding looking at the dragon as he continued advising the others.

"We saw in Mira's book that the shadows swallowed him and the others he was talking to. Maybe they didn't come back..."

Cyn's voice went quiet as she looked from the group Thierry was talking to and the small amount of weapons they had managed to put together. "They look like children on the playground with cardboard swords and shields. Even I can tell they're going to die."

Minutes passed and Fagan made his way around the trees, crouching closer to the group. He wanted a place where he could make out what they were saying and hopefully get a better feel for the current situation that their leader was in. Unfortunately the time for discussion ended as the group broke apart and began leaving the circle of trees with their weapons. It wasn't long before Thierry was alone with the Red Dragon, who glowered at him in the glow of the moss colored stones.

Fagan lifted his hand to motion that it was time to leave but stopped as something in the air shifted. Closing his fist he froze and his eyes scanned the small area, settling on the Storyteller. Something about him and the darkness around him felt off.

Holding his breath, Fagan watched as a shadow curled out from behind Thierry, twisting out from the shadow of the rock he was sitting on. The front part unfurled and it moved forward, resting on his shoulder. Fagan's eyes widened as he realized it wasn't just a shadow, but a very long hand with thin, spiny fingers.

The Red Dragon tried to move away as he saw the hand, stumbling back over the well packed ground. A gathering of small shadow creatures grew out of the ground around him, looking like they were melting in reverse. The creatures were no larger than a squirrel and moved in sweeping, oily movements, like spilled ink slowly creeping down a piece of paper. They might have actually been cute if not for the razor sharp horns on their faces and long, spiny fingers that dripped at the ends. Their faces shifted, eyelids snapping open to reveal bright, white eyes with sickly edges of a yellowish green. One of them moved toward the tied up dragon, its face shifting and opening, revealing a mouth full of gooey shadows. The Red Dragon came to a stop as they moved around him, coming to the conclusion that they weren't going to let him get any further as the shadows rose up and laced together behind him.

Thierry remained quiet as he sat on the rock, his eyes cast down. Fagan could now see thin lines of shadows moving over his skin like strings. They moved around his neck and wrists, literally making the Scough look like a puppet. Fagan felt like he was watching a show of power, of dominance, to serve as a reminder to the captive dragon and Storyteller...

... or maybe...

Had their cover been blown? Fagan shook his head. No, it couldn't have been.

Right?

The dark strings around Thierry's neck forced him to raise his head and watch as the shadows danced around the Red Dragon, mocking him. Whispers could be heard in the air, just faint enough that Fagan couldn't make out the words, but the expression on Thierry's face hardened, making it clear that he could hear what was being said and how he felt about the words. A few of the shadows reached out and touched the dragon, taunting him and causing him to struggle in protest. He growled soundlessly at them, even leaned forward and snapped his teeth in a clear threat. A couple of the strange creatures retreated, but others stood their ground, swarming around the dragon and playing with him while the Storyteller looked away and did nothing, the hand still firmly on his shoulder.

Now was the time to leave, they'd seen enough. Fagan had an idea of what they were up against, the situation far worse than he ever imagined. They would be lucky if they made it back to the cave, but the only chance they would have is if they left now. Lifting his hand he signaled to Cyn and Dox.

Before any of them could respond the shadows all stopped and the sound rushed back in around them. They could hear the rain hitting the leaves and ground. It wasn't a gentle tapping, it was more like a cascading stampede, proudly proclaiming their location as if trying to tell the shadows about new prey to pursue. Fagan swore under his breath as pair after pair of those sickly eyes turned in their direction. Hadn't Dox been shielding them?

Fagan turned to look at Dox in question, only to find him standing completely rigid and fully upright, not even trying to hide anymore. Fagan watched in disbelief as the shadow demon stepped into the cluster of trees and stood in full view. His form was changing, melting away before their eyes. Everything became flat, almost making him look like a black canvas of shadows as Dox slowly made steps toward Thierry. The Storyteller was moving, straining against the shadow webs across his skin as he opened his mouth and gave a pained cry.

"Dox?!"

A high pitched cry, almost like that of a feral cat, struck the air around them. Suddenly, all of the eyes turned away to look toward the cluster of trees. Fagan watched as a Scough jumped down from the branches above to land directly into the swarm of shadows. Claws out and down on all fours, he struck out, swiping and darting forward as he tore through them. The shadow creatures ripped apart like water droplets, scattering into the air around the Scough, only to slide back together into inky pools as they hit the ground.

Thierry's eyes widened, suddenly snapping out of whatever hold the shadows had on him, showing more emotion and struggling against the hand's hold. "Jahren, don't!"

Fagan didn't waste the distraction and darted away from his tree. Without hesitating he reached Cyn's tree and grabbed her arm. "We need to go," he hissed quietly. "Now."

Up ahead, Dox was walking again, this time right up to Jahren as the Scough continued to tear his way through the shadows. Cyn watched as her childhood friend tilted his head in an almost curious look, then his arm stretched forward and caught the Scough by the hair, lifting him up off the ground. Jahren barred his teeth and swiped at Dox, but this time his claws did nothing, as if Dox's skin were as hard as metal. Cyn felt herself begin to shake as shadows rippled up Dox's arm. They began to crawl over Jahren, covering him while Thierry struggled to try and do something.

"Jahren!" Thierry managed to stand for a moment but the shadows pulled him back down. "N-no! Jahren!"

As the area grew darker Cyn looked away, struggling with the words she spoke to Fagan. "We... w-we need to go now."

Cyn wanted nothing more than to rush in and stop her friend, but she knew better. Dox had always told her that around his father he couldn't be trusted, no matter what. Taking a deep breath she turned with Fagan and forced herself to rush into the trees as fast as she could with him. She was scared and soaked, and she swore the creepy Lurks were right behind them. She told herself not to look back. Instead she focused on Fagan's hand holding hers and ran faster than she'd ever run in her life.

Silently she promised Dox they'd get him out of there, but she wasn't even sure if she believed it.

It had started with a stomach ache.

The young, blonde haired woman had been feeling sick for a couple of days. She had gone through the process of blaming it on food. Her and her fiancé were eating out a lot lately because he was always busy with work and she was constantly studying, trying to progress her degree from Bachelors to Masters. When they did manage to share a home cooked meal he was the one who prepared it, her tastes going from the fancy French dishes she had grown up with to mixtures of ground beef and noodles. "To be fair, I did get croissants," he would always say.

And she would laugh and say, "Those are crescents, actually. There's a difference."

"Are all French women this picky?"

"Oui." And this would lead to a kitchen kiss that would threaten to overcook the meat.

After ruling food out she had moved on to plan B: some kind of stomach bug. He had even come home from work early on a particularly bad day, making fresh soup – from a can – and grilled sandwiches. He had stocked the fridge up with orange juice and called himself her personal doctor, putting a smile on her miserable face.

Finally, she had to upgrade to a real doctor, her fiancé going to work despite not liking the idea of her being so sickly while at home by herself. He had wanted to go to the doctor with her but she had insisted that she could go on her own.

Then the news was delivered, the doctor smiling brightly. She wasn't sick, no quite the opposite: she was pregnant.

She had wanted to tell her fiancé right away, leaving the doctor's office and heading to the lab where he had gone from having an internship to a full-time position. Traffic had been unnaturally busy for that time of day. The lunch rush hadn't started, everyone still at work or in class, so the bus shouldn't have been forced to crawl at a snail's pace down the street. Too anxious to wait any longer she had decided to get off and walk the rest of the way. It wasn't too far and hopefully she'd get there in time for them to have lunch together.

The walk had been much too loud and she was wishing for a pair of headphones. Sirens and the honking of fire trucks trying to zip by, it had taken her a moment to realize that they were going in the direction of her fiancé's lab. She could feel the dread swelling up in her belly, her steps quickening, but she shook it off and told herself that it was merely a coincidence. Minneapolis was a large city, those trucks could be headed anywhere downtown. She'd get to the building in a panic for nothing and he'd make fun of her for it. But as she got closer the sirens were louder, people crowded around the sidewalk and whispering amongst themselves.

"Fire." Whisper.

"Some lab up the street." Whisper whisper.

"YH Tech, I think."

Now she broke into a run, pushing her way through the crowd until she ran into a man in uniform. He and a couple of officers were trying to keep the crowd at bay, barricades and police cars parked all around. "Ma'am, I'm going to have to ask you to stay back.'"

"My fiancé is in there!"

"Ma'am please.'"

She had tried to run around the officer but he immediately had his arms around her. "Let me go!" She screamed, "My fiancé is inside!"

She could see, up ahead, a glorious blaze of fire. In her lifetime she had been taught that fire was a blend of hot oranges and yellows, but this was all kinds of blue and black swirls of destruction. The building wasn't just burning, fire fighters trying their hardest to put the flames out, but the entire structure was melting away, concrete and steel dripping into liquid puddles from how hot the flames were. The fire fighters up ahead kept spraying water at it, but it only seemed to create a cloud of steam that continued to fan the flames. A switch to white foaming water from another truck also seemed to have no effect.

The flames weren't going out. In fact, she swore that they had a life of their own, licking at each and every corner of the building until they were satisfied. Cars that had been too close to the building started to melt, expensive sports vehicles and worn out rusty vans each dripping, their tires hitting the concrete and being burned into a black tar. Hot, liquid red from one destroyed car, an old brown from another, the cars reduced to a pool thick like paint.

She kept screaming at the police officer about her fiancé, about him being inside, about the fact that she was trying to tell him that she was pregnant. The man held onto her tightly, his eyes heavy in sadness as the fire seemed to roar and scream, not leaving any remaining scraps of the research lab.

"Alix?"

Alix blinked and looked up to see Mira standing in front of him, holding an armful of dry leaves and twigs. Taking a small breath he nodded to the middle of the cave. "Just set them there," he said.

Mira nodded, setting the items down as Alix walked over and knelt down, pulling a lighter from his pocket to start a small fire. Quietly he watched the orange and yellow flame as it struggled to life, content that the color hadn't changed in this world.

Behind him, Mira looked like she wanted to say something. The Hunter had been sitting alone, hand clasping the ring around his neck with his eyes closed ever since Fagan and the others left. She could always write in her book to see what he was thinking about but she was trying not to do that as much ever since Cyn had gotten angry with her about it. Still, knowing Alix's hard demeanor, she had a feeling that he wouldn't speak on what had been troubling him in his unsteady, light slumber moments ago. She walked back over to where Haven was, quietly talking with him as Alix sat in front of the fire, his eyes not leaving the flames. "What does the ring mean?"

The Ice Dragon responded with a shrug, "I have no idea."

As much as Alix would have liked to avoid lighting the fire, he couldn't ignore the chance that Fagan and the others would come back completely soaked. Covered in shadows or magic or not, he liked to be practical about things. He also decided that the fire would keep them warm while they planned throughout the night. Mira had assured him that many other demons used fire, so there was no reason for the smoke to make them stand out.

The conversation between Mira and Haven had changed – thank goodness. Now Mira was saying something about being worried about her father, holding the book close to her chest like she was hugging a stuffed animal for comfort. Alix was actually hoping she would set down the book just once. He wanted to see what it would do if someone else touched it. He knew her father was the Storyteller and not her, but the thought still intrigued him. What if he could pick up the book and it responded? What if he didn't need a Storyteller? What if all he needed was the book? Could he possibly write in it? Tell it to go back in time?

He had thought about all of the possibilities of how he could have things changed. Maybe Roderick wouldn't have gotten that internship in the first place, or maybe it wouldn't have turned into a full-time job. Maybe they could live in a different city, or attend a different university together. After much thought he decided that the most direct way to act was to have the Storyteller change just one part.

Roderick would simply go to the doctor's office with her instead of the lab.

Alixandre DeBenit – the future Mrs. Alixandre Michaels – had never been a selfish woman. She had always been a woman who believed that all things happened for a reason because she'd grown up with parents who believed in thanking a bearded man in the sky for their successes. Alixandre had believed in the same being and she had been content with that.

Until the fire.

That Alixandre was gone now, replaced with the "man" Alix had become to show Xaver how serious he was. He had spent the last few years training and preparing himself to hunt down the demon – or demons – responsible for the lab fire.

The mention of the Storyteller had changed that. What had started as a drunken conversation between a pair of Hunters he and Fagan had encountered back when Xaver was still around had succeeded to burrow through the walls where Alixandre hid. The thought, the hope, had stayed with who Alix used to be and spurred her forward to something that was almost laughable.

The thought that she could, possibly, have Roderick and her child back.

This possibility was better than some anger laced path of vengeance. Sure, Alix could keep hunting until that demon came face to face with the barrel of his gun, but this? Actually having his loved ones back? Actually having that life that had happened once upon a dream? He had to try. No, *she* had to try, for Roderick and their child. Their family.

The situation in front of Alix now was only a part of that. The idea of rescuing the girl's father was just a piece, a step toward that impossible goal. Alixandre may have wanted her family back more than anything, but Alix wasn't a fool. He knew enough stories and tales about people jumping headlong into their wishes and desires without thinking first and how they had suffered for it. No, he would either ask the Storyteller or find a way to get himself some time with Mira's book for more than a few seconds. It was too bad that Haven hadn't gone with the others, but then the Ice Dragon seemed to have appointed himself as Mira's protector.

Interrupting Alix's thoughts, a small shape moved into the cave, pausing just inside to shake off its fur like a dog. A small black fox now stood at the cave's entrance, a hint of gray at the very tip of its tail and ears. Alix quietly un-holstered his gun, waiting to see what the animal would do. It was no larger than a normal human world fox, but he had no idea if foxes in this world had any special powers or abilities – especially considering Mira's talents.

"Zee!"

Mira, on the other hand, was up in a second and running over to the fox. She knelt down in front of it and pulled it tightly into her arms. She'd moved faster than Alix had ever seen and he made sure to make a mental note of it, especially since Haven also seemed surprised at her speed. He also made sure to note that foxes in this world came in a variety of sizes, from standing tall like Mira to being the normal kind that you'd see in the human world. Though perhaps this fox could shift into a form similar to Mira's.

It made Alix wonder about some of the animal life in his world.

Mira slid the book into her bag then proceeded to smother the fox with both arms. The creature let out a happy little *yip* as it snuggled against her like a happy pup.

"Mira, who is that?" Haven was now standing, walking toward Mira carefully.

"She's my friend, Zee. She's been waiting for me to come back this whole time." The smile on her face couldn't be any wider as she finally let the fox go. The fox then wandered over toward Haven, looking up at him quizzically as if she expected the young man to pick her up. Haven responded by crossing his arms and frowning down at the fox. The fox got the point and wandered over toward Alix instead, but Alix frowned at her, too, and kept his hand on his gun. The fox whined a little, edging away, instinctively knowing that it was a weapon. In seconds she was scampering back over to Mira, practically jumping into her lap.

"You're all mean."

"Mira, are you sure that's your fox?"

"Of course I am! Don't be so paranoid, Haven."

He wanted to make a comment, something along the lines of how he couldn't help but be paranoid around her, but he kept it to himself. His dragon chuckled a silent agreement and it made Haven smile a little. "If you say so," Haven muttered, sitting at the edge of the cave to look out into the rain. Sighing a little he decided to change the subject. "Hopefully they get back soon."

Alix nodded a silent agreement and forced himself to relax as he put his gun away and joined Haven in looking outside. What little he could see of the sky was dark and mostly hidden by the leaves and branches outside the cave. Water was still falling steadily and they could all hear small movement in the forest. Most likely small creatures who used this land as their home, nothing that signaled anything larger than the little fox.

"Do we need to worry about any demons in that size?" Alix nodded to the fox now perched on Mira's shoulder like a well-trained monkey. The creature was busy butting her head against

Mira's neck, not stopping until she raised her hand and scratched behind one of her ears.

Mira shook her head. "There's animals in all shapes and sizes here, but they all live in the forest and mostly keep to themselves."

"So… can you turn into that, too?" Alix asked.

Mira smiled and shook her head. "Zee and I are different."

"But you're both foxes."

"And you and Fagan are human, but you're both different."

Alix tried to think of something to say to that but was interrupted before he could.

"I hear something," Haven whispered quietly. Immediately, the small group grew silent. Alix's hand moved to his gun again as he stood up and moved toward the entrance. He and Haven silently took places at either side of the cave opening, their backs pressed to the stone walls as they watched the forest outside. Mira backed up behind the fire, one hand on the back of her fox friend who remained perched on her shoulder and back. The fox growled softly and Mira hushed her, signaling for the creature to stay quiet.

Alix would be surprised about how obedient the fox was later, right now there were more important matters to deal with. He could hear now, clearly, that there were feet moving through the forest, splashing leaves and water around as they came closer. They were loud and rushed, not taking the time to move quietly through the forest. He exchanged a look with Haven who nodded back, one of his hands shifting from dark brown to white as cold mist began building around his palm.

A second later a very soaked Cyn ran into the cave followed by Fagan, stopping only a few inches away from Alix's gun with a scared look on her face. Alix, luckily, had more control than that and the minute he recognized Cyn he raised the gun to avoid accidentally firing. Stepping back, he lowered the gun while Haven let his hand slip into a normal temperature, watching as Cyn quietly slunk close to the fire, shivering from the rain.

"She's lucky I didn't shoot. What happened?"

Fagan opened his mouth to answer but was interrupted when they all heard a noise outside the cave. In seconds Alix had his gun aimed again and Fagan's sword was in his hands, facing the cave. Both watched the dark, wet forest beyond, waiting for the sound again. The forest was quiet for a long moment before a young Scough stepped forward with his hands in the air and his ears pressed to his head in a nervous look. "P-please don't hurt me, I was just-"

"Lyree?" Mira stepped forward. "Don't hurt him, he's a friend."

Fagan nodded, lowering his sword and Alix tucked his gun in the holster. "He must've followed you," Alix said to Fagan.

"Better us than them." This voice came from outside the cave as Saraisai and Amari stepped in, shaking off the rain water clinging to their fur. Lyree made a face at the older Scough.

"That was scary. I thought the humans were going to kill me!"

"Obviously they didn't," Saraisai said, nodding to Fagan and Alix. "You won't be needin' those weapons, we're on your side."

Mira rushed forward and hugged the old Scough before he could say more. She was about to ask them what they were doing there when her eyes caught the pointed sticks strapped haphazardly to each of their belts. "Why... do you have those?"

Lyree frowned. "Your father insisted that we needed weapons… for when the Red Dragons attack."

"But I thought Jahren was going to talk to them, tell them it was all an accident."

The group of Scough hesitated, looking at each other before Amari spoke. "Mira, he did go and talk to them. But… he didn't come back."

"W-what?"

"Your father told us all that he was killed by the dragons." Saraisai spoke much softer than he usually did, a sad frown on his face when he saw Mira's eyes begin to water.

Mira shook her head, a soft whine coming from her throat. "But… m-my book… it showed…"

"It just showed him speaking to them, but not-" Haven stopped himself from finishing the rest of that sentence and placed a hand on Mira's shoulder. "I'm sorry."

"There's nothing to apologize for because they're wrong," Cyn whispered from the fire. "We saw him when we saw your father. He jumped down from the trees to fight the shadows we saw. They took him and our friend."

Lyree smiled brightly. "This is wonderful news! Oh… I mean, about Jahren, not your friend. Well not Jahren either if the shadows took him. I-I mean it's good that he's not dead and-"

Amari lightly smacked Lyree across the back of his head. "You said shadows, I take it he's not all right."

"Nope. He's completely fucked," Cyn muttered.

Haven frowned and watched as Cyn turned away from the group and focused her attention on the fire. From his angle he could see a worried look on her face. Cyn pulled off the now shredded fishnet she had been wearing, leaving herself in just a tank top. Her fishnet shirt was full of large holes thanks to their frantic run back to the cave. She was left shivering in front of the fire in her soaked tank top and jeans as she tried to salvage the shirt, then ended up tossing it aside as a lost cause.

Pulling off his own shirt, Haven used it to help dry off Cyn's arms and hair, leaving himself bare chested.

"You should keep that on. What if it gets colder from the rain?" She asked.

"Think about that for a second, Cyn. There's benefits to having an Ice Dragon," then he smiled, "And, by the way, that's what... five? Six?"

"Huh?"

"The amount of times I've saved you."

Cyn blinked, then her eyes widened when she suddenly realized what he meant. "Three times, jackass," but she smiled back at him, "And I didn't think being chivalrous counted."

"It's double points for being a gentleman, so four."

Cyn laughed, the terrified look disappearing from her eyes. It made Haven feel better, such a scared look didn't suit the girl at all.

Fagan hated to be the one to break the mood, especially since Cyn seemed to desperately need it. "We should start from the beginning," then he looked over at Saraisai and the others, "We saw Thierry, but he was there with something else. Some long, shadowy arm came out of nowhere and kept him from moving. It took control of Do-"

"Don't say his name!" Cyn said quickly. "Don't say either name. There's enough shadows around here that they could hear us."

Saraisai let out an angry growl. "He told us that Jahren was killed. He used it to make everyone angry at the Red Dragons, now they actually want to fight them."

"Meanwhile, the dragons are mad at us, because we have one of them." Amari sighed, "He's pitting us against each other on purpose."

Alix frowned. "This location isn't safe if your friend has changed sides," he said to Cyn.

"He hasn't… this isn't his fault." Cyn was too worried to fret about how pathetic she sounded right now, her voice soft and filled with sadness, guilt, and all of the emotions that her tough exterior always tried to hide. She'd grown up with Dox, he'd protected her and helped her escape a home that had been broken since before she could walk. He helped her leave a father who thought stuffing a demon into a young child's body was "brilliant." And now here they were, in the middle of the demon world, facing Dox's father without taking his feelings into account. He may have said that he would be o.k., but Cyn knew better. She knew how it felt to have a father who treated you like garbage, she should've protested more, should've fought harder for Dox the same way he'd done for her so many times. By coming here they practically handed him over to his father, to the Lurkhamara. Cyn felt like the worst friend in the world.

Cyn stood up, still rubbing her arms for warmth. "He was willing to help, even if he knew his father was involved. He's not going to come back here and hurt us."

"That may have been true before this happened, but now, he's not in control. We can't trust him and right now there's nothing we can do to help him."

Haven frowned from where he was standing next to Cyn. He could feel Alix's words snap across the space of the cave, slapping the girl and cutting into her. Cyn balled up her fists, shaking in anger, but Haven couldn't tell if it was at Alix or herself.

"That's not fair! He helped us! We owe him! And he's my friend!"

"We have a mission to do. We do that first, then we can discuss-"

"NO!" Cyn yelled loudly and the group could feel the ground vibrate with her yell, a couple small cracks forming along the walls. Her shout was a powerful rush of emotion, her eyes narrowed, the ground responding to her with a tremble and protesting groan. "He's the only friend I have! He helped me get away from my father and I owe him. I'm not leaving him there with that thing!"

Alix glared, not seeming shaken by how the cave around them reacted, even if a couple pebbles could be heard dropping from the ceiling. "Then *you* can go after him."

The cave grew silent at that statement. The implication behind it was very clear and Cyn found herself staring at Alix in disbelief. Before this ridiculous mission Alix had actually treated her with a small amount of respect, or at least tolerance. Alix hated demons, but the way he'd acted around her in the gardens and at the warehouse had made her think that she wasn't in that category of disdain. In fact, part of her had thought that the man felt sorry for her. She didn't chose to be a demon, she was forced into it, so it seemed like he was on her side. But now, with the tone in Alix's voice, Cyn realized that she'd said something wrong, burning any – and possibly all – of the bridges they had between them. According to the philosophy of this bitter man, caring about a demon was enough to put you in the same league as them.

"Hn," Saraisai frowned, crossing his arms as he gave Alix a look of disapproval. "It seems that humans have no sense of comradely."

"Excuse me? We're here helping you."

"You're willing to abandon a comrade," Saraisai said with a low growl. "It's distasteful."

"No one asked you!" Alix snapped at the Scough.

Fagan rubbed his forehead. "Alix, stop. We have to deal with this problem because, like it or not, he knows where we live, not just where this cave is. It's advantageous for us to get him back, whether you like it or not." He glanced over at Cyn then back at Alix, looking between the both of them, "Let's keep the fighting down to a minimum. We need to figure out how we're going to deal with this because we just lost our best source of information."

"No, you did not."

No one recognized the quiet, but firm, voice that had spoken from behind them. When they all turned, the only person they saw was Haven, who was now standing as far away from the fire as possible. Cyn was the first to speak, "Haven?" But even as she spoke his name she knew, somehow, that it was the wrong name to speak.

The most striking difference was the chilly white in his eyes. His fingers, Fagan noted, were longer and pointed, much like the claws he'd seen on the captive back with the Storyteller. Streaks of white and silvery blue slid through his braids like rippling water. He now stood before them completely confident, acting as if he expected them to regard him with a sort of reverence. It was the kind of stance and presence that only the oldest and wisest of creatures ever gained.

"Haven?" Cyn spoke again, a worried look on her face that she didn't bother to hide. On top of Dox being gone and Alix treating her like dirt, the last thing she needed was for something to happen to Haven.

Mira frowned, her hand slipping inside of her pouch to rest on her book. "You don't sound like him. Are you…"

"No need to turn to your book, I am his dragon."

Mira blinked, her hand faltering against the thick binding of her book. "I wasn't going to-"

"You rely on it too much," then suddenly Mira could feel the cover of the book growing colder, slick ice forming underneath her fingers. "It's meant to be an unpredictable weapon, not a tool for you to cling to." Haven leveled Mira with a disapproving glare as frost began to grow from his claws and tickle at his wrists. The entire area around him was cold, a misty chill starting to surround the cave. Even the flames of the fire started to protest, swaying around in an unseen wind and ready to go out.

"There's no need to be so mean," Mira said with a pout, pulling her hand out of her bag.

Surprisingly it was Saraisai who stepped closer to Haven, his eyes wide as he spoke. "An Ice Dragon? How can that be? The last one I heard of died with Hanzo."

Haven responded with a quiet nod. "We have bigger problems than where I came from." He turned his attention to the others, frowning. "This is against my better judgment," his voice was deeper now, more serious, "However I recognize what the situation warrants, now that he is involved." The single word "he" was almost growled out through Haven's lips, leaving no mystery behind the fact that the dragon had encountered the Lurkhamara before and didn't like him one bit.

"I-lyan, that was the name," Saraisai said with a grin. "You were one of Hanzo's advisors."

The Ice Dragon glared at the old Scough, hissing softly in distaste at being recognized. "And you will all keep that name to yourselves."

"Didn't you say that Hanzo was important?" Alix asked Mira.

"I did," then she gave Haven a questioning look. "Haven, you had someone so important with you and didn't say anything?"

"I do not share everything with him for a reason. It's for his own protection. That's why I did not want him here in the first place. But now that we are here and the situation is so grim, I have no choice but to step in," then he turned to address the others. "This creature you encountered, I know of him. Once Anasia – the Reina – realizes that he's behind it, she'll be even more determined to fight. She has a deep hatred for that creature, a hatred that's stronger than my own."

"But my father has done nothing wrong!"

"No, he hasn't. Unfortunately, this creature has wronged many people, particularly those of us who survived Hanzo's fall. The captive they have is her son. The Reina has many, but he is her first. She will kill to protect him. I suggest you find a way to free him before she arrives here."

Fagan decided that it would be best to get right to the point. "What do we need to know about him to get her father back and get out of this place alive?"

The Ice Dragon turned his piercing look to Fagan and regarded him with what looked like an amused expression, but he didn't laugh. "Eegil will be of assistance. It will protect you from the things he controls where other blades would fail. He will use the shadows to his advantage and you may be able to fight them. More than likely you will lose. You will be lucky if he kills you."

Fagan didn't bother asking how the Ice Dragon knew about Eegil.

Strings of frost extended to the edge of Haven's eyes, giving them an almost reptilian shape. The transformation between Haven and I-lyan was constant, as if neither could decide what form to stick to. His braids would go from their normal dark color to shades of ice, his eyes thin and narrow at times then rounder, friendlier during other points in their conversation. The hard voice remained the same, making everything I-lyan said sound condescending.

"No wonder he doesn't like you," Cyn frowned right back at the dragon, his piss poor attitude snapping her back into her normal, cynical self. "You're an asshole."

The dragon laughed, the sound moving through the air like a cool morning breeze that fogged up car mirrors. A puff of cold air swirled around him from the reaction and for a split second it almost looked like wings furling behind him. "And I see why he likes you."

"He likes-" Cyn shook her head and went back to frowning at him. "N-Never mind that, you're still an asshole."

Mira giggled but immediately stopped when Cyn glared at her.

"So we've bitten off more than we can chew, but abandoning this mission isn't something we can accept. Humans are stubborn like that," Alix added with his own grin. "Now how can we face that creature and get the girl's friend out of there?"

Both Fagan and Cyn gave Alix a look of surprise. Wasn't it him who insisted on leaving Dox behind? Now he wanted to save him? Fagan couldn't help but frown at Alix. His mind had to be on the Storyteller somehow.

The dragon stood silently, taking a moment to look over each of them as if sizing them up. The frost moving across his skin was now veins up and down his arms and chest, slowly creeping up his neck and over his cheeks. The cave around them was growing colder again and Cyn found herself shivering, clinging tightly to

Haven's borrowed shirt. The fire behind her had become a few struggling embers that hid under the remaining charred log.

I-lyan sighed and finally nodded his head. "You will be fighting two creatures aside from the one you know. The smaller ones are of no consequence in small numbers, but they will quickly multiply. They serve as his eyes, ears, and messengers over distance. The larger ones will look more like his son, though dead and lifeless. They'll move as quickly as shadows and attempt to pull you in. Everything that is a shadow will be your enemy because he will control all of it. You would do better if you have a source of light, which is where Eegil will assist you."

Mira nodded and pulled out her book, her ears perking up happily. "I can help with that, too!"

"Good for you," Cyn muttered, "You want a treat, little kitty?"

"I told you I'm not a cat!"

The dragon chuckled. He was really starting to like this Cyn girl. "You can't win against him," he said, going back to the original topic, "The only option you have is to make him think that you are not worth the effort. You may not be able to get his son away from him. When they're near each other he has complete control over him. He created him out of shadows and life ripped from another being, but he is still a shadow and only has as much will as his father allows him."

The group nodded, a sad frown crossing Cyn's face. She had known that to a certain extent, but she hadn't realized that it was that serious. Dox never said much about his father, just that he was dangerous and that if he ever came around to run.

"I assume we also have to worry about whatever the Storyteller is capable of," I-lyan said as he looked at Mira. "That is when you should cling to that book of yours."

"... right," she whispered. She wasn't looking forward to having to face her father but she had a feeling it would come to this. Who else could handle a Storyteller but his very own child? Fagan walked over and put a hand on her shoulder. "You might not have to fight him much. He was trying to fight it, so that should buy us some time."

Mira smiled up at him and nodded. "Thank you for telling me that."

"If I see that you are losing this battle and that Haven will be hurt I will leave with him. I gave my word that he would not be harmed. You're lucky I let him come back to this world at all."

"But..."

I-lyan's eyes narrowed. "This is not up for discussion, young Storyteller," he snapped at her, the Scough girl scampering back behind Cyn.

"Understood, thank you for your assistance," Alix said with a nod.

With those last words, the chill in the air faded, Haven's eyes sliding shut as he crumbled forward. Cyn moved before her brain could catch up with her feet, the girl shoving past Alix and running to Haven. She held her arms out and caught him, dropping to her knees and keeping a tight hold on him. The fire behind them exploded with a sudden heat, the crackling loud and echoing around them. The frost that had been covering Haven's skin melted around him, the cold wetness dripping from his skin and onto Cyn's arms as she held him. Soon, Haven opened his eyes, smiling a little as he whispered, "Nice catch."

"So two points, right? For being chivalrous?"

"That only works if you're male."

"Oh whatever, you sexist prick! I'm making it three points since I had to catch you. Four because you got my clothes wet after I had managed to dry off from the rain outside."

"Wet?" Haven looked down and made a disgusted face as he realized his skin was dripping wet from the remnants of the frost that had covered his body. He stood up, stepped closer to the fire, and redid the tie in his hair to keep his braids from dripping water into his eyes.

Cyn followed him and handed him back the shirt he had loaned her earlier. "You might actually need this now."

"I suppose I was the one who said that I wouldn't, huh?"

"To be fair no one expected your dragon to melt all over you."

Haven chuckled, then he winced for a moment. Apparently his dragon didn't find Cyn's comment at all funny. "Keep it, I'll be fine."

Cyn nodded and turned to face the others. "So... what's the plan now?"

"Sleep. We leave at sunrise."

Alix frowned at Fagan and the man didn't have to say a word for Fagan to know he wanted to leave now. The silent argument between the two stretched out for a couple minutes before Alix finally turned away and pushed past Fagan, stepping away from the group. The worst part was that Alix knew Fagan was right. They wouldn't stand a chance if they went in right now.

"Are all humans so angry?" Amari asked, watching as the two Hunters walked off.

"No," Cyn said, "Just the French ones."

"French?" Mira asked.

"Never mind. I think Fagan has the right idea, it would be nice to get some rest," Cyn said.

"Then we best take our leave." Saraisai walked over the Mira and smiled, a rare occurrence for the old Scough. "You be careful, o.k.? We'll do what we can back home, but it won't be much. He's always watchin'."

Mira nodded. "I'll be careful. Thank you."

Both Amari and Lyree nodded to the girl, smiling before they stepped out of the cave. Saraisai let out an annoyed sound as soon as the rain hit his fur and Mira giggled, watching as Amari made some comment about his age before he took off running, the elder Scough growling and chasing after him with Lyree in tow.

Haven walked to the edge of the cave and closed his eyes. "I'll seal the entrance. If something attacks we'll at least have some warning." It only took a moment for ice crystals to form around the entrance, lining the edges and connecting like light blue webs until a thick wall started to form. The wall closed off the cave save for a small sliver at the top so the smoke from the fire could still escape.

"So we leave tomorrow?" Mira whispered, watching as wild drops of rain splattered against the ice.

"Sounds like it," then Haven smiled, lightly tugging on her ear. "Don't look so worried, it isn't like you."

"H-hey!" She batted his hand away, smiling. "Don't do that!"

"It got you to smile, at least... it doesn't look right when you look so serious," Cyn spoke softly, not willing to make such an admission out loud.

"Awwwww! That means you do care!"

"Wha-ACK!" Cyn's eyes widened when she felt the girl wrap her arms around her. "Let go! Right now! I swear I'll kill you!"

Haven tried very hard not to laugh at the two, but he couldn't keep the smile off of his face.

———————◆◆◆———————

"I'm sorry, Ms. DeBenit."

"Sorry? What do you mean?"

"Your child, she…"

"Yes?"

"I'm sorry… she didn't make it."

"W-what?"

"She didn't-"

The laugh was so sudden and loud that Alixandre didn't even know where it had come from. As it echoed around the hospital room she soon realized that it had originated from her own mouth. "Didn't make it? You mean she's dead."

"It… you had a miscarriage. I'm-"

She laughed harder, the sound cruel to her own ears as she began shaking, tears stinging her eyes. "Sorry? Of course you were going to say that. You're required to say that to all of your patients. Tell me, doctor, how many babies have you seen die? How many times have you actually meant what you said?"

Her voice was cold, completely cutting off any kindhearted reply the man could attempt to give, but he still wanted to try. "Is there someone I could call for you?" He asked softly.

"Sure there is. You could call my fiancé. He works over at YH Tech, you know, that destroyed lab that burned so badly that it melted?"

The doctor winced. "I see," he spoke softer. It didn't take much to figure out what happened to her fiancé. "Is there anything-"

"No," she said through the sobs that suddenly tore past her throat. "Just leave me alone."

"Alix."

Alix looked up from where he was sitting on the cold ground, away from the rest of the group toward the very back edge of the cave. The ring was clutched in his hand, his eyes looking tired and worn out as he looked up at his partner.

Fagan sat next to him, frowning softly, "Alixandre-"

"Don't." He had meant for it to sound harsher but it sounded so small, so exhausted.

Fagan sighed and wrapped a large arm around his shoulders, pulling him close. "Just shut up for a moment."

"Fagan, I said-"

"No," and in seconds Fagan was holding him. "Just breathe, Alixandre."

What Alix wanted to do was shove the man away, tell him that they were leaving right now, goddamnit. He wanted to snap at him, tell him that he refused to stay in this dreadful world for longer than he had to. He wanted to finish off that hideous Lurkhamara, save Dox – if he absolutely had to – and get the secrets he needed from Mira's father.

Instead, Alix closed his eyes and rested his head against Fagan's shoulder. Instead, Alixandre DeBenit clung to Fagan's shirt and whispered, "If you tell anyone I did this, I'll shoot you before you can even reach that sword of yours."

Fagan smiled, the man running his fingers through her hair. "Of course," he whispered, selfishly enjoying this rare side of Alix that no one but him had ever seen.

"Fagan?"

"Yeah?"

"… I'm sorry about Xaver," she said as she curled closer to him. It was a rather sudden thing to say, but something they both realized should have been said much sooner.

"Yeah," he whispered back, holding her a bit tighter than he meant to, "Me too."

"Have you thought about… asking the Storyteller to…"

"Bring him back?" Fagan chuckled.

"He can rewrite things. He can-"

"I know. And no, I haven't thought of asking for that."

"Why?"

Fagan glanced up at the ceiling of the cave and shook his head. "Xaver wouldn't want that. He'd want us to move forward."

"… is that what you think I should do?"

"That's completely different, Alixandre. I'm leaving that up to you. Xaver would, too."

"Yes, but-"

"Don't worry about it," Fagan said, closing his eyes. "We have a war to stop in the morning, get some rest."

"Right…" she whispered, closing her eyes. "Goodnight, Fagan."

Fagan didn't respond, opening his eyes to look down at the woman in his arms. She drifted off to sleep easily enough, lightly snoring against his chest. He sighed and glanced up at the cave ceiling again, letting her even breaths help him relax.

He never did say goodnight.

He had a feeling that he would never want to.

———————◆◆◆———————

"Can't sleep?"

Cyn looked up at Haven from where she was sitting, her knees pulled up to her chest with her arms wrapped around them. "I don't ever sleep much. Nightmares, all that jazz."

"Ah." Haven took a seat next to her. "The first time you owe me for."

"You know that whole thing is getting kind of old," Cyn spoke softly as she stood up, walking over to add a few more twigs to the fire. "I think we should call it a draw."

"A draw is unacceptable. I was taught to win. This can't be over until there's a winner."

"Fine. You win. What was it, a kiss or something?" Cyn walked back over to him, knelt down in front of him, and actually slammed him back against the wall. "That was the prize, right?"

Haven wasn't intimidated by the sudden angry look in Cyn's eyes. Instead he frowned sadly and whispered, "How worried are you about all of this?"

"Excuse me?"

"You're worried. And scared. Your close friend is gone, and Alix said all that stuff-"

"I don't need a play by play I know what happened," she snapped, "and you've got it all wrong."

Haven sighed, "It's the same way he use to act."

"Who?"

"Xaver. When he was worried or upset about something he'd act angry to cover it. And he was always angry before a hunt."

Cyn frowned and slowly let Haven go. "I... a lot has happened in the past couple of hours, I'm just tired."

"Tired. Yep. He'd use that one, too."

"Damnit, stop comparing me to other people!"

"Stop acting like him then." Haven flashed an impish smile at her.

"What are you, five?"

Haven blinked. "Five? No, I'm-"

"Just forget it. I-I'm fucking worried, o.k.?" Cyn moved to sit next to him, not looking happy about admitting her feelings.

"Well at least you admit things faster than he did."

Cyn watched Haven quietly for a moment. She watched as his eyes stayed focused on the floor, his fingers trembling a little as he talked with her about Xaver. "No one's said it to you, have they?"

Haven blinked and looked up at her. "Said what?"

"Sorry for your loss. That's what people are supposed to say when you lose someone."

Haven frowned and looked away from Cyn, trying to ignore the sudden tight feeling in his chest. "It's not like any of you guys know me personally like that, except for Mira. Fagan tried to say it before, back when they brought me to the warehouse so… i-it's been said, kinda."

"Still… I mean, you know… I'm sorry. You two were close, right?"

"We, I-I mean yeah but-" then Haven stopped and frowned at her. "You know, he did *that* too. He would always try to change the subject and-"

"O.K. you know what? I was trying to be genuinely nice but forget it!"

Haven smiled, happy to have the subject off of Xaver and back to something easier to deal with. "I know. And so am I. You don't have to be angry and yell all the time around me. You can take a minute and be scared."

"… just a minute, right?"

Haven nodded and slid closer, wrapping an arm around Cyn's shoulders. "And not a second longer," he whispered to her.

The minute was spent with Cyn resting her head on Haven's shoulder, whispering about being scared, about being worried about Dox, about not thinking they could save him, about not wanting to be alone. Haven let her get it all out, his hand gently rubbing her arm, listening to her until she finally felt comfortable enough to stop. "That was a minute, right?" Cyn asked.

"I believe so," but neither had a way to tell time, "Why? Did you want to keep going?"

"Just a few more seconds." Then she frowned, "Alix is an asshole."

Haven laughed and held Cyn a bit closer. "He is. You told the Scough it was because he's French?"

"I was just being nice so I wouldn't give them the wrong idea. Studies actually show that most humans are, indeed, assholes."

Both of them were chuckling now, the mood shifting into something warmer, friendlier. This was the same feeling they felt when they were up on the roof, talking and starting that ridiculous point system. "So are we really ending our little game?" Haven asked.

"Hell no. Besides, we're tied aren't we?"

"I think we should lay out some actual rules."

"Later," she said as she leaned forward and gently pressed her lips against his.

Haven stared at her with wide eyes, too surprised to react as he got lost in the feeling of warm lips and a lingering taste of the rain from outside. The crackle of the fire, the beating of the raindrops against the thick sheet of ice, it all faded away for Haven as the two shared the sweetest of kisses. Cyn's lips were surprisingly soft despite her prickly exterior, sweet like the rich chocolate chips of the cookies that he had tried once, back when they had first met Mira and Xaver exploited her door opening skills into grocery stores.

His first real kiss was over much too quickly, Cyn pulling back with an uncharacteristically cute smile on her face. "You win this time."

"I... o-oh," he cleared his throat, glancing away from her as his cheeks felt warm. "Um... y-yeah..."

"You're stuttering."

"I am not!"

Cyn laughed, a playful look on her face. "Are too."

"Am not!"

"Are too!"

"What are you, five?!"

Cyn blinked, then blinked again, then she started laughing, "So you do understand that insult?"

"I get the jist of it," he muttered.

"Haven…" Both Cyn and Haven turned to see Mira walking over to them, rubbing her eyes and yawning. The Scough girl pouted at them and said, "I'm sleepy." At her side stood her fox companion, the creature opening her mouth and letting out a small yawn.

"Then go to sleep," Cyn said. "It's not that hard of a concept."

"I didn't want to interrupt you two."

"Huh?"

Haven smiled a bit. "Mira sleeps with me."

"What?!" Cyn glared at Mira then at Haven. "You two are sleeping together?!"

"Yes, is that a problem?" Mira asked.

"I just kissed him, you're damn right it's a problem!"

Both Haven and Mira stared at Cyn, boggled at her outburst. After a moment Haven connected the dots and started laughing. "It's nothing sexual, we actually sleep next to each other." And now he suddenly realized why Xaver had reacted the way he did when Mira had brought it up that one time.

Mira tilted her head, her tail wagging curiously behind her. "Sexual? It's just sleeping, does 'sleep with' mean something else in the human world?"

Cyn opened her mouth to protest but stopped, remembering the Scough they'd seen curled up in the nest. Oh, so that's what Mira meant. She could feel her cheeks turning red with embarrassment and quickly looked away from the two before they noticed. "Forget it. Go to sleep."

"You can join us. The more people sleeping in the group the better I sleep," Mira said, already curling up against Haven as he laid down. Zee curled up above Mira's head, the girl using the side of the fox's body like a pillow. From Cyn's experience, most animals would be annoyed, but Zee seemed content to have her so close.

"Good to know..." and Cyn laid on the other side of Haven, her back to him and her arms crossed at her chest, a permanent frown on her face.

"You're kinda cute when you're jealous," Haven said with a chuckle.

"Fuck off."

Chapter 8

The sleeping arrangements had somehow changed overnight.

Cyn woke up to arms tightly wrapped around her from behind. Something was nuzzling the back of her neck and when she glanced behind her she could recognize Mira's thick hair resting against her shoulder. Zee was nowhere around them. The fox had moved to the ice wall, sitting in front of it and watching, waiting. Was she guarding them? Cyn supposed that made sense. It was obvious that the fox and Mira were close and animals could be rather protective when it came to their caretakers.

Haven had moved from sleeping with both girls to being curled up on the ground in front of them, protecting them from whatever lay beyond the ice wall. The way Haven slept now reminded Cyn of the cat that used to sleep at the foot of her bed when she was much, much younger. The fluffy gentleman cat, Mr. Pots, was what she had called him. The feline was always content to sit with her dolls and bears as she danced around her room in frilly dresses.

A shudder ran through Cyn's body as the sound of her childish humming echoed through her ears. Why was she thinking of *that* time, all of a sudden?

Cyn somehow managed to squirm out of Mira's arms. Her back made a terrible sound when she stood up and stretched, a not so gentle reminder that she had been sleeping on a cold cave floor. The still sleeping Mira started whining and reached for someone to hold onto. Cyn knelt down and watched, a bit fascinated from the small yips that left the girl's mouth. Was she really having trouble sleeping because no one was sleeping next to her now?

"They sleep in packs. She told you that."

Cyn looked over, surprised to see that Haven's eyes were watching her with a steely, cold stare. "Good morning to you, too. Do you always sleep like that?"

"It is no concern of yours as to how I sleep," the dragon said as he sat up, still frowning at her.

"I take it from the eyes and piss poor attitude that I'm not talking to Haven right now."

"I do not have a poor attitude," then he smirked at her, "Besides, I thought that was a quality you could appreciate."

"Haven't you heard? I don't have a poor attitude, it's called being goth."

"And what is this *Goth* you speak of?" His voice almost sounded like he was mocking her, but she couldn't be sure.

"It's a phase you go through when you realize your father put a demon inside of you."

"Is that so?"

"It is for me," Cyn said, moving to sit next to the dragon and leaving Mira to curl up against the cave wall. The area around Haven was cold, just like last time, wisps of cold air brushing against Cyn's arms. "It's my own personal protest. If the bastard ever sees me again he won't recognize his 'precious little girl'."

"I see," I-lyan said with a nod.

"So what's your story? How did Haven become your master? Someone as old as you, what made a kid so interesting that you decided to attach yourself to him?"

"So you do know a bit about demons after all."

"Scattered bits from my father, other parts from Do-... my friend. Mostly it's just me being observant. The way you spoke to us and the way you carry yourself, you definitely have a lot of knowledge and have been around for a long time. You also said that you gave your word about him being protected, which makes it sound like you're doing this for someone else. So I guess the real question is-"

I-lyan smiled and leaned forward to whisper into Cyn's ear, "Perhaps another time, we have other things to worry about."

The cold tickling her ear made the girl tremble for a short moment. She swore that she could feel lips touch the edge of her ear but the feeling was gone in an instant. Before Cyn could speak to I-lyan again Mira was sitting up, rubbing her eyes and pouting. "Why did you move?"

"Because I was awake," Cyn said with a frown as she crossed her arms at her chest. "I never said you could snuggle against me while you slept."

"But you're comfy!" Mira pouted at Cyn, then she turned her attention to Zee when she noticed her at the front of the cave. "You moved, too?"

Zee trotted back over to Mira, nuzzling her head in her lap. Mira smiled and scratched behind her ear, enjoying the small yips the fox let out.

"Mira, we should be getting ready anyway."

Cyn turned to look at Haven, surprised to see the icy white gone from his eyes, the young man yawning in an attempt to wake up more. "What happened to I-lyan?" Cyn asked.

"My dragon?" Then Haven frowned, mentally whispering a soft *I wish you'd stop doing that.* Cyn could just imagine the dragon responding with a devious smile on his face.

Mira stood with a grumpy expression on her face from having to get up. Zee whined when she stopped petting her but stood obediently at her side. Cyn found herself chuckling, it was about time the happy girl stopped smiling, even if it were for a moment.

"Should we get Alix and Fagan?" Mira asked. "The sun will be up soon."

"Oh yes, *him*," Cyn grumbled. She still remembered their brief argument yesterday. If it weren't for Dox needing to be rescued Cyn would've loved to leave the pompous ass stranded in the world he hated so much. "I suppose we should."

"No need. We're already awake."

Both Fagan and Alix walked over to the others, Alix's annoying look of determination even fiercer than it had been yesterday.

"Mira and I will head out first. The rest of you will follow Alix and stay hidden. Move in when he says and only then. Our priority is to free the Red Dragon then we can focus on freeing your father. It's obvious that something is being done to keep him there, we can't risk the Storyteller being able to do more than just hold him hostage."

The group nodded, ready to go as Haven melted the ice wall covering the cave. Alix snuffed out the fire, kicking dirt over the embers as Fagan touched Mira's shoulder. "Can you see how close the Reina is? I want to know how much time we have."

Mira nodded and pulled out her book, opening it to a blank page. A collective breath was held as she touched the page and a picture formed. Rocky terrain traced across the bottom of the page with several Red Dragons standing before one on a platform. The woman on the platform was dressed like them in simple leather clothing with a collection of jewels covering her right arm from her wrist to her shoulder. Tight, small braids covered the right side of her head while the other side was a barely tamed mane of dark hair held back from her face by pointed and pierced ears. Even in the faint sketch, they could all make out the old scars crisscrossing her skin.

"It's hard to believe that she's in charge of all of them," Alix murmured, watching as Anasia addressed her guards in the silent picture, obviously giving them commands.

Mira blinked. "Why?"

"Just… she's a woman, and normally that's not how it goes."

Mira shook her head. "Maybe in the human world, but for the Red Dragons, she's their Reina. Only a woman can be the Reina and only she can watch over them. She watches over all of them like an old and powerful mother."

Cyn smirked. "That's kinda badass. Not in this case, I guess, since she could probably burn all of us alive."

Fagan looked over at Mira. "How long do we have until she makes her move?"

Mira watched as Anasia nodded to two dragons in the group, the two walking over and bowing down in front of her before they walked off, the other dragons staying behind. "It looks like it's just her and those two dragons heading toward our area. Why just three?"

"To scout out the area, the same way we did," Alix frowned. "She's smart."

"Which means we should hurry. If she gets here during the fight, she'll be able to handle herself. I'd like to live long enough to tell her we're on her side." Fagan couldn't help but notice the scars she had along her body. She hadn't bothered to cover any of them up, wearing them with the type of pride that rivaled Xaver and the scars he had collected over years of hunting. This was a leader who could handle herself and he had no doubt that if they didn't act fast, Mira's people would be completely wiped out.

"... what if... he uses-" Cyn stopped herself, not saying the name, "*Him* against us?"

"Our goal is to take out his father, save the Storyteller and Red Dragon... and save that creature's son, too, just like I said last night."

Cyn turned to look at Alix in surprise, staring at the man as he looked away from her, his eyes focused on the burnt twigs from the fire instead of the girl in front of him. Fagan offered Cyn a small smile and nodded to her. "We don't plan on leaving without him. He helped us get here, we're going to help him get out."

"I... t-thank you. Both of you. But damn, I guess that means I can't hate you," she said to Alix.

"Not right now. Maybe later."

"Oh my, was that a joke?"

Alix shrugged his shoulders and walked over to the cave entrance. "You're right, you know."

"Huh? About what?" Cyn asked.

"It's too early to be doing anything right now," then he glanced over at her and Cyn swore she could see the slightest hint of a smile. The tension between them slowly faded and Cyn considered that maybe, just maybe, Alix had a reason for his terrible attitude and, perhaps underneath all that, he wasn't that bad of a guy.

At least for now. Cyn reserved the right to let her feelings change on the subject at a moment's notice.

—————◆◆◆—————

Much to Zee's dismay she was told to stay behind. "It's too dangerous," Mira said, kissing the top of her head. With a sad whine the fox watched the group leave, pacing back and forth in front of the cave until they disappeared from sight.

Mira and Fagan crossed the woods together, making their way back to the Scough camp. Mira led the way as Fagan stoically followed behind her. Instead of having Eegil strapped across his back, he'd adjusted the belt to sit securely around his waist in its normal form, making it quicker to reach. The two were expecting a fight and though Mira walked without a weapon, her ears were perked and her tail was stiff, listening to the woods and leaves around them.

This time they took a well beaten path which wove between larger clusters of empty nests. A small group of Scough children ran across the path in front of them and cheerfully welcomed Mira back. Mira smiled and took time to pet each of their heads. Despite the terrible battle that lay ahead Fagan found himself smiling, each child lovingly addressing Mira as "Mi-mi" and telling her how much they had missed her. Fagan noted that the children's clothing was made of a mixture of leather, fur, and the wires he'd seen around the captive the night before.

One of the Scough children became distracted and darted away from the group, chasing after a rabbit for a morning meal. The other two children followed after, but all three of the young ones came to a halt when another creature came from the bushes, pouncing on the rabbit and sinking its teeth into its neck.

"Hey, no fair!"

"Yeah we saw it first!"

"Takin scum!"

Fagan watched as the creature released the rabbit, growling at the Scough children. It was as small as the others, wearing the same leather and fur combination only it fit more like a dress. It had a wild, long head of hair, the dark brown locks reaching past the creature's backside. On either side of its forehead were the beginnings of horns that would, one day, fully emerge from its head. "Too bad," the *Takin scum* said. "I caught it, it's mine."

The children all growled together, baring their fangs as they approached the creature. Mira quickly walked over and stood in front of the lone child. "Enough, you three. The Takin are our friends."

Friends? Fagan made a mental note of there being more creatures in the area besides the Scough.

"But she took our meal!"

"Yeah!"

"We were going to share the rabbit with you, Mi-Mi."

Mira smiled and knelt down, petting each of the children again. "That is sweet of you, but I have some business to take care of. We can eat together later. As for the Takin, she caught it fair and square, o.k.?"

The Takin girl behind her stood up and moved forward, tugging at the end of Mira's dress. "I-I can share with the boys. They did start the chase, I wouldn't have caught it without them startling the rabbit."

Fagan walked over to join the group, nodding to the children. "That sounds like a good idea to me."

All of the children – including the Takin – stared up at Fagan. They had been so distracted with Mira that they hadn't paid too much attention to the man who had been walking with her.

"Who are you?"

"What are you?"

"Why are you so big?"

The Takin girl frowned, returning to all fours in a defensive stance. "He's a human, my father told me about them."

The children all turned and stared at Fagan, their eyes wide in wonder. Meanwhile, Fagan couldn't help but laugh. He never realized that being human was such a big deal.

"He is a friend," Mira giggled. "We have to take care of something back at the camp."

"Actually, I have a job for you kids, if you want to help."

Mira blinked. "A job for them?"

Each of the children nodded to Fagan. It was good to see that demon children were as eager as human ones to help adults, least at this age. "We think there might be a fight. We need you to tell the other creatures here to stay on guard, especially around shadows."

"Only up to the circle of trees where my father is. We're going to take care of that part. If you see that area getting too dark, make sure everyone stays away from it."

All of the children agreed eagerly as Mira and Fagan continued their walk into the camp, the children running around them and playing together. The Takin girl held onto the dead rabbit, occasionally making fun of the Scough boys for failing to catch it. Fagan kept his eyes on the few shadows around them, thankful that they remained still. To the living darkness around them, the children were simply playing.

Their presence was gaining looks, but not as many as he expected. A couple of the Scough would glance their way when they heard footsteps, then, when they noticed Mira, they went back to whatever they had been doing. Some of the Scough were carrying around the same weapons Saraisai and the others had, others letting the sharp sticks rest against the side of their nests. There was a thick tension in the air, the coming of a fight that Fagan could tell these creatures weren't ready for. Fagan noted the hesitation in their eyes, even as they watched him and Mira. Whatever Thierry had been telling them wasn't preparing them for battle, it was scaring them. Real warriors would've at least attempted to stop him and Mira – or at least him – but all of the Scough they passed seemed to be too nervous to try.

Fagan couldn't help but wonder what they thought of him. It couldn't be common for a human to be walking around like this, much less with one of their own kind. Perhaps his sword made them assume he was something else. He obviously didn't have a tail or ears, but he'd seen some very human looking demons before – Haven being a recent example save for when his dragon took over. Perhaps they just assumed he was one of them.

Or maybe they thought Mira had captured him. There was the Red Dragon, after all.

The children were good at the job Fagan had appointed them with. Every time they passed one of the other Scough, one would break away from the group, giggling and running around one of the older demons. They'd scamper around with their childlike innocence, whispering their secret to each of them. *Mi-Mi says to stay here* and *stay away from the circle of trees.*

As the two came closer to the trees Mira couldn't help herself. Quickening her steps, she practically pounced Thierry as soon as she saw him, nuzzling into his shoulder as he looked at her in surprise. The Red Dragon sat at his feet, just as he had before, his eyes looking around the area and watching the shadows. It was foolish for the girl to be here, let alone with a human, the dragon frowning up at Fagan in an attempt to get that point across. The Hunter simply shook his head, trying to ease the Red Dragon's concerns.

It wouldn't be long now, he was sure.

In the morning light, Fagan could see that Thierry looked as if he hadn't slept in days. No matter how tired the Storyteller was he couldn't help the small smile on his face as he embraced his daughter. Thierry looked like he was struggling between being concerned about Mira being there or being happy to hold her in his arms again.

After another minute he settled on being concerned. "Mira? Why are you back here?"

"I came back to see you, with help from the other world." She smiled brightly at him, the words so simple coming from her mouth.

The captive dragon stared at Mira, quickly looking around at the shadows and tugging at the restraints around his wrists. Fagan could see the creature was trying to talk but no words escaped his lips, just like the other night. The Hunter knew that if he himself didn't know that this was part of their plan he would have called the girl foolish. The way she had said it sounded so natural, the naivety easily slipping from her lips. It made him wonder if she was really that innocent. She had certainly seemed clueless when she met them, but when he took a moment to think about the bigger picture, she *did* manage to get all of them to help her.

That cute smile of hers she had originally greeted them with suddenly felt incredibly deceptive.

Thierry frowned, let go of his daughter, and looked at both of them. "You need to go. Now."

"I brought help, father. It will be fine."

Thierry looked at Fagan, ready to insist that he leave once more, then his eyes widened. "Eegil?"

"So you recognize it," Fagan said, smirking a bit as he placed his hand on the hilt.

"Of course I recognize Eegil, but even his services won't be enough."

There was no time to say anything else as the air around them began to grow darker. Fagan frowned and gave a small nod toward the trees. He wasn't sure if Alix and the others had arrived yet, all he could do was rely on years of working with his partner to know that he was there, quietly watching with Haven and Cyn.

The first shadow moved fast, shooting out from the tree trunk behind Fagan like a well-placed sniper shot. The Hunter felt a surge of power from his sword as a warning and managed to step to the side just in time, the shadow creating a deadly string to the tree in front of him, past Thierry's side. Mira immediately took a guarded stance in front of her father and the Red Dragon, her bag flung to the side and her book in her arms.

"Be careful with that book," her father said. "Remember what happened with it last time, back in their world."

Mira nodded and Fagan frowned. He shouldn't have been surprised that Thierry somehow knew what had been going on with Mira after she had left this world, but it was still taking some getting used to, dealing with people who knew things without needing to be there.

"It's all right, father. We have a plan."

Fagan's response after that was more ingrained than anything else. Pulling the sword from its sheath, he spun around and cut directly into the string of shadows and a handful of others that shot toward him. Years of practice and comfort with Eegil helped him block and slice through the shadows at a speed few could rival. Behind him, Mira threw her book open, a protective wall of loose pages flying around her, her father, and the captive dragon. The shadows around them began to move and twist, a couple darting into the wall of paper and trying to pierce it with sharp points. The sound echoed around them, like rocks being tossed against steel, showing that despite its frail appearance that wall wasn't going to break.

Fagan moved forward quickly and swung his sword at the shadows in front of the paper wall, Eegil slicing through them and eradicating each of them with ease. Once it was clear the wall crumbled away, both Fagan and Mira standing in front of the Storyteller and Red Dragon together.

Shadows shot out from around them, twisting and racing up the trees like small creatures scurrying away from a flame. They didn't disappear into the leaves, instead they grew bigger, their shapes flattening and spreading between the trees, adding to the darkness of the canopy around them. Sunlight faded all around them and Fagan's ability to see faded with it, the shadows shading the small circle of trees in a deep darkness.

Normally Fagan would have panicked as the world disappeared around him, but they had prepared for this. Fagan yelled the name "Eegil" and light erupted around them, throwing the shadows back as the dark stone of his sword bathed the circle of trees in a thick, blue light. Mira quickly wrote in her book, ignoring the dark edges that licked at the pages. The Lurkhamara had bested her with this trick before, but she wouldn't let it happen a second time. In seconds her book was surrounded by a film of light and a loud screech erupted from the pages, as if the shadows that tried to attack it were in physical pain. Slowly, the pitch black that Fagan was standing in melded into something visible, the shadows unable to make it any darker.

"How is the darkness fading?" The captive dragon blinked, his eyes widening when he realized that the words he spoke were loud and clear. "How am I...?"

Mira giggled and looked down at the dragon, smiling at him.

Fagan wasn't sure what Mira had written down. As the power surge from his sword died he found he could still see just as she said he'd be able to. The darkness was still there but he could see well enough to not stumble over his own feet when he took a step forward. Fagan struggled to not raise his sword as he watched the shadows ripple at the edges around them. Darkness seeped into those edges and eyes began to form just like the night before, all watching and waiting for something larger.

Something more powerful.

And then, finally, there he was.

Across from them, Fagan could see the wall of shadows twist and blow out like a bubble. The darkness in that area popped with power and a tall figure moved into sight. The creature was so thin that it almost looked two dimensional, standing at least two feet higher than Fagan himself. It had long, spiny arms that were the length of its entire body, if not longer. It moved slowly, the pale, gray skin barely clinging to its bones in an emaciated style that made it look like it had never eaten in its life. Unlike Dox, this thing had real eyes rather than endless black holes.

Fagan recognized the long, spiny hand as the one that had grasped Thierry on the shoulder before. It was obvious that this was the Lurkhamara, the creature they were looking for. Fagan held his breath, waiting until the thing moved closer to them before he moved his sword with perfect accuracy, stopping it right at the creature's throat.

The Lurkhamara chuckled softly and his voice unnerved Fagan. Creatures like this were supposed to have deep, sinister voices, but the Lurkhamara sounded too young, too friendly. It reminded Fagan of Dox, especially when he would calmly speak to Cyn. "I see your daughter has brought protectors," he said to Thierry, not even bothering to address Fagan.

"My father won't be listening to you anymore and neither will anyone here. You need to leave." Mira added an angry, animalistic hiss at the end of her words, glaring at the Lurkhamara and bearing her teeth.

"I have no intention of letting the Storyteller go."

Thierry's eyes widened and he suddenly cried out, stumbling away from Mira as he clutched the side of his head. Mira reached for him but her father shoved her away, shaking his head as he screamed, "D-don't! Don't come near me!" Strings of shadows twisted around him, pulling him back tightly enough to cut into his skin.

"Father!"

The Lurkhamara laughed, the image of Thierry melting into the darkness. Fagan stared as words bled off of the Storyteller's skin, becoming lost in the shadows. His ears and tail dissolved away until there was nothing left, the Lurkhamara letting out a dreadful and deep laugh. His voice no longer sounded like a child, the laughter cold and all too familiar.

"F-father?"

"Interesting," the Lurkhamara whispered, his voice perfectly mirroring Thierry's. His hand wasn't as long as it had been, taking on more of an actual shape, a structure, like Thierry had had before. "He's not a Scough at all."

"What?" Fagan looked over at Mira in question, "What does he mean by that?"

"The Storyteller..."

"Is a shapeless creature," Yvonne growled as he stood up next to them. "He was only hiding among the Scough."

"It was the first creature he saw when he left that place."

"The library," Fagan whispered in realization, remember the things Alix had learned about the creature. "He wasn't supposed to leave, was he?"

"No. And this is why," Mira said sadly.

The three watched as the shadows moved behind the creature, showing the unconscious forms of Jahren, Saraisai, Amari, and Lyree. Mira stared at each of them, crying out their names. Fagan settled on frowning, now realizing why they hadn't seen those three that morning. They were now the Lurkhamara's hostages, just like Dox.

"And these were your best attempts against me," the Lurkhamara said as he smirked at Fagan, "These pathetic Scough, a captured Red Dragon, a human, and a child? You'll have to do better than that."

"Gladly."

Fagan wasn't surprised when Alix broke cover. He was counting on it, watching the surprise on the Lurkhamara's face as Alix moved toward him. Alix was moving before he stopped speaking, aiming his gun and firing nearly point blank at the creature. There was a loud sound in the darkness and Fagan and the others barely had a chance to shield their eyes as light exploded around them, the thick shadows actually cracking and starting to shatter.

Fagan really wanted to read over what Mira had written down, she was getting more creative by the second.

That gunshot started the battle immediately. Mira moved back from the shadows while Cyn and Haven ran over to them.

Alix was standing next to the Red Dragon in a second, pulling a knife from his belt and cutting at the tangled cords around his wrists. "I take it those long claws aren't just a fashion statement and you can fight?"

Yvonne nodded, flexing his claws as he let Alix cut away the wires. A small flame appeared in his palm, dancing across his fingers as he smirked. "You have my assistance."

The Lurkhamara was glaring at them, its arm extending out as shadows leaked from its fingers and dripped onto the ground. Instead of speaking a command, the words *attack* and *destroy* appeared over the darkness as loud screeches began to pierce through the air. The small, round creatures were quickly scurrying after the group like rabid parasites. None of them had eyes to see, instead they were made of toxic shadows that killed the plant life and land they touched. As they got closer Fagan could see that a few of them had large holes that served as mouths, sharp teeth dangling and ready to strike.

"Alix, backup! Now!"

"Allow me." Yvonne smirked, stepped past Fagan, and pushed his hand out. What was once a small flame at his fingertips surged forward, bursting in a wave of yellow and red flames. The strange shadowy creatures wailed in protest, their bodies instantly melting from the heat.

Alix moved next, standing next to the dragon and firing at another group of the dark creatures. The bullet pierced into the shadows before erupting into rays of light, shadow bits and pieces flying into the air like a grotesque spray of blood.

"You seem to be quite the warrior yourself. Alix, was it?"

"Yeah. We can save proper introductions for later," then he nodded to Fagan, "We should let the dragon attack from back here, we'll get anything that he misses."

Yvonne chuckled. "Miss? I don't miss," and to demonstrate he sent another hot flash of fire after the tiny creatures.

"Good to know," Alix said, quickly firing at a stray shadow that had escaped the pack, "But just in case," then he smiled sweetly at the Red Dragon.

Fagan chuckled when he saw the look on the dragon's face. "Don't worry, it annoys me when he does that, too."

On the other side of the battle Cyn and Haven stood in front of Mira, each of them carefully watching the area around them. Just ahead of them Dox appeared with two tall and thin shadows, their bodies looking like they hadn't been completely formed. The deep pits of Dox's eyes swirled with warped shadows, wide and shallow as he looked at the others.

One of the shadows next to him only had one eye, the other side of its face a solid wall of black. Its mouth was long and remained open, its jaw hanging loose with two thin strings of shadows. The other shadow looked normal – if such a word existed for these things. It, at least, had both of its eyes and its mouth was actually closed. One of its arms, however, pulsated and bubbled like a pot of thick soup as the words *sharp* and *blade* appeared within the shadows. Its arm erupted and split in half, the shadows tying together at the end to create the sharpest weapon that Haven had ever seen.

Mira quickly looked down at her book and spoke the word, "Lurai," to identify the creatures. Haven nodded after receiving a confirming hiss from his dragon.

Cyn didn't care about the creatures, all of her attention focused on Dox as he watched her. He opened his mouth, trying to speak but words slid over his lips, creating lines over his mouth like stitches. *Silence* and *obey*. He managed to let out one soft wail of Cyn's name before his mouth was forced closed. She considered shouting at Dox, maybe having one of those emotional moments of trying to reach her friend with desperate pleas of *remember me* or shouts of *snap out of it!* She never got the chance to act on those urges as Dox extended a hand out, pointing at the group. The Lurai both nodded to their master and soon one was rushing forward, swinging its sharp blade right at Cyn's head.

Haven moved quickly, a thick sheet of ice wrapping around his arm as he knocked Cyn out of the way and blocked the Lurai's blade. The sharp metal collided with the ice, the blade clanking up against it before Haven shoved the creature away from him. "As much as I love saving you, I'd prefer it if you didn't get yourself killed." In seconds ice blades were forming in the air around him, both blades spinning before one quickly shot out and pinned the creature to the tree by its shoulder to keep it still. The Lurai let out a cry of protest, trying to pull free as ice began wrapping around the old tree bark to keep it in place.

Haven's second ice blade shot after Dox and the second Lurai, catching Dox in his arm and slicing through it as the second creature melted out of the way. There was a large gap in Dox's dark skin, but the shadows slid over the hole, mending it back together with the word *heal*.

Cyn looked at Haven in surprise for a moment, realizing just how close one of those shadow blades came to slicing her in half. "Thanks," she whispered as she turned to face Dox. The Lurai with the single eye appeared next to her friend, hissing at her.

"Look, I know it must be hard since Dox is-"

"Don't worry about it," then Cyn knelt down on the ground, pressing her hands against the dirt. "Just cover me."

Haven wasn't sure what the girl had planned, but he decided to go along with it. Cyn certainly sounded determined enough. He faced both Dox and the Lurai, nodding. "This better be good, Cyn."

"Oh trust me, you'll be impressed."

"How many points is this going to be worth?"

"Enough to get you to shut the hell up," then she closed her eyes, trusting Haven to cover her.

The words that had stitched Dox's mouth shut shifted and freed his lips, the letters scattering to create new words. *Hurt. Break. Shatter.* The words slid into his mouth before a smirk spread across Dox's face. "What are you trying to do, Cynthia?" He chuckled as he crossed his arms at his chest. "Are you really going to fight me?"

"As you can see, Haven is doing that for me." She opened her eyes to glare at Dox, "And don't call me Cynthia."

Dox waved his hand in the air, the second Lurai rushing forward like a wave of dark liquid. "Haven is going to be busy, it'll give us a chance to talk."

Ice shot down Haven's arm, extending out of the palm of his hand into a solid, ice blue sword. He sliced into the Lurai, cutting it in half, the two halves of shadows falling to the ground with a thick splatter. Haven took a moment to look over at Cyn and asked, "Did he just call you Cynthia?"

"Shut. Up."

"Little Cynthia Maddson, dressed in frills with cute, blonde pigtails." The shadows pooled out around Dox's feet, forming scattered lines that began to connect together along the ground.

Pictures. They were sketching a picture in the same way Mira's book did so many times before. A little girl, smiling brightly, hair pulled back into tight pigtails that bounced against her shoulders when she moved.

Cyn closed her eyes again, whispering a soft, "I said shut up," as she tried to feel for the roots and plants beneath her feet. Taking a deep breath and forcing herself to concentrate, she clenched her hands together and willed the roots to move.

Nothing happened.

"Cynthia's father experimented on her, put a demon inside of her, but he was upset because she wasn't using her new power."

Haven frowned, watching as the image on the ground changed. An operating table. Needles. Little Cynthia's arm filled with small holes like chicken pox. He started to move toward Dox but was forced to stop when shadows came up and wrapped around his legs. Below his feet he could see a dark puddle, a single eye pulsing out to reveal the second Lurai he had thought he gotten rid of. The shadows that held him worked like quicksand, the more he struggled the more he sank into the darkness. "C-Cyn! Cyn concentrate!"

Words slid over Haven's legs now – *Sink sink sink* – and he felt himself being pulled into the darkness faster, his dragon growling in protest.

"Then Cynthia's father had a thought," Dox moved toward Cyn, now kneeling in front of the trembling girl. Eyes squeezed shut, she was gritting her teeth, trying to get the ground to listen. "What if... I pushed her?" Dox whispered, his hand brushing against the side of Cyn's face.

Push. Push. The letters spread across her cheeks like shy little freckles.

"But how could I push her? What could I do to make her lose control?"

"Cyn!" Haven shouted at her, cold wisps of air starting to surround him. His hair slowly started to change, the dark strands freezing as his eyes flickered from blue to ice cold white. The shadows at his feet started to freeze over, cracking and creaking, close to being broken as the words stopped moving over his legs and froze in place.

"How did he decide to do it, Cynthia?" Dox asked, his fingers brushing through her hair as he leaned over and whispered in her ear. Haven wasn't sure what the dark shadow said, but whatever it was it made Cyn's eyes snap open. They were rounder, brighter, a sickly yellow that didn't look right. Haven swore that, for a second, he saw Dox smile and a strange thought crossed his mind.

Had he been trying to set her off on purpose?

"Damnit move!" Cyn yelled as loud as she could, forcing the frustration and anger she felt through her body to gather at her hands. The words on her skin *push, push* changed shape, grew larger and more hateful. *ANGER! RAGE!* The words were moving down her neck, flowing over her arms like living tattoos. *Little Cynthia Maddson* and *frilly dresses and blonde pigtails.* The name swirled around her mind, fresh images of her childhood that led to a cold laboratory in the basement, her young body strapped to a table. *Injection. Injection.* So many injections. So tired, *"So tired, daddy,"* and his comforting smile, *"Relax, Cynthia,"* before another round of injections.

Sharp. Painful. "Daddy stop, stop it!" Then, *"Shhhh,"* and a gentle kiss to her forehead, *"Just relax,"* before another series of injections.

Dox's question lingered in the back of her mind. *"How did he decide to do it?"*

Her eyes widened, pupils getting smaller and less human by the second. *"How did he decide to do it?"*

Haven could do nothing but watch as the image across the ground changed again. After midnight, sleeping in her bed, dressed in a pink nightgown.

"How did he decide to do it?"

She was the picture perfect image of the sweet, innocent girl, except for the needle marks scattered down her arm. She had stopped going to school a while ago, taken out after the first series of experiments, leaving behind friends like Suzie Anderson and Lindsey Carmichael. They used to come to the house, used to ask if she could come outside, but she always felt so weak after all of those tests that her father would tell them no.

"How did he do it?"

Isolated, kept in her bedroom with her toys and gentlemanly cat. Said fluffy kitty slept above her head every night, curled up and purring against her blonde hair.

"How did he-"

Her bedroom door creaked open as a man silently slipped into her bedroom. Pink walls and stuffed animals watched as he approached her bed, slowly pulling back her covers, his eyes lingering.

The sound that came out of Cyn's mouth wasn't the same voice Haven had gotten used to. This was something raw, powerful, a throaty noise that echoed around them. Her thin arms suddenly looked like they were made of scales instead of human flesh, her fingers melding together to create two large, flat hands that stayed firmly pressed to the ground.

In the corner of his eye Haven could see Mira watching. "Do something! Help me get out of the shadows so I can help her!" He screamed.

Mira looked down at her book, her eyes widening for a moment before she shook her head. "No."

"Damnit Mira!" Haven struggled, the ice starting to break as he began to slowly pull himself free. "Stop with the book and-"

"Wait."

"Are you kidding?!" There was no way he was going to watch Cyn suffer like this.

"I said wait!" The words came out like a harsh command, something Haven wasn't used to hearing from Mira. Her voice hit him like a physical punch, keeping him in place and not allowing him to move.

In seconds the ground beneath Haven's feet rumbled, the frozen bits of shadow breaking enough to let him loose. Up ahead he could see Fagan, Alix, and the Lurkhamara stopping their battle, each one looking confused from the sudden earthquake that rocked the area.

For a moment Haven thought it was coming from Mira, but she stood still, her eyes on...

... was she watching Cyn?

Was all of this coming from Cyn?

Little Cynthia Maddson imagined the power inside of her. She willed it to gather and move through the earth beneath her. She pictured a scene from one of her favorite childhood movies, remembered the fantasy world where spells were shouted in the middle of intense battles. She put herself in the wizard's shoes, made up some fancy spell in her head where pure magic could be welled up in her hands before she let loose a stream of power. In the movie, the magic had ripped over the ground in plastic blue CGI waves complete with lightning and thunder sound effects. But this wasn't a cheap effect added by some computer savvy geek who sat in front of an expensive machine. This wasn't something created for a movie studio, lines digitally placed into the scene to represent thick waves of power. This was something real, something Cyn could taste at the tip of her tongue, a slow smirk crossing her lips.

Power, like thick, mud filled water, flowed over her body and into the packed dirt beneath her. Nothing happened for a second, then there was a high pitched squeal like the old wooden floor in a hundred year old house. Suddenly, more whining filled the air and the dirt under her feet shuddered in protest. The trees around everyone started to shift, swaying around and creating an uncoordinated dance. The shadows around the trees tried to hold on, tried to keep them from moving, but soon cracks smeared across the thick sheet of black until the shadows shattered, falling to the ground to disappear into themselves. Sunlight shot through the darkness, illuminating everything around them as the barrier of shadows was broken.

The sudden wave of sunlight forced everyone to shield their eyes. The Lurai that had been pinned to the tree by Haven's ice blade started shaking its head, the light hitting its body. The creature's skin immediately started to burn away, crackling into ash that quietly fell to the sky. The single eyed Lurai who had been a puddle of shadowy gunk on the ground let out a harsh cry, its skin evaporating until nothing was left. The Lurkhamara quickly moved away from Fagan, Alix, and Yvonne, working to slip into the shadows. The light wouldn't kill him, not that easily. He'd lived for too long and had forced himself to adapt to the sunlight. However, standing in it for a long period of time would certainly hurt, even weaken him, and he couldn't afford any moment of weakness against these humans and the Red Dragon.

Dox remained where he was, wincing from the sunlight but he didn't move. Instead, he watched as Cyn slowly lifted her hands from the ground, the scales crumbling away from her skin as her hands reverted back to their previous appearance: small, and nails painted black. Suddenly, Cyn clutched onto her forehead, shaking as she started to scream. Haven winced, recognizing the sound from that very first night he had been brought to Fagan's warehouse, Cyn's painful cries slamming into him and urging him to help her. He moved quickly, kneeling in front of the girl and gently taking a hold of her hands. "Relax Cyn."

Just relax, Cynthia.

Cyn forced herself away from Haven, glaring at him as she growled, "Don't touch me! Don't fucking touch me!" The pounding of her head and the jumbled rush of memories made it hard to concentrate. She tried to tell herself to focus, tried to tell herself that this was a friend in front of her – *Haven, it's Haven* – but the image was blurry, the memories and powers of the demon inside of her knocking into her brain.

Just relax just one more injection little Cynthia Maddson. This wasn't a friend in front of her. This was her father, beard full and smile deceiving. This was the man who hurt her, the man holding that needle.

Cynthia, Cynthia.

Dox took quick steps toward Cyn, the sunlight still burning into his skin. Small hints of smoke lifted from his back like he was being set on fire, but he was desperate to get to his friend so he could try to do something. Suddenly his steps stopped, the whispers of his father still lingering and pulling at him. Behind the trees the tall shadow stood, watching Dox and moving his long fingers, urging him to turn and walk back toward him.

Alix turned quickly, aiming his gun at the shadows and walking toward them. "Come and fight us, coward," he said.

There was no response for a long moment but soon Dox was lunging forward, stumbling after Alix, the words *fight* and *kill* flowing over his skin like a written rush of water. His arm stretched out, shadows extending toward the Hunter in an attempt to grab him and swallow him whole. Fagan was on the move but to his surprise Yvonne jumped in front of Alix, claws at the ready to protect him. It turned out that neither one of them was needed as Mira dropped her book and raced forward, pouncing onto Dox's back so he landed on the ground. The Lurk twisted under her, turning to attack, but suddenly, he froze in place.

Focusing on his deep, black eyes, Mira whispered softly, her words not coming out in sounds but as actual green light in the air. The light moved, sliding through the air to rest on Dox's wrist, wrapping around it and forming words. *Release him.* Mira watched the words and slowly pulled back, kneeling next to Dox, waiting to see what happened.

The shadows that had rushed after Alix dropped away in large, messy clumps, pooling around the ground near the Hunter's feet. Alix slowly walked forward, his boots squishing into the unmoving shadows. "What did you just do?" He asked.

Mira looked up at him, confused. "I-I'm not sure."

"You're not sure?" Fagan asked. He kept his eyes on Dox, waiting to see what he would do.

"I just... I felt the need to do something."

"Let's get him out of the sunlight," Fagan said.

As Mira knelt down to grab her book her eyes widened when she saw a picture of both Dox and his father, his father resting his long fingers against his shoulders. Soon, the fingers were actually broken away, letting Dox walk off and ignore the things his father was trying to tell him to do. "I separated them," she whispered.

Dox looked up as soon as she spoke the words *separated them.* The change was immediately noticeable as he looked at everyone else. Now, instead of the bottomless caverns they were all so used to, they could make out the actual shape of eyes in a dark gray with deep, black irises. He sat up slowly, looking over his arms, marveling at the fact that he could move them on his own. "What... did you just say?"

"I separated you from him," Mira said again, her voice still soft as she looked down at her hands. It had felt so natural, as if she possessed the ability for her entire life. "You can still hear him, but you don't have to listen. S-since when could I-"

Her statement was interrupted as Cyn let out another loud scream. Dox quickly rushed to her side, stumbling as he continued to hear his father's insistent whispers. But Mira was right. He didn't feel the desperate need to listen anymore. The pull was gone.

Ignoring the hiss of the sunlight that hit him, Dox moved to Cyn's side. He could deal with the sunlight, all that mattered at the moment was helping Cyn.

"She won't listen," Haven said, a concerned look on his face. "I keep trying, but she won't respond."

"Cyn, listen to me. Look at me." Dox pressed his forehead against hers, his voice soft as he spoke to her. "It's me, Dox," then he added, "Haven is with me."

The girl kept shaking her head, trying to move away but Haven moved behind her. He wrapped his arms around her shoulders, his skin cold as he spoke to her. "Cyn please, listen to us."

Without warning a wave of darkness rushed after the group. Dox could hear his father chuckling lowly, a sinister sound that echoed in his mind as the wave grew larger. Alix raised his gun to fire at it but stopped, his eyes widening when he saw the Scough buried within the shadows. Alix took a step back, watching as an endless cycle of those small eyes appeared in the shadows around the Scough, blinking and watching them as small hands began to reach toward them.

Kill. Kill kill kill. The words were sharp and deadly, the shadows completely blocking out the sunlight. The sun didn't have much effect against the large wave, no signs of the shadows smoking or hissing from the light. It had to be because of Thierry, the words *light* and *harmless* moving through the black tides, completely protecting the large swarm the Lurkhamara was preparing for them.

Jahren, Saraisai, Amari, and Lyree each opened their eyes, one by one. Each set of eyes were completely blank as they began to speak the words out loud. "Kill. Kill kill kill," followed by the threatening laughter of Thierry somewhere in the background.

Fagan glanced over at Dox, "Can you stop it?"

"I can try…" but the uncertainty was clear in his voice.

Mira stood next to him and shouted, "Father please, stop it!" For a moment the shadows wavered. They could hear Thierry screaming, voice loud and piercing, but then the screaming stopped and dissolved into an unpleasant chuckle.

Mira clutched the book tightly to her chest. "I-I don't know what to do."

"There is nothing you can do, child," was the hissed response from the darkness, "That book won't save you now."

"Don't listen to him," Alix said, clutching onto his gun. "You've been helping this entire time, don't lose courage now."

Mira looked a bit surprised to be receiving a compliment from the Hunter, a small smile on her face as she nodded. "R-right! You can hit the shadows and not Jahren and the others, correct?"

Alix nodded, ignoring the constant chants from the trapped Scough. "They aren't the target, that thing is," then he aimed at the large column of shadows approaching. "Everyone ready?"

The Red Dragon nodded, fingers surrounded in soft flames that began to grow brighter. "Yvonne," he said to Alix. "I thought we should have some sort of introduction now, just in case."

"In case of what? Think we can't handle this?" Alix asked, smirking at Yvonne.

Yvonne smirked back. "I prefer to be cautious, but if we survive I'll make sure the second introduction is more proper."

Alix nodded but kept his eyes on the shadows and his gun at ready.

"This has got to be the stupidest thing you've gotten us into," Fagan said, keeping a steady grip on Eegil.

"Guess I win that bet, huh? About who's brought back the most dangerous thing?"

"That's not something to be proud of," but there was a small hint of a smile on Fagan's face. "You better make it out of this to tell Katalynne that you won, Alixandre." He ignored the fact that if they did survive, the Alix he knew would cease to exist.

Alix chose to ignore it as well. He even ignored the use of the name *Alixandre*, opting to nod his head at Fagan. "Deal," he whispered.

Haven frowned at the shadows, shifting so one of his arms was kept around Cyn's waist. She had at least stopped screaming but she couldn't stop shaking as she curled up close to Haven. Haven raised his other hand toward the large wave, watching as Alix went back to firing at it, Mira quickly scribbling words into the empty page of her book.

"Maybe I can separate my father from-" then Mira stopped writing, staring at the book as a picture was drawn on the pages before she could write anymore.

"Mira?" Fagan glanced over at her, frowning. "Why did you stop?"

"I…" but she couldn't find the words, all she could do was stare at the page before she turned her attention to the person the book had sketched out for her.

Haven.

Mira looked up from her book and over to her friend. Haven had his hand raised and was focusing on the wall of shadows. He knew he couldn't create a wall of ice to counter them quickly enough, but maybe he could stop the shadows. Maybe is dragon could freeze them…

Haven…

His dragon's voice was soft, too soft, and if Haven had been paying attention he might have noticed the scared tremble at the edge of it. Haven squeezed his eyes shut and closed his hand into a fist, shouting a command of, "STOP," willing the ice to cover the darkness and stop it from hurting the others. Seconds later, Haven opened his eyes, watching as the shadows stopped a few inches from Dox's body. But they weren't frozen. There wasn't a hint of ice anywhere, the shadows looking like an unmoving sculpture made of black tar.

"It… stopped?" Alix stared at the shadows, waiting for them to move toward them again. When nothing happened he looked at the others in question, but no one had an answer.

The shadows twisted, suddenly moving again, but none of them reached beyond Haven's hand to hurt the others. They just twisted and writhed, whispers coming from deep within the darkness, all speaking one word.

Era.

Jahren and the others were saying it, too. "Era… Era…"

Haven stared at the darkness. He remembered that word, remembered Mira using it when she told him and the others about Hanzo. She said that an Era was a rule. Why were they using the word right now? Were they… talking to him? *What's going on?* He mentally asked his dragon. He wasn't surprised when I-lyan didn't respond, having gotten use to his tendency to not share information with him, though the circumstances were so strange that Haven felt that, maybe, his dragon didn't have an answer. That was, until, he felt a wave of regret hit his stomach, the feeling curdled with something else.

Guilt.

I-lyan?

The word *Era* completely engulfed the frantic screaming that had been going on earlier, drowning out the occasional, frustrated yell from the Lurkhamara. Dox quickly looked over at Mira. "Now's your chance. Separate your father from him."

Mira finally stopped staring at Haven to write in her book. They could all hear a scream tear out of the shadows, but whether it was from the Lurkhamara or Thierry was hard to determine. Words started to melt off the large, black wave, the letters littering around the ground.

Thierry. Storyteller.

Alix and the others quickly stepped away as the light tore into the darkness, large clumps of black falling and smashing into the ground. Soon, all that remained were the bodies of Jahren and the others, the Scough slowly trying to push themselves up as the shadows slid off of them into a sizzling pool of black that melted away.

Mira quickly ran forward to hug Jahren when he finally managed to sit up, ignoring the wet feeling the shadows had left on his clothes and skin. The disoriented Scough took a moment to gather his bearings before he slowly wrapped his arms around Mira. "You're o.k.," he whispered.

Mira nodded and nuzzled her nose against his neck. "I was so worried about you. About all of you."

Amari and Lyree quickly joined in on the hug while Saraisai smiled at them, actually letting himself be pulled in by an insistent Amari. Jahren smiled and laughed with them, taking a moment to nuzzle in their fur and gently kiss the edge of their ears.

After a moment Jahren began to look around, realizing that there was a particular Scough missing. "Your father, where-"

"Here."

Everyone watched as Thierry stepped over to them. He looked incomplete, as if someone had been in the middle of a thought, only to be interrupted and forget where they had left off. His eyes looked like a sketched drawing, hair not long enough and body only possessing a few splotches of color. It only took a few seconds before the words started to come together to complete the image. *Ears. Tail. Fur.* The Scough stared in shock as the creature they had believed to be just like them literally put himself back together via the letters that moved across his body. Jahren was the first to speak, his voice barely above a whisper, "A shapeless creature..."

Thierry nodded. "The Storyteller is, yes."

Mira turned to face the others. "My father created me. I am a part of him."

"Was it to throw everyone off?" Alix asked.

"From what we've been told so far the Storyteller is only one creature. That would make sense," Fagan said.

Amari smiled, "That's amazing."

"Amazing?" Saraisai frowned, his good mood instantly turning sour. "He's been deceivin' us. Told ya' somethin' was off."

"Has he?" Jahren asked as he stood up to walk toward Thierry. "We always knew that there was something different about him and Mira even if we never voiced it out."

Thierry took a moment to reach forward, his fingers gently scratching behind Jahren's ear. The motion was familiar and comfortable, exactly what he needed after everything that just happened. Jahren smiled and stepped closer, curling up against Thierry as his friend whispered, "I was worried about you."

"I was worried too," Jahren said. "When Mira suggested going to their world... I didn't think..."

"That she'd succeed?" Thierry smiled at Mira. "We're going to have to rely on Mira more. She is the Storyteller, after all."

"What?" Mira quickly shook her head. "What do you mean by that? You're the Storyteller."

"Not anymore."

Jahren looked up at Thierry, a confused look on his face as he spoke to him in. "Since when? Since now? With the Lurkhamara?"

"No. Since Mira was created."

Alix clenched his fists at his sides. "You mean the Storyteller has been with us this entire time?"

"No, that's not..." Mira shook her head, "I-I'm not-"

Thierry chuckled before he took hold of his daughter's hand. "That is something we can discuss in greater detail later."

"No, it is something we need to discuss now." Alix narrowed his eyes. "We did this-"

"To find me. And you have. And we will talk, later."

Mira still looked troubled by his words. "I... am the Storyteller?"

Thierry gave his daughter a reassuring smile. "Surely you must have noticed how impressive that book is, Mira. You possess it for a reason. You possess it because you are the Storyteller."

Mira clutched the book tightly, not looking up at her father. How could she be the Storyteller? And how did she not know this entire time?

Fagan spoke up now, putting all of the pieces together. "I get it, now. He was protecting you. He let himself be captured to stop them from finding out that it was actually you. That's pretty smart, actually. I wonder how many people your father has sent to hide in the human world."

Thierry tilted his head, an innocent look on his face that reminded Fagan of Mira. That explained where she got it from. "I have no idea who else you would be talking about," Thierry said.

Alix immediately turned to Dox. "You. He's talking about you. He helped you to our world, away from your father."

Dox nodded. "Thierry led me to the doorway a long time ago. I told him it was foolish since it would expose him to my father, but he insisted that it needed to be done."

Thierry smiled at Dox. "It's good to see you away from him."

"This is a really nice story, honest, but-"

"Yes yes I know," Thierry said to Alix, "You want to talk to me. To us. And you will, you have my word. But for now I believe a huge thank you is in order, to all of you. Especially you, young

Era," he said to Haven, "It could not have been easy coming back here."

"There it is again. Era." Fagan frowned before he turned to look at Haven. Unlike Alix, who had come here for his own purposes, Fagan wasn't really gaining anything from this trip except for a sinking feeling that it was far from over. Part of him didn't want to ask why the Storyteller – *former* Storyteller – was calling Haven an Era, but another part reminded him that this boy was with Xaver in his last days and that, somehow, that meant he needed to know as much about the boy as possible. "What exactly are you, Haven?"

Haven looked at the remaining shadows and swallowed. As he reached out to touch them he could see the shadows start to curl around his fingers like a cat leaning into its owner's hand. The movement seemed natural, but something about it made the back of Haven's mind shudder.

A moment later he realized it wasn't his mind shuddering. It was his dragon.

Something about the shadows moving around Haven's fingers scared I-lyan and he could feel him curling up tightly in the back of his mind. What in the world could possibly scare his dragon so badly? "I-I... I don't know how to answer that," Haven said to Fagan.

Alix glared at him. He was getting tired of these creatures keeping secrets. First the Storyteller, and now this? "What do you mean you don't know? It's obvious that you're like Dox."

"T-that's not-"

"You used the shadows in the same way," Fagan said. He didn't sound too pleased and it was starting to remind Haven of Xaver when he would get angry about something. "You could have told us going in that you were one of these things."

That's not what you are! I-lyan screamed in his mind so loudly that Haven winced. *You are nothing like them!*

"Then what the hell am I?! You haven't told me anything!" Haven snapped back, not caring about the others staring at him for yelling at himself.

"I-lyan? You never told him?" The compassion in Saraisai's voice was surprising, especially to the Scough around him. "The boy doesn't know what he is?"

"I-lyan? I've heard that name, my mother has spoken it before." Yvonne's eyes widened as he looked over at Thierry. "This boy… is he really the Era?"

"He is," Thierry said, smiling at Haven. "I knew you could stop the shadows."

"My book did, too," Mira whispered. "It showed me."

Haven looked at everyone for a moment before focusing his attention on Fagan. He didn't like how frustrated the man looked, it brought together memories of Xaver that he didn't need to be dealing with right now. "I-I really don't know what any of this means, honest. My dragon never told me."

"You are one of the last remaining Kurai, but then… you don't know what that means either, do you?" Thierry asked.

"Mira has mentioned them, but that's about it."

Thierry nodded before he continued. "You are the same type of creature as the Lurkhamara, though not twisted by sickness and need for power. I-lyan is your protector, given to you by your mother when the others were killed. You are the Era. I believe the term used by humans would be a prince."

"Your land was destroyed long ago, young Era," Yvonne said. "It was a great tragedy for us all. My people used to inhabit that land until it was destroyed. My mother barely survived and quickly saved as many Red Dragons as she could. I was but a boy at the time."

Alix looked at Mira in question, but the Scough girl shook her head. "I didn't realize what Haven was. The book showed him to me, but that was all." She frowned sadly at Haven, her ears drooping down and pressing against her head. "I swear, I didn't know that you were... I-I would've told you-"

Thierry shook his head. "It wasn't your job to tell him, he was supposed to find out. I know you wanted to protect him, I-lyan, but it's time for him to know the truth."

Now things were starting to make sense to Haven. Why his first memory was of his dragon telling him to leave. Why his dragon always advised him to be on the move. Why it always felt like he was running away from something, or someone, some force that his dragon never spoke about.

Haven silently spoke to I-lyan, mentally coaxing him out of the corner he was hiding in. It was unnerving to Haven to feel his dragon like this. He was used to I-lyan being confident and knowledgeable. It was childish, but he thought that I-lyan wasn't afraid of anything. *You were protecting me from this. That's why you never told me anything.*

His dragon hissed softly but it wasn't an angry sound, it was more like a sigh of defeat. *I gave her my word that I would protect you. If nothing else, you would be safe.*

Her?

I-lyan hesitated. *Hanzo's daughter was your mother.*

Haven turned his attention to the others, letting the weight of the information sink in.

Hanzo.

His mother.

He had a mother, a real life mother who, no matter how hard he tried, he couldn't picture. Had he ever seen her, perhaps as a young child? Or a baby? Had she ever held him? Cared for him? Or did she give him to I-lyan right away? He had so many questions for his dragon, but he could tell that now wasn't the time to press him for more. Instead, the Storyteller and the Red Dragon would have to do.

The question was, where should he start?

He wanted to ask about his mother, but they had both said that Hanzo and his land had been completely destroyed. Would they know anything about the woman? Chances are they wouldn't, but they probably knew the cause of all of this. "The person who destroyed it… are they still around?"

Yvonne looked unsure but Thierry spoke, a deep frown on his face. "Unfortunately yes."

Saraisai let out a low growl. "The coward disappeared after the attack. No one has seen him since."

"In your stories, you called him Atticus. The Lurkhamara helped, too, but Atticus was the main cause." Amari hadn't been alive at the time but they all knew the story. They had no choice but to know it. Lyree remained quiet next to him, not speaking up, as if too afraid to say the name.

"That name has come up too," Alix said, "Back when Mira first showed up and talked to us, she mentioned him being the cause of the destruction in this world."

"We all thought there weren't any Kurai left. That dragon helps you hide your true heritage. A good thing, really, because if Atticus knew…" Yvonne's voice trailed off.

Haven frowned, his eyes suddenly hard and angry. "If he knew he would want me dead, wouldn't he? Just like the others? The Lurkhamara was about to start a war with the Red Dragons, right?

The ones who survived the first time? This Atticus person would want to finish things, too, wouldn't he? What if... he figured out I was alive already?"

Haven could feel his dragon hissing in protest. *There is no way he could know that!*

"It's possible," Haven said in response to his dragon. "After all, the Lurkhamara did have access to Thierry."

Dox frowned. "That's assuming that my father was still working with Atticus. Still... it is a possibility."

Fagan's eyes widened a bit, a sick knot settling in the pit of his stomach. "Xaver..."

"Who is Xaver?" Saraisai asked.

"He was a friend, but he was killed. He told me and Haven to stay inside, he protected us." Mira looked up at Fagan, her tail nervously swishing behind her. "Do you think Atticus..."

"No," Saraisai growled. "How could he have gotten into the human world?"

"I did," Dox whispered.

Lyree finally spoke up, "Yeah, but Thierry helped you, right?"

"That may be, but it's not impossible to get into our world. We encounter demons quite often, that's why we do what we do," Alix said.

"Xaver told me to stay inside, no matter what," Haven whispered. Xaver had kept Haven a secret from the other Hunters up until the night he was killed. He had taken Haven in, let him travel alongside him without knowing how important he was to this world or that someone was after him.

No, that wasn't right.

Somehow, Xaver had known, or at least sensed how important Haven was. Why else would a Hunter let a demon travel with him when his entire purpose was to get rid of them? Haven felt a hard lump rest inside his throat. There were a lot of things Xaver could handle, Haven knew that. He'd seen Xaver fight and he'd heard his battle tales thanks to the effects of beer and how it made Xaver much more talkative. Haven used those times to ask him about the demons he'd fought, slowly learning about a world he knew his dragon would never share with him.

Xaver had fought all kinds of demons... but a creature capable of destroying an entire land? Xaver never would've stood a chance, no matter how good he was. That thought made Haven feel worse and, in spite of his victory in the battle against the Lurkhamara, he felt like his dragon at that moment. He wanted to back away from the others and curl into the corner, hiding away until he could process it all.

"Great. A smug dragon and a prince."

The sullen mood was broken as Haven looked down to see Cyn frowning up at him, no longer clutching her head or looking like she was in any pain. If anything, she looked annoyed, almost embarrassed, as she pulled away from Haven. In the whole mess of learning the secrets of his past he had almost forgotten that he had been holding onto her in the first place. "Nice to see you back to normal," he said, trying his best to hide his warring feelings.

"Yeah..." she looked around and frowned. "Where did the shadow asshole go?"

Suddenly, Alix was on the move, nodding to Fagan to follow. In all the commotion with the giant shadow and freeing Thierry and the Scough they had lost focus on their target. As the Hunters looked around the trees they found no sign of the Lurkhamara. "He's gone," Alix said, frustrated with himself. He had gotten too caught up in this story about Haven. It wasn't like any of that mattered, not when he had his own plans with the Storyteller.

"Of course he is. He knows when he's beaten," Thierry said.

Dox sighed. "He'll go back to recover and try to come up with some other way to get the best of us. It could take days, weeks…"

"No matter how long it takes we'll be ready," Fagan said, putting his sword away. He walked over to Haven, who was busy looking down at his hands, watching as the shadows still lingered around his fingertips. "Hey kid."

Haven glanced up at Fagan, immediately pulling his hands away from the shadows as if he had been doing something wrong. "Y-yeah?"

Fagan smiled at him, "Good job," then he clasped a large hand over Haven's shoulder.

The tension and confusion of the moment slipped away at his touch. In that moment, Haven was reminded of Xaver, but in a different way. The man had always looked intimidating and seemed like he would be the most unfriendly person you could run across. But there were moments when you'd catch a smile or a laugh, times when he'd place a hand on Haven's shoulder and say the same words Fagan had just spoken to him. Haven remembered the times the two would spar, how Haven never did manage to knock the blade out of his hand until Mira controlled his movements, but Xaver would always give him that smile. *"Good job kid, good job."*

The rough and strong hand felt comforting on his shoulder and Haven was finally able to relax. The situation with the Lurkhamara, Cyn's frantic outburst, this new revelation on the Era, the Kurai, all of that could be explained later. For now, Haven closed his eyes, allowed the weight to sag off of his shoulders as he leaned back against Fagan, whispering a soft, "Thank you."

Now that the shadows were gone around them and the Lurkhamara had disappeared into the darkness, they could all see beyond the trees around them. The Scough in the area were gathering, watching the exchange in curious silence, their ears twitching and tails swishing back and forth as they watched the group. Standing with the Scough were a few other animals who were just as furry, only they had curved horns on either side of their head. Fagan remembered the name *Takin* from earlier with the small children. There were small murmurings amongst the demons, a couple whispering *Red Dragon* and *Yvonne* before they started to frown, eying Fagan and Alix and growling out the word *human*.

Alix was quickly on edge, his hand resting on his gun before Yvonne reached over, taking his hand and shaking his head. "They will not harm us," then he nodded to the small group of children that ran over to Mira, smiling and hugging her legs.

"Mi-mi!"

"You're all right!"

"Yay!"

Mira smiled and knelt down, petting each of the children. The Takin child walked over to Fagan and smiled. "We did what you asked us to do. We kept everyone away."

"Ah." The Hunter knelt down and pet the girl on top of her head. "I see that. Good job."

Seeing Fagan speak with the child seemed to put the other demons at ease. They slowly walked over, surrounding the small group. "The shadows? Are they gone now?" One of the Scough asked.

Thierry nodded, brushing his hands over his arms to make sure that the strange shadow strings were truly gone. "Yes," then he smiled at Alix and the others, "Thanks to all of the people here."

"But isn't he a Lurk?" A Takin asked, frowning at Dox.

"No."

Everyone turned to look at Cyn from where she stood next to Haven. She hadn't spoken to Dox since the fight, not quite able to make herself look him in the eye. The words he spoke still lingered quietly in her mind, bringing up memories that she always tried hard to forget, but she had a feeling that she knew why he had done it and she would bring it up to him later. For now, it was time to take up her self-appointed job of defending her friend from people who mistook him for being an asshole like his father. "He's different. He was under the Lurkhamara's control just like Thierry was, but he isn't anymore. He's the reason why we're even here."

"Cyn…" Dox frowned, and now Cyn could see the emotion on his face better than she'd ever been able to. When Mira had separated him from his father she'd done more than she realized. Dox's eyes looked real – albeit oddly colored – and emotion filled his face like any normal creature. "About what I said before, I-"

"I know," Cyn whispered, actually smiling a little at him. So much for not bringing it up, but it comforted her to see the regretful look on Dox's face. "You needed to push me, I get it."

"So you weren't under his control at that point?" Haven chuckled a little, "I knew it."

"I… no, I was, I mean… I-I could hear him, and he kept screaming at me to hurt all of you. I was trying to work around that, somehow. I realized that maybe if I hurt Cyn in the right way, then the whole situation would backfire on him and help you. My father gave me my own mind, so I had to listen to him, but I could still think on my own." He flashed a guilty look at Cyn. "I'm really sorry I used your past like that. I know I promised to never-"

No one was surprised when Cyn quickly walked over to Dox, her fists clenched at her sides as Dox's apologies died off. Haven had considered holding the girl back but she was already several steps away from him and this wasn't one of those situations that someone should intrude on. Haven and the others found themselves staring when the girl threw her arms around Dox's shoulders, holding him as tightly as she could. Dox remained frozen in shock for a moment, Cyn trembling against him as she whispered, "Don't you ever call me Cynthia again."

Dox took a deep breath and exhaled, one arm tight around her waist, his other hand buried in her hair. The last time he had held her so tightly was back when she had been Little Cynthia Maddson. He had been tucked away in her closet that night, ready to rest when he had heard her door creak open. He hadn't recognized the man as her father, any of his colleagues, or the people in white coats who would check up on the girl after one of her father's sessions. Dox had watched, horrified, as the man removed the blankets around her, letting out the sort of noise that was meant for a man who desired a woman.

Little Cynthia Maddson had woken up screaming and the man hadn't bothered with covering her mouth. He had let her scream as he climbed on top of her, his hands sliding underneath her nightgown to tug at her panties. *"Just an experiment,"* he had said, *"Be a good girl, your daddy wants to try a new experiment."*

Before the vile man could get any further the shadows had roared to life. Dox had yelled her name back then, he'd called her Cynthia and he'd promised, after that, when she'd asked him to cut away her curls forever, that he would never call her Cynthia again.

"I won't break that promise again," Dox whispered, trembling as he held Cyn tighter.

Thierry smiled and wrapped an arm around his daughter's shoulders as they watched Dox and Cyn. "Come on. We should head back to the camp," then he glanced over at Alix, "I believe dinner is in order, along with some discussion, yes?"

Alix's eyes widen and he watched as Thierry urged the other demons to follow him. Dox and Cyn had finally stopped hugging, walking back with Thierry as Cyn kept a tight hold on Dox's hand. Haven still looked a bit unsettled about everything, but Fagan was walking with him, offering a silent form of comfort.

Yvonne glanced over at Alix. "You are joining us, right?"

"A-ah, yes, I will catch up."

Yvonne nodded as he turned to follow after the group, leaving Alix with his thoughts.

Once he was alone the Hunter took a deep breath, his hand clasping the ring around his neck. His heart was pounding loud enough to cancel out the rest of the sounds around him – the light conversations between the Scough, the rustling of the leaves through the trees. His fingers trembled around the ring, palm sweaty as he tried to prepare himself for the one thing he wanted since that fire, since Alixandre lost everything in that cold doctor's office.

This was it. This was finally it. The Storyteller was going to talk to him.

And Alixandre could finally get her life back.

Chapter 9

The smell of roasted food cooking over a large fire hung in the air, rising up with the smoke to meet with the light of the late afternoon sun. After the events of that morning, the camp of Scough and Takin had gone from staying in their own little groups to becoming a full circle. Mira's fox companion had returned from the caves they had been hiding in, yipping happily when she saw that her friend was safe and sound. The children were busy running around the fire, some sort of animal hanging over the flames on a stick. Both Fagan and Alix could tell that Thierry and the others were attempting to be being generous. Most of the Scough had already started eating chunks of uncooked meat, claws and teeth sharp enough to tear the animals they caught for dinner apart. Fagan couldn't help but be amused. "Wonder if Zach would still think she was cute," he said to Alix, nodding over to Mira as she sunk her teeth into what had once been a demon world rabbit.

"This. Is. Disgusting."

Haven glanced over at Cyn, trying not to smile too much as she made a face at the Scough around her. *So says the Earthmover* his dragon chuckled in the back of his mind. "My dragon made some comment about you being an Earthmover."

"Mmfh mower?" Amari said around a mouthful of his food, tilting his head. "You don't look like one."

"I hide it well," Cyn muttered, not wanting to get into it. "What matters is that all of you are gross. It isn't even cooked."

"That's surprisin' to hear comin' from an Earthmover," Saraisai said, smirking. "You should see the things you guys eat."

"Mm! Mmhm!" This came from Mira as she finished off the last of her food, licking away a couple of stray drops of blood. "Earthmovers eat all sorts of things, like-"

"Shut. Up. Otherwise this shaky friendship we have is over."

"Wait, you actually think of me as a friend?" Mira smiled brightly, "Sweet!"

"Sweet? How is that sweet, it's not a flavor..." Amari scratched behind his ear, confused.

"It's a flavor and a compliment in the human world, just something else I learned while I was over there," Mira giggled.

"Really? Sweet!" Lyree giggled and Saraisai rolled his eyes, grunting out a disapproving remark toward the Scough, as always.

Suddenly there was a small commotion in the crowd. Alix and the others turned to see the three Red Dragons they'd been expecting earlier. A hush fell over all conversation as the Reina walked up to the main group who were eating closest to the fire with Jahren and Thierry.

In the book the Reina had been impressive, but in person she was downright intimidating. Tall with legs that could rival Katalynne's, the woman easily matched Fagan's height in her bare, clawed feet. Her skin was a dark bronze, like her son, speckled with scars that had long since faded to faint black lines. There was a particularly nasty looking scar curved around her neck that was decorated with a faint white paint. It was an obvious sign of how close she'd come to death and how she'd conquered it.

The two men behind her were younger by several years, closer to Yvonne's age. A handful of jewels hung from their necks and around their wrists, but not nearly as many as the woman or Yvonne. Long, sharp pieces of smooth metal were affixed to their hands, exaggerating their fingers into claws that looked like they could easily cut through anything.

The Scough grew silent, all watching with nervous tension. Yvonne stood, walked up to the woman, dropped to one knee and took the woman's hand to kiss the back of it. "I welcome you, my Reina. It is good to see you."

"And you as well, my son."

Alix tried not to stare but couldn't hide the shock on his face. Mira had mentioned to them that the leader of the Red Dragons was female, she had even shown it to them in her book, but it was still hard for him to grasp the concept. The level of respect the Red Dragons showed the woman and the fact that all of the demons watched her carefully proved to Alix that not only was this woman in charge, but she was something to be feared.

Alix had a feeling that, if a fight were to start, she wouldn't even have needed the two dragons with her.

"I trust you have an explanation for taking my son, Thierry?" The woman asked as she looked over at him.

Thierry nodded. "Of course, Anasia."

"It wasn't his fault, honest!" The sudden outburst surprisingly came from Lyree. The young Scough gave the woman a pleading look, ears pressed tightly to his head. "A-Anasia, I-I mean Reina, please!"

Anasia stared at the young Scough in surprise, watching as he bowed down in front of her. After getting over the shock of his outburst she chuckled and patted him on top of his head. "There's no need for that. I came for an explanation, not a fight."

Lyree looked up at her hesitantly. "R-really? Saraisai is always saying how ill-tempered Red Dragons are and-"

"Shut up!" Saraisai growled at Lyree, then he turned and swiped his claws at Amari when he started to laugh. "Shut up, all of ya!"

"Please excuse them, Anasia. I promise, they mean no harm," Thierry said.

"Oh I can tell," then she smiled at Lyree, scratching behind one of his ears. "This one is kind of cute, actually," and she smiled more when she saw the blush on the young Scough's face.

"Anasia. Behave."

"Oh hush, Thierry."

Unlike the others, Thierry didn't feel the need to address her with a title. Even stranger, Alix and Fagan realized, was that no one seemed bothered by this – not even Anasia. In Alix's mind, this completely cemented his position and power in this world, even if he claimed that Mira was the true Storyteller.

Anasia and Yvonne joined the others while the two guards remained standing off to the side, still watching the area even if the danger had passed. Once the food was cooked Jahren offered it to Alix and the others. Cyn gave the Scough a blank stare. "How do you expect us to eat it?"

One of the Scough children giggled, "You just bite into it, silly."

Mira whispered to both her father and Jahren. "They use things to eat their food off of. I saw it while I was there."

"Oh... I apologize," Jahren said, giving Cyn a sheepish smile.

Thierry chuckled a little. "The Scough don't-"

"Eat like normal people? Yeah, I noticed," Cyn said.

"She's got quite the attitude," Anasia chuckled. "I think I like it."

Haven wasn't sure why he felt the urge to sit closer to Cyn. Something about the way the woman looked at her, lips curled into a smirk, her eyes just a touch bit playful. Anasia took notice of it and gave Haven a sweet smile. "Is she already spoken for?"

"I... what?" Cyn looked at Haven, then at Anasia. "What the hell are you talking about?"

Dox considered explaining it to Cyn, but he was having too much fun watching the confused look on his friend's face. He settled for staying silent, the occasional light chuckle leaving his lips.

Yvonne spoke up, sounding more than a little amused himself. "My mother finds you appealing, but it appears that you have already been claimed."

"E-excuse me?!" Both Haven and Cyn spoke at the same time, both of their faces flushed in embarrassment. Cyn was the first to speak, "I am not some *thing* you can claim!"

"But the Reina being interested is quite the compliment," Lyree said, the wonder and awe clear in his voice. "Being a chosen companion is a great honor."

"You seem to know a lot about me, young Scough," Anasia smiled.

"Oh, well..." Lyree fidgeted, feeling his cheeks get warm once again. "I- I hear a lot of stories from the older Scough like Saraisai, and... y-yeah..."

Jahren laughed as he began to help the Scough gather pieces of thick cloth in an attempt to create a sort of plate for the meat. "Why are you so flustered, Lyree?"

"Are you interested in the Reina?" Amari teased.

"N-no! I mean… w-who wouldn't be? I-I mean… s-shut up, Amari!"

"Hmph. Maybe now you'll stop laughing at my expense when he's irritating," Saraisai muttered.

"Perhaps two companions are in order," Anasia smirked at Lyree and Cyn. Lyree quickly looked away from the woman, still squirming under her gaze, while Cyn settled for glaring and trying to fight the annoying flutters in her stomach.

"Can we just get to the part where Thierry explains things, please?! And you," Cyn pointed at Anasia, "stay right there."

"I do not intend to leave my seat for the moment." Anasia only sounded a bit sincere, her eyes sparkling with mischievousness. Cyn could tell that this was a woman who appreciated teasing her opponents no matter what form of prey they were – to be killed or to be pleasured-… no, Cyn shook her head, she was not going to think about *that*.

"I suppose I could explain now," Thierry said, tail wagging in amusement.

Jahren took a seat next to Thierry, smiling as he tried a cooked piece of meat now that it had been torn apart in ragged chunks by their claws. "Not bad, actually, if you're patient enough to wait."

Thierry leaned over and took a bite out of Jahren's food, the Scough leader making a face at his friend. "It is quite good."

"See? I know what I'm talking about," Cyn said to them. Anasia chuckled, eating her own food before she gave Haven a curious look, "I'd like to know how you managed to find an Ice Dragon."

"I-lyan has always been with me," Haven said, "He never really explained-"

Anasia's eyes widened and she interrupted him, "I-lyan? I have not heard that name in years." Rising from her seat Haven stiffened as the woman took a step closer. He was surprised to see her drop to one knee, bowing her head to him as she spoke that word again. Era.

Haven stared at her and quickly shook his head. "Y-you don't have to bow down to me. Really, no one does."

"Yes, I do," she whispered, "And please forgive me for attempting to court your chosen companion."

Whatever the story was with the Kurai and the Era, it had to be important. Mira had given them small bits of it, but certainly not enough to warrant this woman bowing down in front of him. Haven had never been addressed in such a way, especially by someone who was also supposed to be royalty herself. He knew, in a battle, he could never hope to stand up to this woman. The very idea that she was bowing to him now…

He was starting to feel how important this whole Era thing was and it was a bit overwhelming.

Don't let it intimidate you. Hanzo was important to this world, and so was your mother. These people respect you, Haven, and they have good reason to.

Part of Haven wanted to yell at his dragon, wanted to know why it had taken so long to tell him the truth. For years he had been living alone without a simple explanation as to why. He had no clue about what he was, about his family, about this Atticus person or the Lurkhamara. Protecting him was one thing, but keeping him completely in the dark for so long – especially after Xaver's death – was inexcusable.

The other part, however, decided that being angry wasn't worth it. They were at this point now and there was no avoiding the subject anymore. As upset as he was, he could feel how this was affecting his dragon. He had put his life into protecting Haven and there was a sense of guilt, of failure, that Haven could taste at the tip of his tongue. Even through all of I-lyan's regrets over the situation, he was still taking the time to talk to Haven to try and make him feel better about everything.

So instead of being angry, Haven decided to grant his dragon a little kindness. *Thank you, I-lyan.*

"Um, about me being his 'companion'?" Cyn frowned at Anasia, trying her best not to blush. "That isn't-"

"I forgive you," Haven said, cutting Cyn off as he tried his best to sound confident. "You had no way of knowing." He was fairly sure he failed, his voice trembling a little.

Cyn glared at Haven and whispered to him, "You. Are so. Dead."

Haven decided that keeping his laughter to himself would be best; he didn't want to draw Cyn's anger back toward him.

As the group fell into a comfortable silence while eating, Thierry began to explain the situation to Anasia. The Lurkhamara had been trying to start a war, but instead of directly stirring up trouble, Thierry had been used as a scapegoat. Thanks to the shadows and Thierry's abilities, he'd captured Yvonne and brought him to the Scough. Originally, the Lurkhamara had wanted to leave Yvonne's body dead in the forest for Anasia to find, goading her into a battle with the "poor, defenseless" Scough. Anasia would have never expected the Storyteller or the Lurkhamara to be in their camp and he would have killed her, spurring others into fighting and killing what little remained of her kind.

Even Anasia had to admit in such a situation, she would have lost.

The plan changed, however, when Lyree had stumbled onto Thierry, forcing him to bring Yvonne back to the Scough's camp.

"The Lurkhamara is aware of your hatred toward him," Thierry said to Anasia. "It would have been his chance to take you out or attempt to get a hold of you to use you in the same manner he was using me. Either outcome would have been bad."

"Thankfully these Hunters, as you call them, came in time," Yvonne said.

Mira smiled proudly. "I knew they could do it, the book told me so."

"I admit I had my doubts, but this all actually worked out," Jahren said as he leaned against Thierry.

"Hunters?" Anasia turned her attention to Fagan and Alix. "I have heard of Hunters, but I've never heard of them acting in such a way. These two humans are responsible for saving you, Yvonne?"

"Not just us," Fagan said, nodding to Cyn and Haven, "They helped as well, along with Dox and Mira."

Anasia looked at Dox and chuckled, "Betrayed by his own son. That's quite amusing."

"I've never liked listening to him. I'm not sure why."

"The reason doesn't matter. What matters is that you were a great help. Still..." Anasia looked over the group, "Such a small group dared to battle against the Lurkhamara? That is very impressive."

"It helps that we're all idiots," Cyn muttered, picking at the cooked meat in front of her as she decided that she was actually hungry enough to eat it.

"Impressive indeed," Yvonne said, smiling at Alix and ignoring Cyn's comment. "You have my thanks."

"Oh... right." Alix knew he should've cared about the story and the explanation of what they'd just been through, but he couldn't quite focus on Thierry's words. His food sat in his lap, untouched, and despite how hungry he was he couldn't make himself eat. There were so many other things he wanted to discuss with the Storyteller, but he would need to do it alone. With all of these demons here, eating and talking, Alix's stomach churned with impatience. It was sheer force of will keeping him from standing up and dragging Thierry away from the group to talk.

"You seem to know a lot about me," Haven said to Anasia. "Can… you tell me anything?"

Anasia frowned sadly and shook her head. "I don't really know about you, in particular, just about the Kurai. Before the land was destroyed, the Red Dragons stayed in the same area. We had formed a good alliance with the Kurai thanks to Hanzo. The Red Dragons actually helped raise him after his mother died, he and I were very close." She smiled and slowly moved her fingers over his braids. "That is why my dragons wear them. A symbol of honor for Hanzo and the Kurai."

Haven watched as she looked over the tips of his braids, a small frown on his face. He hadn't realized that wearing his hair in such a way meant something. He remembered that, one day, his hands had seemed to move on their own, his dragon guiding him through the motions of braiding his hair. He hadn't thought much about it at the time, too young to really care about the state of his hair, but now he felt foolish for not asking.

"Just how old are you anyway?" Cyn blurted out, interrupting Haven's thoughts.

Anasia laughed, "Quite old, my dear."

"You don't look like it."

"That's rather flattering, but most dragons retain their youthful appearance."

"Unlike Scough, right Saraisai?"

"Quiet Amari!"

Anasia chuckled at their bantering before she continued. "Hanzo was a good ruler, and a dear friend. I-lyan was an adviser to him. The Ice Dragons were older than my people and not as numerous," she stopped, the sadness growing in her eyes. "Of course, after the battle, my people are no longer numerous and the Ice Dragons are practically non-existent. The land was destroyed by a man we all thought we could trust. I barely survived. I... thought that none of the Kurai had survived, but it appears that you did."

"I've been with my dragon for as far back as I can remember. He always tells me to stay on the move, like someone is hunting us down. I... suppose I finally have an explanation as to why."

Fagan spoke up at this point. "A friend of ours was killed recently. We believe he was trying to protect Haven. This person who destroyed this land Haven comes from? We have a feeling that it might be the same person."

Anasia growled lowly, clenching her fist. "Atticus," she hissed.

Haven could feel his dragon shudder again when Anasia spoke the name. It brought up images of destruction, harsh screams echoing in Haven's mind that he couldn't recognize. He could see stones of buildings built long ago crumbling as if they were nothing. The people around him were in the middle of a battle and he suddenly felt like he had known them all for years.

There was the man who he would spar with on occasion when Hanzo was too busy. He watched as that man twisted the shadows in the area, trying to attack some force that was too powerful to battle. The shadows actually turned against him, wrapping around him and swallowing his screams as they crushed him into nothing. To the right of the commotion were the dancers that performed during dinner, the women screaming, each one being killed one by one in front of him. Darkness and destruction were everywhere he looked and he couldn't stop it.

Even with all of his power he couldn't stop this.

Suddenly, he was racing down the hallway, pushing open a set of large, double doors. Hanzo's back was to him as he helped a young girl walk through a hidden passage in the wall. *"Just go! Your mother and I will catch up, I promise!"*

But he had broken that promise.

Hanzo had never caught up and neither did the girl's mother. Haven could now feel the choking sting of sadness against the back of his throat, could taste the regret, the anger, the fear. He knew that these feelings were coming from his dragon, but they were so strong that they gnawed at his stomach as if they were his own. He was the one who couldn't protect his friends and family from this man, this man he did and did not know. This man, this *Atticus*, who floated above everything as the entire area crumbled around him. He could hear him laughing, the sound reverberating through his mind and his entire body.

Cyn placed a hand on his shoulder, whispering his name softly and breaking the memories. Haven's breath caught and he looked at her in surprise. When had he started breathing so hard? When had he clenched his fists up so tightly? "S-sorry," he whispered, trying to calm himself down.

"It's fine. It's a lot to take in."

"I didn't mean to cause you any sort of distress, young Era," Anasia said, a guilty look crossing her face.

"It's all right," then Haven smiled at her and Cyn. "I wanted to know, so thank you for telling me."

Anasia nodded before addressing everyone else in the group. "If it is him who is pursuing you and who killed your comrade, consider the Red Dragons as allies. I want nothing more than to get rid of that creature."

"Same here," Saraisai said. "I might not be as strong as the dragons, but Atticus is something we can all agree about. He needs to be destroyed."

"I never thought you'd volunteer for something so dangerous."

"I don't need your jokes, Amari."

"I'm being serious." The younger Scough placed a hand on Saraisai's shoulder, "If you're willing to become an ally to these people, so am I."

"Me too," Lyree said.

"I'm sure all of the Scough would agree, we owe you our lives," Jahren added.

"Then it's settled." Thierry smiled at Fagan and Alix, "It appears that we are all on the same side now."

Fagan had never thought about having demons as allies. Their entire purpose was to hunt these creatures down. Now that they'd actually taken the time to sit down and talk to them civilly, they all seemed to have a common enemy. Faced with this new, dangerous situation, having such a powerful group of allies was comforting, for lack of a better word. Fagan never really considered himself to be the vengeful type. As a Hunter, he knew the risks involved and understood that any mission could be his last. But Xaver's death seemed to be leading to something bigger than himself.

As Fagan looked over at Haven he could see how Xaver got attached. There was an urge to protect this boy, to keep him safe as he stumbled through his life, unsure about everything. Having a group of powerful dragons to help didn't seem like a bad idea at all. And while the Scough weren't exactly battle ready, they did seem to be rather crafty and intelligent in their own right. Mira might have come off as a walking bundle of incapable sunshine and happiness, but she had more than proven herself in the earlier battle and had even, somehow, managed to get humans and demons together in one place.

Fagan held his hand out and smiled at Anasia. "You have my thanks for any assistance you can offer. That goes for the Scough, too."

"And you have my thanks for saving my son," Anasia said. "I see why Eegil chose you."

Fagan said nothing at the mention of his sword – again – but kept it in the back of his mind. "I suppose we will simply have to adjust to having demon allies."

Alix stared at his partner. What in the world was he doing? Alix generally trusted Fagan's decisions, but going so far as to accept assistance from these demons? Not only that, he was actually conversing with them, bantering back and forth in the same manner he used to with Xaver. There had really been no choice in the battle, but now that it was over it would be best to just leave the demons in their world and end all ties, Xaver's killer be damned.

Still, if Alix got his way, this lifestyle of his would be over, wouldn't it? Then there'd be no reason to care about what Fagan decided to do. Alixandre would have no need for Hunters or missions. Alixandre would be concerned with decorating the baby's room, picking out cute pastel outfits and falling asleep in her fiancé's arms. So Alix sat and watched as the woman took Fagan's hand in hers, nodding to the Hunter.

Soon, none of it would matter.

The group had dispersed after that. The Scough were talking in small groups, eating in peace as they enjoyed the defeat of the Lurkhamara. The children were still running around but their movements were a bit more sluggish, showing how tired they were becoming. Eventually, they ran off to their nests, the Takin disappearing somewhere in the woods, presumably to return to their own home. Saraisai and Amari were bantering back and forth about something, while Mira was sitting next to Jahren, telling him about what she'd seen in the human world while Zee finished off what was left of her rabbit leg.

Cyn stayed sitting next to Haven, with Dox sitting on the other side of her. Haven was still speaking with Anasia, asking what the Kurai were like and absorbing as much as he could. Surprisingly, I-lyan remained quiet in his head, silently enjoying the praise and respect Anasia was giving to the now fallen race of shadow users. Lyree was sitting next to the Red Dragon, looking quite happy that she had invited him over, content with listening to her talk about a world before his time.

Dox would chime in sometimes, mentioning the small amount of knowledge he had on the Kurai. All of his facts had come from his father – which wasn't necessarily the best source of information. What he knew was that his father had somehow been created from a Kurai, twisted and torn apart, only to be put back together as the Lurkhamara. The Lurai were morbid representations of what the Kurai had been, a proud race of shadow users being replaced by screeching, melting, shadowy messes of their former selves, all mindless minions to his father and long past saving.

The Lurkhamara and Dox were the exceptions, Anasia pointed out. "You especially," she said to him. "In fact, you remind me of what the Kurai are supposed to be. They were noble and protected their own in whatever way was needed, no matter how severe."

Surprised by her words Dox could only stare at the woman, whispering a soft, genuine, "Thank you."

Cyn couldn't help but smile. Finally, someone understood that Dox was different and didn't hold what he was against him. Maybe now Dox would stop holding it against himself.

Near the edge of the circle of trees Fagan was speaking to Thierry about something. Alix couldn't catch the details from where he was leaning back against his own tree. *Not that I care, all of that is going to change soon.* He forced himself to ignore the faint whisper in the back of his mind, the one that asked if he honestly wanted to give up this life. Obviously, he did. How could he want a life where he was on edge every day when *she* could be Mrs. Roderick Michaels?

How could he... right?

"May I see it?"

Alix looked up in surprise at Yvonne who was now standing next to him. "See what?"

"That." Yvonne pointed to the ring that Alix held between his fingers.

Alix looked down at the ring. He hadn't even realized that he had pulled it out again and was toying with it. "I would rather not. It is important to me."

"Of course," but the dragon's gaze was still directed at the ring.

Alix's first reaction was to, perhaps, repeat himself, but he couldn't get the words out of his mouth. The way Yvonne was looking at the ring was genuine, almost respectful, as if he were quietly honoring the gold plated metal between Alix's fingers. "What interest do you have in my ring?"

"You and your companions assisted in protecting me. I would like to properly repay you, if you will allow me."

Alix hesitated for a moment before he slowly pulled the necklace over his head. He handed it to the dragon, but kept a hold on the thin strip of leather it hung from. Yvonne took the ring, carefully turning it in his fingers like an age old artifact from a lost civilization. "I am not familiar with humans, but I have heard they value the stones as we do." The dragon tilted his hand and plucked one of the smaller stones from his hand piece. The jewel shimmered with a deep orange light, reflecting from the fire behind them. Holding Alix's ring, Yvonne pressed the stone lightly onto the top. Alix watched in surprise as the small, bent pieces that had once held a diamond twisted back into place to hold the orange jewel. The dragon bowed his head to Alix then handed him the ring. "This stone is rare and will serve as a sign to my kind and others in this world. You have our protection, because I am in debt to you."

"… thank you," Alix whispered, slowly turning the ring in his fingers. It wasn't the same as the diamond that had been there all those years ago, but it gave a new life to the old and tarnished ring. The ring now brought warmer memories to Alix, that *once upon a time* when a handsome young man got down on one knee, spoke words of marriage, and held a happy Alixandre DeBenit in his arms.

"Before the battle I spoke of proper introductions." Yvonne dropped down to one knee and took Alix's hand, actually kissing the back of it. "I am Yvonne, son of the Reina, Anasia."

Alix stared at the dragon before it occurred to him that he should pull his hand from the creature's lips. "I already know your name."

"I am aware of that, Hunter Alix." He spoke the word *Hunter* as if it were a title, a thing to be earned and respected. Alix couldn't deny that he liked the sound of that. He could feel a smirk spreading across his face until Yvonne spoke again, "This is the proper way to address a strong woman."

Alix could feel the color draining from his face. "W-what did you call me?"

"A woman. That is what you are, correct? Or do humans have a different way of saying-"

"N-no," Alix hissed, frowning, "We do not have a different… w-what makes you think that I'm a-"

"I do admit that your breasts aren't as large as some of the women I have seen, but the way you carry yourself speaks of a strong woman's grace."

The color, at least, had returned to Alix's face, far more than he was comfortable with at that moment since it was being replaced with a burning red. "My b-breasts…" he struggled to say the word, to admit that that body part existed somewhere beneath the layers of clothing, "T-they are not something you can speak about!" Much to Alix's annoyance that came out as a squeak, an embarrassing quirk that only Roderick had managed to unearth while they were engaged.

"Well they are very small…"

"It's called a compression shirt! A-and why are we even discussing-"

"So you hide them?" Yvonne tilted his head, confused. "Why would you hide one of your natural assets? Women are beautiful, powerful creatures who are to be respected. There's no need to hide anything about your true nature. I do not understand why you would wish to be seen as a man."

Alix tried hard to think of another reaction besides staring, but every time Yvonne spoke it left Alix speechless. Finally, Alix looked away from the dragon, making sure to cross his arms at his chest. "Y-you can stand up, you know."

"As you wish," then Yvonne stood up.

"You were really waiting for me to tell you that you could stand up?"

"I already told you that women are to be respected. It's how my mother taught all of us."

Somehow Alix managed to gather his wits and steady his voice. "I... would appreciate you not speaking of my... secret."

"There is no need to keep it a secret."

"Nevertheless, I have my reasons. So please?"

Yvonne frowned. "I still see no reason to hide your true nature," then he stopped, sighing, "But, if you insist, I will do this for you. I do owe you my gratitude, after all."

"Thank you," then Alix nodded down to the ring he was holding, "And thank you for this as well. I appreciate the gesture. I will keep this with me."

"Of course. It is the least I can do."

Alix decided that it would be best to change the subject. "It looks like things are settled with your mother and Thierry?"

Yvonne nodded, moving to take a place standing next to Alix instead of standing in front of him. "Things have been settled to an acceptable degree. The Lurkhamara has been a mutual enemy of ours since the destruction of our homeland."

"I thought someone else was behind that."

"Ah, you mean Atticus? He was the primary cause behind it but he had some assistance. Due to the Lurkhamara being a twisted version of the Kurai, his hatred for them gave him reason to help."

"Who created him?"

"I cannot say for sure, unfortunately." Yvonne's gaze wandered over to where his mother sat with Haven and the others. "You don't need to worry yourself over that right now. You have a good group of warriors at your side who will be of great assistance in keeping the young Era safe."

"I... oh, yes of course." Alix looked away from the group, turning his attention to where Fagan was still talking with Thierry. "Fagan is a good man. I'm sure he will be able to help with all of this."

"As will you."

"... yes... about that..." Alix tried to put together the words to finish that sentence. *"About that, I don't plan on being a Hunter anymore,"* or, *"About that, I'm going to get my real life back."* No matter how hard he tried Alix couldn't say it. He couldn't make himself actually speak the words. Hadn't all of this been for a chance to start over? It certainly hadn't been for helping that fox-like girl, or that ice kid, or that pissy goth and her shadow friend. It sure as hell hadn't been for "the sake of the hunt," or some overused message of finding a "thrill" in "the chase."

It had all been for a chance to be a wife, a mother, to have a normal life as Alixandre. But as he looked at Fagan he still couldn't make himself say the words to Yvonne.

"Are you worried about what will happen to Thierry now? Is that why you've gone quiet?"

That was half true, in a sense, and Alix decided that it would be best to agree. "I should go speak with him, actually."

"Before you go, may I ask you something?"

"Yes?"

"When we were fighting the Lurkhamara, your partner spoke a name. Alixandre, I believe?"

"…yes… but why-"

"Is that the woman you hide from everyone?"

"Not for long. Now, if you'll excuse me-"

Yvonne frowned, speaking up before Alix could leave. "There are stories about the Storyteller, about the things he can do. *She*, I suppose, since it's Mira. I know I barely know you, so I have no right to speak on the subject, but-"

"You're right," Alix whispered, pushing away from the tree, "You don't have a right to speak on it at all."

In seconds Alix was walking over to Thierry. The weight of the ring felt heavier on his chest, serving to remind him of the most important thing in his life. Suddenly, any sense of hesitation was gone. Suddenly, he knew exactly what he wanted and, goddamnit, he deserved it. He had cast aside his entire perspective regarding demons. He had ignored the queasy feelings in his stomach every time he had to talk with them, fight with them, hell, they even stayed in the place he called home.

Yvonne's words didn't matter. Fagan's decisions to continue to aide them didn't matter. Nothing mattered but the Storyteller.

When Alix reached Thierry the Scough simply greeted him with a smile. "Ah yes, I believe we have something to discuss." Thierry spoke as if he knew this conversation had been coming. Part of Alix felt that, perhaps, this creature did know.

The other part decided that he didn't have time to analyze it. "Yes, we do."

"Alix…" Fagan wasn't the best at speaking words, especially when they mattered and were centered on his feelings. He wasn't a man who could spout out meaningful words of *don't leave* or *your life is fine the way it is*, he was a man who used his sword and fists to communicate. Besides, he knew that if he said anything like, Alix would knock every single one of his teeth out. He – no, *she* – was too determined about this whole thing. Fagan knew going in that if Alix ever had a chance he would turn back the hands of time, but Fagan had always clung to the fact that such a thing wasn't possible.

As a Hunter, he should've known better.

Now that the moment had arrived Fagan would've preferred it if Alix stayed. In spite of his brash attitude and tendencies to annoy the ever living crap out of him, Fagan had gotten used to his partner. He dared to think that Alix not only liked working with him, but that he actually cared about him.

So Fagan opened his mouth to speak, forced his brain to come up with something worthwhile to say because you could only do this sort of thing once. Before the words could leave his mouth Thierry placed a hand on his shoulder, a warm smile on his face. "Go on, it'll only be a moment."

"But–"

"Trust me." The look on his face was sincere and, for a moment, Fagan let himself feel hopeful. Maybe there would be something he could keep after this mess of a mission. Fagan responded with a nod and turned to leave. He looked at Alix one more time before walking off to sit with Haven and the others.

He found himself wondering if this world had an equivalent to beer because it would've been a godsend right about now.

"Should I leave too, father?" Mira asked.

"You're fine, Mira. He wants to talk to the Storyteller. That's you, remember?"

Mira hesitated. "You still haven't explained–"

"And I will. Trust me." He gave her a reassuring smile before he turned his attention to Alix. "I believe you have a request you would like to make?"

Alix gave a short nod. He could figure out the finer points between Thierry and Mira later. "I have heard that the Storyteller has the ability to change someone's past. I want you to change one thing about mine."

Thierry reached forward and brushed his fingers against Alix's arm, sending a small shiver down his back. Thierry's silverish hair shifted into a thick, cinnamon brown, tossed around his head as if he had just gotten out of bed. His golden eyes melted into the color of dark cocoa, a comforting smile on his face that made Alix's knees feel weak.

Alixandre recognized that smile. It brought back memories of her walking into a classroom, books in hand and that smile directed at her from a seat in the middle of the room. It brought back memories of cold nights in the winter; that smile greeting her with a warm cup of tea. She whispered a name, "Roderick," and to her surprise the name swirled into the air in a green mist, "W-what is–"

"Shhh." This came from Mira as she watched the two of them, "He's reading you."

"Reading?"

She could feel fingers moving along her arm, words lifting off of her skin. Another name, her own – Alixandre DeBenit – then the name split itself in half. Alix Andre DeBenit.

"I see. You would like the story to be changed so he was not in that accident." Thierry pulled his hand away, the brown turning back to silver and gold. Alix frowned softly, lightly rubbing his arm where Thierry had been "reading" him. He felt like he was dusting away letters, words, different storybook passages of Alixandre's life – love, engagement, pregnancy, fire.

"It should be simple enough. Just make it so he never died."

Thierry frowned softly and shook his head, speaking in a softer voice. "This is the extent of my powers. I can read other's stories from a touch and my body automatically changes to fit in with those around me. I can also show people things, in a similar manner to Mira's book, only her abilities are far more advanced that my own. I can no longer change a person's story."

Alix's eyes narrowed, "And that's where she comes in?" He turned his attention to the younger girl who was now shifting nervously beside her father. She looked shocked and unsure, her ears perked and her tail unmoving as she watched her father. Zee, who had been resting by Mira's feet, was now looking up at Thierry, too.

Thierry reached over and gently started to scratch Mira behind one of her ears to calm her. "When I created you, I gave you the majority of my powers. I was waiting for the right time to tell you, but then this situation with the Lurkhamara came up. But it appears that there is nothing for me to explain. This fight with the Lurkhamara showed you what you're capable of. It showed you that you are, indeed, the Storyteller."

"But... I can't... h-how am I more powerful than you?"

Thierry smiled even more. "Don't start doubting yourself now. You know I'm telling the truth, you know that the power is yours, not mine."

Mira took a deep breath before she looked at Alix. "So I am the one who can give him what he wants?"

Thierry nodded. "If you touch her, you should be able to summon her book."

"Her?" Mira blinked, confused, and was about to correct her father but he was already urging her to step closer to Alix. He took Mira's hand, placed it on Alix's arm, and slowly guided her fingers over the Hunter's skin. Once again the words appeared beneath her fingers, but she could feel a small weight to them, like something waiting just beyond what she could see. Mira closed her eyes and silently pulled at that weight, feeling it move to settle into her hands. When she opened her eyes and looked down, she could see a thick book there, just as he said it would be.

The book was blue, the thick cover made of the finest dyed leather. The name Alixandre DeBenit was written across the cover and down the spine in sweeping calligraphy. The book was in pristine condition except for the edges of the cover, which were blackened from what looked like a fire. Mira looked from the book to Alix and noticed he was trembling just a little, but she couldn't tell if it was the shock of seeing that one's entire life was merely a story to be read, or if it was anticipation of what he was asking for.

Wait, her father hadn't said he. He'd said *she*.

Mira opened the book and turned a couple pages to look over the story. The pages she turned to were written in a script much like the front cover. As she glanced over the words she could see scenes unfolding before her in shadowy figures. She could see a young girl no more than ten years old playing around in one of her mother's dresses. The girl's parents were sitting in a lavishly decorated living room, discussing a future filled with a college education and a well off, promising young man. Mira blinked and looked at Alix in a new light.

"Alixandre," she whispered, "You're not a man, you're a woman."

Alixandre frowned at her. "That's not important," she snapped. "I want you to bring him back. Bring Roderick back. He shouldn't have died that day."

Mira turned more of the pages, letting her instincts lead her to the right page. As she turned them the ghostly image of the little girl grew up and changed from stealing her mother's clothes to wearing plaid and private school uniforms. Blonde hair grew longer and Mira could see her speaking with friends and teachers and attending classes. Most of the things were unfamiliar to her, but with this woman's book in her hands it all felt like she'd always known it. She knew what universities were and how much faith humans put in educating their young and preparing them for the world. She knew that Alixandre was one of the smartest of her kind and had gone through many long hours of school to become that way.

Then, in college, Alixandre met him.

Mira knew this man was Roderick, and she took a moment to watch him and Alixandre in the image. They were decorating an apartment together, Alixandre filling the kitchen with fancy, framed pictures of cafe chairs and the Eiffel Tower. Roderick was asking her what the point of decorating the kitchen was when neither of them really cooked. She was frowning at him, suddenly turning on the kitchen water and grabbing the attached hose to spray it at him. He was laughing, fighting back by grabbing her, easily lifting her and pulling her out of the kitchen and into their bedroom. The bedframe wasn't put together yet and the mattress was on the floor, but Roderick was pinning her down to it and tickling her, their laughter bringing life to the apartment.

Mira could feel her eyes watering as she read, the scenes changing. Roderick was getting an internship. Alixandre was studying to further her education more than she already had.

They were eating take-out together, making plans for the future, watching movies, making love night after night until-

Mira closed the book and took a deep breath, her hands shaking. She brushed her fingers against the burnt edges of the book, wiping at her eyes. As she looked up at Alix she suddenly understood the Hunter's attitude toward demons and the world in general. She understood how Alixandre had transformed into this mean spirited young man and how he grew to hate anything that wasn't human. Mira could feel the hatred, how Alix had struggled to work with all of them, how he fought to keep his focus on that hatred and not lose himself in this sudden realization that demons weren't as terrible as he thought. But Fagan had taught Alix about balance, about hunting the ones who deserved it instead of running around and killing anything with too many arms or a tail.

Mira glanced over at where Fagan sat, the other man watching her. He had been watching the entire time, she could tell, his eyes focused on them and waiting to see what would happen. Mira knew that this wouldn't just change Alix's life, but Fagan's as well, and suddenly she could feel a terrible weight on her shoulders. If she did this, Fagan would lose a good partner and friend. But how could she not help Alix?

Mira wanted that pain to go away. Mira wanted to make this man – this *woman* – feel better. Alix had suffered through all of this to save her father, it was the least she could do, right?

"Mira?" Thierry began to rub her back. "Take a minute," he whispered. He remembered what it felt like to read someone's life and he knew from the brief contact he had with Alix that this particular book would be drenched in sorrow.

"I'm fine, father," Mira whispered as she opened the book again.

"Did you see him?" Thierry's voice was quiet as he watched his daughter look through the pages.

"Bring him back." Alix's voice was quiet, pleading.

Mira glanced up at him – her, she could tell that this was Alixandre. This was the woman that Alix had tried his hardest to keep hidden until this very moment.

Mira quickly read through the pages, determined. Fire. Unborn child. Training. Hunting. Lurk. Xaver's death. Ice Dragon. Storyteller. Mira read the words quietly, searching, then suddenly her eyes widened.

"Bring him back. All you have to do is change one small thing. Just make it so he doesn't die."

Mira watched the woman sadly as Alixandre reached forward and snatched the book away. Soon the woman was stumbling back, dropping the book and staring down at it. "W-what is this?" She whispered, shaking her head. "What is this, why is it empty?"

Thierry frowned. "You can't read your own book," he whispered to Alix. "You live the words, so you can't read them."

"What?" She picked up the book, frantically flipping through the pages. There had to be something. Something! Anything! But there wasn't a trace of any words or sentences, each page was painfully blank no matter how many she flipped through. Alixandre narrowed her eyes at Mira and shoved the book in her hands. "What does it say?"

"I-"

"Never mind, it doesn't matter," Alixandre whispered, cutting her off, "I can't read it, that doesn't matter, I don't need to. Just do as I say. Bring him back!"

Mira was fairly certain that the shout was supposed to be louder. Instead it had come out as a harsh, throaty choke that made Mira's heart hurt. Suddenly, Mira was letting the book go, watching it for a moment as it disappeared before hitting the ground. Moving forward, Mira hugged Alixandre and caught her completely off guard.

"Bring him back," Alixandre's voice was shaking now with her trembling body. The feeling of Mira's arms around her killed her anger and desperation, making her feel exhausted. This was her only hope. The Storyteller had to be able to bring him back, she couldn't let go of that hope. She couldn't have been following a lie this whole time.

"I'm sorry, Alixandre, but I can't bring him back." Mira smiled as she leaned forward and whispered softly, "He isn't dead."

Even Thierry looked surprised when he heard that bit of news, staring at his daughter. "Are you sure?"

Mira nodded. "I am sure, father."

Alixandre stared at the girl and she could literally feel a sick lump falling into the pit of her stomach. The words echoed through her mind. *"He isn't dead."* That only made the lump harden, her throat feeling impossibly tight as her heart came to a stop. She felt her legs weaken until they completely gave up, forcing her to collapse against the young Storyteller. Mira kept her arms around her, holding her close, one of her hands running circles over her back.

Mira could see Fagan stand up from where he was sitting, Haven and the others looking up at him in question. Mira shook her head at the man, smiling as Fagan slowly made himself sit back down.

Alixandre had so many questions, so many things she needed answered. Had her entire life up until this point been based on a lie? But that couldn't be true. She had seen the fire with her own eyes, had tasted the smoke and heat as she watched the lab crumble and melt onto the streets of Minneapolis. Was he sleeping somewhere in some hospital bed or some simple apartment like the one they'd shared? Was he just down the street, carrying on his normal life like nothing happened? She had to know and each question that filled her mind crushed onto her shoulders with the weight of a thousand needs she never thought would be fulfilled.

Alixandre tried to focus. The questions could be answered. There was someone right in front of her who could give her the answers. Now wasn't the time to be emotional. Now was the moment where Alix could be the most useful, could stand tall and get the answers Alixandre so desperately needed.

"How?" Alix whispered. "How is that possible?"

Mira smiled, her tail swishing behind her as Alix's book reappeared in her hands. She turned it ahead, her eyes eager to share this new information with the person who had helped her save her father. She opened her mouth to say something, but stopped as her father stepped forward and placed a hand on her shoulder. He gave Alix an understanding look, but shook his head.

"Father, why can't we?" Mira asked.

"It does not work like that." Thierry stepped closer to Alix, keeping the conversation quiet. "We can tell you things about what has happened because it is already written. But the pages in the future, they shift and change. If we tell you what will happen in detail, it may change and never happen."

"C'est des conneries!" Alixandre snapped in an angry hiss, "You've told Jahren and the Scough things! Why can't you tell me?"

Thierry flashed Alixandre a knowing, sad smile. "Actually, I've never told them anything that would affect their stories in such a huge way. That's how Jahren knew something was wrong, because the Lurkhamara tried to use my powers in a way that I never would."

"You told them about Anasia coming to invade your territory!"

Thierry shook his head. "No, that was the Lurkhamara twisting things. Even so, if that were actually going to happen, I would warn them because of the danger involved and we all would have left, not fought back. This is different. This is a large part of your story, Alixandre. If she tells you, it might not happen the way it needs to."

"T-that's not fair!" Alixandre let out one last cry before she lowered her head. "That's not fair," she whispered, feeling the overwhelming weight of the situation crush into her.

Thierry placed a hand on Alixandre's shoulder, giving her a look that he hoped came across as comforting. He had a feeling that no matter what he tried right now she would see it as the exact opposite. "He taught me, when I took this power, to be vague," then he nodded to Mira, "Go on."

Mira took a deep breath. "The book showed me that he is still alive. He survived that fire. You will see him again, and it will be soon."

"I want… I need more than that. I need to see him."

"And you will. Please, trust me," Mira whispered.

Alixandre wanted to continue pleading with them. If that didn't work she would resort to grabbing the two Storytellers by their ears and forcing them to read the other pages to her so she could find Roderick and ask why he'd abandoned her all those years ago. Not a single phone call or anything of the sort, surely he had to still be concerned for her, right? Or had he tried looking for her, coming up short because Alixandre DeBenit no longer existed? But, somewhere deep in the questions and pain, the other side of Alixandre caught something important.

Alix had caught something, a single phrase that Thierry had said.

He taught me.

Thierry said that someone had given him this power, this power that his child now had. Someone had taught him how to use it. There was someone else out there with more power than the two creatures in front of him. If they couldn't help it was simply a matter of finding the person who could.

Determination welled up inside Alix, the same determination that had fueled him to stand in from of Xaver Knoxton with raggedy hair and a pair of old jeans, proving to him that he could handle anything that he threw at him. Alix had become stronger, had learned how to shoot a gun and fight. He had even survived battles against demons, including this battle in the demon world. It all welled up inside of him now, and instead of begging and pleading, he found himself simply nodding and walking away.

Alixandre knew what she would have to do, what *Alix* would have to do, and nothing was going to stop either of them from doing it.

"Father, can't I?" Mira looked up to him as Alix walked away from both of them without another word. The young Storyteller felt sorry for the woman and could see the pain that burned through her very existence. The whole story was just so sad and she'd seen that things would change, that it would get better. "Can't I just tell her a little bit more? You know, to make her feel better?"

"No Mira, that's not our place. We guard and retell the stories, we don't write them."

"But that's not writing it, father."

Thierry watched his daughter and smiled, petting the top of her head. "It is, in a way, because it could potentially change what happens if we tell her about future events."

Mira stuck out her bottom lip and pouted. "She's right, though, you do tell them things," then she nodded over to where Jahren was still sitting with Lyree and Anasia.

"Jahren is different."

"Uh huh. That's because you care about him."

Thierry lightly tugged on Mira's ear. "Even if that is the case, I would never tell him something as important as this information is to Alix."

Mira batted his hand away, frowning. "That's still not fair."

"I think I said the same thing, too, when he told me about these powers."

Mira was quiet for a moment, thinking those words over before she spoke again, "Do we *really* have to listen to the smiling man on this one?"

That brought a laugh to Thierry's lips and he hugged his daughter close. "You did a good job Mira, just like I knew you would."

Mira curled up in her father's arms. "So... I'm really the Storyteller?"

"Yes, you are."

"Will I be a good Storyteller father? Did he say? Or can you not tell me?"

Thierry smiled as he remembered the man who had helped him create his daughter and give her the majority of his powers.

"I can tell you this, it's fine," then he held her closer, whispering into her ear, "He said you'd be perfect."

Mira's eyes lit up when she heard those words, the worry melting away into a happy sigh, her tail happily wagging behind her.

As Thierry watched Alix sit next to Fagan, he smirked a little and whispered to her once more. "He also told me something else."

"Oh? What's that?"

"You have got to be kidding me."

Alix stood at the doorway with Fagan. He'd originally thought that Mira had accompanied them to open the door and let them go back to their world. When he heard otherwise, the frown on his face was rock solid.

"But I want to come with you."

"For what reason?" Alix asked.

Mira giggled, "Just cuz."

Alix's frown, if possible, got more serious. "I have already assisted you. Our business is over." Alix had already determined he didn't need this girl. His search for the one who'd taught her father could continue without her annoying peppiness.

"But I want to learn more about your world!"

"Read that book of yours. It seems to be good at telling you things that you aren't willing to share with others."

Mira sighed, trying to ignore the harshness of Alix's voice. "I already explained that to you! And your world was a lot of fun, I want to go back."

"It's not all that great," Cyn muttered. "Trust me, you're not missing much."

"Besides, if you want to explore our world, go ahead and do it. No one says you have to be with us," Alix said.

It wasn't like Cyn to agree with Alix, but she was more than happy to nod her head. The last thing she wanted to deal with was Mira's bright smiles and bounciness on a normal basis.

"But Haven is going to be there and he's my friend!"

"That was Fagan's decision, not mine," Alix snapped.

Fagan smirked at Alix and whispered, "I was under the impression that I was going to lose a partner, so I thought I could make my own decisions."

Alix decided to not respond to that.

"Come on! I won't cause any trouble, I promise! And neither will Zee!"

"Zee?" Both Fagan and Alix watched as Mira stepped to the side, revealing her fox companion standing behind her as she let out a large yawn.

"I had to leave her behind last time and she missed me so much!"

"No. No no. No. Absolutely not, I am not babysitting you and your pet!"

"But you're babysitting Haven!"

"What does that even mean?" Haven asked, feeling that he should somehow be offended.

"It means that they're going to be watching over you and taking care of you. It's a term reserved for children," Cyn said, smirking at him.

Haven frowned. "I am not a child."

"Neither am I!" Mira shouted in protest.

"I'm not sure I like the idea of keeping an actual pet fox. Katt would have a fit." Fagan could just hear the woman demanding a raise for dealing with fur and fox droppings. "Why can't she stay here with your father?"

"There's still some loose ends between the Scough and the Red Dragons, no one has time to play with Zee or anything. She'll get lonely," Mira whined.

"Isn't it odd for a fox to keep a fox as a pet?" Cyn asked.

Mira sighed. Alix had brought this up before, too. "Zee is more than a pet. She's my friend and I love her," then Mira knelt down to hug the fox, Zee letting out a happy yip to emphasize her point.

Cyn rolled her eyes. She really needed to stop asking Mira questions.

"Look. This isn't up for discussion. Fagan only agreed to Haven, not to the rest of you."

"Well that may be true, but Cyn is my chosen companion according to Anasia. She should stay with me," Haven said with a sly grin.

"Watch it," Cyn hissed at him. "I'm not feeling very sympathetic toward you right now despite your shitty Kurai backstory, which means I won't feel bad about kicking your ass."

"Oh, so you want to leave me?" Haven asked, an annoyingly sweet smile plastered to his face.

They could all hear Dox chuckling from where he was leaning against the wall of vines. Cyn glared at her friend. "Shut up! I'm not feeling terribly sympathetic toward you, either!"

"So you do want to leave then?" Dox asked.

Before Cyn could answer Alix glared at all of them. "It doesn't matter what she wants because all of you are not staying! The mission is over!"

"No, it is not. Xaver's killer is still out there," Haven said.

"So is my father," Dox added.

"And what about Roderick? You're not sure how any of that will happen, what if you need me to be there?" Mira asked.

Cyn blinked. "Who the hell is Roderick?"

"Shut up! Just shut up!" Alix turned to face the doorway, "Now... let's go before I change my mind."

"Clearly, you can't, because we all just said why you need us to be around you," Dox said.

"Je déteste démons."

Epilogue

A few wires, hooked up to perfection. A couple of dials turned to just the right angle. Doors closed and a laptop sitting on the desk with speakers that looked too scuffed up to function, each one put in just the right place. It was the stereo equivalent of a well-worn pair of tennis shoes, mud stained and falling apart but oh so comfortable. Zach looked over his set up like a parent whose kid just made the honor roll. Taking a breath, he reached forward and hit the enter key.

A split second passed before the sound ticked through the speakers and filled the room around him. Zach grinned and turned off the lights before he dropped onto the couch a couple feet away from Katalynne's desk, listening to the loud and perfect sound that danced through the room. He had been right. After his brother's renovations of the entrance lobby to the warehouse it was now the perfect shape to make his music sound just right. The beating drums never sounded this good back at home, and even if they did, his parents would always come through the door and yell at him to study and turn down that ear splitting piece of garbage.

Zach closed his eyes and relaxed on the couch, listening to the music and letting it envelope him. Nothing could break his new found freedom here.

"Zach! Turn this crap off NOW!"

The lights snapped on as Zach heard his name above the tunes and words of his favorite artist, reminding him of one sure fact: his brother had inherited their father's temper.

Zach considered protesting then changed his mind and jumped up. He stumbled over a couple of cords before he made it to the desk. He was just about to close the laptop when he noticed the fox girl from before, her ears twitching as she listened to the beat of the music. Suddenly, her tail was swishing back and forth with the rhythm, a curious look on her face. "What is this?"

"WHAT?!" Zach couldn't hear her over the bass, cupping a hand over his ear.

Behind her, Zee started to make noises along with the music as if trying to sing along. Mira giggled and shouted to Zach, "What is this! It is rather catchy! Even Zee likes it!"

Zach would've turned his attention to the yipping fox if it weren't for the cute girl in front of him. He smiled brightly as he made his way over to her. "It's my favorite band! Move your hips a little, the way your tail is moving!"

Mira blinked and moved her hips from side to side, giggling, "This is fun!"

Cyn rolled her eyes. "No, this is crap. This group is terrible."

Zach gasped. "How dare you! You're lucky you're hot or I'd be really pissed."

"Oh no, I wouldn't want that," Cyn muttered.

"Damn right you don't, because-"

"ZACH!" Fagan screamed again, interrupting him, "Either turn this shit off or I'm breaking the damn laptop!"

"Right, right!" Zach made his way back through the wires and closed the laptop, the music unceremoniously snapping off as he flashed his brother his best, practiced, innocent smile – the only thing he had inherited from their mother. "Welcome back."

Fagan regarded his brother without the slightest bit of amusement as he crossed his arms and glared. The slight wear from the battle they'd fought only served to make him look more threatening and he knew it. "What the hell were you doing?"

"I was bored. Your lovely secretary left me alone here so I had to amuse myself."

"What?" Fagan frowned and pulled out his phone, dialing Katalynne.

"So… are all of you staying here?" Zach asked, stepping over the wires to talk with Mira and Cyn.

Mira smiled, "Yep!" And Zee let out a small yip, agreeing with her.

Zach smirked, "Awesome." He already had an arm around Mira's shoulders as he shifted his smirk over to Cyn. "What do you say, ladies? Why don't we get together and-" he stopped when Haven was suddenly next to Cyn, an arm wrapped around her waist. Cyn was about to protest then realized that Zach had his hands raised in the air. "Cool, cool, I get it."

"Don't you mean sweet?" Mira asked.

"Not exactly… I'll explain it later."

"Your possessiveness is a pretty nifty trick," Cyn whispered to Haven.

"How many points does it get me?"

"I promise not to break your wrist, how about that?"

"Deal."

To Cyn's amusement Zach had taken a couple of steps back, bumping right into Dox with a surprised cry of, "W-what the fuck?!"

Dox chuckled, his arms crossed and the shadows thick around his feet, showing that he had just materialized behind Zach. "My apologies, I thought you saw me."

"N-not cool! We have to talk about boundaries, man!"

"What for?" Alix asked, frowning at Zach. "You don't live here."

"Well…"

Fagan's eyes narrowed at Zach. He was just about to ask what exactly his little brother meant by that when Katalynne finally picked up.

"Good evening, boss."

Katalynne's voice sounded like thick and rich velvet over the phone, more so than usual. Fagan could hear faint voices behind her and the clinking of glasses with inebriated laughter. She was sitting in a bar, enjoying herself, which didn't improve his mood one bit – partly because he would've liked to be sitting next to her, especially after the mission he'd had. Even worse, he realized, was that she had obviously been expecting him to call. He dared to think that, from the tone of her voice and the chuckle hidden just behind it, she had been looking forward to this.

"What the hell is he still doing here?"

"Oh, it's very simple. Your dear brother forgot to tell you something very important before you left. He was kicked out of your parent's house and has decided that you, being his loving older brother, would happily take him in."

"What?" Fagan turned to look at Zach, letting him see the fury on his face. Alix decided that now would be the best time to leave, quietly urging the others to follow. Part of him had wanted to rub it in Fagan's face, a sort of revenge for Fagan agreeing to help a certain Ice Dragon and turn their warehouse into a demon motel. He had a feeling that he knew what Katalynne had just said over the phone, he could tell from the dangerous look in Fagan's eyes as Zach seemed to shrink away from him. That look also urged Alix to save any mocking for later, Mira waving to Zach who was too busy mustering up as many nervous smiles as he could.

How did Zach always end up in these situations? It seemed like, since the day Zach was born, Fagan had gotten the prestigious job of cleaning up his brother's messes. That time he had gotten into a fight in fifth grade, that other time he got caught in some girl's room in high school, every single argument he had with their parents – even after Fagan had moved out.

"Have fun, boss. I'm on a date with a hot woman. A really, really hot woman and she's about to get me very drunk. Catch up or something, like brothers do."

"Date?" That was a foreign word to hear from Katalynne. Fagan had never heard of her actually taking someone's offer – unless if she had been withholding information from him. But then there was a second word that caught his attention, his eyes widening. "W-woman?!"

"Oh! Is it the hot girl from the bar?!" Zach asked.

Fagan glared at him. "Who gave you permission to speak right now?"

"N-no one, sir."

Katalynne laughed, "I should go. I'll talk to you later."

"Wait! You're actually... I mean... w-we had a moment before, remember? Before the mission?"

"I do remember," she smiled, "And I'm glad you're back safely. But, right now, I'm off the clock and in a tight little black dress and high heels."

"Wait, Katt-"

"Later boss," then she hung up the phone and covered her chuckle with her hand to keep it from going hysterical. She could just imagine Fagan's dumbstruck face as he was left standing there with a silent phone, staring at Zach as his little brother tried to come up with an explanation. She remembered Zach trying to explain the situation to her. *"Parents are unfair,"* and, *"They don't understand me."* Instead of listening, Katalynne had decided that it would be in her best interests to cash in that rain check from Harper.

She had no doubt that when she went back to work Zach would be a permanent fixture. It would make her life and work harder, but in that moment it wasn't something to worry about. Turning off her phone, she tucked it into her purse and turned to smile at her date.

Harper was behind the bar, just as she had been when they first met, finishing up the last of her night shift. In the course of the eventful week she'd gotten a haircut and she was now practically bald save for a small buzz of blonde hair. Katalynne let herself admire the many tattoos sweeping over her arms as the hands on the clock above the bar reached midnight.

One more minute now and they would be out on that date.

The stool beside her pulled out as the final hand of the clock moved into place. Harper's replacement had already stepped in and seamlessly took up her orders as she moved to the computer in the back and logged herself out of the system. Katalynne stood up to leave with her, raising an eyebrow as the new person seated at the bar stool stood up and waved her hand to catch Harper's attention.

The woman wore wire framed glasses, the lenses tinted a hazy blue to perfectly match her eyes and the plaid colored headband that rested on top of her long, blond hair. There was a sort of old fashioned feel to the girl, like she belonged in the fifties in an ad for a malt shop, sitting on top of a baby blue Cadillac. It would have looked out of style on anyone else, but this young woman managed the look effortlessly. She was the type where everything matched, right down to the sparkling sweet smile and the painted French nails.

Katalynne was more curious than jealous. At least that's what she told herself.

"I wanted to catch you before you left." The girl's voice was thick with a French accent caressing her words. More than a few men at the bar glanced her way, mentally flipping through their pickup lines to find one that might possibly work.

"Good timing," Harper smirked, stepping around the bar without her apron. Katalynne took the moment to admire the tight fitting jeans and simple blue and black striped tank top paired with knee high boots that curved up over her legs. "Natalia, this is Katalynne. Katalynne, meet my roommate."

Katalynne smiled and nodded to the girl. "Oh good, because I was assuming she was an ex."

"Me and Harper?" Natalia chuckled, "No, that wouldn't happen."

"Nat is a bit too academic for me, she's always studying when she should be out partying"

Natalia smiled, "There is plenty of enjoyment to find in a book."

"Wow," Katalynne said, "I thought girls like you were extinct."

Harper laughed, "She does technically have a boyfriend, but he's just as brainy as she is." Harper made sure to say it loud enough for the men behind Natalia to hear, each of them frowning and giving up on the mental images of the blonde haired woman spread across their beds. Harper smiled at Natalia. "Now, you wanted to catch me about something?"

Natalia stuck her tongue out at both women. "Forget it, it can wait. Enjoy your date."

"I can wait, it's fine," Katalynne said.

"Well I can't." Harper hooked an arm around Katalynne's arm, "Let's go before she changes her mind."

Natalia laughed and waved to both of them. "I'll see you tomorrow. Nice meeting you, Katalynne."

"Likewise."

"See you, Nat," then Harper smirked, "Although hopefully it's not until later tomorrow, or even the day after."

"Ha ha. We'll see if you get that lucky." Katalynne didn't even try to keep the smirk off her lips as she fished out her keys.

"Says the woman who stood me up for her boss. You owe me, dear."

Katalynne leaned forward and brushed her lips against Harper's cheek in a very teasing movement before she turned and headed for her car outside. Harper followed with a laugh and final wave to her roommate.

As they left Natalia spun a little in her seat, pulling her phone out of her pocket. The bar was filling up and it was quickly becoming a bit too full for her tastes. Jumping down from the seat she headed to the back room as if she were an employee, easily shaking the two men who had started to head in her direction with some line about her being too young and cute ready to fire.

Stepping through the door, she wove her way to the back stockroom and pressed one of the auto dial keys on her phone.

"Good evening. I was expecting a call from Harper." The voice on the other end of the phone sounded slightly annoyed, but Natalia knew it wasn't directed at her.

"She didn't get a chance. She's on a date for the night." She paused to see if he had a response. When he didn't, she decided to add more information. "With her target."

"I see. Then I'll expect a report by tomorrow afternoon. Though, this time, I'd like her to call me."

Natalia smiled sweetly into the phone, letting it leak into her words with a tone of perfectly crafted innocence. "I'll let her know. Goodnight, sir."

End

About the authors

In 2001, during her freshman year in college, Briana Lawrence joined an anime mailing list and met a girl named Jessica Walsh. They ended up chatting aimlessly and writing fanfiction together until, one day, they realized they weren't just friends anymore. In 2002, the two women met in person at an anime convention – Anime Central – and have been inseparable ever since. A long distance relationship of internet chatting gave way to characters, stories and adventures filling thousands of log files.

The crazy idea to turn those logs in to an actual readable novel series during a National Novel Writing Month spree gave birth to the Hunters, a series of book that begins with, "Seeking the Storyteller." Thanks to Jessica's knowledge of different cultures and Briana's Creative Writing background, the two have become an imaginative couple out to produce a series of books unlike any other.

Below are the authors' websites, where you can find information on their other books and the Hunters series:

Main Website:

http://www.sewntogetherreflections.com

Briana Lawrence:

http://www.facebook.com/brichibicosplays
http://brichibi.wix.com/whisperedwords
http://www.facebook.com/BrianaLawrencesPenAndPaper

Jessica Walsh:

http://www.facebook.com/snowcosplays
http://snowtigra.wix.com/jessicawalsh
http://www.facebook.com/storytellerhuntersseries

Stephen Raffill
Front and back cover artist

http://www.rain-arc.com/

Made in the USA
Columbia, SC
29 November 2017